Prais

"Kennedy Ryan pours he ... ything she writes, and it makes for books that are heart-searing, sensual, and life affirming. We are lucky to be living in a world where she writes."

—Emily Henry, #1 *New York Times* bestselling author

"Few authors can write romance like Kennedy Ryan."

—Jennifer L. Armentrout, #1 *New York Times* bestselling author

"Kennedy Ryan has a fan for life."

—Ali Hazelwood, *New York Times* bestselling author

"Ryan is a powerhouse of a writer."

—*USA Today*

"Kennedy Ryan is a true artist."

—Helen Hoang, *New York Times* bestselling author

"Ryan is a fantastic storyteller and superb writer."

—NPR

Reel

Entertainment Weekly's Best Romances of the Year

Washington Post's Best Romances of the Year

BookBub's Highest Rated Books of the Year

"Kennedy Ryan is one of the finest romance writers of our age, and she offers readers another marquee title with *Reel*."

—*Entertainment Weekly*

"*Reel* is alive and pulsing like a beating heart. This romance is a triumph of art and emotion."

—Talia Hibbert, *New York Times* bestselling author

"Emotional, layered, sexy, and deeply satisfying, with stunning prose and a sweeping storyline, *Reel* is everything that has Kennedy Ryan fans devouring her books."

—Lexi Ryan, *New York Times* bestselling author

Also by Kennedy Ryan

The Skyland Series

Before I Let Go

This Could Be Us

The Bennett Series

When You Are Mine

Loving You Always

Be Mine Forever

Until I'm Yours

All the King's Men Series

The Kingmaker

The Rebel King

Queen Move

The Hoops Series

Long Shot

Block Shot

Hook Shot

"The Close-Up"

(A Hollywood Renaissance/ Hoops Crossover Novella)

The Soul Series

My Soul to Keep

Down to My Soul

Refrain

The Grip Series

Flow

Grip

Still

REEL

KENNEDY RYAN

FOREVER

NEW YORK BOSTON

Forever
Hachette Book Group
1290 Avenue of the Americas, New York, NY 10104
read-forever.com
twitter.com/readforeverpub

Originally published as a print-on-demand edition in 2021 and as an ebook by Forever in February 2024

First trade paperback edition: November 2024

Forever is an imprint of Grand Central Publishing. The Forever name and logo are trademarks of Hachette Book Group, Inc.

Library of Congress Control Number: 2024941213

ISBNs: 978-1-5387-6962-1 (trade paperback),
978-1-5387-6964-5 (ebook), 978-1-5387-6963-8 (hardcover edition),
978-1-5387-7319-2 (Barnes & Noble signed edition)

Printed in the United States of America

LSC-C

Printing 1, 2024

Dedicated to the stars who shone brightest when it was dark

Frankie Manning Leon James
Billie Holiday Sarah Vaughan
Lena Horne Dorothy Dandridge
Big Bill Broonzy Ma Rainey Duke Ellington
Josephine Baker Eartha Kitt Fredi Washington
Louis Armstrong Adelaide Hall Pearl Primus
Clarence Muse Charles Sidney Gilpin
Ella Fitzgerald Count Basie Cab Calloway
Langston Hughes Johnny Hodges
Charlie Parker Art Tatum Thelonious Monk
Dinah Washington August Wilson
Dizzy Gillespie Bessie Smith Nella Larsen
Ethel Waters Blind Lemon Jefferson
James P. Johnson Willie Smith Miles Davis
Gladys Bentley Chick Webb
Erroll Garner Nina Simone John Coltrane
Edith Wilson Claudia McNeil
Jules Bledsoe Sidney Bechet Ossie Davis
Harold Nicholas Fayard Nicholas Pearl Bailey
Diahann Carroll Harry Belafonte
Hattie McDaniel Leslie Uggams Nat King Cole
Sammy Davis Jr. Nichelle Nichols Ruby Dee
Zora Neale Hurston Claude McKay
James Baldwin Lorraine Hansberry
Gwendolyn Brooks Lead Belly Bud Powell
Mississippi John Hurt Albert Ammons
Hazel Scott Pete Johnson Paul Robeson
Fats Waller Coleman Hawkins
Joseph "King" Oliver Carmen McRae
Oscar Micheaux Louise Beavers Cicely Tyson
Bill "Bojangles" Robinson Sister Rosetta Tharpe
Jeni LeGon Edna Mae Harris Lillian Randolph

And on and on and on…

"If you kin see de light at daybreak, you don't keer if you die at dusk. It's so many people never seen de light at all."

Zora Neale Hurston,
Their Eyes Were Watching God

PROLOGUE

Canon

At 20 Years Old

It's the magic hour.

Gold dust smatters the horizon, gilding the fine line dividing earth and sky, bathing the shore in light and shimmer.

"It never gets old," my mother whispers, the awe in her eyes as new as the unfolding sunset.

After a thousand sunsets from a thousand rickety piers, she, a veteran photographer, still holds on to wonder for this view.

A brisk breeze slips beneath my unzipped windbreaker.

"It *is* beautiful, but we should probably go inside. It's getting cool out here."

"It's not cool out here." Mama's eyes, alive in her weary face, snap to meet mine. "Don't treat me like an invalid, Canon."

"I'm not. I…I'm not." I study the wheelchair she spends most of her days in now, the camera in her lap, cradled lovingly in unsteady hands. "I'm sorry. I didn't mean to."

The irritation eases from her expression a little, but her lips remain set. "Ever really consider that word? Invalid? In-valid. Because someone can't walk or get around easily, we invalidate them? We don't see them, don't respect their wishes?"

"Ma, I didn't mean to do that. We been out here for a while. It's been a long day and I just want it to end well."

The camera, when she lifts it to her eyes and aims it at the sun, shakes in her tenuous hold until her tightening grip steadies it. "Every day that ends with me still breathing has ended well."

Her words grind into my heart and I draw a sharp breath through my nose, never prepared for the idea that my mother won't always be around. May not be around much longer.

"Don't talk like that, Ma." I shift my feet, feeling as unsteady as the waves lapping at the legs of the pier.

She tears her eyes away from the camera, from the burnished horizon, to cast me a shrewd glance and scoffs. "Boy, we all gonna die. Question is, how did you live? *Did* you live or just wait for death to come? Not me. I ain't waiting for nothing."

She turns back to the sunset. "Except this. I'll wait for the magic hour every time. It's waiting for a miracle, but knowing it'll come through. Like clockwork, it'll come through. A miracle you can count on."

I don't have the heart to tell her I've given up on miracles. She'd only say I'm too young to abandon faith and hope and the luxury of naiveté, but the disease ravaging my mother's body has accelerated her aging and mine.

"Where's your camera?" she asks, her sudden question finding me over the sound of sloshing waves.

I slide the backpack from my shoulders and pull out my handheld video camera. I know what she wants. More and more she's been documenting this journey of hers. Of ours. While it hurts to hear some of the things she tells the camera, things she doesn't say to me, I never stop her. I'm always ready to capture every word, every glance from the remarkable woman who raised me.

"You are my boy for sure. Couldn't ever find me without my camera either." She peers over the camera, up at me. "It's the love of my life, but as much as you love your art, Canon, I want you to find someone you can love more."

I laugh and taste salty air. "You didn't, but you want me to?"

A sad smile sketches fine-line parentheses around her mouth. "We always want more for our children than we had."

I won't tell her that me loving someone more than my art *would* take a miracle. Life has stolen enough of my mother's illusions. I can't bring myself to take more.

I turn the camera on. I turn it on *her*.

"Oh good. It's on?" She lowers her camera and squints into mine, resolve as bright in her eyes as the sinking sun setting the ocean on fire. "'Cause I got something to say."

PROLOGUE

Neevah

At 18 Years Old

I should have known this day would suck.

At breakfast, I knocked over the salt. Late for school, I paused long enough to scoop up a handful and toss it over my shoulder to counter the bad luck, but the damage had already been done.

First period, Mr. Kaminsky called on me just when I realized I'd left my AP English assignment at home. At lunch, I dropped my tray, spilling chocolate milk, mashed potatoes, and my fruit cup all over the cafeteria floor. And the worst part of this day? I dropped a line in rehearsal for the final school play, *Our Town*. I had that monologue down. How did I forget?

"Do any human beings ever realize life while they live it?" I recite my character Emily's words under my breath and pull Mama's old Camry into our driveway. "Every, every minute?"

I scoured my brain for those words, but for the life of me couldn't find them anywhere when I needed them. I even knew the line that came next, the stage manager's response, his answer to the question I couldn't come up with.

"Saints and poets maybe."

The theater department is the best thing about our little high school. I wouldn't have a full scholarship offer to the Rutgers drama program without everything the drama club and classes have taught me.

I put the car in park and bang my head against the steering wheel, still mad about forgetting those lines today. "Damn salt."

When I look up, Brandon's F-150 is parked up ahead under our car porch. My boyfriend—correction, my fiancé since we got engaged over

Christmas—always seems to come right when I need him. He's not thrilled about the Rutgers offer, even though I haven't decided if I'll go or not. He hopes I'll attend a school closer to home, though none of them have offered to pay my way. Despite our recent tension over my future plans, this bad day just got better knowing he's inside waiting, even though I didn't expect him.

I love it when he comes over after his shift at Olson's, his daddy's garage, where he's a mechanic. Brand's got a knack for cars—always has. When no football scholarships came through, he took it in stride and started working at Olson's without complaint. He always smells like Irish Spring, the soap he uses to wash up after work. No matter how hard he scrubs, stubborn traces of grease usually stick under his nails and in the creases of his hands. I don't mind as long as his hands are on *me*.

Brand was my first. My only. Secretly, I've been leaning toward staying, maybe studying drama at our community college instead of going up north because I can't stand the thought of being away from him four years.

I hop out and head for our ranch-style brick house.

"I'm home!" I pocket my keys and close the front door behind me.

Brandon always waits in the living room. Mama would skin us alive if she ever found us in my bedroom, though we've gotten away with it a time or two.

I head up the hall, stopping short when I see my sister, Terry, seated beside him on the couch. They were both juniors when I started high school. Terry is so beautiful, everyone tries at least once with her, but as far as I know, Brandon never has. I couldn't believe it when he asked me, a freshman, out.

"Hey, guys." I walk in and flop onto the couch since they're squeezed onto the love seat. Brandon holds himself stiffly beside her, sitting straight as a pole, fists clenched in his lap. Terry, with her quick smile and that fat ass, is the life of every party, but right now her brows pinch, her face twisted with what looks like misery.

"Who died up in here?" I blow out a laugh, which fades when Terry's eyes drop to her lap, and Brandon looks away altogether. My father died of a heart attack when I was twelve. I've been paranoid about losing someone else ever since.

"*Did* somebody die?" I sit up straight, fear thinning my voice. "Mama? Aunt Alberta?"

"No," Terry cuts in. "Ain't nothing like that. We, uh..." She shakes her head, presses her lips together, and closes her eyes.

"We have something to tell you." Brandon's voice is gravelly, grave. "We...well, Terry—"

"I'm pregnant."

Her words drop like a stone into the small living room, and I blink at her stupidly. For a second, even though I know this must be the last thing Terry wants since she just finished cosmetology school, I feel joy. I'm going to be an auntie! Terry and I have laid on my bed dreaming on Saturday afternoons about my wedding to Brandon, and how I'd probably have babies before she did because she'd take forever to settle down. We'd laugh, me on the floor between her knees while she braided my hair.

The joy, short-lived, evaporates like steam exposed to air.

We have something to tell you, Brandon said.

We.

They are not a *we*. Brandon and I are a *we*. Terry and I are a *we*, but they've never been joined by anything but me.

"W-what's going on?" I sputter. "Why are you...what do you mean..."

That's all I can manage before my voice gives up. My insides turn to rock, bracing for something my brain hasn't caught up to yet.

"It's mine," Brandon chokes out. Jaw flexing, he reaches up to massage the back of his neck and stands, pacing in front of the fireplace. I catch sight of the gold frames lining the mantel, some so old they're tarnished, all displaying photos of my family. Several of me and Terry. From snaggle-toothed and pigtailed to celebrating and sullen. A parade of stages and years and emotions we've experienced together. Sisters.

My sister is pregnant by my fiancé.

We.

A landslide of fury and confusion and hurt crush my insides to rubble.

"No." I shake my head, stand, and back away a few feet, putting space between me and these traitors. These selfish traitors who were supposed to be mine, not each other's. "When?"

"The first time," Terry says. "We—"

"The first time?" I hurl the words at her, outrage and pain wrestling for dominance in my heart. "How many...how long...What have you done, Terry?"

I turn wet eyes, blurred with tears and burning with anger, to Brandon. "What have *you* done?" I ask him, too, unsure whom I hate most right now. Who has hurt *me* the most.

"You weren't ready," Brandon's voice is defensive and laced with blame. "I told you it's hard for a guy to wait, but you...you weren't ready."

He was older and all his friends were having sex with their girls, but I wouldn't be rushed. He begged, telling me how tough it was for guys to go without. I felt guilty and he felt frustrated, but we got through it. He waited until I *was* ready, and it was worth it. It was good—at least, I'd thought so. I never suspected he cheated. And with my sister?

"That was almost two years ago, Brand," I shout. "You've been fucking Terry since my junior year?"

Terry's eyes, widened with panic, shoot to the living room entrance. "Shhhh! Jesus, Neev. You want the whole neighborhood to hear?"

"Really, T? That's your main concern? I'm pretty sure everybody'll know soon enough. Unless you plan to—"

"It was one time," Brandon interrupts, eyes pleading. "The summer before we...before you and me started doing it. It was an accident. I told her it could never happen again, and it didn't."

"I'm not great at science," I say, sarcasm pushing its way through the pain. "But it must have happened again if she's just now turning up pregnant two years later."

Their guilty quiet following my words suffocates even the faintest hope for a miracle. For the impossibility that it had only been once, which is bad enough, but to think they would do it again. That he'd do it when I thought we were happy. That she'd do it when she's my sister and she knew. She *knew* how much I loved Brandon. How could she not have known, and how could she do this to me?

"It's only been the last few weeks," Terry admits, tears slipping from the corners of her eyes. "You gotta believe that I never—"

"I ain't gotta believe nothing," I spit at her.

"You've been rehearsing so much for the play," Brandon says.

"So again it's my fault?" A derisive laugh leaps out. "I have to rehearse after school for a play a few days a week and you can't keep your dick away from my sister?"

"Neev, damn!" Terry shoots to her feet, a scowl marring the smooth prettiness of her face. "Keep your voice down."

We're all standing now, the tension triangulating between the three of us. I've wrapped myself in anger, but the protective layers are fraying, and pain, sharper and heavier than I think I can take, pounds in my temples and thunders behind my ribs. My knees wobble and my head spins.

I could faint.

I rack my brain for a play where a character faints, and all I can come up with is Shakespeare's *The Two Gentlemen of Verona,* and that's such a bad example. This is the last thing I should be thinking about while my life burns to the ground in my living room, but somehow it refocuses me.

I still have the stage.

Here I was considering staying, giving up my scholarship, possibly my dream of performing someday on Broadway, for him. For *this*. There's an acceptance letter in my desk drawer to a great theater program. My ticket out of here. My passport out of what has become hell. Rutgers can pay for a fresh start, far away from here; from them. From this wicked *we* staring at me with lying, tear-drenched eyes.

It feels like they've taken everything, but they haven't. I have a lot.

I have opportunity.

A weird calm falls over me. It doesn't dull the throbbing, pulsing pain in my chest, or ease the churning nausea in my stomach—I'll throw up when I make it to my room—but it does give me the strength to do what needs to be done.

Leave.

"Jazz washes away the dust of everyday life."

—Art Blakey, Renowned Drummer

ONE

Canon

(Present Day)

I blink when the lights come up in the Walter Reade Theater, brightness assaulting my eyes after nearly two hours spent sitting in the dark. The packed room seems to draw a collective breath and then release it as thunderous applause. And then they stand. I'm sure some folks stay seated, but I only see a roomful of people standing, clapping for the documentary I poured the last three years of my life into. Warmth crawls up my neck and over my face. I will myself not to squirm in the director's chair set center stage. It's not my first time screening a documentary at the New York Film Festival, but I'll never get used to the attention. I'm much more at home behind the camera than in front of an audience. I'm like Mama in that way.

I hope I'm like her in a thousand ways.

Charles, the moderator, clears his throat and shoots me a grin, mouthing *I told you so.*

I roll my eyes and concede his point with a dip of my head and a wry smile. He predicted a standing ovation for *Cracked,* my documentary examining America's war on drugs, mandatory minimums, and mass incarceration, and contrasting the current largely suburban opioid crisis.

My usual lighthearted fare.

I gesture for everyone to sit, and for a few seconds they ignore me, until in small waves, they take their seats.

"I think they liked it," Charles says into his handheld mic, causing a ripple of laughter through the theater.

"Maybe." I look out to the crowd. "But I'm sure they have questions."

Do they ever.

For the next hour, the questions come in a quick succession of unrelenting curiosity and mostly admiration. A few challenge my largely critical stance of the government's so-called War on Drugs. I'm not sure if they're merely playing devil's advocate, or actually believe the points they raise. Doesn't matter. I enjoy a good debate, and don't mind having it with three hundred people watching. It's a great chance to further clarify my points, my beliefs. And maybe learn something in the process. We aren't usually one hundred percent right or informed on anything. Even if I don't agree with someone, I never discount the opportunity to learn something I hadn't considered.

When I'm sure we've exhausted this discussion and I can start thinking about the mouthwatering steak I've promised myself, another person approaches the mic set up in the aisle.

"One last question," Charles says, pointing to the freckled guy with red hair who's sporting a Biggie T-shirt.

"I'm a huge fan of your work, Mr. Holt," he begins, his blue eyes fixed and intense.

"Thanks." I ignore my stomach's protest. "'Preciate that."

"As much as I love your documentaries," he continues, "I miss your feature films. Did the experience with *Primal* put you off directing movies?"

Shit.

I do not talk about that disaster. It's been discussed enough without me ever addressing it publicly. *Everyone* knows not to ask me about that movie. And this little joker has the balls to ask me *now*? After a standing ovation at the New York Film Festival for the hardest documentary I've ever made?

"Some stories should be told by other people," I say, keeping my tone flat and shrugging philosophically. "You find the stories you're supposed to tell and move on if it becomes clear a story is not for you. It's not personal."

"So I think that does it," Charles says. "Thank you all for—"

"But it *was* personal," Redhead cuts in over Charles's attempt to shut him down, pressing on despite the color flushing his cheeks. "I mean, you were dating Camille Hensley, and when you guys broke up, she had you fired from the movie. Does it get more personal? Do you have advice for us young filmmakers who might find ourselves in similar awkward situations?"

Yeah, don't fuck your actress.

I don't say that out loud, of course, though it *is* the lesson I learned the hard, humiliating way.

"I guess the lesson is that art takes precedence over everything." I force an even tone. "That story turned out exactly as it was supposed to..."

Trash.

"And performed the way it was supposed to..."

Flopped.

"Without me. I think we all know personal involvements can complicate what is already the hardest thing I've ever done—make great movies, whether they're true stories of lives ruined by a government's ill-conceived policies."

I gesture to the large screen with the *Cracked* logo behind me.

"Or stories born purely from imagination. Storytelling is sacred. Story must be protected, at all costs. Sometimes at personal cost, so when it became apparent my involvement with that project could potentially compromise the story, I bowed out."

Railroaded is a more accurate description for how Camille leveraged her mega-star status to get me off the project. The movie being butchered by the new director and the rotten tomatoes hurled at the film did little to soothe that wound. I didn't need the movie's failure to vindicate me. I knew I should not have mixed it up with Camille. Not even great pussy is worth a wasted opportunity.

But it's hard to call anything "wasted" when you learn your lesson this well.

~

"You looked like you were two seconds off jacking redhead up."

Monk's comment makes me grin, but I'm too focused on my crab cake to speak. After all that craving for steak, P.J. Clarke's crab cake turned me.

"I mean, it *did* take balls to ask." Monk winks and takes a bite of his steak.

"Punk ass is lucky he's still got 'em." I wipe my mouth and toss the napkin onto the table. "He's gotta know I don't talk about that shit."

"You've barely talked to me about *Primal,* much less a roomful of strangers, so I thought you not strangling him on the spot was damn near commendable."

"Hmmm." I offer a grunt in case Monk gets it in his head that I want to discuss this further. I do not. *Primal* is a sore spot. I've built my career and reputation on thoughtful, groundbreaking documentaries. When I direct features, it's because the material grips my imagination and incites my convictions. *Primal* is a reminder that I strayed from that once and paid in pride. I wasn't lying up there. Storytelling is sacred to me. Jeopardizing my integrity as a storyteller for a woman?

Won't happen again.

"I get the message," Monk says, taking a sip of his beer. "You don't want to talk about *Primal,* so let's talk about your next movie. I know you're into that."

I glance up from my plate and nod. I believe in economy of words. Talking too much usually means saying things I didn't want to or shouldn't have.

"I've got a million ideas about the score," he continues, not waiting for me to speak.

Wright "Monk" Bellamy is one of the best musicians I've ever met. He plays several instruments, but piano is what he's best known for. His obsession with Thelonious Monk gained him the moniker, and his towering skill as a pianist backs it up. He's that rare classically trained beast who can seamlessly cross into pop, contemporary, jazz. You name the genre. He can probably hang.

"So you *are* free to work on the movie?" I take a sip of my Macallan. I didn't realize how anxious I was about the documentary's reception until that standing O. Most of the tension drained out of me after that. This drink is handling what's left.

"I can shuffle a few things." Monk's dark eyes twinkle with humor. "For the right price."

He's as intense as I am, but he disguises it with a laid-back persona and good-natured smile. I don't care enough to disguise anything. You get what you get.

"We got budget," I mutter. "This time. I hope I don't regret letting Evan convince me to do this with Galaxy Studios."

"It's a period piece. And a huge one at that. Considering the costuming, production, scope of this thing, it ain't gonna be cheap. Evan was right to go the studio route."

"I'm sure he'll be pleased to hear it. Though if there's one thing you never have to tell Evan, it's that he's right."

My production partner, Evan Bancroft, deserves a lot of credit for our success. He "indulges" me my documentaries, and makes the films between count, ensuring the movies we do make us a lot of money. The guy's too smart to be poor. Not that he's ever been. Evan grew up in the business with a screenwriter for a mother and a cinematographer for a father. He bleeds film.

"Still no closer to finding your star?" Monk asks.

I put the drink down and lean back in my chair, watching Lincoln Center glow through the window as the first layer of darkness blankets the city. Finding a great story is only the first hurdle. Getting the money to make it? That's another. Casting the right actors—one of the most important steps in the dozens you take to make or ruin a film.

"I'll know her when I see her," I tell him.

"How many have you seen so far? A hundred?"

"The studio put out this huge casting call that's been a joke. I like to be a lot more precise than this. It's a waste of time and money, if you ask me, but they didn't. They just started looking at all these actresses who are totally wrong for the role."

"Well, in their defense, you have been searching for six months without one callback, so they're probably just trying to help this baby along."

"But it's *my* baby." I glare at the passersby on the street like they're the suits safely ensconced in their Beverly Hills homes. "I found this story in the middle of nowhere. They have no idea what it will take to make it what it should be. All I want is their money, not their ideas."

"Silly them, thinking they should have some say about how their money is spent."

"I've been doing this a long time. I know how it works, but there are some things I know only with my gut. And casting this movie is one of those things, so I need the studio execs to stay the hell out of my way while I find the right actress."

"It's still kind of a miracle how you got *Dessi Blue*. Like, once-in-a-lifetime."

I'd been traveling from one interview for *Cracked* to another. Driving through a rural Alabama town, I almost missed the small roadside marker.

Birthplace of Dessi Blue (1915–2005)

Driving, I didn't have time to read all the fine print beneath the heading that told more about her life, but the gas station in the tiny town where I stopped was on Dessi Blue Drive. Inside, I asked the cashier about Dessi Blue, and the rest is history. That sent me on the winding road that has brought me to the most ambitious movie I've ever attempted—a biopic about the life story of a hugely talented jazz singer most have never heard of and never knew.

"Darren's writing the script?" Monk's question jars me from that pivotal memory.

"Uh, actually, no. I really think this story should be written by a woman." I pause, leaving plenty of room for the bomb I'm about to drop. "I want Verity Hill."

Monk's knife stops midslice into his medium-rare steak. He looks up, blinking at me a few times. His knife and fork clatter when he drops them on his plate. A muscle works in his jaw.

"Look, I know you two have a past," I say.

He answers with scornful laughter and sits back in his chair, making no move to return to his steak.

"You don't know shit about our past," he says, his voice even, but his usual good humor absent.

"I know you dated in college and—"

"Don't speculate, Canon."

"I mean, she didn't say it would be a problem for her, so I assumed you'd be—"

"You already asked her? Before you asked me?"

"Sorry, bruh, but the studio was more interested in who would write the script than who'd do the music. She's in high demand since she won the Golden Globe."

"Yeah, I get it."

"I needed to nail her down, get her attached as early as possible."

"I *said* I get it." Monk's words are diced up into tiny pieces, but it sounds like he's choking on them. "She's fine. I'm fine."

"Yeah, she didn't seem to have a problem with you."

"She shouldn't," he mutters under his breath, but loud enough for me to hear it.

"So it was a bad breakup?"

"It was college." Monk picks up his fork and knife, slices into the tender pink meat. "We grown, and we're professionals."

"Make sure, because I don't like personal shit messing up my movies."

"Oh, you mean like Camille and *Primal*," he says with a sudden evil grin.

"Man, if you don't—"

"Okay, okay." He puts up both hands in surrender. "You drop Verity and I won't mention Camille."

"Bet." I flick my chin up and lift my empty glass so our server can see I need a refill. "We got our studio. Our writer. Our music. Now if I can just find Dessi. I don't want to cast the guy until I know who Dessi'll be. I need to see who she'll have chemistry with."

"Makes sense," Monk says distractedly, looking down at the phone by his plate. "Oh, damn. Good for her."

"Good for who? What's up?"

"A few weeks ago, an old friend begged me to step into this gig for him in the Village." He picks up the phone, smiling. "His wife went into labor and he didn't want to leave the band hanging."

"So he asked *you*?" I blow out an impressed breath. "Must go way back."

Monk's a big deal. Asking him to sub at a local gig is like bringing in LeBron for a pickup game on the playground.

"It was fun. Whatever." Monk shrugs and smirks. "So there's this chick singing with the band that night and she was phenomenal. Sick with it. Like 'star' written all over her. It's only a matter of time with this one."

"What's her name?"

"Oh, you've never heard of her. Neevah Saint. I started following her on Instagram after that gig. Anyway, she just posted that she's in that Broadway play *Splendor*. She's an understudy, and apparently the lead actress is on vacation so she's stepping in tonight for the first time."

He glances at his watch and then to me. "What you got going on? You wanna catch a show?"

"You think we can get tickets day of? With such short notice?"

He gives me a *do you know who I am* look. "Bruh, I always got a hookup."

"I was gonna look at first passes Verity sent over of the script."

"Screw that. We're in New York. Come on. You work too hard."

"Look who's talking."

"Yeah, but I play hard, too. Extract the stick from your ass at least for tonight."

"Wow. You really know how to charm a guy."

"Bruh, we way past charm. I'm dragging you down to this show."

I stare glumly into my empty glass. "Aw, hell."

"Aw, hell, my ass." He signals to the server who never made it over with my refill. "Check, please."

TWO

Neevah

"Calling to wish you luck tonight, Neevah. Sorry I can't be there."

Listening to my mother's voicemail, I hear the regret in her voice, but it doesn't lessen my disappointment that she's not here.

"I had surgery and you know my knee ain't been right ever since," she goes on. "Traveling that long on a bus would be hard. Anyway, I'm so proud of you. We all are. I love you."

She doesn't fly.

I'm only in the role for a week.

She has obligations at home.

I rehearse the litany of reasons my mother cannot be here when I need her, like I have many times over the last decade. Like I did my first semester in college. And when I was struggling after graduation. I toured with a play once and we did a show in Charlotte. It was a small role, but Mama came. She beamed with pride over the couple of lines I had onstage for only a few minutes. How would she feel tonight seeing me on Broadway as the star of the show?

"You got this," my hairstylist and best friend, Takira, says, jarring me from my thoughts and bringing me back to the dressing room as I prepare to go on.

Her words echo the mantra I've been chanting internally ever since I found out I'd be stepping in for the lead actress tonight. I've actually known for a few weeks because her vacation was planned, but this is the first night I'm actually *doing* it. On Broadway. Stomach in knots. Possibly vomiting.

"I'm gonna ruin this costume with these big ol' sweat circles." I laugh and lift my arms. "My nerves. Oh, my God. I just want to get this over with."

Takira sticks another pin in to secure the long wig I'm wearing for the part.

"I repeat." She catches my eyes in the mirror, resting her chin in the crook of my neck and squeezing my shoulders. "You got this. Truth be told, I thought Elise would never go on vacation 'cause she knows her understudy can sing her out of the water and act her under the table. She didn't want folks seeing how good her backup actually is." She winks at me. "But tonight they will."

Will they? I don't care if anyone thinks I'm better than the principal. I like Elise. She's truly talented. I just want to get through this and not embarrass the director or let down the cast. Or disappoint the people who paid to see Elise.

"I'll be right back," Takira says. "I'm gonna go grab you some of that tea they had in the green room."

The walls of Elise's dressing room seem to clamp around me like jaws. While she's on vacation, I get to borrow hers, but the one I share with three other understudies is a glorified broom closet four flights up. This much larger room is tastefully decorated, with gorgeous rugs, plush furniture, and abstract paintings gracing the walls. Plenty of space for my doubts and fears to make themselves comfortable.

A few minutes later, there's a knock at the door. The understudies cluster in the hallway, their eyes lit with excitement.

"Good luck out there," Janie gushes. "There's nothing like it."

She's been on before. As swing, she understudies for several actors, so her chances of getting onstage are greater than mine.

"You guys," I say. "I'm so nervous."

"You're gonna be amazing," Beth reassures.

They crowd around me with their topknots and varying shades of leotard and sweatpants, squeezing me. I slump into their arms, finding solidarity and a few seconds of borrowed confidence in their tight grip.

"Half an hour, ladies and gents," the stage manager's disembodied voice reminds us through the intercom system.

My heartbeat seems to triple.

"Okay. Almost time. Let's get out of here, girls," Janie tells the other two understudies.

"It's your night," Beth says. "Show 'em what you got."

"Thanks." I offer the three of them a smile and wave when they file out of the dressing room. I'm left with my reflection in the mirror and the waiting quiet. I do a few deep breathing exercises, some vocal warm-ups. None of my routines seem to quell the anxiety blossoming in my chest.

Takira opens the door, startling me as she enters carrying a steaming mug.

"Here you go." She reaches in her bag and pulls out a bottle of water. "Room temperature. Wasn't sure which you'd prefer so I brought both."

"Thanks." I'm mentally rehearsing the monologue from the final act, barely paying attention.

"Let me check your hair one more time and then I'll leave you alone." Takira comes over and adjusts a few hairpins. "Your scalp looked good, by the way."

That does get my attention. I turn to search her face. My hair has been…an issue. After showing up for a few gigs and finding no one on set who knew what to do with Black hair, I started making sure I was prepared to do it myself. I found Takira, who has taken care of it recently and helped keep it healthy. I could have handled it tonight, but having her meant one less thing to worry about.

And Takira's my girl. With so much distance between my family and me—not just the miles separating North Carolina from New York, but the chasm yawning between our hearts—I've collected a few good friends through the years. I've needed them.

There was a time when I couldn't imagine a night like this without Mama and Terry, and now it's hard to see them in any part of my life. Hard for me to imagine fitting into theirs. Especially Terry's. I have a niece, Quianna, I barely know and can hardly bring myself to look at because each time I do, I see *them*.

"Stop it," I tell the girl in the mirror with the heavy stage makeup and the silky wig spilling down her back. "The past is shit. The future is uncertain. All you have is now."

"That's what you always say." Takira laughs, her wide white smile contrasting with her flawless brown skin.

"I literally forgot you were there." I chuckle, allowing amusement to pierce my nervousness for at least one moment.

"Well, I'm getting out of your hair, so to speak." She picks up her bag, stuffed with supplies, from the floor and pats her cap of natural curls. "I'll be watching from the balcony."

"You're coming to dinner after, right? I think some of us are heading to Glass House Tavern."

"Sounds good. I'll meet you back here." She grins. "I want to see you signing all the autographs at the stage door."

"Pffft." I swallow the anxiety inching up my throat. "I doubt it."

"This role has never been played by a Black woman." Takira's smile fades and her look grows more intent. "Understudy or not, tonight's a big deal, not just for you, but for the little girls out there who need to see *us* onstage. Tonight's not just your night. It's all of ours."

I huff out a laugh and rub the back of my neck. "No pressure, huh?"

"Girl, you were born for pressure." She leans in to lay a kiss on my cheek.

I catch and hold her hand, hold her stare. "Thanks, T, for everything."

"You know I got you."

"Fifteen minutes," comes over the intercom.

Sweat sprouts around my hairline and my breath stutters.

"Bye," Takira says, and slips from the dressing room.

And then it's just me, sitting with a cup of tea, room temperature water, and all the possible ways I could screw this up. The faint buzz of preparation beyond my door sifts into the silence. The bees working in the hive backstage while the patrons wait, bellies full from a pre-show dinner, or relaxed after a drink or two. I watch theater on an empty stomach and completely sober. I don't want a thing dulling my senses or making me slow. There could be something I miss. I consume a show like a starved animal, like a tremoring addict chasing a high. Hard to believe I thought I wanted a different life when now this, performing, is everything to me.

Since graduating from Rutgers, I've done regional tours, some commercials, done swing for a couple of smaller shows, but this is my first time stepping onto a Broadway stage. In the years since that awful day with Terry and Brandon, I've learned a lot about myself. My view of the world, of what was possible, was so limited then. It's like I was looking at life with one eye open. I might have stayed in my small town, done community theater, married Brandon and been content with two or three kids. Maybe taught drama at our local high school. That is a path my life could have taken and I might have been fine.

They ran me from that life, though, Terry and Brandon. They kicked me out of the nest and sent me soaring. On some level I'm grateful things happened the way they did, but most times when I think of them, it's hard to find goodwill, and as much as I hate to admit it, grace has been scarce. A wound left untended festers, and that's what's happened with my family.

"Five minutes," the stage manager intones over the intercom.

I close my eyes, blocking out old hurts and moldy memories. Even cutting off the roads my mind would take to the future and what doing well tonight, this week while Elise is on vacation, could mean for my career. I whittle my thoughts down to one thing.

Splendor.

This play. This character. This performance. This moment.

I've been in the wings, backstage every night for months. Always prepared, but never put on. Every line and lyric lives in my pores now, runs through my veins. I want to give myself to that stage tonight. I want to pour out every emotion this story demands.

Theater has the power to transform, to transport. For every person waiting for curtains to rise, this story is the vehicle to escape the mundane, the grind, the pressures life imposes on us. I know because I feel those same pressures. I feel the weight of life and I want to be lifted as badly as they do. For someone tonight, I'm the getaway.

And just like that, my perspective shifts and it's not about the tightness in my chest or the shortness of breath or the sweat running down my back. It's not about my fear of what could go wrong for *me*. It's about what I can do for *them*. What we can create together tonight.

I stare at the same girl in the mirror, but now in her eyes, there's a mingling of peace and fire.

"Places, everyone!" the stage manager urges. "Places!"

THREE

Canon

I prefer film.

I like months to mold a story into my preferred shape, to manipulate with light or reconstruct with editing.

I like takes.

A few chances for my actors to find their best.

I like time.

Theater is immediate. With a movie, I'm bringing something to life. With theater, it's breathing on *me*. It's already alive. I know it takes months, sometimes years bringing a work to the Broadway stage, so I respect the process and appreciate its rigors, but the experience is very different from film.

And I prefer film.

But from the moment *she* steps onstage, this understudy, something kindles inside me. At first, it's merely a flicker of recognition. Not that I know her or have seen her before. I recognize this *feeling* of finding something unexpected and exceptional.

Discovery.

After a while, beauty blurs. In my business, you've seen one pretty face…so for me, a well-constructed face doesn't necessarily hold my attention the way it did when I was younger. Surgeons can construct a great face. Beauty can be bought.

This. What she has, what she *does*, is not about beauty.

She's attractive, I guess. Even under the thick layer of stage makeup and the wig and the costume, there's an arresting quality to her.

I mentally strip every performer when I meet them. Remove the makeup, costume, whatever identity they've assumed to examine what lies beneath. The bones under the skin. The soul under the flesh. It's a knee-jerk response after years of casting for movies. I automatically disassemble them into their smallest parts. Even when I'm not working with an actor, I assess them to see what's there for me to use.

There's so much here.

If she were a room, all the windows and doors would be flung open. There is an unboundedness to her, even as she exhibits the restraint of craft. She's obviously well-trained and disciplined, but her spirit gallops like a horse given its head, lengthening the reins until it runs wild. Her face tells the story before she delivers one line. She's adularescent, the glow of a stone that comes from beneath the surface—like all the brightest parts of her aren't available to the naked eye, and onstage she brings it out for the audience to see.

For much of the play, she interacts with other characters, but near the middle, the stage clears until she stands alone in the spotlight. The stage is vast, and she seems so small, it could easily swallow her, but it doesn't. She commands the space, and when she reaches the pivotal monologue, anyone else onstage would only be in her way.

Splendor
There's splendor in our kisses
And awe in every breath
When you touch me, just like that,
just like that right there, the world stops
Beneath your fingers, I shiver. I crumble. Your caress leaves me boneless, weightless
One glance from you, the sun stands still in my chest
High noon, high rise, high on you
My field of poppies, my field of dreams
My splendor in the grass
Splendor, splendor, splendor
Chase me. Catch me. Wrap me in your fantasies.
Feed me from the storehouse of your love.

Let's sustain each other. Let's enjoy each other. Let's find forever.
Each and every eternity.
I'll trade my heart for yours.
And we will be splendor, you and me.

She and I are not alone in the theater. I know hundreds of people around me hear her words, too, but somehow, it feels like she delivers the words to me. To only me. I wonder if everyone listening feels that way, too.

That's the alchemy of this actress. She *reaches* you. With an audience this large, she makes it personal. In a story that is pretend, she makes it feel true.

And in a moment when I wasn't looking, I've found exactly what I was looking for.

FOUR

Neevah

When the show reaches its climax, at the very end, the song pries the final note from my diaphragm, pulls it from my throat and suspends it—leaves it throbbing in the air. The theater goes quiet for the space of a breath held by eight hundred people and then explodes.

Applause.

The relief is knee-weakening. I literally have to grab the lead actor John's arm for support. He doesn't miss a beat, pulling me into his side and squeezing.

"Bravo," he whispers, a broad, genuine smile spread across his face. The last song made me cry, and my face, still wet from those tears, splits into a wide, disbelieving grin.

I did it. I survived my first Broadway performance.

The lights drop and we rush backstage, a cacophony of laughter and chatter filling the hidden passageways. When the curtain call begins, the cast return to the stage in small waves, the applause building as the principals take their bows.

And then it's my turn. On legs still shaky, I leave the safety of the wings, the long skirt of my costume belling out around me. I take center stage. The applause crescendos, approval vibrating through my bones and jolting my soul. Someone thrusts flowers into my arms and the sweet smell wafts around me. Every sense, every molecule of my being, strains, opens, stretches to absorb this small slice of triumph. I can't breathe deeply enough. The air comes in shallow sips, and I'm dizzy. The world spins like a top, a kaleidoscope of colors and light and sound that threatens to overwhelm me. The whirl of it makes me giddy, and I laugh. Eyes welling with tears, I laugh.

These are the moments a lifetime in the making. We toil in the shadows of our dreams. In the alleys of preparation and hard work where it's dark and nothing's promised. For years, we cling by a thread of hope and imagination, dedicating our lives to a pursuit with no guarantees.

But tonight, if only for tonight, it's all worth it.

I'm still floating when Takira bursts into the dressing room.

"Neevah!" she screams, throwing her arms around me and rocking me back and forth. "You did it. You chewed that performance up and spat it *out*. You hear me?"

I laugh and return her squeeze, new tears trailing down my cheeks. It's relief and reward and, in some tiny corner of my heart, regret. Regret that my mother isn't here to hold me. Regret that if my sister were here, I wouldn't even know where to start wading through our shit so we could celebrate together. You know what? Tonight is about *tonight*, not past drama with Mama and Terry, and I'm determined to enjoy it.

"Thank you." I pull back to peer into my friend's face. "I can't believe it."

"Well, believe it. You served notice." She snaps her fingers and grins. "Neevah Saint is *here*."

"Now to do it seven more times." I laugh and start taking pins from the wig, which is as hot as a herd of sheep on my head.

"Oh, you got it, unless Elise hears how amazing you were and cuts her vacation short."

"Not happening. She was ready for a break, but she'd never missed a show."

I strip off the costume and stand in only panties, unselfconscious. Modesty is one of the first things to go in this business. I've undressed hurriedly in a roomful of actors and dancers in smaller shows where there was *a* dressing room, so we get real communal real fast.

I tug on skinny jeans with a tight-fitting orange sweater, and layer it with a brown leather jacket, scarf, boots. I wipe away the heavy stage makeup. It feels like my skin can breathe for the first time in hours. I assume there will be some fans at the stage door, even if it's just a few.

They'll have to get the real Neevah because I don't want anything more than a slick of lip gloss and a bit of mascara. A brown, orange, and green plaid newsboy cap covering the neat cornrows I wore under my wig is all I'm doing for hair. Slim, oversized gold hoops in my ears finish the look.

"Ready?" I ask Takira, hefting a slouchy bag on my shoulder.

"Let's do this. Hopefully your adoring fans won't take all night, 'cause your girl is starving."

We're still laughing, and I'm so preoccupied with my empty stomach, I'm completely unprepared for the crowd at the stage door. Are they here for John? For some principal player? Because surely they're not all here for the understudy.

"Neevah!" a young girl, maybe ten or eleven, calls. "Can you sign this?"

She thrusts a pen and a *Splendor* playbill toward me. She glows, her smooth brown cheeks rounded with a wide grin. Her eyes shine with...pride?

"Oh, sure," I mumble dazedly, taking the pen and signing my name.

She's the first in a long line of girls, all shapes and colors and ages, saying what it meant to see me onstage. Mothers whispering how impactful it was for their Black and Brown daughters to be in the audience tonight. The impact is on *me*; what could feel like a weight or burden or responsibility feels like a warm embrace. Feels like strong arms encircling me. Supporting me. The first time I saw someone who looked like me onstage, it planted a seed inside me. It whispered a dream.

That could be you.

It makes me emotional to think I might have done that for any of these girls tonight, and I spend the next twenty minutes scribbling my name on playbills through a film of tears.

"Neevah!" a deep male voice calls from the back of the now-thinning crowd.

I squint at the tall man, frowning until I place him.

"Wright!" I take a few steps and he meets me halfway, giving me a tight hug. "Oh, my God. You were here tonight?"

"Was I here?" When he pulls back, a warm smile creases his handsome face. "You blew it out of the water. I knew you were good, but damn."

Laughter spills out of me and I don't think this night could get more perfect. I randomly met Wright Bellamy a few weeks back at a gig when he subbed for the pianist, giving the audience more than they bargained for with such a famous musician tickling the ivories that night.

"Thank you." I step away and shove my hands into the pockets of my jeans, huddling in the leather jacket against the chill of an October night. "I was nervous as hell."

"Didn't show. Your voice is spectacular. I knew that from the gig we did, but I had no idea you were *that* good. Wow. Glad I saw your post on Instagram or I would've missed it."

I'm stone-still, shocked that he came tonight specifically to see me perform. "I'm so glad you made it. You're still in LA, right?"

"Yeah, but I'm here for some stuff. Heading back home in a few days."

Takira walks up, linking her arm through mine. "Girl, if we don't get some food," she whispers.

"Oh, yeah. Sorry." I turn back to Wright. "Takira, this is Wright Bellamy. Wright, my friend Takira."

"Nice to meet you," Takira says. "You got any food on you? I'm about to eat your hat."

As usual, Takira never meets a stranger and has us laughing right away.

"We're actually headed to Glass House Tavern," I tell Wright. "Come if you want. It's a group of us from the show. Just some of the cast celebrating, but you're welcome. We can catch up."

A small frown dents between his thick brows and he glances over his shoulder.

"I mean, no pressure, obviously," I rush to assure him. This is one of the biggest names in music, and here I go, inviting him to dinner with a group of strangers.

"No, it sounds cool," he says, looking back to us. "Lemme check with my boy. Can he come?"

I glance over his shoulder and spot a tall man turned away from us, his broad shoulders and back straining a wool blazer, a hoodie pulled up to cover his head and face in the cold. His hands burrow into the pockets of his blazer and he's nodding like he's talking to himself.

"He's on the phone," Wright explains. "But lemme see if he wants to roll."

He steps away toward the man and Takira immediately squeezes my hand and squeals.

"Shit, Neeve." Her eyes are wide and bright. Mouth dropped open. "That's Wright Bellamy."

"I know. He's cool as a fan."

"You know him? How—"

"We're in," Wright says, stepping back up beside us. "He's finishing a call, but we're ready. Lead the way."

It's just a few blocks, and the three of us chat about the show and what Wright's been doing in New York. All the while his friend's deep voice rumbles a few paces behind. I don't want to be rude or nosy and look back, but the rich timbre, his towering height, his face obscured by the hoodie—I'm intrigued. He hangs back on the sidewalk, still on his call, when we enter the restaurant.

Our friends already have a table and a shout goes up, congratulating me on popping my White Way cherry. My three understudy buddies came. John's here, too, and one other principal. A few from the stage crew. Our little troupe has become a family and, as if eight shows a week isn't enough time together, we gather and eat every chance we get.

"You're not paying tonight," John says, holding out the seat beside him. "And drinks are on me."

"Aww." I plop into the chair and drop my bag to the floor. "You're so sweet. You don't have to do that."

"You were fantastic," John says, baby blue eyes sincere and smiling. "Let's do it again tomorrow."

Takira is already sitting beside me, so Wright takes the seat next to her.

"Hey," he says to Janie across the table. "Could you hold that seat beside you for my friend? He's wrapping up a call, but'll be in soon."

"Sure." Janie blushes. "I love your work, by the way. The score of *Silent Midnight*...gah."

"Thank you. That was a special project. Lots of fun," Wright replies with a smile. "Now tell me about the show."

Wright's a genius, but he's so unassuming and modest. A man as famous as he is could easily make this conversation about him, let everyone at this table give his ego a real nice hand job, but he doesn't. He talks about our show, compliments the performance, asks John about his process. I liked him when we did that last-minute gig, and we've interacted some on social media since. My impression of him holds up. He's a good guy.

Not to state the obvious, but also fine. Like *fine*.

He has this Boris Kodjoe vibe. Real smooth. Kind of golden brown. Clean-cut, close-cut. I can objectively recognize his appeal, even though he's not my type.

Not that I have a type lately. I'm so deep in this dick drought I'm past the point of thirst.

At first, I thought it was merely the grind. Auditioning constantly, taking craft classes, doing commercials and voice-over work to not just keep bills paid, but to save. This business is feast or famine. I'm eating now, but I've been hungry before. Not again. I'm thirty. Too old to still be living gig to gig and buying into that starving artist thing. I need health insurance and regularly scheduled meals, thank you very much. So yeah, the grind could account for my semi-disinterested libido, but I suspect it's more.

Maybe *I'm* disinterested.

I've always been guarded with men. It only takes your fiancé sleeping with your sister once for you to be wary. It's beyond my cynicism, though. I need a man who doesn't think that because he has a dick and I don't that I should defer to him—shrink my dreams down to a more manageable size. I almost did that with Brandon. I dreamt of something else; something that brought me to New York, to that stage tonight, to this moment. And I almost reneged on my dreams for a man who cheated on me and got my sister pregnant.

So, yeah. I'm cautious not only about who I share my heart and body with, but I'm also protective of my dreams; of my ambition. I won't endanger my future for a man who can fuck. Though...a man who can fuck? I wouldn't turn it down, but it will take more than that to pique my interest.

"What are you getting?" Takira asks, leaning over to read my menu instead of hers. "Anything here meet your high standards?"

I roll my eyes. My standards aren't that high. I've just cut out red meat and stopped drinking as much alcohol. My health demands it. "You're the one who said my scalp would thank me if I changed my diet," I remind her.

"Yeah, but you took it to that next level." She elbows me and flashes a grin. "Always being extra."

"I'm thinking about the salmon, but I—"

A chair scraping across the floor catches my attention. Wright's friend has finally come inside to join us. The table shrinks immediately when he settles his imposing frame into the seat beside Janie. He peels the hood away from his head and I bite off a gasp.

It's Canon Holt.

Like *the* Canon Holt.

The director I, and probably every actress at this table and in this dining room, would sacrifice a pinky toe to work with. Canon Holt is at my table sitting across from me.

Takira's expression doesn't register this massive earthquake of a revelation, but she kicks me under the table and hisses from the corner of her mouth. "Did you know?"

I pretend I need to reach for something on the floor so I can whisper back, "Do you think I would have kept my shit together this long if I knew?"

"True. True." Takira casually glances up from her menu and smiles in Canon's general direction, but he's not looking at her. He's studying his screen. He's apparently in an exclusive relationship with his phone, and no one at this table tempts him to stray.

Which means I can look at him.

Good. God.

He's not that handsome, but that's irrelevant. Some might even call his features, examined on their own, unremarkable.

They'd be wrong.

It's a Maker's sleight of hand. Now God knew this man did not need lashes that long and thick, a paradox against the hard, high slant of his cheekbones. Canon hasn't looked twice at anyone here, as far as I can tell, but I've stolen enough glances to know there's a fathomlessness to his dark eyes that is arresting. His unsmiling mouth is wide, the lips full in the blunt elegance of his face. A five o'clock shadow licks the ridge of his jawline. There is a geometry to him—angles, lines, edges—that disregards the individual parts and illuminates the compelling sum.

Our food comes out on steaming platters just as he lays his phone on the table.

"Excuse my reach," the server says to him, distributing plates and drinks to the rest of the table. "Is there anything I can get for you, Mr. Holt?"

He doesn't even blink when she calls him by his name.

"Macallan?" he asks. "I don't see it on the menu, but—"

"We'll figure it out," she assures him with a smile.

I'm sure folks just go around figuring things out for him all the time at this point in his career.

"So, Mr. Holt," Janie says, all pink and flustered, "I loved your last documentary. I heard you're working on a movie next. What's it about?"

"It hasn't been announced." He truncates the words, his expression shut down. He looks over his shoulder like the restroom might offer an escape from this banality.

"Oh, you can tell us," Janie cajoles.

One dark, imperious brow elevates. "But I don't want to."

Okayyyyy.

An awkward silence falls on the table. Seemingly oblivious, or uncaring, he picks his phone up and starts typing again.

So fine as hell, but a jerk.

My lady parts shimmy back into their shell. I don't have time or patience for narcissists who think the sun and stars were made for them. I may find it hard to stop looking at him, but it's increasingly easy not to like him.

"So when did you know you wanted to be on Broadway, Neevah?"

My fork is halfway to my mouth when Wright asks. I'm too hungry to forego this bite, so I take it, chew thoughtfully, and consider his question.

"You know," I say and sip my water, "it wasn't as much Broadway specifically, as it was that I knew I wanted to perform. That I wanted to be an actress."

"So when was that?" Wright presses.

I shuffle through my memories to locate all the scents and sounds and sights that made the experience singular.

"I was eleven years old," I begin, recalling everything good about that summer. "We'd have family reunions every June."

"Us too," Takira pipes up. "Whoo. The Fletchers can throw a reunion, and I got a whole line of family tree T-shirts to show for it."

"So do I." I laugh. "My cousins lived in New York at the time, and they'd always come down to North Carolina for the family reunion. When I was eleven, they suggested we come up north for a change. We got a bus and drove. They took us all over the city, and on our last day here, we got tickets to *Aida*, the original cast."

"Oh, Dame Headley," Janie breathes reverently.

"Exactly. When Heather Headley sang 'Easy as Life,' I don't think I breathed until she finished." I shrug helplessly. "She had this monstrous talent that devoured the whole room. When she was done, I just sat there and everyone around me seemed to be as stunned as I was. That's when I knew what I was supposed to do with my life. I was supposed to perform and make people feel the way I felt in that moment. And it didn't go away. Not when the show was over. Not when I got back home to North Carolina. Not when my parents told me acting was a long shot and I needed a backup plan. From then on, it was only ever this."

When I look up from my plate, my gaze collides with Canon's dark eyes fixed on me. Ever since he sat down, his glance has skidded over everyone, never settling, like a bee who can't find a flower worthy of pollination. But he's looking at me now, and I'll be damned if I can look anywhere else. My breath is snatched under his scrutiny. It's intent and discerning, his stare. I feel like something under glass he may add to his collection.

"Refill?" the server asks, snipping the chord stretching between Canon and me.

"Uh, yes." I offer her a smile and my empty glass.

By the time I look back, Canon is on his phone again. Maybe I imagined that moment. Not that we shared a glance, but that it was somehow as intense for him as it was for me.

I shake off the effects of that exchange and demolish my meal, digging into the food with relish. It's a good group, and our camaraderie is infectious. Wright fits in easily, telling jokes and stories that crack us up. You'd never know this man has Grammy awards and Oscar nominations and platinum records to his credit. He's down to earth and more "normal" than most artists I know. Much less intense and off-putting than *Le Directeur* across the table hooking up with his phone.

But every once in a while, Canon actually does talk with John and even thaws some with Janie, who is, no two ways about it, trying too hard.

Once the plates are cleared, I reach for my bag so I can pay my portion, despite John's offer.

"Don't bother," Wright says, placing his hand over mine. "Canon already got the bill."

"Oh."

I look at Canon, whose wide mouth curls at the corners, head inclined toward Janie's as she tells him something I can't hear. He doesn't quite smile, but at least he's not scowling.

We file outside and cluster on the sidewalk. By nature I'm a people watcher, and I find myself observing the pods of conversation going on around me. Takira's embroiled in a passionate discussion about *Dreamgirls*, for some reason. John is laughing with some of the crew over a missed cue from tonight's show. Wright chats with one of the cast members who's working on a new album. I catch snippets of their exchange. *Coltrane. Miles Davis. Genius.* The cast member is a jazz enthusiast, so I can see how they'd click. Janie is still working her angle with Canon, and his expression says his long-suffering may be on its last legs. How can Janie even bring herself to keep talking with him looking at her that way? It's actually pretty comical, and before I catch myself, I'm chuckling under my breath.

"What's funny?"

I look up by centimeters, certain he can't be talking to me because he hasn't all night, but he's looking right at me. Head turned away from Janie, who has wandered over to join Takira's small circle.

"What?" I manage, stalling.

"You laughed. What's funny?"

"No, I—"

"So you didn't just laugh, standing here by yourself?" he asks, no smile in sight.

"Not laugh, exactly." I bite my lip and shove my hands deeper into my jacket pockets.

His brows raise knowingly.

"Okay, so I chuckled. Maybe snorted. I snuckled."

He tilts his head, and lo and behold, those full lips twitch at the corners the slightest bit. "So what made you snuckle?"

I shake my head and hope he'll let it go.

He doesn't.

"Tell me," he says, crossing his arms over his wide chest.

Incidentally, that blazer and hoodie really is a very good look for him.

"Oh, good grief," I huff. "It was the look on your face."

"When I was talking to…" He tips his head in Janie's direction and I nod. "What was the look?"

"It wasn't impatience, exactly."

"Are you sure?"

"And not irritation."

"It may have been."

"It was more this kind of…forced tolerance."

His almost-smile deepens a little. "That does sound accurate."

We stare at one another for a few seconds, the plumes of our breath mingling in the cold night air. And then we grin together. It's the first full-fledged smile I've seen from him. It's dazzling, sketching grooves into his lean cheeks, and I feel such a sense of accomplishment, winning that smile. I retract everything I thought about him not really being handsome.

Because when he smiles, he is. He so is.

"Dude, you ready?" Wright asks, walking up beside us.

"Yeah." Canon breaks our stare, his smile disappearing as quickly as it came. "I'm whipped. Let's go."

"Neevah, so good to see you again." Wright pulls me into a side hug and squeezes. "Congratulations."

I look up at him, offering a smile. "Thank you again for coming."

"Wouldn't have missed it. You were great. If you're ever in LA, don't hesitate to hit me up."

"Will do." I studiously train my eyes on Wright's face, and do my best to ignore his taciturn friend.

The two men turn and take the few steps that lead them away from me and this extraordinary night. I'm about to join my friends and head toward the subway when I feel a light touch on my arm. I look up and shock rolls through me. Shock and a thrill. It's Canon.

"Did you forget something?" I ask, my breath refusing to push in and out as per normal respiratory patterns.

"You were exceptional on that stage," he says softly. "The best in the show."

Vines sprout from the sidewalk and wrap around my ankles, trapping me where I stand. Immobile. I should say something, not just stand here like I'm starstruck, though there is a part of me that is.

"What you said tonight about making people feel when you perform," he says, his eyes never straying from my face. "Keep that."

And then he turns and walks away.

FIVE

Canon

"You were especially pleasant tonight," Monk says when we climb into the Uber that met us at the corner.

"I was, wasn't I?" I settle back into the seat and close my eyes. "Thank you for noticing."

"You were on your phone the whole time." His voice holds little sting because he knows I don't respond to that guilt shit, especially not when it comes to being social.

"I was convincing Mallory to fly out to New York as soon as possible. Lots of protests and texting back and forth."

"Your casting director? Why does she need to come to New York?"

"I want her to see some auditions out here." I open my eyes and grin crookedly. "I found my Dessi."

"What?" Monk's brows shoot up. "When? Who?"

"Tonight." I hesitate, watching his face for a reaction. "Your friend Neevah."

Flabbergasted.

"The fuck?" he says after a moment of his mouth hanging open. "Neevah Saint?"

"Yeah. The one we watched perform. The one we had dinner with."

"First of all, *we* did not have dinner. I had dinner with them folks. You were the same antisocial bastard you usually are, and they *still* were all up your ass."

"They're actors. I'm a director. They want work, so the forecast is always partly fawning with a high chance of kiss-ass."

"Second of all, you barely looked at Neevah, much less spoke to her. When did you decide she's Dessi Blue?"

"Pretty much as soon as she stepped onstage."

"It's the way she looks? That's why you want to cast her?" Censure, though unspoken, lurks in his voice.

"Get the fuck outta here. You know me better than that. You think I find the story of a lifetime, put my whole-ass career on the line to tell it, take almost a year to fund it, then search for the right actor for six months, only to cast a girl because she has a great ass?"

"Oh, so you did notice her ass."

And every other part of her, but that's not pertinent.

Her ass. Her tits.

Her flawless coppery skin. A face so expressive it's like a blank canvas she paints every emotion across in vivid color, in broad strokes. Big brown eyes that in one moment offer everything and in the next seem to hoard a thousand secrets. A man would ransom his soul for those eyes, for those secrets.

Each of her physical features is remarkable.

And completely irrelevant.

If all it took was a pretty girl, I could have cast this part six months ago. *Dessi Blue* requires more than a pretty face.

I want that *light* Neevah lets out when she sings. I want that *conviction* behind every word she spoke onstage. I want that little volcano of a woman to erupt on my set. I want everything she has to give because I knew immediately she was one of those who gives everything. And I'm the man to get it out of her. The right director (me). The right story (mine). And she'll be touted as a rare talent. It didn't take me all night to know that. I knew it right away.

And it's never happened to me before. Not like this.

"Her ass won't tell my story," I respond after a few seconds. "The studio wasted all that money and time looking for Dessi the last six months and I found her making her Broadway debut. Randomly."

"Not sure they'll agree. What did Mallory think?"

"Let's just say she's skeptical. She's never heard of Neevah, so of course she's got reservations."

"You mean that Galaxy won't trust a budget that big on an actress no one knows on the strength of... what? Your gut?"

"Don't underestimate this gut." I pat my stomach and wink. "It knows. And, yeah. The studio will give some pushback."

"Forget the studio. You won't get it past Evan."

He has a point. Evan won't be feeling this, trusting the project of a lifetime to an unknown with little to no movie experience.

"You let me worry about Evan. Once he sees her, he'll agree with me. That's why I want Mallory to come out here immediately. Catch Neevah onstage this week before that other chick returns from vacation or whatever. Then get a screen test with her as soon as she's back to doing standby. I don't want to throw too much at her when she's got this Broadway thing going on."

"This Broadway *thing* is her dream. Were you not listening?"

"Were you? Performing is her dream. That's what I heard. So you telling me I offer her the starring role in a Black biopic with a monster budget and *me* directing, and she turns it down to play backup on Broadway? Shiiiiiiit."

"Do you *know* you're a narcissist?"

"Of course. Narcissism comes with the territory. You aren't the dude who believes he *should* get millions of dollars to tell a damn story if you aren't just a little bit of a narcissist."

"The only thing that saves you from being a complete asshole is your mama raised you right."

That she did.

Whenever I'm smelling myself, as Mama used to say, her voice in my ear is the dose of humility that reins me in. She tethers me to my past. She prepared me for my future. Everything, *anything* good in me, Remy Holt put there. Thanks to my first documentary, everyone knows it.

I took all that footage Mama captured, all her sunsets and soliloquies, and bundled them into *The Magic Hour,* my first professional documentary. It took the grand jury and directing prizes at Sundance. I sailed through that awards season with her as the wind at my back every time I accepted a new, unexpected honor. It was her indomitable spirit that inspired audiences all over the world. Her fierce commitment to art even when her body betrayed her. It was her sage advice lit by the golden hour setting the world on fire that year.

I only wish she'd lived to see it.

"So Mallory is coming," I say, needing to shift this conversation from something I'm emotional about. Over the years, I've become an expert compartmentalizer. This life requires almost unsustainable, singular focus. My therapist earns his keep.

"When's she flying in?" Monk asks, linking his hands behind his head.

"Her daughter has a recital tomorrow, but goes to stay with Mallory's ex this weekend. So she'll come then and can still catch Neevah before she goes back to being understudy."

It's criminal, *that* woman being anyone's backup, but that's okay. I'll fix it.

"You want me to let Neevah know you guys are coming?"

"Hell no. Imma find the darkest corner of the theater to hide in. I don't want her to know we're there. Why do you think I ignored her all night?"

"We covered this already. You're an asshole."

"That too, but mostly I didn't want her to know I noticed her. She would have started auditioning. She would have started *acting* again. I wanted to see her *being*."

"Neevah is fantastic. I don't think you're wrong about what she could do with the role. I'm just surprised that since this movie is already a huge financial and commercial risk, you would, on the strength of a single performance, not even on film, cast her in the biggest movie you've ever directed."

"That's why I want Mallory's feedback. And I haven't cast her yet."

Through the car window, the velvet blanket of the city's skyline is stitched with lights and stars, and its vastness seems to reflect all the possibilities I felt after seeing Neevah onstage tonight.

"But I want her."

SIX

Neevah

"Crap." With my legs flung over the side of the couch, I frown. "I just got an alert that my phone has a virus from adult sites I visited."

"So Pornhub gave your phone an STD?" Takira pauses in chopping onions for the soup she's making. "You had unprotected surfing and now your phone has herpes?"

"Shut it. Does incognito mode mean nothing?"

"Long as it's been since you had that Vitamin D, no wonder you're banging your phone every day. You were bound to get infected."

"Could you stop being gross about my sex life?"

"What sex life?" Takira starts chopping again. "Social services will be by soon to pay your vagina a wellness visit."

I hurl a pillow across the room at her, missing on purpose.

"I'm here to check on Neevah's *pussy*," Takira says in her professional voice. "The neighbors are concerned. There's been no sign of activity for months. We're making sure the cat still purrs."

"I hate you," I grit out, but the struggle not to laugh is real.

"You won't hate meh when you taste this lunch, gyal," she says, easily slipping into her Trinidadian accent. "Diz iz meh grandma's famous corn soup."

"It does smell good." I walk over to stand by her at the counter. A short walk since our apartment has the square footage of a Porta Potty.

"And vegan." She proffers her knife. "Put them little hands to use. You on peppers."

"Yes, ma'am." I slide my phone into the pocket of my lounge pants. "On it."

It's my day off. My last show as the lead was last night, and when I return to the theater tomorrow, Elise will be the star again. I don't begrudge her that. She's a great singer. Outstanding actress. It just felt good to stand in the spotlight for a week. It's okay. My time will come. I just gotta keep grinding and pay my dues.

I'm slicing red peppers when the phone in my pocket buzzes. It's a number I don't recognize, but it could be a callback for something. Ya never know.

"Hello." I trap the phone between my ear and shoulder and keep cutting.

"Neevah?" a vaguely familiar, shiver-inducing voice says on the other line. "It's Canon Holt."

I drop the knife.

Dammit.

This man should not call me when I'm holding a knife. I could lose a finger.

"Uh, hey?" My curiosity and general state of shock lilt the words.

"I hope it's okay that I called. Monk gave me your number."

"Uh-huh." I send a slightly panicked look to Takira and mouth *Canon Holt*. Her eyes saucer and she catches a squeal with one hand. "I mean, sure. It's fine that you called. That he gave you this number. Wright. Monk, I mean. Yes."

Am I Kanye's Twitter account right now? I'm barely coherent. Good Lord.

I should sit down. I walk back to the couch and lower to the cushions carefully, waiting to understand what this is about. I mean, we *did* have a moment on the sidewalk, right? Is he still in town? Is he asking me out? What will I wear? I have to wash my hair and shave my legs. I need a Brazilian!

Oh. My. God.

I can't go on a date with Canon Holt with a furry pussy. What if we... my brain explodes at the thought of sex with that huge man. He would break me.

It would be fantastic.

"There's a small part in my next movie I'd like you to audition for."

I believe the thalamus is the part of your brain responsible for erotic stimuli. It fizzles when I realize Canon is not indeed looking to mate, but then all the other rational parts of my brain combust because he wants me to *audition*.

Calm your tits. Be normal. Act like this happens all the time to thespians like you.

"Oh really?" I drawl, sounding like fucking Bette Davis. "Sorry. Wow. That's great. What's the movie?"

"It hasn't been announced."

That's what he told Janie at dinner. So top secret. I'm intrigued.

Who am I kidding? I'm panting.

"My casting agent, Mallory Perkins, is in town. Can I put her in touch with your agent? They can discuss all the details."

"Sure. Yeah. That sounds great."

It's quiet on the phone for a few electric seconds.

"So...can you give me your agent's info to pass on to Mallory?"

"Yes! Of course. Is this your cell?"

That sounds so intrusive. I shouldn't have this famous director's number, especially not when I was just thinking he would break me if we were to ever copulate. He should file a restraining order. Immediately. But he doesn't need to know that.

"Yeah. This is my cell," he says. "You can share the contact here and I'll send it to Mallory. That work?"

"That works, sure."

"Sounds good. Bye."

He doesn't wait for me to respond. He's gone almost as quickly as he called. I flop onto the couch and stare at the ceiling, waiting for my particles to settle back to normal.

Takira rushes from the kitchen to hover over me. "What'd he say?"

"He wants me to audition for a part."

"Ayyyyeeee!" Takira jumps onto the other end of the couch and pumps her legs. "This is amazing."

It *is* amazing and not something I ever could have seen coming. At least once a day every day since I met Canon, I've thought about him. His intense, infrequent stare. That magnetic pull. His indifferent brand of charisma. The surprising words of encouragement he shared before he left. I have deliberately not talked about him, but my thoughts? I have less discipline where they're concerned. I thought more about the undeniable attraction I felt, not an opportunity. I didn't dare imagine this.

I shoot a text to my agent telling her to expect a call from Mallory Perkins, Canon Holt's casting agent. Of course, she calls right away with a dozen questions I have no answers for. I nearly forget I need to text her info to him.

Me: Hey! Great talking to you. Here's my agent's contact.
Canon: Thanks.

That's it? *Thanks?* Guess we're not at emojis yet. I get it.

"Ewwww!" I screech and sit up straight. "I just sent a text to Canon Holt from my porny phone."

Takira cackles and kicks me lightly. "You probably gave his phone crabs."

"Heifer," I laugh and lie back, wearing a wide smile. It's surreal. I'd filed that night away as *that one time I met Canon Holt and he called me exceptional*. Even though I've thought about it often over the last week, I accepted that I'd probably never see him again. It was something cool that happened with someone I admire and respect, but that was the end.

What if it was just the beginning?

SEVEN

Neevah

Of course, the elevator isn't working.

I punch the darkened button seven more times just to make sure the universe is indeed conspiring against me. As if this day has not found every way possible to make that clear.

I woke to a petulant day with pouting clouds downcast in a moody sky, so I brought my umbrella just in case.

My period came early.

Like three days early. Probably triggered by the stress of this oncoming audition. Yes, oncoming, not upcoming, because it feels like a train barreling toward me for a collision.

So...I have cramps.

I chipped a tooth eating a bagel.

Who chips a tooth eating a bagel? Now, in my defense, that bagel was tough. Fortunately, it was a back tooth. It and my dentist will have to wait until this audition is behind me.

Then the subway stalled. Only for a few minutes, but between the chipped tooth, the stalled subway, and now the out-of-order elevator, I'm running late.

"This place *would* be on the fifth floor," I mutter, flapping my arms a little so I don't sweat too badly. At least I'm dressed comfortably. The casting agent said come wearing little to no makeup and street clothes. My ballet flats have gotten a workout today, schlepping through Manhattan to get to this old building with its broken elevator.

I release a long, relieved breath when I reach the fifth-floor landing. A door opens to a studio with a long table and three chairs. Autumn sunlight streams through the floor-to-ceiling windows. A camera rests on a tripod in the middle of the room. A gray-streaked brunette, maybe in her late forties, turns from contemplating the street below to smile at me.

"Neevah?" she asks, walking forward and extending her hand to shake.

"Yes, hi. Ms. Perkins?"

"Call me Mallory, please." She gestures toward the table. "Would you like to put your things down? If you had to walk up five flights of stairs like I did, you must be out of breath." She looks me up and down and grins wryly. "Though it looks like you're in better shape than I am."

I drop my bag and umbrella on the table and wait for instructions. She didn't send sides in advance and didn't ask me to prepare anything, so I assume this is a cold read. I also assume Canon won't be coming.

"Is it, um, just us?" I ask.

"Yeah, just me today." She turns the camera on. "Canon generally doesn't do these."

"Of course," I rush to say, not wanting her to think I expect special attention from him.

"He prefers to see auditions on tape."

She takes one of the seats behind the table and slides a script toward me. It's well-worn and malleable in my hands. How many girls have stood in front of Mallory Perkins, heart in their throats, like I am right now? Clueless and hopeful, uncertain. How many girls got a surprise text from Canon Holt, and felt flattered that the great director had handpicked her, only to show up and discover he'll watch them on tape later? Then they never hear from him again because whatever he *thought* he saw actually wasn't there.

"Find page seventeen in the script," Mallory says, jotting a few words on a legal pad. "You can read the part of Dessi and I'll read Tilda. Let's start with the—"

"Sorry I'm late."

My head swivels to the door, and I nearly swallow my tongue when Canon strides into the room. He looks *scrumptious* in an army jacket worn over another hoodie, this one with *USC* emblazoned across the front. I refuse to be distracted by this, and immediately imagine him wearing an Oscar Mayer Wiener costume. They say envision your audience naked, but the last thing I should do is imagine Canon naked.

The wiener also doesn't help.

He's still really attractive.

And I still have a job to do, so I force a casual smile like I'm not completely thrown by his sudden appearance.

"I didn't think you were…" Mallory tilts her head and squints at him. "I mean, you don't usually—"

"I was close by." He walks over to the camera, closing one eye and peering through the lens. Adjusts a button on the side and sits at the table beside Mallory. "I have an appointment in thirty minutes three blocks away."

In other words, let's get this over with.

Mallory must hear the unspoken command same as I do. "Right," she says. "So on page seventeen—"

"Do you know why I want this cold, Neevah?" Canon interrupts.

I look up from the script in my hands to find his dark, disconcerting gaze trained on my face.

Is this a trick question? If so, it's working.

"Um, I guess—"

"Let me just tell you because again, I'm short on time. When I do a documentary, it's with real-life subjects—people with true stories to tell. You don't know anything about this movie, but it's a true story. It's a life story, and though I'll take some creative license, I'm looking for someone true. In a documentary, the subject usually doesn't rehearse to be on camera because it's about honesty and about instinct and immediacy. There usually aren't takes. You've never read what's on page seventeen, so I'm not judging if you trip over words or anything like that. I'm looking for truth—who you really are as an artist and as a person. That's more important to me than if you can memorize lines for an audition and polish up real good to impress us for ten minutes."

That's the most words he's ever spoken to me and I'm trying to absorb them. Trying to use what he just gave me to do my best. To show him who I actually am and to tell the truth.

"Okay," he says. "Now in the script, turn to page seventeen."

EIGHT

Dessi Blue

DESSI BLUE

Screenplay by: Verity Hill & Canon Holt

Story by: Verity Hill & Canon Holt

WORKING SCRIPT

P. 17

EXTERIOR - LAFAYETTE THEATRE - NIGHT

132nd Street & 2nd Avenue: Odessa Johnson stands outside the Lafayette surrounded by hundreds of people waiting to get in. The lit theater marquee sign above reads *Macbeth*. Scalpers wave tickets to the mostly Black theatergoers, men in their coats and sharp-brimmed hats, women dressed in their finery with freshly pressed hair. Odessa cranes her neck, trying to see above the crowd, obviously looking for someone. She's jostled by several people.

DESSI

Hey! Watch it!

She clutches her hat when it's almost knocked off her head and she's shoved into a girl in the crowd.

DESSI

'Scuse me. Everybody's trying to get in.

TILDA

It's alright. And if they ain't got a ticket, they can forget it. 'Lessen they plan to pay five dollars.

DESSI

I was kinda hoping I'd get one. A friend of mine was bringing me some money she owes me so I could buy a ticket.

Dessi cranes her neck again.

DESSI

But I ain't seen her. Not that I could find her in this crowd anyway.

TILDA

Hmmmph. I got a ticket I'll sell you. My old man bought 'em, but he late. Bet I'd find him with that other one.

DESSI

He cheating on you?

Tilda offers a mischievous grin.

TILDA

Yeah. With his wife.

Both girls laugh.

DESSI

I'm Odessa Johnson, but you can call me Dessi.

TILDA

Matilda Hargrove. Everybody calls me Tilda.

Dessi looks around at all the people elbowing each other and trying to get into the theater.

DESSI

Harlem is on fire tonight.

TILDA

Where you been? Harlem's on fire every night.

DESSI

This is different. I never seen the likes of this.

TILDA

What watermelon truck you fall off, girl? You sound as country as Mississippi.

DESSI

Alabama, I'll have you know.

TILDA

You want this ticket, Bama?

DESSI

How much?

TILDA

How much ya got?

DESSI

A dollar and some change.

TILDA

Girl. Where you work?

DESSI
The Cotton Club.

TILDA
Stop lying. You ain't yellow enough to work at the Cotton Club.

DESSI
Not onstage. I wash dishes.

TILDA
Oh. You like it?

DESSI
What you think? It's white folks' dishes.

The girls laugh again and Tilda looks at Dessi, assessing, head to toe.

TILDA
You dance, Bama?

DESSI
I do.

TILDA
Lindy?

DESSI
I can do 'em all.

TILDA
I might have something better than white folks' dirty dishes. Ever been to the Savoy?

DESSI

Couple of times.

TILDA

I'm a hostess there. We looking for new girls.

DESSI

Hostess? Do hostesses keep their legs closed?

Tilda touches her chest, feigns shock.

TILDA

Lord, Bama! Well, I never.

DESSI

I'll ask your old man if you ever.

They cackle, and both are jostled from behind, pushing them into each other again. Dessi grabs Tilda's arm and they stare into each other's eyes for a long second. Tilda clears her throat and takes a ticket from her stylish purse.

TILDA

I may be a cheat, but I ain't no whore. Tell ya what, Bama. Looks like Daddy got hemmed up with his old lady. Take the ticket and we'll talk about the job after the play. How's that sound?

Odessa's eyes widen and a smile breaks out on her face. She snatches the ticket.

DESSI

Perfect!

NINE

Canon

God, I missed LA.

Give me seventy-five degrees and sunshine in October over cold, gray New York. And you have to walk *everywhere*. Or take the subway. I mean, I get the appeal, but I grew up in San Diego County, in Lemon Grove, with beaches and mountains and canyons all in easy reach. Where rain is rare. I'm a Cali boy, born and bred. I didn't dream of going anywhere else for college. Plus attending the USC film school kept me close to Mama when she needed me most.

She would have liked Neevah.

I bat away that useless thought when I enter the office of Scripps Productions. Most people assume my company name is a play on words, me ghettofying *scripts*, but Scripps Pier was actually one of Mama's favorite places to watch her sunsets.

"Boss!" Graham, our assistant, says when I walk through the door. "Welcome home. We missed you."

"Missed you, too." I fish a Statue of Liberty figurine from my messenger bag and place it on her desk. "I got you something for your landmark collection."

"It's pink!" She snatches it, eyes bright with delight over the cheesy thing.

"Yeah. I figured that was unusual so I grabbed it."

She crosses around the desk to hug me. "I've never seen a pink one. Thank you!"

I squeeze her back briefly and then pull away to head toward my office.

"It's nothing," I call over my shoulder. "Is he in yet?"

Evan and I don't come to the office all the time, but we agreed to meet here today. I already know he'll try to talk me out of casting Neevah. That's his job—to make sure my creative impulses don't bankrupt us. But every once in a while I have to remind him it's my creative impulses that have gotten us this far. Today is one of those times.

"Said he's grabbing a smoothie from that place around the corner and is only a few minutes away," Graham shouts from the reception area.

"Cool. Let me know when he's ready."

I close the door and sit at my desk. I haven't been here in weeks, which is not unusual. I'll probably be in New York a lot more once we start shooting *Dessi Blue*. So much of the story takes place there. I did the spec script to sell the concept and get Galaxy onboard, but Verity is already reworking it now that she's attached. Evan will coordinate with the director of photography and the production designer to scout locations once the script is more final, but I can't imagine we *won't* be filming in New York. That would make things even easier for Neevah.

I haven't even offered her the part, but how could she turn it down?

I pull the headshot she brought to the audition from my bag.

I quickly skirt over the fact that she's beautiful. Who isn't, in this business? She has that indefinable quality you can't teach, can't Botox or artificially enhance into existence. She was born with it and has cultivated it, and now it's come to my attention.

And I'm going to use it.

Someone taps on my door.

"Uh-huh," I grunt, reaching for the bottle of water Graham always stocks in my office.

"You're back."

If there was ever a picture of Hollywood privilege, it would be my production partner Evan. Bronze- and gold-streaked hair falling in perfect-cut waves. Year-round tan. Chiseled bone structure and tall, lean frame. Even though he has a Hollywood pedigree dating all the way back to the heyday of MGM and RKO and the studio system, he set out to make a name and fortune for himself. He probably didn't think it would be with the kid from Lemon Grove, but you never know how life will mix it up.

"My dude," he says, walking farther into the office and dapping me up. "Welcome home. I thought you were doing the film festival and coming right back."

Holding his smoothie in one hand, he plucks Neevah's headshot from my desk, raising his brows and slanting me a knowing glance, even though he doesn't know shit. "I can see how you might have gotten a little… distracted."

"It ain't like that." I grab the photo and toss it onto my desk. "I mean, I did stay longer to audition Neevah, but… it ain't like that."

"It better not be. We can't afford another *Primal*."

"If I hear one more word about that damn movie." I sit and take a long draw of my water.

"Believe me. You getting fired from a huge movie over pussy is the last thing I want to discuss."

"Evan." His name is a guttural warning in my throat.

"And you better hope it doesn't come back to bite us that you didn't at least allow Camille to audition."

"Auditioning Camille would have been a steaming pile of wasted time. We all know I would never cast her—certainly not after what she did, but probably not even before. She's not right for Dessi."

"You injured her pride."

"What about *my* pride? Getting fired from a movie I could have directed with my eyes closed because we had a bad breakup? Are you fucking kidding me? What good would it have done to go through the motions like she even had a chance at the role?"

"We've seen Camille has a vindictive streak. Just saying… hope it doesn't streak all over us. Turning down one of Hollywood's hottest names right now, we better cast this right."

"Neevah *is* right."

"I haven't seen you this set on a particular actress this way… well, ever," he says, taking the seat across from me. "Don't make the same mistake again. You aren't—"

"Dating her?" I finish for him through tight lips.

"I was gonna say fucking her because I know you aren't really the dating type, which was why you dating Camille was such a—"

"At some point in this conversation, should we discuss the fact that I found the actress we've been searching six months for? Or you gonna just keep talking about useless shit that won't make us any money?"

"I'm not sure you *have* found the actress we need for *Dessi Blue*."

I take a long draw from the water bottle, cooling my aggravation because you never win a fight with Evan being ruled by emotion. "You saw her audition tape?"

"I did."

"You watched the reel her agent sent?"

"Yup. Man, that girl can sing. Gorgeous, too."

"And?"

"And no one knows who the hell she is. You can't expect Galaxy to sign off on some no-name understudy who just had her first turn on Broadway for a film of this scope. This is a lot of money. It's a huge investment and they want to make their money back. We need a big name."

"What we *need* is the right actress, and I found her. Figure out how to convince the studio."

"Don't dig your heels in with me, Canon." He leans forward to set his smoothie on my desk and gives me a direct look. "You may intimidate everyone else with your grunts and glares, but not me. This is my business, too."

"This is my story."

"You're a producer on this, too. Not just the director. Not just an artist, so act like one and hear me out."

No one talks to me like this and gets away with it.

Except Evan.

We met at USC, and knew each other casually, but didn't keep in touch after graduation. Once *The Magic Hour* won so much critical acclaim, I expected all the doors to fly open, but that's not really what happened. I struggled to find the right projects for a couple of years, served as assistant director on a few projects, paid my dues. Finally, I managed to make an indie film on a shoestring budget, which garnered more attention. Out of the blue, Evan reached out to congratulate me and proposed we work together. I had the stories, but Evan had a lot to offer. He grew up in the business, had money to invest and perfect instincts.

Most of the time. This time he's wrong.

"I *am* thinking like a producer," I grit out. "If we cast some big name who isn't right for the part, *Dessi Blue* will flop. Like Francis Ford Coppola *Cotton Club* flop. It could easily become some overblown, overbudget albatross that checked all the boxes—right director, lots of money, big-name stars—so no one can figure out why it failed."

"We won't let it fail."

"You damn right it won't fail. I found this story literally on the side of a country road." I pound my chest for emphasis. "*I* interviewed Dessi's family. *I* got them to tell me all the things the world doesn't know about this woman."

"I understand that, Canon, but—"

"I don't know if you *can* understand. Do you have any idea how many Dessi Blues there are? Black artists who shaped our culture, made our music, but whose contributions have gone unacknowledged? Their stories just slipped through the cracks. People who, by all rights, should be household names, but *nobody* knows their names? All they have to show for what they did is a plaque in their hometown or a line on Wikipedia, *if* that."

"You're making this personal."

"Black artists getting their due is personal for me. All my life I've seen their talents mined and appropriated, even while being told they weren't as good. They paved the way for me to be sitting in this office arguing with my bullheaded privileged business partner."

Lips twitching, Evan drops his head back, releases a heavy sigh, and stares up at the ceiling. "I hate it when you do this."

I chuckle, making a conscious effort to loosen the tight muscles in my shoulders. "You hate it when I what? Be right? Or be Black? I'm one most of the time and the other all the time."

He lifts his head to glare at me, but relents with a smile. "I'll set up a meeting with Galaxy. They assigned an exec to us as our contact. New guy named Lawson Stone. We'll start there."

TEN

Neevah

"So how are we looking, Doc?"

Dr. Ansford filters my hair through her fingers, touches a few tender places on my scalp.

"Better," she murmurs.

"I promise not to say I told you so," I tease, looking up at her over my shoulder.

"I will admit you're doing well without the drugs, but we're not out of the woods yet. I still see some spots here along your crown. Tell me what you've been doing."

"I cut out all red meat, gluten, and dairy, like we discussed. Eating lots of wild-caught fish, leafy greens, avocado. Taking my supplements. Fish oil, vitamin E. All of them. I've always had to stay fit for my job, so I was already exercising, and that seems to help."

"Good. Good." She runs a cool finger along a small bald patch at the base of my skull. "This seems to be healing nicely. What are you using on your hair?"

"All natural products. Lots of jojoba oil and shea butter. My roommate is a hairdresser. She mixes them for me herself. I wear protective styles like braids as much as possible."

"And no sign of the malar rash again?"

The butterfly-shaped rash over my nose and cheeks, often an indicator of lupus, was one of the most telling symptoms that prompted my primary care physician to refer me to Dr. Ansford, a rheumatologist, who subsequently confirmed my diagnosis.

She pats my shoulder approvingly. "Your blood and urine look good. Antibodies under control. Lupus isn't easy to manage. You're doing great."

"Discoid lupus," I correct. "Right?"

I always hold my breath when I wait for her answer. I got the lupus diagnosis about eighteen months ago. It was a relief to understand the fatigue, rashes, and hair loss, but the word *lupus* struck fear in me immediately. My aunt died from lupus, so I know how dangerous it can be. Dr. Ansford assured me it was discoid, which is not life-threatening, not systemic, which was the kind my aunt battled. Knowing my family history actually helped identify an accurate diagnosis faster than it otherwise might have been. We knew where to look.

"Right. Discoid." Her brown eyes are kind and reassuring when she takes the seat behind her desk. "I don't see any signs of systemic lupus as of now and from what I can tell, everything is under control. I was concerned the stress of performing in the show a few weeks ago might have triggered a flare-up."

"I know, but I meditated every night before I performed, and I tried acupuncture."

"Oh, good. I'm glad. How was that? You think it helped?"

"I guess? To be honest, that week is a blur. I was more stressed about *getting* stressed than I was about the actual show, if that makes sense."

"It does." She chuckles and peers at me over her rimless glasses. "You were brilliant, by the way."

"You came?" I cover my mouth with one hand.

"Twice. Best seats in the house." She grins and flicks the locs over her shoulder like she's fancy. "My husband and I came the first night, and I brought my niece later that week."

"You should have come to the stage door. I would have loved to meet her."

"She had a train to catch. She had to get back to school in Connecticut."

"Next time."

"Next time it will be for *your* opening night." Her gentle smile fades, her expression sobering. "You are incredibly talented, Neevah. I really had no idea. I'm sure you'll have people banging on your door after this."

"Well, I don't know about banging." I grimace and shrug. "My agent's gotten a few calls. Commercials. Auditions."

I don't mention that *the* Canon Holt asked me to audition for his next movie. Only my agent and Takira know. He said it was for a small part, but who even knows if I really have a shot?

"It will happen. Especially after seeing you perform, I have no doubt. I know it was demanding." She gives me a probing look. "How's the joint pain?"

"Manageable. I'm doing yoga and taking turmeric. It seems to be helping."

"And if your ANA levels start spiking and I recommend a steroid or something stronger like prednisone, will you listen?"

I set my jaw mulishly. I've done the research. Some of the drugs most people take with this diagnosis are as hard on your body as the disease itself, with side effects like osteoporosis, weight gain, and eyesight issues. I'll do everything in my power to manage this naturally for as long as I can.

"It won't come to that," I reply after a few seconds.

Dr. Ansford's raised brows beg the question again.

I roll my eyes and heave a resigned sigh. "If it comes to that, then yes. We'll try it your way."

ELEVEN

Canon

"Do we really need to have dinner?" I ask as Evan and I climb the steep driveway of Lawson Stone's house in the Hollywood Hills. "I just want him to sign off on Neevah so we can offer her the role."

"Shit gets done at dinner," Evan reminds me. "Besides, I hear he has a kick-ass wine cellar."

"I'm sure he can't wait to show it off." I ring the doorbell. "I actually am hungry. This food better be good."

"Even if it's not, you need to—"

The door opens and a breathtakingly beautiful woman stands at the entrance. Her face is delicate and sharp, fragile, like it was etched from porcelain, but with a bold nose and amber-glazed skin stretched taut over flaring cheekbones. She can't be any taller than maybe five-two, and her black hair is shiny, center-parted, and hangs in textured waves to her elbows.

"Good evening, Mr. Holt," she says, smiling at me somewhat stiffly before shifting her glance to Evan. "And you must be Mr. Bancroft."

"Uh, yeah…that's me. I am," Evan says. He's usually a little smoother than that, so I shoot him a surreptitiously curious glance. He's looking all dazed and confused.

"Welcome." She steps back to allow us inside. "I'm Law's wife, Linh. He's wrapping up a call. Please come in."

We enter a grand foyer with an intricate stone chandelier suspended from the ceiling.

"That piece is incredible." Evan tips his head back to study the light fixture.

"Thank you," she says. "My father made it."

"Your father?" I ask, looking from her to the chandelier. "Wow."

"He's a sculptor. Chap Brody. It was a housewarming gift."

"Chap Brody is your father?" Evan's mouth hangs open in uncharacteristic awe. It takes a lot to impress my jaded production partner, but apparently this does it. Chap Brody is the only Black sculptor I know by name. Real talk, he's the *only* sculptor I know by name, period. That's not really my thing as much as it is Evan's.

"You've heard of him?" Linh asks with a pleased smile.

"Of course." Evan looks almost boyish in his enthusiasm. "I'm kind of an architecture geek, and I've come across his work in a lot of cool spaces. He's a genius."

"So he keeps telling me." She laughs, leading us down a stark white corridor lined with vases and busts and various other pieces displayed in dimly lit alcoves.

Lawson collects beautiful things—the most beautiful of which is his wife. He's one lucky man. By the way Evan can't take his eyes off Linh, he must agree. We're trailing her into their living room and I elbow him, giving him my *what the hell* face. Seriously? He's going out like that in the man's house? He gives me a confused look, like he has no idea what I'm talking about, but he knows.

"Wine, or something stronger?" Linh asks. "I have appetizers here, too, while we wait for Law."

The appetizers are various combinations of vegetables, fruit, and seafood. Also some kind of dumpling in a brown sauce, all of which Evan and I devour. We load up small plates and sink into the luxurious white couch at the heart of the living room. Through a wall of glass, an aqua-blue infinity pool glitters under strategically placed floodlights, but Evan seems more interested in the view *inside* the house than out. Linh's Black and what I'm guessing to be Asian ancestry blend beautifully. I can count the times he's looked away from her.

"Mom, I'm stuck."

The statement comes from a young girl, maybe ten or so, standing at the foot of a staircase. She's a replica of Linh, but with fairer skin and silkier hair.

"Oh." Linh rises and tops off our wine. "I'll be right back. Algebra calls."

As soon as she leaves the room, I turn on Evan. "You do know she's Lawson's wife, right?"

"Uh, yeah." He looks at me like I'm crazy and he's clueless. "And?"

"And you're all up in her grill. Stop it."

"A man can look. She's gorgeous."

"You're asking for trouble. Stop that shit." I suck my teeth and reach for another dumpling.

"Gentlemen." Lawson enters the living room. "Sorry to keep you waiting."

He's a typical Hollywood exec. Since he's home, he's shed the shiny suit for the studied casualness of a button-up and slacks. Linh has melanin working for her, so it's hard to discern her age, but I'd put Lawson Stone in his late-forties, early fifties. The work he's probably had done may have firmed his jawline, but he wears the years in his eyes and his too-uniformly black hair.

"I see Linh got you started," he says, holding up the bottle. "How's that pinot noir? It's Linh's favorite."

"She's great." Evan takes a sip of his wine and mock toasts. "I mean, *it's* great. Delicious."

"Good." He scans the room. "Did she go check on dinner?"

"Your daughter needed help with homework," I tell him.

"Ah. Algebra." He reaches for one of the appetizers. "We both suck at it, but Linh sucks a little less. Thanks for coming tonight."

"Thanks for having us," Evan replies. "We're looking forward to discussing next steps in pre-production on the project."

"Yeah, now that we've found our Dessi," I say casually, studying my drink, "we can fill out the rest of the cast. Verity's retooling the script and—"

"We need to talk about this girl before we get ahead of ourselves." Law stuffs a dumpling in his mouth, chewing around the words. "We're not sure she's the right fit."

I set my glass of wine on the low table by the couch and straighten. "What are your reservations?" I ask, keeping my voice low, even, reasonable.

"Isn't it obvious?" Law barks out a laugh. "No one knows who the hell she is, for one."

"Did you watch her audition tape?" I ask. "And her reel?"

"It has nothing to do with her talent. Obviously she's talented. So are half the contestants on *American Idol,* but I'm not offering them the lead role in a film of this scope either. We've drafted a list of suitable actresses with the kind of drawing power this budget merits." He extracts a folded piece of paper from his pocket, offering it to me.

I don't accept or even glance at it, but keep my stare fixed on him. I sense Evan tense on the couch beside me. "I won't be needing that."

"Excuse me?" Law's brows jerk into a frown and the hand holding his little slip of paper drops back to his side. "These actresses—"

"Will not be in my movie," I say with a calm that disguises the anger roiling beneath the surface.

"*Your* movie?" he asks, brows lifting. "Our money—"

"Your money is funding my movie, but you don't control it, and you don't control me. If you have any illusions about that, I can go elsewhere."

"Now let's not be hasty," Evan says. "I'm sure there's a middle ground."

"There's not." I stand and face Law. "Neevah Saint is a nonnegotiable. I've given you six months to find the lead, and you haven't."

"There are several acceptable options on this list," he says, extending the paper toward me.

I ignore it again.

"Neevah Saint," I say. "Or we walk."

Evan growls a protest, which I also ignore.

"Think long and hard before you say more, Holt." Law's polite veneer is thinning and his irritation, his condescension, starts to show.

"You think I need you badly enough to let you ruin my movie?" I scoff and shake my head. "Do you know what Spike Lee did when the studio tried to pull the money for *Malcolm X* because they wanted it shorter?"

"No, what?" Law answers cautiously.

"He went to Black leaders, entrepreneurs, creatives, athletes and asked for help. He secured the financing himself from the community who most wanted that story told. I assure you I will have no problem raising money to tell this story."

I nod to the piece of paper hanging limply from his fingers. "You try to give me that list one more time, and I don't stay for dinner. I walk out that door and take my movie with me." I bend down to grab another dumpling. "So what's it gonna be?"

TWELVE

Neevah

When Canon called a few weeks ago, I saved his cell in my phone under CH…just in case he ever called again. I'd know it was him and be less likely to run off a road, dismember myself somehow, or generally lose my shit once I answered and heard his rumbling voice on the other end.

So when CH appears on my screen on a Thursday afternoon while I'm preparing to leave for the theater, I know who it is.

"Hello?" I answer with a question because I don't want *him* to know *I* know.

"Neevah," he says. "It's Canon."

I know!

"Canon, hi." I will my molecules to stop vibrating and sit on the couch, plunking my bag on the floor.

"I want to offer you a role in my upcoming movie," he says without further greeting. The words slam into my chest and crater behind my breastbone, leaving no space for air.

Trembling, I offer a silent prayer of thanks to my patron saint, Audra McDonald. This is a Canon Holt movie. This is a break. Even if it's not a big role, I'll do my best and make something of it.

"Neevah? You there?"

"Oh. Sorry. Yeah. I was just…wow. I guess I'm a little stunned. Thank you so much for this opportunity."

"Don't you want to know what the role is?" he asks, a tiny bit of humor sneaking into his usually sober voice.

Third cow from the left? Girl who walks in field? Skipping marionette?

I'm pretty sure any role he casts me in will be one I accept.

"Sure," I answer like a more reasonable person.

"It's Dessi Blue."

Hold up. Wait a minute. Put a little crazy in it.

"Um...but when I auditioned...it seemed...wasn't the main character named Dessi?" My lips have gone numb and my brain is firing molasses instead of synapses, but I do remember that much.

"It is. I'm offering you the lead."

My butt slides right off the couch and I land on the floor.

"Holy shit," I mutter.

A dark silk chuckle unfurls from the other line. "Is that a yes? The role is yours if you want it."

If this moment were a hand, I'd never wash it again.

In an instant, I go from shell-shocked to completely, emotionally verklempt. I look around our shoe box of an apartment, remembering all the tuna I've eaten straight from the can when money was tight. All the past due notices I've stuffed to the back of my mind and the back of a drawer over the years, struggling to make art my living. Knowing this is what I was supposed to do, but sometimes unsure how to do it. Unsure of how this story, *my story*, would end. Only to find a beginning. After the last year of being Elise's standby with only one week in the spotlight, the very week Canon was in town, it's a miraculous new beginning.

"I-I, well..." *Do not cry. Zip it up. Hold it in. Be professional.* "Yes. I'll do it."

"Good." Canon's voice doesn't hold surprise, because who would turn this down, but he sounds satisfied. "We'll reach out to your agent to discuss the details. I hacked a script just to pitch and get it sold to a studio, but Verity Hill is writing it. What you read was our rush job. I promise it'll be better by the time she's done with it."

"She's incredible. I loved that last show she wrote for."

"Agreed. And Monk's doing the music."

"Oh, wow. That's so exciting. I have to thank him for dragging you to my show, I guess."

"He's really looking forward to working with you."

"When do we start or…I just want to make sure I give plenty of notice to the team at *Splendor*."

"It'll be a while. I wanted to cast Dessi first because she's the center of the whole thing. I need to build around her. Around you."

I can't even breathe right. This conversation is a high-speed car chase and I'm barely keeping up. I force myself to focus on his words despite the tires screeching in my head.

"Mallory's working on casting everyone else. As soon as Verity delivers the script, we'll start scouting locations in earnest. We've done some prelim work, but I want the script before we nail it down. I hope to shoot in New York since so much of the story takes place there."

"I just realized I don't know the story. I don't know anything about Dessi other than what I read on page seventeen."

"It's fascinating. Dessi was an incredibly talented singer and dancer from the thirties and forties who led a remarkable life, but like so many Black performers back in the day, she's gotten lost."

"You love history, don't you?" I don't know what makes me ask that in the middle of this discussion about the project, but I don't regret it.

"I'm interested in the stories lost in the crevices of history, yeah."

"So many of your documentaries focus on historical figures, so that makes sense."

"Winston Churchill said history is written by the victors, but I would amend that to say it's often written by liars. History is fact. You can't change what happened, but you can edit it. People lie and leave out the truth, bend it to suit their needs. I like to tell stories that excavate the facts and expose the truth."

"I love that."

There's a loaded pause before I clear my throat and he does the same.

"Yeah, well, so," he says. "About the movie."

"Oh, sure. Sorry. You were telling me about Dessi Blue."

"I'd rather you learn about Dessi for yourself. You up for a field trip?"

"A field trip? When? Where?"

"As soon as you can get some time off. Just a few days, but Dessi still has family in the small town where she grew up. Her parents moved to New York from Alabama during the Great Migration when she was sixteen, but some of their family stayed behind. Her daughter lives in Alabama and essentially oversees the estate—what there is of it. I'm optioning Dessi's life story through her. I think it'd be great if you got to know Dessi through someone connected to her."

"That would be super helpful."

"Verity will come, too. Great opportunity for her to get as close as we can to source material."

A road trip with Canon Holt, even chaperoned, sends a secret thrill through me, one I suppress immediately.

Focus.

"This all sounds amazing," I say. "It's a true biopic."

"Yes, and we don't get enough of those about Black folks who did big things. It will be a demanding role with singing, dancing. You will act your ass off for me. I'll do whatever it takes to get the best out of you. I'm not easy to work with. You might hate me by the time it's over."

"Why me?" I ask softly. "I mean, this is obviously a huge budget and a once-in-a-lifetime role. I'm . . . a standby."

"No, you're a star who was standing by waiting for me to find her."

I let his low-voiced encouragement sink in before replying.

"That sounds very Svengali. Are you planning to mold me into exactly what you want?" I release a breathless chuckle. "Good luck with that."

"I don't want to change you. I think you're fantastic exactly as you are."

All humor fades to dust at the certainty in his rough-smooth voice. A man like Canon, a director like him saying I'm fantastic as I am—I need to savor this. Roll it around in my mouth like candy. Suck on it for a second and swallow all the affirmation hidden at the center.

"This role will change you, though," he continues. "Inevitably and irreversibly. The learning curve will be steep, and I won't go easy on you. You have no film experience."

"I know," I say, the enormity of this undertaking flattening my high.

"But what you do have is Dessi's spirit. There's not much left, but I've seen old photos and some rare footage of her performing. She had an inextinguishable light. Trying to cast this role the last six months, I've seen so many actresses. Many of them were great, a lot of them already famous, but I didn't see that light until I saw you perform a few weeks ago. I want it. I want that light. I want that heart and that vulnerability and strength. There is so much inside you, Neevah, and I'm warning you now that I want it all."

And in this moment, sitting on the floor of my dingy apartment, on the cusp of the greatest opportunity of my life, I want to give it to him.

THIRTEEN

Canon

"I feel like we've been driving through the set of *Deliverance* for two hours."

Verity has been saying things like that for the last ten exits or so. Not that we've seen many exits. I've heard of back roads, but this route through Alabama seems to be *behind* the back roads, a stretch of nothing but rural landscape punctuated by the occasional house hungover from another era.

Neevah whistles *Deliverance*'s famous dueling banjo tune from the back seat, and Verity aims a grin over her shoulder at her. I can already tell the two of them will be trouble.

"When can we stop?" Neevah asks, catching my eyes in the rearview mirror. "I need to pee."

"You have the bladder of a beetle." I try to sharpen the words, but they come out half-amused. Neevah seems to have that effect on me. "We *just* stopped for your bathroom break."

"Excuse me for staying hydrated."

"Hydrated? More like waterlogged."

"I think two hours is a perfectly reasonable time between pisses," Verity interjects.

"Thank you." Neevah pokes her tongue out at me and giggles.

I'm glad Verity came with us on this trip since she'll write the script. Not to mention, it's not a good idea to be alone with Neevah for this long. It wouldn't look right, and after the *Primal* debacle no one seems prepared to let me forget, the last thing I need is anyone thinking I'm romantically involved with my actress.

Camille was an aberration. Crafty enough to figure out exactly the kind of woman who could make me break my rules. Chameleon enough to fool me into thinking she was the answer. A great actress, she could pretend to be that kind of woman, but couldn't sustain the charade. I realized too late she wasn't who I thought she was.

She could never be.

To be honest, I don't know if the woman I thought she was even exists.

"Oooooh!" Neevah points frantically to a building not much better than a hut with two gas pumps. "We can stop here."

"You *want* to sit on a toilet in this place?" I ask.

"I *need* to pee, and I won't sit on it. Duh. I hover."

"I don't need that visual." I pull into the gas station's gravel lot. "Be quick."

The back door flies open and Neevah dashes off, disappearing into the hovel-ish structure.

"I like her," Verity says, smiling. "She'll be fun to work with."

"What about Monk? You still okay working with him?"

The amusement on her face burns to ash, a frown kindling between her thick brows. Verity is striking, with the rich undertones of her smooth skin and the jet-colored hair adorning her shoulders in two fat, silky braids. She's smart as all get out and has a dreamer's soul. Monk was probably a goner as soon as he laid eyes on her.

"I told you the first time you asked, I'll be fine," she mutters through tight lips, folding her arms across her chest and staring out the window. "I can't speak for Monk. I barely know him anymore."

"When was the last time you saw him?"

"Golden Globes a few years ago." Her shrug dismisses the incident or him or both.

"I don't actually care if you two hate each other with a passion, or if you fuck the first chance you get."

Her head snaps around, her eyes slits of outrage.

"Keep your shit out of my movie," I tell her, my face set in stone. "I don't need personal history messing up my project."

"And did you have this little talk with him, or just the woman in this scenario?"

"Of course I did. I might be an asshole, but I'm not a misogynist. The most talented, capable people I've worked with have been women. A woman needs to write Dessi's story, and I think that woman is you, but I also think the score of this movie is trapped in Monk's head. Setting aside whatever beef you guys have, you know the man's a genius."

"He is that," she says, her voice grudging, her gaze shifting to her lap.

"We have the chance to do something extraordinary. I don't want to screw it up with personal complications."

Neevah comes out running. She left her natural hair free today, and the breeze tosses the textured nimbus cloud around her face. Her body is toned and firm, not thin. There's a ripeness to her, and she moves with a dancer's easy grace; there's a natural sensuality in the swing of her hips and arms. A confidence in her stride. I don't usually allow myself to look at her much in case I look too long and my dick ever gets hard. There's no coming back from that.

But I look now.

"Hmmm," Verity huffs, tipping her head toward the window and giving me a knowing glance. "Speaking of making things personal."

I shoot Verity one of my best glares.

"That doesn't work on me, boss," she says. "You got this reputation for being all mean and broody and artistic. I know your secret."

"Oh, you do?" I cock a brow at her, genuinely curious. "And what's that?"

"I saw *The Magic Hour*. You're a mama's boy, and they're all bark, no bite."

"Oh, I bite. Let this shit with Monk affect my movie, you'll feel it."

"Fair enough." Verity glances back to Neevah, who has almost reached the car. "Make sure you heed your own advice."

FOURTEEN

NEEVAH

It's an odd experience, sifting through the detritus of Dessi Blue's life. Dog-eared books and diaries, faded dresses from bygone eras, letters so old, parchmented like they might crumble in my hands. Her daughter, Katherine, has given us complete access to everything left in the house after Dessi died. She said she hasn't gotten around to looking through half this stuff because her parents were pack rats and held on to every little thing documenting their colorful lives. She hasn't made time to pick through their past or to dispose of it.

It's like stumbling into a pharaoh's tomb, the walls lined with riches and treasures. It's mundane and magnificent. Worthless. Priceless. So many things I need to know about the woman I'm to portray. I'm eager, but also feel like a Peeping Tom, glimpsing another woman's nakedness through the window of her past.

"Finding what you need?"

Canon stands in the doorway, his wide shoulders filling the frame. His eyes curious in the sharply hewn face. I drag my gaze away from him and to the stack of letters tied with string I'm holding.

"Yeah," I say. "More than what I need. It's kind of overwhelming and I'm not sure where to start."

He walks in, his usual confident stride slower. He's always guarded, but his expression seems almost wary when he sits beside me on the bed in what Katherine affectionately calls the "back room." A box of old photos rests on the floor, and he bends to retrieve a few. A tarnished silver frame displays a happy, smiling couple on their wedding day. The style of Dessi's dress and her rolled upsweep hairdo indicate early twentieth century, maybe late thirties, early forties. It's a black-and-white photo, but it's clear that she's fairer than her groom. They make a beautiful study in contrasts, him darker and her smaller, slim and elegant next to his imposing height. Shunning the camera, they stare into each other's faces, noses nearly touching, love radiating from their expressions.

"Cal Hampton," Canon says, nodding to the photo. "They got married in London while they were touring Europe. He was a great trumpet player."

"They look so happy. According to the family Bible, they were married forty-five years until he died of lung cancer in 1985."

"All that smoking caught up to a lot of them later in life." He hands me the photo. "They do seem happy, but there was a lot of heartbreak in those years. Mostly from living in a country that wanted them to sing for their supper, but use the service entrance to come and go. That's why so many of them left for Europe. Who can blame them?"

"I remember watching Halle Berry's Dorothy Dandridge movie. That scene when Dorothy dips her toe in the pool at the hotel where she's performing in Vegas."

"And they drain the pool." Canon's full mouth hitches into a cynical bend. "You know how many people had no idea who Dorothy was before that movie?"

He bumps my shoulder, and the rare ease of a gesture like that from him makes me smile.

"We're gonna do that for Dessi Blue," he says.

"Thank you again for choosing me, for casting me."

"We searched six months before casting you, Neevah. I knew as soon as I saw you onstage you were right for this part."

"And the studio was okay with an unknown carrying a film like this?" It's occurred to me more than once, but I haven't asked him or Mallory. I was too afraid they might think about the huge risk they're taking and change their minds.

"The studio is thrilled." He bends to grab another box from the floor, and I can't see his expression, but his voice sounds sure. Then again, when doesn't Canon sound sure?

"Look at this," he says.

Dust stirs from the jewelry box when he opens it, and a ballet dancer pops up. An old tune warbles from the box, so faint it's barely music, and the figurine executes a turn, her pirouette shaky and uneven. Canon picks through a few pieces of jewelry—a black velvet ribbon choker, a cocktail ring shaped like a star and studded with rubies, diamond-flecked hairpins. There is a small tear in the floor of the box. I pull the base up, revealing a hidden compartment.

"Look at you, finding the secrets," Canon says, lifting the base out completely and extracting a stack of papers, frayed and falling apart. He spreads them on the bed between us. There isn't much, but you don't hide things that mean nothing.

I angle my head to study the newspaper clipping of a wedding announcement.

Harlem nightclub owner Hezekiah Moore weds Matilda Hargrove. The ceremony took place at Abyssinian Baptist Church, with reception following at the Hotel Theresa.

Beneath the photo of a stern, stout man and a gorgeous woman of medium brown complexion, wearing a waxen smile with her wedding dress, are the words *I had to. Forgive me,* in neat handwriting.

Canon and I exchange a quick look of speculation.

"Matilda was Dessi's roommate in New York for a few years," he says. "The scene you did with Mallory showed how they met. Katherine said when Dessi left to tour in Europe, they lost touch completely."

I flip through a stack of letters, all written in the same neat handwriting from the newspaper clipping. "Looks like she was wrong about them losing touch."

The edge of a faded maroon paper peeks out from beneath the newspaper clipping so I pull it out to see it fully. It's a playbill for *Macbeth,* but obviously an adaptation that, based on the graphic, seems to have African or island influence.

"Says the play was presented by the Negro unit of the Federal Theatre Project." I flip the playbill over, scanning the details. "I've never heard of it."

"Yeah. In the scene you read, that's the show they were waiting to see. The Federal Theatre Project was a New Deal stimulus program that funded plays and live performances."

"New Deal as in FDR's New Deal?"

"Yeah. After the Great Depression. It put actors, playwrights, and directors to work. Orson Welles adapted *Macbeth* with an all-Black cast at the Lafayette Theatre in the thirties. Maybe '36? They called it Voodoo *Macbeth*."

"*The* Orson Welles?"

"Yeah, and he was only twenty years old at the time. Wasn't even really making movies yet." Canon shakes his head. "Genius, man."

I open the playbill and there's a newspaper clipping inside showing a huge crowd outside the Lafayette. "Says here people lined up for ten blocks on Seventh Avenue. Over ten thousand people trying to get into the theater, and only twelve hundred seats."

Canon leans closer to read for himself, and the clean scent of him invades my senses. I try to stay focused on the work, on what this opportunity means for my career, and not think about how drawn I am to him, but sometimes…like *now* times, when he smells so good, and his body radiates warmth, I just want to…

Stop it, Neevah.

He tilts his head to read the fine print beneath the photo, and his head bumps mine.

"Sorry," he says, glancing up from the pile of faded memorabilia. Our eyes hold, and I hope mine don't tell him everything; don't tell him that I'm fighting this most ridiculous, inappropriate, ill-fated attraction every time I'm around him. And I *am* fighting it. I know it's wrong and will only make this job harder.

His eyes search mine and drop to my mouth, and I feel his gaze like a hot, tender touch. My lips part on a caught breath, and I have to lick them. I have to stop before I make this weird and uncomfortable for him. He's my *boss*.

I let the playbill fall from my fingers to the floor, seizing the excuse to bend, to break the hot connection between our eyes. It's hot to me. I'm burning up, but when I sit up, Canon's eyes are cool, his expression inscrutable. I want to apologize for disrupting the easy rapport between us, but I didn't do anything. It just happened. My body inconveniently reminded me that Canon Holt is exactly my type, and I didn't even know I had one. Big and brooding and brilliant.

"Saints and poets?" he asks.

For a second, I have no idea what he's talking about. He's staring at my hand holding the playbill, at the ink scripted along the outside of my thumb.

"Oh, my tattoo. Yeah. It's from—"

"*Our Town*. The stage manager says that."

I glance up to smile, but can't hold it when I meet his eyes. There's an intensity about Canon that I don't think he even cultivates. It's simply who he is—hungry to know, to understand, and his intellect and curiosity consume everything in his path. Every story, every project, every conversation. *This* conversation. And when you are the subject of his lens, you feel like he's hungry for you. Like he wants to understand exactly what it is he's looking at. And I can't help but wonder how that hunger would feel in a kiss. Would he crush me against him like we couldn't get close enough? Like the taste of me was driving him wild? My fingers burn with the need to scrape across his shadowed jaw, to trace his brows and lips.

"It was, um…" I clear my throat, desperate to rein in my rebel thoughts. "It was the last play I did in high school. That line stuck with me."

"Where are you from?" he asks easily, apparently oblivious that I'm struggling to maintain some semblance of non-kissing normalcy.

"A-a tiny town in North Carolina you've never heard of. Clearview."

"You're right. Never heard of it." He almost grins, yielding the slightest curve of his lips, and I realize how seldom he smiles. "So you had a burning desire to spread your wings and you struck out for New York City, diploma in hand?"

"Not quite." The shard of Terry and Brandon's betrayal pricks my heart. Not as much as it used to, but it may always draw a drop of blood.

"I might have been content to stay there and do community theater. Get married. Have some babies."

"But?"

"But things happen." I shrug and force myself to meet the probe of his stare. "And it was off to Jersey, not New York. I had a scholarship to Rutgers, the drama program."

"It would have been our loss. You might have been content to stay hidden away in Clearview, but it wouldn't have been right. You were made for the spotlight. Whatever happened to make you leave was a blessing in disguise."

My breath stalls. There's so little space separating us, and the air seems to pulse in time with my galloping heart. And this time, now, I don't wonder if he feels it, too. I know he does. It's in the way he frowns and his eyes darken and his jaw tightens. It's like a wavelength between us in the taut silence.

He clears his throat and leans away, inserting a few more inches between us. "So this play, Voodoo *Macbeth*."

"Oh, yeah. The play. The play."

"Right, before Orson Welles did this play, most had only seen Black actors in vaudeville or in blackface. There was even a national tour after the New York run, so this was huge."

"I can imagine." I need something to do with my hands, some way to reroute this conversation to neutral ground. I look down at the playbill and pull a photograph from inside. It's of two young women posing in front of the Lafayette, both dressed well, smiling, glowing. Dessi and Tilda.

Canon flips through the small pile of papers and pulls the wedding announcement out again, placing it beside the photo.

I trace one finger over the handwritten words on the newspaper clipping.

I had to. Forgive me.

"For someone who supposedly disappeared from Dessi's life," Canon says, lifting his brows, "there's a lot of letters from her hidden here. There's a story here. Now we have to find it."

FIFTEEN

Dessi Blue

May 8, 1936

Mama,

I'm sorry it's taken me so long to write, but a lot has happened and I haven't had time. I can hear you saying I just didn't make time! You right, but I do have a lot to tell you.

I'm not working at the Cotton Club anymore. I know you hoped one day they'd find me in the kitchen washing dishes and decide I should be onstage, but that never happened. I wasn't "Tall, Tan, and Terrific" enough for them! They want that high yellow. I would still be there washing dishes if it wasn't for my new friend Matilda Hargrove. We met at the Lafayette Theatre. I know you and Daddy used to go see the bands down there. Well, they did a Shakespeare play with all Black folks. Macbeth*! Can you believe that? I never seen so many people trying to get into one place. I went down there opening night to get me a ticket. They were selling them outside for near $4! Some of them even five. Too rich for my blood, so I gave up, but I met Tilda, who gave me one of her tickets. Her beau never showed. But we got to talking and she set me up with some work.*

Now I already see your face, Mama. I ain't got a pimp and I ain't hustling. It's honest work down at the Savoy Ballroom. Tilda works there, hostessing. We teach the men who come in there who don't know how to dance. We just show them the steps and they pay us! Better than washing dishes, I tell you the truth. Pay is better, too.

I know you been worried about me up here by myself since you moved back home, but I couldn't go back to Alabama, not after New York. It ain't perfect here for Black folks, but they ain't hanging us from trees. We had that riot last year in Harlem, but it's not as bad as down South. I'm never living down there.

I know you miss Daddy. I do, too. I understand why you wanted to go back and be with family, but I can't. And see? I found a new friend!

I left the boarding house, too. Me and Tilda put our money together and we're in an apartment down off 139th Street, not too far from the Savoy. We in the middle of everything. Everybody comes through. I feel alive, Mama. I've been so sad, what with Daddy passing and you leaving, but working at the Savoy, this new place with Tilda, it feels like things are looking up.

Tilda's cousin takes pictures for The Crisis. *He took this one of us at the* House Beautiful *that night. Ain't we pretty? I'm also including $20. I'll send more when I can. I hope it helps. Kiss Granny and Aunt Ruth and Cousin Belle. All of them. Tell them hey and I love you all.*

Yours,
Odessa

SIXTEEN

CANON

The trip to Alabama was enlightening and broadened our understanding of Dessi's journey, but I'm glad to be back in LA. I got off the plane and came straight to the production offices. The things we found in Alabama have changed everything. Dessi's family always assumed she had two great loves: Cal Hampton and music.

Turns out there were three.

Tilda Hargrove was Dessi's *first* love. Before she met Cal Hampton while she was hostessing at the Savoy. Before he discovered Dessi could sing like an angel. Before she performed at Café Society, joining greats like Billie Holiday, Sarah Vaughan, Lena Horne, and Hazel Scott. Before Cal and Dessi struck off for Europe to tour with a band and eventually married… before all that, Dessi loved Tilda Hargrove. And Tilda Hargrove loved her. In addition to the newspaper clippings, Dessi saved love letters they exchanged while she was touring Europe and Tilda remained in Harlem.

Not shocking. Many of the women from that era sang openly about their bisexuality. Ma Rainey, Bessie Smith. Hell, even Billie had at least one documented affair with another woman, Tallulah Bankhead. Unearthing that as part of Dessi's story made sense and simply adds depth to what I know about her as a character as we tell her story. For a family member, though, especially one from the Bible Belt, who may or may not want that known about Dessi, it's not as simple.

Surprisingly, Neevah was the one who broached the subject with Katherine.

One of Neevah's greatest assets, and she has many, is how she makes you feel you've known her all your life. There's this accessibility that comes across not only when she performs, but any time you're around her. I saw it in how quickly she and Verity clicked. I observed how much Katherine trusted her after a few hours of conversation out on the front porch, just the two of them and a pitcher of lemonade. Discussing the things we found about Dessi with Katherine could have been awkward, but Neevah had already paved the way, lowering Katherine's guard with her easy smile and open manner. When I first approached Katherine about optioning Dessi's life story, I think she saw an opportunity. Financial, yes, but also a chance to celebrate her mother's contributions; to bring her the recognition she deserves. When she looked at Neevah, she saw a friend. Someone whom, after only a few hours, she trusted. Seeing their natural rapport, I tasked Neevah with discussing our discoveries and asking Katherine if we could include them in the movie.

We can.

And I know I have Neevah to thank for that, at least in part.

That moment in the bedroom was a close call. Not that I came close to doing anything about the attraction, which is growing and—I suspect—mutual. But I almost showed my hand.

Shit.

Did I hide it?

It's her heightened sensitivity that fuels her brilliance as an actor. She's emotionally astute, which puts her in touch with not only how she feels, but how others are feeling, too.

I'm not a conceited guy. Many of the women who approach me see a role, an opportunity, a chance to get ahead. It's part of the game, but Neevah…I haven't known her long, but already I can tell that with her, there are no games. There's a sincerity to her—a humility and realness that the more I see, the more I admire, especially in a business like ours powered by ego and artifice.

Surely Neevah knows anything more than a professional relationship between us would spell trouble, so she's fighting this pull. So am I, but if Verity picked up on it, Evan will. And the last thing I want is a daily lecture from that dude about keeping my dick in my pants.

"Welcome home," Evan says, walking into my office, sipping on his smoothie. "How'd it go?"

I look away from the colored cards of the storyboard on my wall to Evan.

"Great trip." I tip back in my chair and prop my feet on the desk. "We have a whole other story we didn't know existed."

Over the next twenty minutes, I share all the things we learned about Dessi and Tilda. Evan sits across from me, his eyes lighting up as he realizes this story is even better than we first thought.

"And the daughter is okay with us putting all this in?" he asks.

"She is. Neevah talked to her to make sure." I shuffle a deck of multicolored index cards. "They really hit it off."

"Sounds like Neevah will be an asset in more ways than one." Evan casts a cautious look at me from under a slight frown. "Which brings me to something we need to discuss."

"Shoot." I keep my tone casual, but I know that look. I've met that frown before. This is some shit I don't want to hear.

"Lawson Stone called," Evan says.

"And?"

"And Galaxy is not happy about you casting Neevah."

I shrug, belying the tension in my shoulders. "Not surprising. We knew they would take some convincing."

"Lots of convincing." Evan looks me square in the eye. "And some compromise."

I lower my feet and swivel in the office chair. "My least favorite word. Well, one of them. What kind of compromise?"

"If you get to keep Neevah as Dessi—"

"And I do," I say, my voice unyielding.

"Then they get to choose the guy. They have someone in mind for Cal Hampton."

"Who?"

"Trey Scott."

"He's a pop singer," I say, not bothering to disguise my distaste. "He's on Nick at Nite."

"Those are reruns and that was years ago. He's all grown up now. Plenty of big-name stars begin as child actors. Hilary Duff, Miley Cyrus, Zac Efron, Selena Gomez. The list goes on and on. The cache of this film will bring in the over-thirty crowd. Trey will draw a younger audience, even though he's now over thirty himself. He still has that fandom."

These are not the things I wanted to consider when casting my movie, but I do recognize Galaxy is taking an enormous risk with Neevah.

"You got tape of him?" I ask curtly. "He still has to audition like everybody else, and if he's trash—"

"I do have tape, and he's actually really good. Don't let the Disney vibe fool you."

"Send it to me." I turn back to my storyboard. "We done?"

"Well, I know you wanted to shoot in New York."

I whip around to face him again. "Of course, I do. Most of the story takes place there."

"Yeah, but Trey will be doing double duty in the fall when we need to shoot."

"Double duty?"

"He'll shoot with us during the day, and we can be strategic about his scenes for night shoots," Evan says, lowering his eyes and toying with his keys, a sure sign he doesn't want to tell me the rest. "He'll be hosting a live game show here in LA three nights a week."

"Are you fucking kidding me? They think I'm shooting my movie in LA instead of New York because he's hosting *Family Feud?*"

"It's not. It's—"

"I don't give a damn what it is." I stand and pace from my desk to the windows overlooking the city. "You outta your damn mind, Evan. His game show won't dictate our locations."

"Not all of them and not all the time. We're still forming the location list, but I think it could work."

"How? How could it work?"

"We could use Galaxy's back lots. Most of the scenes will be interior and we can grab pickup shots in New York. Also keep in mind a lot of those buildings from Harlem in the thirties are either demolished or look really different. We'd have to create our own with models and other tricks anyway. We have to re-create the Savoy Ballroom, a massive undertaking. A back lot is ideal for that. That's not to say no shots in New York. Just from October to January, we need to—"

"That's ninety percent of the shooting schedule. Shit, Evan. We don't need their money that bad. Not to ruin my movie."

"First of all, we do need the money. This is a big project with a huge price tag. Second of all, I actually think back lots could give us that old Hollywood vibe. Might be perfect for this period piece."

That does give me pause. I prop on the edge of the desk and fold my arms over my chest, daring Evan to convince me. "Go on."

"You said you want to shoot on film, right?"

"Some, yeah, sixteen millimeter for certain sequences. I know it's expensive, but I'm not compromising on that, Evan. It's bad enough they want to cast a Mouseketeer."

"He wasn't a Mouseketeer. And no, they think film is genius, but it gives even more credence to using old Hollywood back lots. Layering that nostalgia in on every level."

I hate that it's starting to make sense.

Evan's slow smile tells me he knows it. "Can I tell them Trey's in?"

"Not until I see his tape. He's not getting in without an audition."

"Well, Neevah Saint practically did."

"Neevah did a damn Broadway show *and* killed her audition with Mallory."

"I'll send you his tape. Mal's working with his agent. The team's coming together. We got Verity on the script. Monk's in for the score. Neevah's in for Dessi. Costumes will be a huge part of this. We need to start looking at costume designers."

"Yeah?" I turn back to the storyboard, only half listening now. "Alright, whatever."

"Lawson Stone has a suggestion."

Something in Evan's voice makes me study him over my shoulder suspiciously. "Don't tell me. His second cousin is a seamstress."

"Even better." Evan fights a smirk unsuccessfully. "His wife."

Now *that* I wasn't expecting. "Linh? His wife we met? Whose dad is the sculptor?"

"Yeah, pretty sure he's only got the one wife."

"And if he's willing to get rid of her, you'd be in line."

"Me? The last thing I want is somebody's wife."

"But you think she's pretty," I tease.

"I think she's gorgeous and sexy as hell, but she's married to our studio exec. There's plenty of pussy in the sea."

"Nice with the mixed metaphor. You seen her stuff yet?"

"Yeah, man. She's terrific, actually. She's worked on several period pieces but under someone else's banner. Now starting to branch out on her own."

"Send it over. I'll take a look."

"You mentioned needing to see the chemistry between the two actors," Evan says. "What do you think about flying Neevah out to do a screen test with Trey?"

This is a sound suggestion, but the thought of seeing Neevah again gives me pause and also, unfortunately, a dangerous thrill of anticipation.

Be smart.

Be cautious.

"Canon?" Evan asks, one brow lifted. "Think we should bring Neevah in for Trey's screen test?"

"Sorry, dude. My mind is all over the place today. We can ask her, sure."

"Okay, well, since you've been dealing with her and she and I haven't actually met yet, you want to do the honors?"

"Yeah. I will."

"Cool." Evan heads for the door. "I'll coordinate with Trey's agent."

Once he's gone, I consider the phone on my desk. I know I need to make this call, but I'm bracing myself for that husky-sweet voice of hers, and how the sound of it hits me like a shot of whiskey. And I need a clear head.

"You don't have time for this shit," I mutter, grabbing the phone and dialing. "It's just a call."

She picks up on the second ring.

"Canon?" she asks, sounding a little breathless.

"Hey, yeah. How are you?"

"Good. Great actually." There's a slight hesitation on the other end. "Is something wrong? Or did you need something for the movie?"

"Not wrong at all. We—my production partner, Evan—and I wondered if you're available to fly out for a few days."

"Oh, wow. To LA? Of course. I can make time. What's going on?"

"We're casting Cal, and it would help to see your chemistry with one of the actors we're considering."

"Do you know when? I just need to get time off from the show."

"Right. We're coordinating with him and his agent now, but we'll work around you, I'm sure, since we all live here in the city. My assistant, Graham, will reach out to you and make the arrangements."

"Oh, Graham, so will he—"

"She," I correct with a smile because everyone assumes that. "I'll make sure she has your number so we can go from there."

"Cool."

I should hang up now, but do I?

"So how have you been?" I ask...stupidly.

"Um, great. And you? Not working too hard, I hope."

"I always work hard, but I'm trying to take it easier before we go into production."

"Katherine let me take some of Dessi's diaries and letters. She didn't even know half that stuff was back there. I thought it might be useful as I prepare. Verity took some, too."

"Oh, I didn't even realize that."

"I'm sorry. If we weren't supposed to—"

"It's fine. I grabbed some stuff, too. Katherine's been really generous." I shuffle a stack of the multicolored cards I keep for storyboarding.

"Thanks again for talking to her about including some of the new things we discovered."

"It was nothing. She's sweet."

"You're good with people."

"Not all people," she says, something like irony inflected in her voice. "Sometimes it's easier to be good with people you don't know than the ones you do. Than the ones who know you."

My hands still, and I'm not sure how to respond to that. Everyone tastes my impatience at some point, especially when I'm working. Neevah will probably find that out for herself.

"Well, you were good with Katherine," I say. "And it'll help us in the long run."

"Thanks."

"So you're still with *Splendor.* How's that going?"

Why am I extending this conversation?

"Yeah," she replies. "Same. Still understudy, but I have gotten onstage a few other times. The lead had a stomach bug—not that I wanted her to be sick or anything. I just meant—"

"Of course not. So you're staying busy."

"I've been gigging a little more, too, when I can. Like singing some here in the city."

"You have a beautiful voice." *Unnecessary compliment.*

"So do you," she says.

"Me?" I breathe out a surprised chuckle. "I can't hold a note in a bucket."

"Oh." Her laugh dips low and has me gripping the phone tighter. "I meant…talking, I guess. I like your voice when you…talk."

It's quiet on the line for a few seconds while I play that back, irritated with myself for wanting to ask her what else she likes about me because that doesn't matter. It can't. Even separated by thousands of miles, tension coils between us—a rubber band that if pulled too hard, will pop. I'm honest enough with myself to acknowledge it, but doing anything about it? No damn way. Hell, I should have let Evan or Graham handle this, though that would have drawn their curiosity.

"Uh, thanks," I say abruptly. "So look for the details and travel arrangements from Graham in the next day or so. Verity has reworked the script. We'll send over what you guys will read for the screen test, though it won't be much."

"I can't wait to read Verity's changes."

"It'll keep evolving, I'm sure, but it's getting there. We want to get a little with you and Trey to see how you vibe. Graham will send the scene over." This has got to be the most pleasant, stilted conversation I've ever had, but I need to end it. "I gotta go."

"Oh, sure. Of course. I'll be on the lookout for the script. I guess I'll see you soon."

"Yeah. See you soon. Take care, Neevah."

And then I do what I should have done five minutes ago.

I let her go.

SEVENTEEN

Dessi Blue

INTERIOR - SAVOY BALLROOM - NIGHT

Two shot - Dessi and Tilda. They are in the employee's coatroom, preparing for their shift as hostesses at the Savoy. Both wear loose 1930s-era dresses. They hang up their coats. Tilda starts to walk out, but Dessi catches her arm and snatches the slouchy hat from her head.

DESSI

You gonna dance with that hat on?

She hangs the hat on a nearby hook, looks around, checking for any witnesses, and pulls Tilda into her arms.

DESSI

And you forgot my kiss.

She cups Tilda's face and kisses her, rubbing her back intimately.

TILDA (WHISPERING AND PULLING AWAY)

You crazy! You gonna get us fired, Bama.

DESSI

Buchanan don't care 'bout two girls kissing.

TILDA (WHISPERING)

I'll kiss you when we get home. I need to find a man to kiss tonight so we can make rent.

DESSI

Don't say that, Till. Don't do that. I told you we'll figure it out. You don't have to—

TILDA

Look, I been on my own since I was fourteen and I been knowing what's what since then. Don't make me no never mind if I gotta give a little something up to get a little something back.

DESSI

What about a rent party? Folks from the third floor raised all their rent in one night last month.

TILDA

You ain't gonna find my hand out asking for something I can get myself. They oughta be ashamed, charging Negroes twice as much when we ain't got half what they got.

DESSI

Well, we know shame don't come in white.

TILDA

Sho don't.

She gestures to the red dress hugging her curves.

TILDA

But rent come in red.

Dessi pulls Tilda into a hug and kisses her neck.

DESSI

How about you let me find a way? Give me tonight to raise the rent. You know he can't do it like I can.

They exchange a heated glance before Tilda shakes her head.

TILDA

That don't pay the rent, Bama.

DESSI

Gimme 'til tomorrow. I'll raise the rent. Come home with me tonight. Save all your kisses for me.

A tall black man dressed impeccably walks in and they pull apart.

CHARLES BUCHANAN

You girls ready? We got a crowd out there tonight.

DESSI AND TILDA IN UNISON

Yes, Mr. Buchanan.

VIEW OF SAVOY BALLROOM FLOOR

Dessi and Tilda rush out into the beautifully decorated ballroom, packed with dancers. The atmosphere is electric. Both bandstands are filled with musicians.

CHARLES BUCHANAN (TOUCHING DESSI'S SHOULDER AND POINTING TO A TALL MAN ACROSS THE ROOM)

Got you one.

Dessi's head turns in the direction Buchanan points and she spots the man. She takes Tilda's arm and whispers in her ear.

DESSI

Don't forget. Gimme 'til tomorrow to get the money. Meet me back at the coatroom when the shift ends.

Tilda hesitates, nods, and then heads off for the man she's supposed to teach to dance. Dessi approaches the one Buchanan pointed out, a tall, well-dressed man.

DESSI

Wanna dance?

He looks down at her, his smile widening.

CAL HAMPTON

I do now. I'll follow your lead any night.

DESSI

You know this is just for a dance, right?

CAL

Might start that way. You never know.

DESSI

Oh, I know. We dancing?

Dessi starts teaching Cal the basics of a few dances. They laugh when he steps on her toes and can't get the steps right.

DESSI

You're no good at this.

CAL
I'm good at other things.

DESSI
Not at flirting either.

CAL
I mean, my horn. I'm a trumpet player.

DESSI
Oh. A musician, huh? I don't believe you.

CAL
I can prove it, but I had to leave my trumpet in the coat check. Come with me to the Radium Club when you get off. See for yourself.

DESSI
When I get off? We don't shut down 'til three o'clock in the morning.

CAL
Night's just gettin' started. Jam sessions and breakfast 'til the sun comes up. Just over off 142nd Street. Whatta ya say, doll?

DESSI
I say don't call me doll, and I don't think so. Me and my roommate gotta get home.

CAL
If you change your mind...

DESSI

I won't, but thanks for stepping on all my toes with your two left feet.

They laugh and Dessi leaves for the next customer. Cal stands on the sidelines and watches her go with a smile.

VIEW OF DANCE FLOOR

Dance sequence/montage showcasing the Lindy Hop, the Flying Charleston, Snakehips, and Rhumboogie. Cal stands by all night, not dancing again, but watching Dessi from the sidelines. At the end of the night, Dessi thanks her last customer and looks around for Tilda. When she doesn't see her, she heads for the coatroom, collects her hat, and exits the building.

EXTERIOR - LENOX AVENUE - OUTSIDE THE SAVOY - NIGHT

Dessi stands on the street, scanning the well-dressed people leaving the Savoy. Cal approaches her, holding up his trumpet case for her to see.

CAL

Told ya I was a musician.

DESSI

Hmmmh. If you say so.

CAL (LAUGHING)

I'll show you if you come with me to the Radium. You been on the track all night. Come have some breakfast.

DESSI

No, I ain't—

She spots Tilda with a well-dressed man headed in the opposite direction. Tilda looks over her shoulder at Dessi guiltily and then shrugs. Dessi glances down at the sidewalk and blinks away tears.

CAL

It'll be a good time. Best music in the city. White boys show up, too. Benny Goodman and Harry James came last week. And the best grits you ever had.

Dessi looks in the direction Tilda went, seeing her red dress swallowed by the late-night crowd. She forces a smile and looks up at Cal.

DESSI

Did you say grits?

CAL (LAUGHING)

Best in Harlem. Come on.

EXTERIOR MOVING SHOT on Cal and Dessi talking inaudibly with a jazz music bed under the shots as they walk the few blocks to the Radium Club.

INSERT shots of Harlem nightlife, buildings lit up, Tillie's Chicken House, The Log Cabin, the Theatrical Grill, well-dressed white patrons entering the Cotton Club, and finally ending on the entrance to the Radium Club.

INTERIOR – RADIUM CLUB - NIGHT

When Cal and Dessi enter, the club is filled with smoke and people and music. A dimly lit stage sits in the center of the room, and a small band tunes up.

CAL

I gotta get up there. I was waiting for a certain hostess to finish her shift and now I'm late.

DESSI

Oh, you in the band?

CAL

I am tonight.

DESSI

What y'all playing?

CAL (PULLING HIS TRUMPET FROM ITS CASE)

"Body and Soul" is the only one I know for sure. We kinda just figure it out as we go some nights.

Dessi starts humming "Body and Soul."

DESSI

Oh, I love that song.

CAL

You sing?

DESSI (LAUGHING)

For an audience of none.

CAL

You sound like you can do a li'l something.

DESSI (SHRUGS)

I'm okay, but I get scared.

CAL

Well, order you some breakfast and I'll be back on our first break.

Cal heads up to the stage. Time lapse of Dessi eating and enjoying her pancakes and grits while Cal's band plays. Montage ends with the sun rising outside, illuminating the room.

CAL (INTO MICROPHONE ONSTAGE)

Looks like we're the last ones standing. Well, I think we saved the best for last. I got a special treat for you.

Turns and whispers to the band members, who nod.

CAL

Making her debut right here at the Radium Club singing "Body and Soul," my very good friend who I just met tonight, Odessa Johnson.

Dessi gapes at him with a mouthful of grits.

CAL

Don't be shy and don't make me look like a fool up here. Come on, Odessa.

The few patrons still remaining give Dessi encouraging applause and wolf whistles. Dessi stands up like she's headed for the stage, but dashes for the door. Cal runs, catches her around the waist, and drags her to the stage.

DESSI

You crazy? I can't sing.

CAL

I heard you. I think you can, and you won't know 'til you try.

Cal hands her the mic and picks up his trumpet, standing beside her.

CAL

I'll be right here, and there's hardly anybody still around. What you got to lose?

The first strains of "Body and Soul" begin. Dessi holds the mic awkwardly, flicking nervous glances around the club. She begins haltingly, and continues with growing confidence.

DESSI

My days have grown so lonely,

For you I cry, for you dear only,

Why haven't you seen it,

I'm all for you, body and soul

I spend my days in longin',

You know it's you that I am longin',

Oh, I tell you I mean it,

I'm all for you, body and soul

I can't believe it,

It's hard to conceive it,

That you'd throw away romance

Are you pretending,

It looks like the ending,

Unless I can have one more chance to prove, dear

My life a wreck you're making,

You know I'm yours for just the taking,

Oh, I tell you I mean it,

I'm all for you, body and soul

My days have grown so lonely,

For you I cry, for you dear only,

Oh, why haven't you seen it,

I'm all for you, body and soul

By the end, people are applauding and Cal gives her a hug onstage. Covering her face with both hands, Dessi laughs.

EIGHTEEN

Neevah

"So what'd you think of Trey during the screen test?" Canon's production partner, Evan, asks.

"He was great." I sip my virgin mojito. "I mean, I thought so. What'd *you* think?"

"Totally agree." Evan glances around the incredible rooftop restaurant, Open Air, where we're having drinks and an early dinner. The Olympic-sized pool is positioned as the aquamarine centerpiece of the roof, accessorized by lounge chairs and VIP curtained pods offering additional privacy. "Galaxy loves him, too. I'm not the one who needs convincing."

"Let me guess. Canon."

"You got it. It took him forever to cast your part. I don't expect him to be that picky on Cal's role, but it's Canon, so..."

He leaves the comment unfinished like it's self-explanatory, and I guess it is. Canon's reputation for being exacting precedes him and makes him casting *me*, an unknown, that much more miraculous.

"He's en route, by the way." Evan glances at his phone. "He had to speak across town at this event where he was being honored."

My heartbeat hiccups.

Stop doing that.

This crush, attraction—*whatever it is*—has to be put down before it causes any awkwardness and costs me this opportunity.

"I, um, don't want him to feel like he has to rush to get here," I say, twirling the miniature umbrella from my drink. "I don't want you to feel like you have to entertain me either, hanging out tonight."

"You kidding me? I need the break and you fly back tomorrow. It's a chance for us to get to know each other. Besides, I love this place. I don't come here enough."

Graham booked me in The V, a boutique hotel in the heart of downtown LA. It screams class and money like a dog whistle. The rooftop restaurant is the cherry on the literal top of the spectacular building.

"This place is something else." I take in the crowded outdoor dining space, which resembles a high-fashion photo shoot. "Does everyone in this town look like a supermodel?"

"It's LA and this is a popular spot to be seen, so everyone always looks their best. You never know when you might be 'discovered.'"

With my hair scraped back, wearing only light makeup and a simple sundress, I feel a little underdressed compared to everyone else on the roof. I expect Tyra Banks to pop out from behind a potted palm tree any minute and order me to smize. I work in theater, in New York, so there are always beautiful people around, of course. *These* people, though, set against the balmy glamor of the LA skyline, glitter like a tray full of diamonds, everyone in on a beauty secret that makes them glow.

"Monk's on his way, too," Evan says, glancing up from his phone. "He texted me. He was in a session, but he wants to see you."

"I wouldn't be sitting here if it weren't for Monk dragging Canon to see me in *Splendor*."

"Things happen like they should, I guess."

I'm not sure I've believed that in a long time. The things that hurt you most—it's sometimes hard to accept that those are the result of fate or a deity's deliberation. Much easier to believe the universe means us good, and good will prevail. Either way, I'll always be grateful for Monk's role in getting me here.

"This is actually my sister's place," Evan continues. "Well, stepsister."

"This place belongs to your sister? Uh, stepsister?"

"Her family owns the hotel and the rooftop is kind of her pet project."

"Some pet. This place is gorgeous."

"It's even better when it's empty. It doesn't open 'til five, so occasionally she lets us up here before the madness starts. Can't beat a gorgeous view of the city and the best mimosas in town."

"Nice. You said she's your stepsister. How long have your parents been married?"

"Oh, they're not anymore. That particular marriage only lasted about nine months. My father is, shall we say, indecisive. He just remarried again." Evan raps his knuckles against the table. "Knock on wood, sixth time's the charm."

"Six? Wow. Is she your only stepsibling?"

"I have..." He counts on his fingers and squints. "Twelve."

I laugh and gape at him. "How do you keep up?"

"I just start calling them by reindeer names," Evan says, flashing an unabashed grin. "Growing up, there were only a few I actually lived with or got to know. Arietta and I stayed in touch even after our parents parted ways. I'm closest to her."

"No blood siblings?"

"One half-brother. My father wasn't married to my mother much longer than he was to Ari's." He grins over my shoulder. "Look who's here."

I glance toward the door, my stomach flipping at the sight of Canon. I was braced for standard fine-ass Canon, but wearing a dark gray suit with a slate blue button-up open at the collar, he is not playing fair tonight. The sun is not quite gone for the evening, so he still wears sunglasses as he scours the rooftop for us.

What in the GQ is happening right now?

I'm not sure what to *do* with this buzz transported through my blood like oxygen and dispatched to my tingling extremities. This low hum of attraction that thickens the air when I'm around him under the best of circumstances. Him showing up looking like this? Not optimal.

And then I notice *her.*

Accompanying him is a woman beside whom every one of these glittering diamonds appears a little dull. Large, dark soulful eyes and long black hair that clings to her bare arms and shoulders. The kind of breakneck curves you find on a race track and a white, wide smile revealed when she laughs up at Canon, her arm looped through his elbow.

Heifer.

I have no right to this auto-petty response, and seeing that impossibly beautiful woman with Canon...it shouldn't affect me. We have nothing more than a business relationship. He hasn't given me reason to think differently. There are a hundred obvious reasons why me plus him would equal bad, but I don't like seeing him with *her.* I'll have to sort through this on my own time in the privacy of my hotel room. For now, let me paint on a plastic smile and pretend I don't want to pull this woman's hair out.

Again. I. Have. No. Right.

"Look who I found," the woman practically purrs when they reach our table.

I hate her voice. It's all deep and sexy and pleasant. *Yuck.*

"About time," Evan says, standing and hugging her. "We were starting to worry."

"Event went a little over," Canon says. "Sorry I'm late." His eyes meet mine briefly, then flick away. "Enjoying yourself, Neevah?"

"I am," I reply, my voice sounding unnaturally high and breathy, a la Marilyn Monroe.

"The place is jumping tonight." Evan kisses her cheek and sits back down.

"I know," she says with a slight accent. "I need to check in with the staff, but I had to meet the woman who finally managed to satisfy Canon."

She turns those beautiful dark eyes on me and extends her hand. "I'm Arietta, Evan's sister. I'm so glad they finally found you. So nice to meet you."

Evan's sister. Of course.

"Hi." I shake her hand, maybe a little too vigorously. "It's nice to meet you, too."

Canon and Arietta take their seats and I remind myself I cannot stare at this man all night. Not any part of the night, actually. I train my eyes on my drink and try to become invisible.

"So, Neevah, what was your impression of Trey?" Canon asks.

Well, that didn't work.

"I thought he was great," I say.

"You guys had amazing chemistry," Evan interjects.

"Yeah, I guess so," Canon says. "But I want to see the tape."

"It was so weird interacting with him as an adult," I admit, giggling a little. "I remember watching him on TV when he was like twelve years old."

"So do I!" Arietta laughs, widening her eyes. "They used to pour goop all over him every episode of that show."

"And he had that thing where he always rang the doorbell that made the goose-honk sound," I add.

"I didn't watch this show," Canon says. "But it sounds pathetic."

"First of all," Arietta teases breezily. "You're older than we are."

"How much older?" I ask before I can stop myself, and then regret it when his dark, assessing gaze lands on me.

"You're what?" he asks. "Thirty?"

"Yeah," I say.

"Same as me," Arietta squeals, giving me a high five across the table.

"I'm thirty-seven," Canon offers.

"Same as me." Evan imitates Arietta's squeal and goes for a high five, which Canon deflects with an eye roll. We all laugh and Canon allows a small twitch at the corner of his mouth.

"You were probably in college or something by the time that show was popular," Arietta continues. "So that's first of all. And *B* of all, your mother wouldn't have let you watch it anyway."

"Now that's true," Evan says. "I've heard you say Mama Holt was strict about that stuff."

"You didn't watch television growing up?" I ask him.

"Some on the weekends." Canon signals for a waiter before looking back to me. "She wasn't a big fan of TV."

"And I thought our television was a relative until I was like five years old." I laugh. "I don't remember a babysitter, but I remember our TV."

"Movies were different," Canon says. "She'd take me out of school so we could see a new movie together. She took me to see *Forrest Gump* the day it released. That movie still gets me."

The Magic Hour, Canon's highly personal documentary about his mother's journey with MS, was the first work of his I ever saw. It's surreal that I'm sitting here with him now.

"That's when you knew you wanted to be a director?" Arietta asks.

"It was a hundred movies that probably showed me that." Canon tips his chin in thanks when the server sets a drink down in front of him. "*The Godfather, Glory, Taxi Driver, Do the Right Thing.* The list is endless, but I definitely knew very early on."

"Did your mother ever want you to be a photographer like her?" I ask.

He doesn't seem surprised that I already know this much about his background, his family, and I'm struck anew by fame and how it cracks open the book of your life for people to read before they've even met you or know anything about the person behind the stories they've heard.

"Never." Canon shakes his head, affection softening the line of his mouth. "She wanted me to be whatever I decided—to be true to that."

"What we doing?"

I turn at the deep voice, delighted to see Monk standing by our table. Without thinking, I stand and give him a tight hug. He rocks me a little and kisses my cheek.

"Hey, superstar," he says, taking the empty seat by Canon. "How you liking LA?"

"It's great," I reply, sitting back down. "I'm glad I got to see you before I leave tomorrow."

"You know I wouldn't miss seeing the next big thing before she blows all the way up." Monk grins. "I haven't gotten the chance to personally congratulate you on landing Dessi. It's a big deal."

"I have you to thank," I tell him. "If you hadn't put me on Canon's radar, none of this would have happened for me."

"I knew at that gig when I heard you sing there was something special about you," Monk says, his usual easygoing expression serious. "I know talent when I see it, and I love when I meet someone before they really take off." He tosses a glance at Canon, the cocksure grin returning to his lips. "Take Canon, for instance."

"I knew this was coming." Canon groans, swiping one big hand over his face. "He tells this story every chance he gets."

"What story?" Arietta leans forward, her face animated. "I haven't heard this."

"I have." Evan stands. "I'm going to the little boys' room. Be right back."

"So I was on the set of this music video," Monk says.

"Half his stories start this way," Canon interrupts. "In case you're wondering."

I laugh, enjoying the dynamic of their friendship.

"It was a video for a song I co-wrote." Monk grimaces. "Not my proudest moment."

"Tell it all," Canon says. "If you're gonna tell it."

"It was 'Grind Up on Me, Girl,'" Monk admits, his smile chagrined.

"Ew," Arietta murmurs. "You wrote that?"

"Co-wrote, thank you very much." Monk tips his head toward Canon. "And guess who directed the video?"

"No way!" I screech before I remember not to be rude. "You did that?"

"In my defense," Canon says, his full lips spread in a self-deprecating smile, "I was twenty-two years old and had bills to pay. A Grand Jury prize does not pay your rent."

"Seriously?" Arietta asks. "I can't imagine you struggling after all the accolades you got for *The Magic Hour.*"

"Hype is not money," Canon says, sobering. "And buzz doesn't keep the lights on. Truth be told, I took all those prizes and awards for a documentary, and it was great, but nobody was beating my door down. It's a haul for anyone in Hollywood, but a young brother like myself fifteen years ago? Man, I was grateful when they asked me to direct the video for that cheesy song Monk wrote."

"Alright now," Monk protests. "I can talk shit about my songs. You can't."

"Bruh, it was bad." Canon laughs. "I think *it's not your tits, but your wits* was my favorite line, and by favorite, I mean that it made me cringe the most."

Monk almost spits out his drink. "I said I *co-wrote.* I do not take responsibility for that line and begged them not to keep it. Don't you put that on me, motherfucker."

"You did win a Soul Train award for it," Canon says.

"So did you, though I at least showed up to accept mine."

"By then I was making another documentary." Canon takes a long swallow of his Macallan. "I was in South America during that awards show. I meant no disrespect. Hell, I may have gotten more mileage out of the Soul Train award than I did from Sundance in some ways. I just had to be more discriminating about what I accepted."

"What part of South America?" Arietta asks. "My neck of the woods?"

"Not Venezuela, no. I've never been there, actually. It was Brazil."

So that's the accent I hear, and it accounts for her beautiful coloring. "You're from Venezuela?" I ask.

"Yes." She waves her hand to encompass the rooftop. "Thus The V. When my father arrived in America, his business associates called him the Venezuelan. He bristled at first, but then embraced it and has turned it into a brand, The V."

"The hotel is amazing," I tell her. "I'm glad Graham booked me here. Can't wait to meet her."

"She'd be here tonight, but had a family commitment. You'll meet her soon. She keeps the ship running," Evan says, taking a seat and joining us at the table again. "Speaking of running, I'm on empty. Can we order some actual food?"

"Agreed," Canon says. "That event had nothing to eat and I need more than this drink."

He slips his suit jacket off and hangs it on the back of his seat. This man's shoulders and the width of his chest...damn. The silvery-blue open collar against the rich hue of his skin is criminal. Some imp inside my head, conspiring with my vagina, obviously, telegraphs an image of me biting into the corded muscle of his throat. When my eyes roam farther up, I meet his gaze, my breath catching. Him watching me watching him. Mortified, I grab one of the menus, using it as a shield while I grapple for my composure.

I'm a professional.

I can sit at a table with the sexiest, most brilliant man I've ever encountered without lusting all over him.

I think I can.

I think I can.

I think I can.

When I slowly lower the menu, I'm glad no one seems to have noticed my lust-lapse. Just as I think I've safely disguised my fascination with Canon, I feel the weight of his stare on me, and when I look up, there is an undeniable knowledge in those dark eyes. A recognition. An awareness. That same pull I felt sitting with him on the bed in Alabama, riffling through Dessi's memories, resurfaces between us, doubling my heartbeat. I cannot look away, and we may as well be on this roof alone, the darkening sky an awning covering just us two.

"Neevah, what looks good?" Monk asks, snapping my focus back to the table and the other people seated here.

"Um, let me see," I say, actually reading the menu this time. "Maybe something with shrimp."

His question dispels the mist fogging my brain and I force myself to concentrate. Everyone discusses their orders, and the easy camaraderie provides cover while I pull my proverbial shit together and suppress the carnal urges the sight of this man in a suit stirs.

I'm a professional.

I chant it in my head a hundred times during the course of the delicious meal. It's a night I'll treasure. These are remarkable people, powerful people in the entertainment industry, but so comfortable with one another in a way that comes with time. It's hard to believe I'll be telling Dessi's incredible story with them.

"It was so nice to meet you, Neevah," Ari says once the plates are being cleared. "These two were so picky about casting Dessi, so I knew you had to be special when I heard they'd found you."

"Canon," Evan coughs into his hand, and then grins across the table at his partner.

"It was great meeting you, too," I tell Arietta. "Your rooftop is amazing. I hope I can come back when I get out here."

"For sure!" Arietta's eyes light up. "We'll hang once you get settled. When do you start shooting?"

"Fall," Canon says, a frown knitting his brows. "September or October. If it works out with Trey, we need to confirm his schedule."

That's still a few months away, and I'm in limbo, suspended between the simple grind I'm living now in New York as an understudy, singing in small clubs, and the great demands of starring in one of the most epic biopics to come along in years.

"I'll walk out with you, Ari," Evan says, standing. "I need to ask you something."

He reaches down to hug me and I squeeze back.

"It was great meeting you, Neevah," he says. "And I can't wait to get started. You'll be a fantastic Dessi."

He's movie-star handsome, and from what I can tell, the definition of rich and privileged, but he also seems grounded by his relationships, the friendships represented at this table. He and Canon definitely have a lot in common, but also seem to provide counter perspectives. I can see how their personalities would blend well in a partnership.

"We'll talk tomorrow about Trey," Canon says, knocking back the last of his drink.

Evan nods, says his final goodbyes, and leaves with Arietta.

"And I actually have a recording session starting in an hour," Monk says. "So Imma pull, too."

I glance at the time on my phone. Nearly ten o'clock. The night is just beginning for studio rats. Recording is such a nocturnal scene.

"Great seeing you again, Neevah," Monk says. I stand to hug him and give him an extra squeeze.

"Thank you again for everything," I tell him, feeling unreasonably emotional as I realize none of this would have been possible had we not met, had he not seen my potential.

"You got the goods." He kisses my cheek. "Can't wait for you to get out here to Cali."

My stomach knots when it's clear Canon and I will be the only ones left once Monk bounces. When I look down at him, still seated, it feels like we are borrowing each other's thoughts—simultaneously realizing that we will be alone if we stay. A muscle tics along his jaw and he reaches for the well-tailored jacket on the back of his chair.

"I'll walk out with you," he tells Monk, standing, towering over me. I tip my head back to catch his eyes as they drop no lower than my face. "Neevah, you're staying here, right? At The V?"

"Uh, yeah." I grab my wristlet from the table. "I'm headed to my room now. I have an early flight back to New York."

As the three of us cross the rooftop and walk to the bank of elevators, I'm cognizant of the heads turning, the attention they draw. I'm flanked by two famous, tall, powerfully built, fine-ass men cloaked in melanin, but only one of them inspires acrobatics inside me, makes my belly turn flips with nothing more than a glance.

Monk's phone rings, and he answers, but continues walking with us.

"I guess you should get used to the attention," Canon murmurs as we exit the restaurant and enter the rooftop lobby.

"What?" I look up, my chest tightening when our stares collide. "What attention?"

"When we walked through the restaurant, all eyes were on you."

I release a startled peal of laughter. "I thought they were all looking at you, not me."

"I wonder how long you'll be able to keep that," he says, his voice a low rumble. "That humility. Once everyone starts telling you how beautiful you are, how amazing you are, it's hard to hold on to."

"Is it hard for you?" I ask softly.

That could be taken in some really pervy ways, but I'm glad that when he looks at me, his eyes sober, he seems to consider the question exactly as I meant it.

"Sometimes you start believing your own press, yeah." He slides his hands into the pockets of his impeccably fitted slacks. "And forget what matters most."

"What matters most?" I ask.

Dear elevator, if you could just not *come until he answers this one question, that'd be great.*

"The story matters most. Always the story." He looks back to the rooftop, still packed with patrons, now bathed in star glow. "And if you're lucky, you find people along the way who keep your feet on the ground—who remind you that real life matters, too."

I know he's referring to his tight inner circle, people like the coterie we just spent the evening with, and some audacious voice inside wonders if I could one day be one of them…to him. Someone who reminds a force like this that he's also just a man.

Our elevator comes too soon, and I savor the last few moments around him. Once I return to New York, I probably won't see him again before we start production. My senses hoard the last of him. His clean, masculine scent. The rich timbre of his voice and the compelling landscape of his features. The intellect and curiosity mingled in his dark eyes. The rare, bright flash of his smile.

I have no right to think I'll miss him, and yet I know I will.

Monk is still on the phone when we board, and neither Canon nor I speak once we're in motion. I sneak a peripheral glance at him from beneath my lashes, watching the shift of his shoulders under the jacket. I think about how I felt when I saw him with Arietta—the unreasonable jealousy. I wonder if he's got a girl, some woman he goes home to or finds solace in or who merely slakes his physical needs. And the thought of it embeds a burning thorn in my heart. How can someone you've known for such a short time inspire this visceral response?

I don't have much time to wonder because we reach my floor and it's time to say goodbye. Still on the phone, Monk whispers *see you soon*. Canon holds the elevator door with one hand, waiting for me to get off.

"Uh, well, I guess I'll see you in a few months," I say, leaving the elevator car. I don't wait for a response but take the first steps toward my room.

"Neevah," Canon calls.

I look over my shoulder, committing his face and the way I feel when I'm around him to memory.

He stares back, his expression enigmatic, but alert.

"Yeah?" I ask, my voice pitched low. Waiting. Breath held.

"Nothing." He frowns, clears his throat. "Good to see you again. Thanks for flying out."

Before I can respond, he releases the door, letting it close between us.

NINTEEN

Neevah

"So they found a new understudy?"

Takira's sitting cross-legged on the twin bed in my tiny bedroom while I purge and prepare to move. We're crammed in here like Tic Tacs. I'm due in LA in two weeks and I'm so ready to leave this place.

But I'm not ready to leave Takira.

"Yeah." I toss a denim jacket I don't even remember buying into a trash bag for Goodwill. "She starts next week, the new girl. I get a few days off before I have to fly out and report to set."

"That's great." She bites her bottom lip and folds a sweatshirt.

We haven't talked much about me leaving. I think we've both been avoiding the subject. I'll still be able to pay my part of the rent since they provide a place for me in LA. She'll have more room, privacy, but I know she'd rather have me here. And I want her with me. When you lose your natural family by blood, the family you choose is that much dearer, and I'm closer to Takira than anyone else.

My phone buzzes on the nightstand, and I grab it to check the text message. A slow grin spreads over my face. It's what I've been waiting for.

"Well, this is good news," I say, waving my phone at Takira.

"Oh yeah?" The forced brightness of her tone does little to disguise the glumness.

"My agent and I had a few things in the contract we needed to negotiate."

"Nice." She pairs up socks and rolls them into a ball.

"I told them that too often Black women get to a job and there isn't someone who knows how to do their hair."

"Girl, facts." She rolls her eyes and sighs. "They don't be checking for us."

"And you already know my hair has... we'll call them special considerations."

Her eyes soften. "Dr. Ansford said everything looks good, though, right?"

"Yes, and I want to keep it that way, so..." I let the smile I've been suppressing break out fully. "I told them I need to choose my own hairdresser, which is not unheard of."

"And?" Takira's eyes hold curiosity and cautious hope.

"They said yes!" I jump on the bed and squeeze her neck. "Girl, we going to Hollywood!"

"Ayyyyeeee!" Her squeal probably wakes the roaches. "*We* are? You and me?"

"Unless you don't want to live rent-free in LA for the next five months and get a movie credit on your resume." I grab my phone and pretend to start dialing. " 'Cause I can tell them right now that you're not—"

"Gimme!" She snatches my phone and rolls from the bed to stand. "Seriously, Neev?"

"Seriously. I need you out there. For emotional support, of course, but also for this hair, which is on a sliding scale from 3B to 4A with a 4C patch in the back." I touch the tender bald spot at the base of my head. "And this scalp is a war zone. You know that better than anybody. This is the biggest opportunity of my life. The last thing I want to be thinking about is my hair."

"Did you tell the studio or anybody about your condition?"

"My agent and I talked it through. As long as I pass the physical for the insurance company, which I did, I've done what they require, and I don't have to disclose anything else."

"Oh, that's good."

"When we requested you as part of my contract, we did tell them I have a condition that affects my skin and hair. Discoid lupus isn't contagious or life-threatening so that's as much as they need to know, but the word *lupus* freaks so many people out. They don't understand it. They make assumptions about what it must mean. I don't want special treatment or anyone assuming I can't do my job. I don't want them doubting me. I got enough doubt"—I tap my temple—"right here. I don't need more second guesses."

"And you've been performing and making a living in this business with no problems since you got the diagnosis."

"Exactly. I mean, I have some joint pain and fatigue, but who doesn't? I probably take better care of myself now that I have the diagnosis than when I didn't."

"What's the doc say?"

"She's setting me up with a rheumatologist out in LA who I can check in with, someone I can see in person if needed, but my bloodwork looks good. My antibody levels are in range. This," I say, pulling at the hair puffing around my shoulders, "is my biggest concern, and that's where you come in."

Takira walks over and wraps her arms around me. "I got you, girl. Don't worry."

I run my hands through my thick hair, delving into the bare spaces hidden by its sheer volume. Don't worry?

Easier said than done.

TWENTY

Canon

"Never be late to my set."

I study every member of the cast and crew, glancing around the large U-shaped table and giving each of them time to look me in my eyes and see that I'm not playing with their asses.

"Come prepared, and if you aren't, don't make excuses. This will be fun. You might even make some friends." I point a thumb to Graham, who, along with Evan, is seated behind me. "Our assistant will make sure we're one big, happy family. She always plans socials and other stuff to bond the team."

"Hey, guys!" Graham says, and I can just imagine her waving and cheesing.

"So Graham's got the fun covered." I slide my hands into the pockets of my jeans. "But this will also be some of the hardest work of your life. I won't go easy on anybody because we are here to serve this story. This is someone's life we're introducing the world to. I don't take that lightly, and neither will you."

I try to smile, to relax, but that gets harder once a movie is out of pre-production. I leave the petting and coddling to Evan and Graham. I don't have time for games or tolerance for bullshit. I know how to get the best out of my actors, and it's not berating them or bullying them. At the same time, I'm not here to make friends.

Though, despite my grumpy ways, that inevitably happens on set.

"Just so you know," Evan says, walking up beside me, "you'll hate this guy at least once before the movie is over. We all do, but then we see what he does, the movie he makes, and we forgive him. I'm going to apologize in advance for the beard."

I smile before I remind myself that is not funny.

"He grows his beard out for every movie and the longer it gets, the more unbearable he becomes," Evan says over everyone's laughter. "We'll try to keep him in line and the beard groomed. I'm Evan Bancroft, one of the producers, by the way. This is Verity Hill, our writer."

Verity looks up from her phone and waves.

"Wright Bellamy is our music guy," Evan continues. "He's writing the score, but for those with music and singing parts, he'll be working directly with you, too."

Monk waves and flashes around a smile that dies when it lands on Verity. She rolls her eyes and looks away. And so it begins...

"We're gonna do a table read," I say, picking up where Evan left off. "Don't show me all your good stuff. I'm not looking for tears. Save that for when the cameras are rolling. Believe me. We'll get there. Today we're just familiarizing ourselves with Verity's brilliant script."

With a sweep of my arm I gesture to the studio back lot we've transformed into 1930s Harlem, sprawled just beyond the corner of the set where we're meeting.

"Look around," I tell them, glancing over my shoulder to the building facades, the apartment stoops and fabricated city blocks, the reincarnated elegance of hotels and clubs long passed away. "This is our new home."

I introduce the department heads—cinematographer, production designer, assistant director, and Linh, whom we did bring on for costuming. Lawson Stone is also present, but I'm hopeful this will be our last time seeing him for a while. It's not unusual for a studio exec to attend the first read-through. It's all hands on deck—the first time everyone involved gets to fully experience the scope of what we're making. Until now they've seen their parts, but I've been living with the entirety of this story for almost two years already. Of what it could be, and now it's time to make it real.

"We are recording," Evan interjects, pointing to the camera set up at the front of the room. It's far enough back to capture everyone seated around the U-shaped table. "So don't be thrown off by that. We have food coming. There's water here. If you need anything, let me or Graham know, and we'll take care of it. Before we start, we'd like everyone to introduce themselves."

Mallory outdid herself casting this movie. I was anal about the role of Dessi, but Mallory and I have been working together for years. I trust her instincts, and they did not fail me. Even Trey turned out to be the right choice for Cal. I don't particularly like the thought of him, all Disney and Nick at Nite, but the reality of him isn't so bad.

I know everyone, so I tune them out for the most part, and flip through the script, marking up places I want to pay special attention to.

Jill Brigston, seated beside me, bumps my shoulder. She's the best cinematographer I've ever met and would have an Oscar by now if she was a man.

"I can feel you vibrating," she leans over to whisper while the cast introduce themselves.

"What do you mean?"

"This crazy energy comes off you when we start a new project," she says, green eyes sparkling with knowing humor under her shock of blonde hair.

She would know. She's worked with me on just about every movie for the last ten years.

"I'm Neevah Saint."

I stiffen, but don't look up from my script. Don't need to. I know exactly where she is in the room. To my right. Three chairs down, seated beside Trey. She's wearing a white sundress that leaves her shoulders bare and smooth, along with a colorful head wrap from which her wild tresses sprout and overflow. There are lingering traces of a Southern accent in her voice, like honey sprinkled into something savory. At this point, it's been nearly a year since I first saw her onstage and a few months since she flew out for Trey's screen test. We've spoken a couple of times about the script, research, making sure she feels prepared, but any nonessential communication has gone through Evan and Graham, as it typically would.

I don't need distractions or entanglements. She could be considered both. Of course, I'll have to interact with her as the director, but I've decided to limit any contact beyond that to only the absolutely necessary.

"I'm really grateful for this opportunity," Neevah says. "And honestly still pinching myself that I'm even here. The more I learn about Dessi, the more I realize what a privilege it is to introduce people to her story, to her life."

I look up to see her spread a warm smile around the room.

"And I do hope to make lots of friends."

That evokes a small murmur of laughter before the next cast members introduce themselves.

"I like her," Jill says, pitching her voice low.

"Why?"

"She's one of those people who pulls you in. Ya know? She's sincere. And I have an instinct about folks." She taps her nose. "I can smell a phony a mile away, and she's the real deal. Good job finding her."

"Monk found her."

"Um, you fought pretty hard for her."

I snap a glance up to study her face. "How do you know that?"

"Evan told me."

"Figures." I roll my eyes. "She's the right choice."

"I believe it and I saw her screen test. I see why you're so into her."

"I am not *into*..." I cut my words off when I realize how closely Jill is watching my face. Dammit. I gave her too much. Jill's as observant as an owl.

"I am not," I finish more evenly, "into her."

Graham shoots us the kind of look reserved for kids talking in church. She puts a silencing finger to her lips.

"I just know talent when I see it," I say in a barely audible whisper.

"Sometimes you just know," Jill agrees, smiling like a sly cat. I don't even want to speculate what that means or what idea has gotten lodged in her head.

Once the introductions are complete, I stand. Jill is right. I'm basically vibrating with the need to get started. I school my expression to implacable, but inside, my desire to tell this story echoes like a voice that hasn't been used in a long time and is ready to sing.

"Alright," I say. "If that's everyone, get out your scripts. Let's read this thing through."

TWENTY-ONE

Neevah

"Will you run lines with me real quick?" I ask Takira.

She's putting finishing touches on my eye shadow. Turned out the chick they hired to do makeup wasn't that great, so Takira offered to handle that, too. She cut her teeth in New York, and has done hair and makeup for TV shows, theater, movies, and commercials. Every possible medium runs through the city, and she has experience in them all.

"Sure." She catches my eyes in the mirror. "Do like this."

She pops her lips. I mimic, evening out the shock of matte red lipstick.

"This old-school look is made for you, Neev," Takira says, smoothing a strand of hair into my updo.

I still double-take when I see myself in the mirror before I go out to set. Standing in my tricked-out trailer, surrounded by every modern accoutrement, including a gigantic flat-screen television built into the wall, I'm an anachronism. My Victory roll hairstyle. Linh's vintage costumes designed with such flair and attention to detail. When I slip on the dresses that swish against my legs, the sheer stockings, or a velvet bucket hat, I'm transported into Dessi's world: a city struggling to drag itself from the Great Depression. Black people, striving to live and love and laugh and sing in a world that sometimes made all those things harder to do. But they carved out a vibrant, spectacular community in Harlem. A time of excellence and style and art. Of fur-trimmed coats and pomade-slicked hair and satin gloves. A place populated with dancers and dreamers and thinkers and agitators and writers and folks just *living*. Making do and making history in the trench of everyday life.

Each time I step out of this trailer, I'm at the corner of then and now. The production team transformed this back lot into a world long lost. Lafayette Theatre. The Savoy Ballroom. 139th Street. Lenox Avenue. The Radium Club. With Monk as their conductor, the ghosts of Duke Ellington, Jelly Roll Morton, and Louis Armstrong play their songs, dousing the air with notes of aching nostalgia.

"You said you need to run some lines?" Takira asks, snapping shut a tray of eye shadows and lovingly stowing her prized collection of brushes.

"Oh, yeah. I'm worried about this scene."

"You're not a complete novice. You've done some commercials and stuff."

I give her my *are you shitting me* face.

"*Commercials and stuff* is not a feature film. The learning curve is steep," I say, grabbing one of two rolled-up scripts from a nearby table for myself and handing her the other. I keep two copies with me all the time because I constantly recruit someone to run lines with me. "And working with one of the best directors in the industry doesn't help my nerves."

"We never actually see him on set." Takira laughs. "How can someone who isn't there make you nervous?"

Canon watches from video village, a tent filled with screens so he can see every camera angle and shot we're capturing in real-time. The assistant director, Kenneth, out on set, is in constant communication with him. Canon is still extremely hands-on, and more than once I've seen him on a crane camera up in the air, checking shots before we start rolling.

He is the kind of man you meet once in a lifetime. Yes, he's sharp and takes no shit, but I want that. To do my best, I need that. We all know he's the magnetic nucleus holding this together. He carries this story and the pulse of it beats inside him. He's protective of Dessi's journey, its chief guardian, but he's also concerned about his actors. For his art, he's obsessive and distracted and focused and impatient and long-suffering. He's a million things and he's single-minded.

It's getting harder not to want him. Every day I stomp on this unfortunate longing, this ill-advised craving, this dead-end desire. And I cannot make it stop.

The knock at my trailer door dispels my thoughts.

"They're ready for you, Ms. Saint," a voice says from the other side.

I didn't get to review my lines one more time. The question is am *I* ready?

TWENTY-TWO

Dessi Blue

INTERIOR - CHICAGO NIGHTCLUB - NIGHT

Dessi sits backstage in a tiny dressing room with a mirror hung on the wall, waiting to go on. She holds a letter from Tilda.

VOICE-OVER OF TILDA READING LETTER:

Hey, Dessi! How is the road treating you? I hope Cal and the band are taking care of my girl. Thank you for the money you sent. It feels good not to worry about making rent, but I miss you, baby Bama. I can't wait for you to come home so I can hear about all your adventures. Everybody at the Savoy sends their best. Mr. Buchanan says to tell you he's holding your spot if this singing thing don't work out! But I know it will. I'll see you when you get home. I'm saving all my kisses for you.

Love, Tilda

Someone knocks at the dressing room door.

DESSI

Come on in.

Door opens. Cal walks in, a worried expression on his face.

CAL

We need to talk before you go on.

DESSI

You look like somebody killed your dog, and I know you ain't got no dog, so what's wrong?

CAL

It's a mess out there. The city's just coming out of those riots, and all them white folks are tight as a bow. Got management worried.

DESSI

And what's that got to do with us?

CAL

They're afraid the light'll hit you just right and the audience might think you're a white girl onstage with a bunch of Negroes.

DESSI (LAUGHS)

Whoo. They come up with some stuff, don't they? And what they want to do about that?

Cal pulls a small tin out of his pocket.

CAL

They...uh, got this greasepaint for you to wear.

DESSI

The hell I am, Cal. I ain't singing in no blackface.

CAL

We got a contract, Dess. They won't pay us, and not only that, but they'll spread the word. Maybe mess up bookings for the rest of this trip. It'll ruin things for all of us.

DESSI

But I'm the only one gotta wear it! Not you. Not them.

CAL

It ain't right, but what choice do we have? What choice do we ever have?

DESSI

Cal, no. If we play down South, I'm pissing in cups and shitting in the woods. Eating on buses. And up here, this?

CAL

It's all America, Dess.

DESSI

Well, I'm good and damn tired of it.

CAL

We all are. Look, I'll take you somewhere nice for dinner. Just . . . put it on? For me? For the band? So we can get paid and get outta here?

Dessi wipes away a tear and nods. Cal squats down in front of her and gently smears on the greasepaint.

CLOSE SHOT ON DESSI

She stares at her darkened face in the mirror before standing and following Cal out.

INTERIOR - THEATER STAGE

Spotlight on the band and Dessi, who sings an upbeat song in the dark makeup, forcing herself to smile.

TWENTY-THREE

Neevah

As soon as Kenneth calls cut, I flee the set, stumbling past the craft foods table and the cluster of cameramen breaking for coffee. My heart is a runaway coach led by a team of wild horses. Rivulets of sweat streak through the thick greasepaint Trey smeared on my face for the scene. I trip up the short set of steps into my trailer and collapse onto the couch. Even seated, my legs still shake, my hands tremble. I touch my face and my fingers come away streaked with paint, smeared with pain and degradation. In my right mind, I know this didn't actually happen to me. It was Dessi's burden, not mine. I'm not in my right mind, though. I'm not in my mind at all.

I'm in *hers*.

And her outrage claws its way from the grave to burrow in my thoughts. Her humiliation lingers in my bones and cages my spirit. I glance up into the mirror, shocked to see my haunted face instead of hers.

A knock at the door jolts me to the present.

I don't want to see anyone, but I left the set without even asking if we needed to do another take. We probably do. I lost it at the end of that scene. Swallowing my tears and trying to steady my breathing, I answer. "Come in."

Canon steps inside, and any composure I had regained dissipates. I figured I screwed up the scene, but his heavy frown and tight lips confirm it. He rarely comes out other than at the beginning and end of each day, or occasionally to adjust a camera shot. We haven't really talked one-on-one much since the rooftop, so seeing him now in these close quarters, his tall frame dominating my trailer, only disconcerts me more.

"I'm sorry," I say in a rush, lowering my head into my hands, seeking refuge from his scrutiny. "I know. I lost control of my emotions. I just... I'm sorry. It won't happen again."

He doesn't reply, and the silence gnaws at my ears, nips at my vulnerability. For a scene like that, I dig into my heart to find someone else's soul, and it lays me open, leaves me bare. I need time to recover myself, to *find* myself again after pouring everything into Dessi, but there is no reprieve. No time to regroup when the man who unnerves me most stands here, watching me. Judging me? Wondering if I'll break? Tears blossom at the corners of my eyes while I wait for him to say something.

He moves, but not toward me. I stare at the rug beneath my feet, but peripherally see him walk toward my vanity. When he sinks to his haunches in front of me, I sit back quickly, my eyes going to his face. He stares back, and the now-familiar electric current passes between us. The same thing I sensed brewing in Katherine's back room, on the roof, stirs the air again.

"I'll do it better," I whisper, stretching my eyes so the tears will stand and not fall.

"You can't."

"I can. I know I can, if you give me the chance to—"

"You can't do it better because it was perfect."

Shock rattles me at his words, and I look up to find him studying me soberly.

"You didn't lose control. You lost yourself. It's what you have to do with this kind of work. It demands it of you. You are stepping into shoes that walked a hard road. Prejudice, disrespect, heartbreak—that was all part of Dessi's life. But so was joy and lots of good. Over the course of this movie, you will absorb the full arc of her existence. Great actors inhabit the character, sometimes so much that the line between fact and fiction, them and you, blurs and you feel *everything*. That's what you're experiencing."

Using the tissue he plucked from my vanity, he gently wipes at the corners of my eyes, then at the heavy greasepaint smeared on to darken my skin. With each swipe away of the offensive makeup, my breath comes easier, my heart settles into a more regular rhythm.

"I've actually asked Evan to bring a therapist on set for you guys."

"You have?"

"We should have from the beginning." He shakes his head, leaving his hand to rest at the curve of my neck. "I was trying to think of everything and missed maybe the most important. Taking care of my actors."

"You *have* taken care of us. Bringing in a therapist—that'll be great." I place my hand over his at my neck. "Thank you."

He looks down to where our hands rest together. I jerk away.

"So," he says, clearing his throat. "Lawson was on set today."

"From Galaxy? From the studio?"

I'm glad for the subject change, but I tense again because the studio execs rarely visit. Lawson Stone *would* choose today, one of the most challenging scenes of the movie.

"Yup. You know what he said to me after he saw you in that scene?" Canon tosses the paint-stained tissue into a nearby wastebasket.

"What?" Dread and anticipation make my voice tight.

"He said, 'Well, you were right. You found the perfect Dessi.'"

That startles a relieved sound from me that is half-laugh, half-sob.

"Scenes like that cost you." Canon takes my hand and squeezes it, looking into my eyes and letting me see the truth, which is rare for him. "You paid the price, but it's worth it. It will be worth it. You're doing a fantastic job."

My heart races but not with doubt or fear, but because I don't think he realizes he took my hand again. He's caressing the ink scribbled along my thumb. My breath shortens, huffing past my lips in pants. The scent of him floods the air around me. Earthy and clean and rich and masculine. His pupils dilate and the fullness of his lips thins into a line. He drops my hand abruptly and stands.

"Canon, I—"

"I better get back out there." He turns and is out the door before I can say anything else. Before I can ask him if I'm imagining this; if I'm alone in this growing awareness, or if he feels it, too. I keep slamming the door on my feelings, but there is a persistent *tap, tap, tap* constantly tempting me to open it.

Daring me to find out what's on the other side.

TWENTY-FOUR

Canon

"This is a waste of time," I tell Monk.

From Evan's balcony, we watch a roomful of partygoers in costume.

"Hey, you might be the big-shot director," Monk says.

"*Might* be? Brothah, I am."

"But Graham knows how to keep up morale. The cast and crew have been working hard. Throwing this party was a great idea."

Graham asked Evan and me about planning an eighties-themed party for Halloween, which Evan agreed to host here at his huge house stuffed into the side of a mountain overlooking LA. The view alone is impressive, much less the minimalist décor and sapphire-colored swimming pool. I think everyone from the cast and crew is here, most costumed with some nod to the era.

"If it's such a good idea," I say, "then why didn't you dress up?"

"Why didn't you?"

"Because I don't need parties to boost my morale. These spirits *stay* high."

"You been by yourself brooding out on this balcony all night. If this is cheerful, I'd hate to see you down."

I sip my Macallan and drink in the night air, refreshing after being inside with that crowd. Monk's right. I'm in a mood. I don't want to acknowledge to myself what's causing it because that would mean acknowledging other things best left alone. Things that would distract me and just all-around not be a good look. Still, despite my best intentions, my gaze wanders back inside to Evan's living room and finds Neevah. Every time I've seen her tonight she's been dancing, but now she's laughing with Trey, her hands animating whatever story she's telling. One of the grips is trying to push up on her hairstylist, Takira. From the look she's giving him, seems like he might be tapping that sooner rather than later.

"Everybody thinks they're already fucking," Monk says.

"I don't know." I set my drink on the balcony ledge and roll a cigar between my fingers. "Takira seems to be holding out a little while longer."

"Not Takira. Neevah and Trey."

My grip tightens around the cigar. I'm still and hot, like a wick trapped in the wax of a burning candle.

"What did you say?" I slow the words so Monk can have no trouble understanding them.

He looks away from me and to the crowd, his expression intent. I follow the direction of his stare.

Verity. Of course.

I snap my fingers in his face to regain his attention.

"Man, don't be snapping at me." Monk turns to me with a scowl. "I ain't no damn dog."

"How else do I get your attention," I ask, tipping my head toward Verity, "when *she's* around?"

"I ain't thinking about that girl. She can do whatever she damn well pleases."

The Monk doth protest too much.

"And I'm sure she will, but you mentioned something about Neevah and Trey."

"Oh, yeah." He looks back to the spot where Verity stood a moment ago, but she's not there anymore. "They're probably sleeping together."

I don't mean to harm the cigar, but it snaps in my hand.

"You alright there, Holt?" Monk's alert stare shifts from my face to the crushed stogy.

"I'm cool." I toss it over the balcony into the yawning canyon below.

"Oh, good. 'Cause for a minute there, I thought you might feel some type of way about Trey fucking our sweet ingénue."

"Stop saying that." I grit my teeth and try to regulate my uneven breathing. "I stay out of my cast's business."

"Right. Right." He taunts me over the rim of his drink. "Well, here comes some cast business now."

Takira and Neevah head toward the balcony, fanning their faces.

"Whew," Takira says breathlessly. "Lawd. I need some air. All them *bodies*. It's hot in there."

"Who y'all supposed to be?" Monk asks, gesturing to their color-coordinated outfits.

"Sidney and Sharane from *House Party*." Takira rolls her eyes. "We realized too late that movie was made in 1990."

"It *released* in 1990," Neevah corrects. "So it was probably made in 1989. So we'd be alright on a technicality."

Takira points to her bright yellow body suit and hair. "You don't spend an hour putting in crinkle curls for a technicality."

Monk laughs along with them, but it's not funny to me. Nothing's funny. Specifically not the thought of Neevah sleeping with Trey. I've made it a point not to be alone with her again since the day in her trailer. I give notes to most of the cast directly, but usually, I send Neevah's through Kenneth. Nothing good can come of this connection between us, so I've steered clear of her.

Apparently, that was unnecessary thanks to Nick at Nite. I take another swig of my drink and turn away from the trio cutting up. I lean my elbows on the balcony ledge and contemplate the glimmer of lights scattered throughout the hills.

"You didn't want to dress up?"

I turn my head to find Neevah beside me, her back to the city, elbows propped on the ledge. Now that I know she's supposed to be Tisha Campbell's character from *House Party*, her vest and bright yellow pants make more sense. She's left her hair out and wild, floating around her shoulders with the slight breeze blown in by the night.

Instead of answering, I pull another cigar from my pocket. Cameo's "Candy" booms from inside followed by a collective whoop from the crowd. I glance at Monk and Takira, who immediately start the steps of the electric slide. My back is to the crowd Neevah's facing, and humor lights her expression.

"Oh, my God! You should see this. They even got old Mr. Anderson out there dancing."

Maybe the thought of the seventy-year-old cameraman doing the electric slide would typically make me smile, but I'm too preoccupied with visions of Trey bending Neevah over a couch in her trailer.

Monk and Takira leave the balcony to join the dancers. Neevah stays.

"You like to dance?" she asks.

"Did you need something?" I carve the words out of stone and show her my irritation with a scowl.

Surprise and dismay mingle on her pretty face. "I-I was just trying to make conversation."

"Go try with someone else. I'm not in the mood for it."

"Wow." Hurt fills her eyes and she presses her lips together, shaking her head. "Sorry I bothered you."

When she turns to leave, which is exactly what I told her to do, like the conflicted motherfucker I am, I reach out, cuffing her wrist to stop her.

She drags a glare from the loose clasp of my hand up to my face. "Did I misunderstand? I could have sworn you wanted to be alone."

"I'm an asshole."

"That's a well-established fact, but no excuse for being rude when I was just trying... well, you told me to go *try* with someone else. So let me go."

"I'm sorry."

"That's better than I'm an asshole." The tight lines of her face soften almost undetectably. "Look, I know how you get kind of lost in what you're thinking and want to be left alone. If you're—"

"It's not. I mean, you're right. I do get like that a lot, especially when I'm making a movie. I'm usually turning the next day over in my head, thinking about the scenes and everything that goes into the shots, but I don't mind some company."

I glance over my shoulder at the packed room, the dancers, the drinking games some of the crew resurrected from their frat-party days. "Not them."

We share a brief laugh, our amusement cresting and falling, leaving us staring at each other with the same intensity I felt on the sidewalk, in Alabama, on the roof, in her trailer. Hell, every time I'm alone with this woman for more than two minutes, this happens. I don't look away like I usually do—don't suppress the rising wave. I let it, just this once, wash over us.

"What I meant to say," I continue, "is I don't mind *your* company."

She swallows, the muscles of her graceful neck shifting with the motion. And it happens. The thing I swore to myself I would not let happen.

I get hard.

I've avoided looking at her ass all night. Breasts have been off-limits since day one. Even this woman's hands, slim and elegant and decorated with ink, have the potential to turn me on, so I never look long. And, damn it to hell, it's her *swallowing* that pours cement all over my cock? Maybe it's the thought of my dick in her mouth. Or her swallowing me down after she—

"I can't do smoke," she says, gesturing to the unlit cigar in my hand. "It aggravates my... I just can't do smoke, and I want to let you enjoy your cigar, so I'll go."

She tugs to free her wrist again, but I still don't release her. Instead, I toss this cigar over the balcony like I did the last one.

"Stay."

It's one word, but it tells her a thousand things I haven't said before.

And we both know it.

Her nod is a little jerky and the pulse at the base of her throat flutters, trapped beneath the delicate skin. Do I make her nervous?

Well, you are still gripping her wrist like some psycho who might tamper with her drink.

I release her and she steps closer again, leaning her elbows on the ledge beside mine and slanting me a look.

"The therapist you guys brought in has been great. We've talked a few times. I wasn't prepared for how some of this would affect me. Thank you."

"That's what a director is for. Just doing my job."

Our eyes catch and hold. It's true. I didn't bring in the therapist just for Neevah, and several have used the service. Taking care of the cast is my job, but I'm not sure how much longer I can pretend that the way I think about *her,* am attuned to *her,* want to be around *her,* is about the job. I need to cling to that excuse for as long as I can. At least until this movie wraps. For both our sakes.

Directors have famously taken advantage of their position of power for sex. It's a problem and a bad cliché. I've turned down many offers. *Every* offer. I don't play that shit. It disrespects the artists and cheapens my craft. That's why dating Camille was such an anomaly. That epic failure only served to confirm that I am oil and my actresses are water, and we should not be shaken together. I won't make that mistake again.

"Well, thanks." Her voice is hushed. "Even if you were just doing your job, it was exactly what I needed."

I nod, but don't respond further. I asked her to stay, but cannot think of anything safe to discuss. Nothing's safe because every time we talk, I find more to like about her. Before I can embarrass myself by bringing up early-twentieth-century film innovations, the music from inside the party changes. Quiets.

"Let's take a few songs and pay tribute to one of the eighties' greatest crooners," the DJ says. "The legendary Luther Vandross."

The opening piano flourishes of "A House Is Not a Home" drift out to the balcony, with Luther's distinctive baritone close on the heels of the poignant notes.

"Oh, this was my jam," Neevah says, closing her eyes and lifting her face toward the sky. Moonlight caresses the high curves of her cheekbones, kisses the ripeness of her lips. Long lashes rest like feathers on her cheeks. She's a druid. An innocent. A hedonist. A cluster of contradictions that somehow all make sense in this woman.

"You weren't even born when Luther made this song," I remind her.

"So?" She laughs and turns back toward the canyon, a small smile teasing the lush line of her mouth.

My grin slips, but doesn't fall completely. "It was one of my mother's favorites. She played it all the time."

"My mom's, too. My favorite Luther is 'If This World Were Mine.' Technically a duet, but…"

"I love that one, too." I chuckle, leaning a little closer, catching the scent hidden behind her neck and ears. "My mom used to say, 'Big Luther, skinny Luther. Jheri curl. Press and curl. I don't care. I'll take that man any way I can get him.'"

"I know that's right. And then he'd bust that note. You know the one."

We look at each other and in unison replicate Luther's famous swelling run.

"Whoooooooooo," we sing together, finishing with her giggling and me smiling wider than I have in weeks.

I no longer feel the need to find something to talk about because the things find us. She's that kind of person. I'd like to think she's this way—genuine and sweet and funny—because she's with me, but I've watched her for weeks with the cast and crew. She's like this with them all. The magic of Neevah is that she's the same with everyone, but still manages to make it feel special for you.

She's that way with Trey. I want to ask if she's kissed him. If she's fucked him. If he's been to her house. I know exactly where Neevah and Takira are staying. As a producer, I have access to all that information, but she's the only one whose housing I've checked or cared about.

"Speaking of your mother," she says, biting her bottom lip, "I wanted to tell you how much *The Magic Hour* meant to me. It's my favorite work of yours."

"A documentary I made on a nonexistent budget when I was twenty-one years old about my mom? Out of everything I've done over the years, that's your favorite?"

"It is. I have a wall of inspirational sticky notes in my bedroom. Something she says in that documentary is up there."

"Oh, yeah? What?"

"'We are artists,'" she quotes softly, her eyes set on mine. "'When there is no joy to be found, we have the power in our hands, the will of our souls, to make it.'"

I hear Mama saying it, looking into my camera and smiling from her wheelchair, the Nikon at repose in her lap. I see a hundred evenings on ancient piers, Mama brandishing the camera like a sword, defying the disease determined to diminish her. Her smile.

God, Mama's smile.

Bright and brave and backlit by the sun. As much as my technique has improved, as large as my budgets have grown, capturing Mama's story with a cheap video camera and no goal but to hear her shout—that remains the best thing I've ever done. Probably will ever do, because it was for her. Not Mama's dying wish, but her *living* one.

"You know," I say after a few seconds, "I think it's my favorite, too."

"What must that be like?" she whispers, her gold-flecked brown eyes dark and deep and curious. "To be your favorite?"

This balcony is not big enough for all the unsaid words collecting between us. The desire, unspoken, hangs heavy all around. The air turns viscous, and her breaths shorten, shallow, quicken.

"Neevah!"

Someone calling her name breaks the tension long enough for me to draw a calming breath and remind myself this isn't a good idea.

"Neevah," Trey repeats, stepping out onto the balcony with us. "I was looking for you. Hey, Canon. I didn't know you were out here, too." He glances between us, speculation entering his eyes. "Am I . . . interrupting?"

Damn. That's the last thing I need—Disney dude starting rumors.

"Not at all." I grab my glass from the ledge and nod to them both. "I was just about to go. Early call in the morning."

Neevah's stare burns a hole in my back as I leave them alone on the balcony, but I don't acknowledge her or the moment Trey just shattered.

I don't look back because I can't.

Not yet.

TWENTY-FIVE

Canon

The Disney dude is good.

But I *did* give him someone amazing to work with.

God, Neevah is even better than I'd thought she would be. Her performance so far is a whole-ass *I told you so* to Law Stone and every Galaxy Studio exec who doubted me when I cast her. She and Trey do have great chemistry, so I'm sure they'll take credit for casting him. I really don't give a damn who gets credit. I just want this movie to fulfill and exceed its potential. And so far, it seems like it will.

Looking at the dailies on my laptop, I scrub back a little in the scene when Dessi and Cal first meet at the Savoy and she's teaching him to dance. I freeze the frame of Neevah's face lifted to the light, her smile coy and teasing. She smiled just like this at me on the balcony at the Halloween party. I've thrown up road blocks in my head so I don't think about that night too much—so I don't think about *her* too much.

"Whatcha doin'?"

I slam my laptop closed and swing my chair around to face Jill. "Sneaking up on me?"

"It only feels like sneaking up if you're doing something you don't want me to know about." She sits down. "Watching dailies? Lemme see."

I hesitate because when I open the laptop, she'll know that I was looking at Neevah, and the last thing I want is Jill teasing me about having a damn crush on our lead actress. Reluctantly, I open the laptop.

"She really is fantastic, isn't she?" Jill crosses an ankle over her knee. "Her skin. Her eyes. God, the woman says more with her eyes than most do all day talking. The camera loves her."

I don't bother answering, but scrub back in the footage. "You wanted to look at the Lafayette scene again?"

"Already did. They emailed me the dailies, too. I got what I needed to see."

"Great."

A tornado of blonde curls hurtles through the video village door toward us, touching down in Jill's lap.

"Mommy, guess what?" Sienna, Jill's four-year-old daughter, asks.

"What?" Jill pushes back the wild curls.

"I had a Popsicle. Look!" She pokes out her tongue, showing off a bright shade of blue.

"Nice! Where'd you get it?"

"They had them for lunch, and Kimmy said I can have one." She holds up a wilted Popsicle. "I brought one for you, too."

"Oh, thank you, baby," Jill says, accepting the drippy offering. "And where's Kimmy now?"

"Here I am. Sorry." Kimmy, one of our PAs, walks in, her usual perky ponytail limp and barely hanging on. "I turned my head for one second, and she was gone."

"She's a handful, aren't you, Sin?" Jill asks her daughter.

"I am." She nods enthusiastically and climbs from Jill's lap to mine. "Are you coming to Thanksgiving dinner, Uncle Canon?"

Technically I'm her godfather, but who could correct her when she looks at me like this?

"Not this year, Sin," I tell her. "But thank you for thinking about me."

"But will you be by yourself?" she asks, a frown dipping her blonde brows.

"I hope so." I laugh. "Maybe I'll come by on Friday *after* Thanksgiving. How's that sound?"

"Come on, Sin. Mommy's working." Kimmy shoots Jill an apologetic look.

"It's fine," Jill assures her. "Okay, baby. Run on and I'll see you in a little bit. I need to look at one thing with Uncle Canon."

"Did Seth have anything to do with her?" I ask as they exit the tent. "She looks exactly like you in every way."

"He got the other two, so it all evens out." She laughs, running a hand through the disorderly hair flopping into her eyes. "Thank you again, on behalf of all the working moms, for the on-set daycare. I wish more directors did it. I mean, Sin's just out of school today, but for the moms in the cast and crew with babies, it's a lifesaver."

"Not a big deal."

"If it wasn't, everyone would do it. Don't get me started on the things that hold women back in this business. You adopting French hours for this film is huge, and I hope more directors follow suit."

"Well, not perfectly. Some folks are still here fourteen hours a day, sometimes more, but I hope the ten-hour workday for most has helped."

"So much. There are a lot of really talented women who give up on this business because they can't disappear for literally sixteen or eighteen hours a day, and can't afford care for their kids that long."

"The adjustments haven't actually been that hard. I'd do whatever it took to get you on set. You're my secret weapon."

I'm not exaggerating. She is, which is why I use her whenever I can. The only projects she's missed were when she was having a baby.

"Well, the ladies say thanks."

"Hey, my mom was a working photographer. A single mom at that. I know how hard it can be."

"Are you spending Thanksgiving with her family? Sienna's right," Jill says, licking the forgotten Popsicle, grimacing and tossing it into the trash can beside the table. "I don't want to think of you alone."

"Nah. I'll do Christmas with them. I *want* to be alone. I want one meal that isn't shoved down my throat between takes or in front of a laptop, and I'd like to eat it in peace."

"You'll swing by on Friday?" Her worried frown remains unmoved by my explanation.

"Sure."

"But what will you eat on Thanksgiving?"

I shrug. "Takeout."

"No. So I have this great place my agent told me about. I'll give you the info."

"Okay."

"I'm just concerned."

"I think you're spelling smothering wrong."

"And I think," she says, turning back to my laptop and pinging a knowing smile between me and Neevah onscreen, "she's fantastic."

So much for keeping anything secret around here.

TWENTY-SIX

Neevah

I'm soaring.

Tossed through the air, wind whipping the skirt past my knees and thighs. A blur of legs and flying feet. My partner's strong hands anchor at my waist, whirling me to his right and then his left. Propelled through his legs, I glide across the floor on my back, hopping up for a flying run into his arms again.

Caught.

Held.

Lifted.

Spun.

I'm a weightless wonder. One in a kaleidoscope of hand-painted butterflies taking flight, our way made straight to a chorus of trumpets. The band blares "Flat Foot Floogie" as a hundred feet stutter through the intricate steps of the lindy hop. Electricity crackles the air, charging our bodies into frenetic rhythm. We move, we dance, clothes clinging to our bodies with the sweet juice of fervor. Sweat drizzles between my breasts, coats my neck and arms like dew. In the thrall of this dance, a syncopated stomp, I drip the wine of winding hips. I dip. I sway in an intercourse of jazz and blues and swing.

"Cut!" Kenneth calls.

The fifty or so dancers roar and clap and laugh, triumphant. We've been practicing this number for hours. Days, really, and finally, it's falling into place. It's one of the dance centerpieces of the movie, and Lucia, the choreographer, has been relentless.

"That was great, Neevah," my partner, Hinton, says, walking with me over to a table loaded with water. "Best so far."

"I hope so." I accept a water bottle and down a long, refreshing gulp. "It took me long enough to get it."

"Most of us are trained dancers. I know you dance, but it's not your primary discipline. You're a natural, though."

I swipe the sweat from my forehead. "This is the hardest thing I've ever done."

"Well, you're doing great."

"You could be better," Lucia says, appearing seemingly out of nowhere.

The woman is a phantom. She haunts my dreams. I'm surprised I don't wake up every night screaming *get that leg higher*. I know I'm the lead, and I feel the weight of that responsibility, but she rides me harder than everyone else. At four feet, eleven inches, with a nest of dark Medusa curls and a plethora of expletives, she's the most intimidating presence on set, second only to Canon himself.

"Something is missing," she says to me now, Puerto Rico and New York thick in her accent. "You got the steps—now I need you to feel them. Stop thinking and just let 'em take you."

I swipe at the sweat sliding from beneath the wig and down my neck, afraid to admit I'm not sure how to do that. "I'll get it. Sorry."

"You are verrrrry close, and much better than when we started. You need to see. Come on."

She walks off without another word. I shoot a startled glance at Hinton and scurry to catch her. She dances like a swan, but walks like a tank. The sea of brightly clad dancers part in her wake. You'd think, since her legs are half a foot shorter than mine, I could easily keep up, but I'm scampering after her like an eager Chihuahua.

"Where are we going?" I ask, waving at members of the cast as we plow through the crowd.

"Video village. It will help to see yourself on camera."

She strides confidently into the large white tent. It's usually a hive of activity—command central, with mounted screens covering the walls, 3D prop models on the center table, and laptops scattered seemingly on every available surface.

The first thing I see when we enter is a digital diagram of the Savoy Ballroom plastered to the wall. The production team re-created the famous ballroom to such exact specifications, you're transported to Lenox Avenue, what Langston Hughes called the Heartbeat of Harlem, as soon as you step on set.

The Savoy spanned an entire city block on Lenox Avenue and could hold up to four thousand people. The team carefully recrafted two flights of marble steps bordered by mirrored walls leading up to a smaller replica of the original ten-thousand-square-foot, mahogany, spring-loaded dance floor. The floor saw so much traffic, the owners had to replace it every three years. The production team left no detail undone, even adding the ballroom's cut-glass chandeliers, rose-pink walls, and two raised bandstands where legends like Benny Goodman and Chick Webb dueled before record crowds.

Being in the room, working for hours and focusing on getting the steps right, I lose sight of how massive the set is. The sketch taking up the entire wall reminds me.

Canon, wearing a frown, stands at the other end of the tent with Jill and Kenneth. He pokes the digital illustration on the wall and grasps the headphones draped around his neck. Everyone teases him about the beard he grows during a movie, but damn, if it doesn't look good on him. It lays close to his face, framing his full lips and scraping the sharp angle of his jaw.

He glances up, the frown deepening when his eyes collide with mine. We're two days from Thanksgiving, and we haven't really been alone since the Halloween party. And why should we be? Because he said he didn't mind my company? Because we shared a few innocuous moments on a secluded balcony serenaded by Luther that felt more intimate than every kiss I've ever had?

Girl, get a grip.

"Hey," Lucia says to a tech scrubbing through footage. She points to the jigsaw of rectangular screens on the wall. "I need to show Neevah something from that last run."

"Sure," he replies. "I'll cue it up. Just let me know where."

"We need to see the whole 'Flat Foot Floogie' sequence," Lucia mutters, eyes already fixed to the screen.

"I think the camera's positioned wrong," I hear Canon say.

I need to pay attention to all the deficiencies Lucia wants to show me, but I can't help it. I glance over to the wall. He's tugging at his bottom lip, something he does when he's working out a problem. He looks up, catching my eye, and I turn back right away like a kid caught with her hand in the cookie jar.

"I'm going to check," he says, walking out without acknowledging Lucia or me.

I release a long breath, able to focus now that he's gone, and tune into what Lucia's saying. She pauses the tape, though, and stares at me for long, disapproving seconds.

"What? Why'd you stop it? I thought you wanted to show me what I'm doing wrong."

"Not wrong. What you can do better."

"Semantics."

"You *seemed* to be more interested in him," she says, tipping her head to the wall where Canon stood seconds ago, "than in the dance. I've caught you looking before."

"Excuse me?" I hope I sound confused and indignant instead of caught. "I don't know what you mean."

I send a furtive glance around the tent to see who might overhear this mortifying conversation. Jill and Kenneth are still engrossed in their discussion about the diagram and the tech is at a laptop on the other side of the tent, leaving us to our own devices.

"Look, you're obviously the real thing," Lucia says, her words lowered so only I hear. "As much talent as two Jacksons and an Osmond, but no one'll notice that if you start screwing your director before your first film even releases."

"I'm not," I grit out.

"This crush, or whatever it is you have—squash it. It will only distract you, and if he figures it out, which, knowing Canon, he already has, it'll compromise your working relationship. He's not gonna ruin his movie over some pussy." She runs assessing eyes over me, head to toe. "No matter how good it might be."

Each crude word congeals my insides into embarrassment. My hands screw into the wide skirt of my swing dress. "It's not like that."

"Good. Don't let it be." The hard, red-painted line of her lips softens. "Look, I get it. That is a *man*. Like, they don't make 'em like that anymore. Every room he walks into, he becomes the center, even when he doesn't mean to."

She's right. There's a reluctant charisma to Canon. Like he doesn't ask for everyone to be drawn to him, but he can't *not* be the thing that draws them.

"He the honey and we the bees," Lucia says. "But he ain't looking for a queen bee. Ya feel me? Quickest way to get your heart stomped is to sleep with him and expect something he never gave a girl before. Canon is loyal, and when he finds someone he likes, he sticks with them. Evan, Kenneth, Jill, me. Through the years, he's built a team of people he trusts. He's just as serious about keeping out the ones he doesn't trust as he is about keeping close the ones he does. You make them eyes at him every time you walk into a room, and guess which side you'll be on?"

"I don't mean to..." I want to deny it, but she just peeped me so thoroughly, I can't. I want to tell her I can't help it—that I'm trying my damnedest not to feel like this—but she either wouldn't buy it or wouldn't care, so I settle for the only thing I hope she'll believe. "Thank you. I appreciate it."

She smiles, nods, and restarts the tape, eyes once again fixed on the screen. "Now let's look at your footwork. I want more Frankie Manning from you, less Megan Thee Stallion."

"Megan Thee..." I laugh at the teasing glint in her eye, grateful for her attempt to ease the tension of our conversation about Canon. "You better stop, and I don't even know who Frankie Manning is."

"Most don't." Lucia nods to the monitor. "That air step you do when

Hinton flips you over his back and you land on your feet? Manning did that. The lindy hop was created right in the Savoy by him and his crew before other folks took it and renamed it the jitterbug. He should be a household name, but whereas Fred Astaire and Gene Kelly went on to Hollywood, he went to work in the post office for 'bout forty years 'til somebody 'revived' him when he was seventy years old. Least he did win a Tony before he died. A little of the recognition he shoulda got. Girl, the way they do us."

"I feel robbed sometimes." I sigh, expelling my frustration. "All the things we don't know, are never taught. Have to dig around to find out."

"History is so picked over, by the time you get to the tree, there's barely any fruit left." Her grin is sudden and bright. "When you get home, look up *Hellzapoppin'*. Watch that clip. I know you've looked at tapes of swing. My fault for not mentioning this clip sooner. You have the steps technically, but dance is more than execution. It's *possession*. You gotta give your body over. Your whole spirit has to surrender. The people who can teach you what I'm talking about are all dead."

Her phone lights up and she grimaces at the text on her screen. "Watch that last run-through. They think one of the dancers may have sprained an ankle. I need to go check."

"Oh, no. You go. I'll be out and ready before the next run."

She nods absently, a frown worrying her brows, and leaves the tent. Before watching my next run-through, I'd love to see the *Hellzapoppin'* clip. Our phones aren't allowed on set, so we usually leave them in our trailers.

"Excuse me," I call out to the tech, who lifts his head. "Can I borrow your phone for a sec?"

I watch the clip on his phone and instantly understand what Lucia meant. The dancers' movements are liquid, their limbs loose and flowing like water. And there is a madness to the energy, but there's also control. The ease is undergirded by so much discipline and skill. When I watch myself, I see the difference.

"Lucia got you watching tape?" Jill asks, sitting down beside me. She's blonde, around forty, with a dozen or so tattoos graffitied on her arms. Chunky silver rings adorn most of her fingers.

"Oh." I pause the tape of our last run-through. "Yeah. She was right. I needed to see myself to know how I could do it better."

"You're doing great, but Lucia knows how to get that last drop of greatness out of her dancers. Even when it looks perfect to us, she sees room for improvement. That's why Canon chose her."

At the mention of Canon, I stiffen and want to change the subject. What if Lucia isn't the only one who's noticed my fixation on the director?

"So you have big plans for Thanksgiving?" I ask.

"Just dinner with my family. My husband and kids, I mean. We'll go see family in Chicago for Christmas. It's such a quick turnaround; we'll save that trip for next month when we can stay a bit. How about you?"

"Same. I mean, about the quick turnaround. My family's in North Carolina. I don't want to do cross country for just a few days, but also, we've been going nonstop. I need to rest and prepare. We have so many big scenes coming up."

"And you're in every one of them." Jill pats my hand, her green eyes kind, sympathetic. "It's a lot of pressure, and you're doing amazing work."

"Thanks. There are two scenes next week after the holiday break that I don't feel ready for. I've been so focused on the dance, I haven't memorized those lines. So that's how I'll be spending Thanksgiving."

"You're welcome to come to our house for dinner. I don't want you to be alone."

"Does it sound crazy that I kind of want to be alone?" I shake my head and scratch under the itchy wig. "My roommate is going home to Texas. She invited me and so did some of the other cast, but I would love to just have the house to myself for a few days and see no one. I know it sounds antisocial, but—"

"Not strange at all. This is a long haul. Whatever self-care looks like for you, do that." She looks at me speculatively. "Tell you what. There's a great little family restaurant in Topanga Canyon that does a crazy-good Thanksgiving dinner. Fantastic view. You'd love it. I always try to convince my family that we should go, but every year I end up slaving over an undercooked bird."

"I don't actually eat turkey."

"This place serves faux turkey, or you eat fish? They do a smoked salmon crepe that's to die for."

"Now that sounds incredible, but do you think they'd have a table this late with Thanksgiving only two days away?"

"My agent knows one of the managers. I bet I could get him to reserve a spot for you."

She digs through the Post-its and mangled scripts cluttering the table until she finds a notepad and pen.

"Honestly, the scenery is as good as the food," she says, jotting down the name of the restaurant. "If I can swing this table, promise me you'll try it."

"Promise. I'm actually really looking forward to it. Thank you."

"Good. You won't regret it."

Her smile is almost sly, secretive, but I'm probably paranoid and take her kindness at face value. The only thing I plan to cook is Mama's apple cobbler because even though I don't often go back to Clearview for the holidays, it makes me feel a little closer to home. Letting someone else handle the rest sounds good to me.

TWENTY-SEVEN

Canon

I'm not sure this was a good idea.

A little sign out front boasted this place is LA's most romantic restaurant. A man dining alone for Thanksgiving doesn't exactly scream romance, but I trust Jill. It's the only way I could get her to stop harassing me to eat dinner with her family. I asked what part of *alone* did she not understand, but finally caved and agreed to give this place a try. Why not? It's just a meal. Since I'm in the thick of filming, today is just another day.

The holidays held less significance after my mom died. I do have extended family still in Lemon Grove—Mama's people. I keep somewhat in touch and typically spend the holidays there. I'll see them at Christmas, but I invest more time in the family I've found through the years. I've collected some of my best friends working on sets, like-minded storytellers and dreamers.

I've barely spent a string of hours by myself since *Dessi Blue* started production, and for someone like me, I need the time alone. It's how I recharge. I'm not at my creative best if I don't get it. So before we enter what will be the toughest stretch of production, I'm taking advantage of this tiny reprieve, and not crowding it with a bunch of people and football.

I mean, I'll watch football when I get home, but in peace. In quiet, with just me and my Macallan 25.

"Mr. Holt," the hostess says with a warm smile. "We have your table ready."

"Thanks."

I follow her through the restaurant and outdoors, where a white tent strung with twinkling lights and flowers oversees a sprawling patio. So this is the romantic part. Just show me the turkey. I don't need romance. I shoot down the image of Neevah, her smile equal parts sweet and seduction. I got too much shit to do. The last thing I need to think about is the actress starring in the biggest movie of my career. I'm not screwing this up. The only thing that derails a movie faster than ego is feelings and fucking, and I suspect with Neevah, you don't get one without the other.

That I cannot afford.

The hostess picks her way carefully past the tented tables and down a steep flight of stone steps. I look back and up at the other diners. Where the hell is she taking me? Do they annex the singles? Shunt them away from the couples and the families gathered around their festive five-course meals?

Fine with me. No one wants to see that anyway.

We reach a clearing with two gazebos. A creek gurgles close by and in the distance, there's the rush of a waterfall.

"Uh, is this me?" I ask skeptically. "I didn't ask for—"

"Your friend Jill thought you might like privacy," the hostess replies, her smile and tone conciliatory. "Would you prefer—"

"Oh. No, it's fine. I just wanted to make sure it wasn't... it's fine."

"Right this way then." Gesturing to the gazebo housing an elegantly set table, she leaves me alone with my menu and the sound of rushing water. Slowly, the tension that's been locked in my shoulders and back for the last month eases. I settle into the padded seat and let the tension drain away—let the burbling creek drown out the voices in my head reminding me of all the work waiting. Jill was right. This was exactly what I needed.

I'm gonna kiss her Monday when we get back to work.

"Right this way, Ms. Saint," the hostess says.

My head snaps around toward her voice. Neevah carefully makes her way down the steps into the clearing, heading for the neighboring gazebo.

I'm gonna kill Jill, and I may not wait 'til Monday.

"Canon?" Neevah pulls up short, the genuine shock on her face convincing me she had nothing to do with this. I have only my matchmaking cinematographer to blame. "What are you..."

In addition to looking shell-shocked, she looks gorgeous. The kind of gorgeous people do everything in their power to achieve, but you can't make it. It's from the inside. The rich coppery hue of her skin glows in the waning sunlight. She's scooped her cloud of textured curls into an updo, a huge flower pinned behind her ear. An emerald-green dress hugs the toned ripeness of her body, paying special attention to the full, uptilted breasts and the glory of her ass. She's lost weight since the movie started. Lucia demanded it for the choreography. Linh prefers it for the costuming, and the studio likes it because they always think thinner is better, but I've been secretly hoping she wouldn't lose that ass.

And look at God. She hasn't.

Neevah glances back over her shoulder, up the steps, obviously as nonplussed as I am, but not as adept at hiding it. "There must be some mistake."

"No." The hostess frowns and nods to the gazebo beside mine. "Here's your table. If it's not to your liking, I can shuffle a few things. Put you up in one of the tents?"

Neevah and I stare at each other, a luxury I don't often allow. She gulps in the extended silence, tearing her eyes away from mine and nodding.

"I think that might be best," she tells the hostess. "I don't want to impose. This is a crazy coincidence, Canon. I'm sorry. I'm sure you wanted to be alone and the last person you want to see is…"

She's rambling. It's cute.

"Well, I'm sorry," she finishes on a rush, turning to mount the steps. "Happy Thanksgiving."

"Stay."

That damn word will be the ruin of me. I said it on the balcony at the Halloween party and could barely concentrate for a week after our conversation.

She pauses, one high-heeled foot on the stone step, the other on the ground, and looks back at me. She really is breathtaking. It kind of sneaks up on you. You think at first she's merely pretty, but up close, midnight lurks in her velvety brown eyes and someone thought it was okay to dust a few freckles into the rich caramel of her skin.

That was not okay.

Those freckles pose a threat to my sanity and make me want to lick them, find out if they taste like cinnamon. Find out once and for damn all how *she* tastes.

"Are you sure?" she asks, her expression as uncertain as her words.

"Yeah." I shrug, like this isn't exactly the kind of situation I've avoided with her. "Why not?"

The hostess leads her to the neighboring gazebo.

"Look, that's ridiculous," I say. "What? We gonna sit five feet apart and eat separately?"

I'm playing right into Jill's schemes, but even I know that would be crazy.

"Canon, I don't want to—"

"It's dinner. It's an hour. I have the rest of the night, hell, the rest of the week to be by myself." I nod to the empty seat across from me. "Join me if you want."

The hostess grins like this is the best idea she's ever heard, and I bet she wrote that damn sign outside. Most romantic restaurant, my ass. After a brief hesitation, Neevah takes the few steps up into my gazebo and settles into the seat across from me, a look of discomfort on her face despite my assurances. The hostess says she'll give us a few minutes to look over the menus.

And then she leaves us alone.

TWENTY-EIGHT

Neevah

"Is this your first time?" I ask in the silence the hostess leaves behind.

This is as awkward as a Real Housewives *reunion special.*

"I just meant..." My laugh tinkles nervously like a fifteen-year-old on her first date. "Have you been to this restaurant before?"

This is not a date. Canon Holt is not your Thanksgiving date. You will not lust after him... anymore.

"No." He studies his menu, his brows furrowed in some serious concentration. "Jill suggested this place and reserved my table."

"She reserved mine, too. So sweet of her."

The look he flicks at me over the edge of his menu says he doesn't agree. "She needs to mind her damn business. Meddling."

"Meddling? I don't understand. She..."

She reserved us tables together at the city's self-proclaimed most romantic restaurant.

"Oh." *Shit.* "You don't think she... that she thought we—"

"Uh, yeah. I do think she thought *we*."

My face catches fire, mortification filling every inch of my empty stomach.

"Canon, I'm... I had nothing to do with this. I promise I was clueless."

"I know that. For an actor, you're not very good at faking."

"Should I be insulted by that?" I ask, smiling in spite of the awkward situation.

"No. Some actors don't know when to stop pretending. You do. You're as clear as glass and don't dissemble well."

"You mean everyone can read my emotions easily?"

"I don't know about everyone." He holds my eyes over the menu. "I can."

That makes me highly uncomfortable because my emotions are in constant turmoil around this man, and right now, on a scale of deep respect to raging hormones, I'm at a twelve. To think I'm transparent to him, that he might *see*...

"I should go." I stand, tossing the linen napkin onto the table.

"Sit down." The gravel-rough command in his voice sends a shiver clamoring up my spine.

"I don't think so. I really should—"

"And where will you go? What will you eat for Thanksgiving dinner?"

"Um, In-N-Out Burger?"

His low-timbred chuckle, accompanied by that rarest of phenomena, a full-fledged Canon Holt smile, catches me where I stand, trapped between coming and going.

"Neevah, sit. It's one meal. We'll survive it."

I check his expression to see if he means it, but unlike me, Canon is opaque glass frosted by his iron control. So I'll take him at his word.

I sit and pick up my menu.

"So, what looks good?" I ask.

Besides you because dayummmmmm.

Neevah, this is why we can't have nice things. If you're gonna stay, you have to stop this inner drool dialogue.

"Do you realize you move your lips when you talk to yourself?" he asks.

I lower the menu, my eyes wide. "Can you hear me?"

"Can I hear what you're thinking? No, even I'm not that good. I'm not Dr. Dolittle."

"I know... Can you make out what I'm saying when my lips move?"

"No, you just say it literally to yourself. I first noticed it on set. You'd drop a line or get a step wrong, and then walk off with your lips moving. Talking to yourself."

I groan and lift the menu high enough to cover my face. With one finger, he slowly pushes it down until I'm forced to face him again.

"Don't be self-conscious," he says, a half-smile playing around his lips. "It works for you. Whatever you got wrong, you always got right after you talked to yourself."

"You're like the eye in the sky back there in video village, with all your screens and control center. Do you always direct from there? Or do you ever come out?"

"It depends. With a movie like this, especially ones with huge dance numbers, I need to see what we're getting from every angle. I like the various camera shots, and I like to see how it's coming out since that's the way the audience will see it. I'll be out there when we shoot outdoors. I'm too particular about light not to be."

"A photographer's son, huh?"

"Definitely. I never took a photography class, but my entire childhood was a clinic. All the best things I know about light and detail and composition, my mom taught me. The woman was obsessed with her camera." He glances up with an ironic grin. "I mean, she named her son after one."

I smile, too, recalling Remy Holt from his first and most personal documentary, railing at the sun, making art and daring her body to stop her.

"She was very wise and very pretty," I tell him.

"She never lost either of those things." Canon's smile dies on his lips. "It was hard for her, losing so much control of her body. They've made a lot of strides with MS now. I wish she'd lived long enough to take advantage of them."

"And your father? I mean, I assume you don't spend every holiday eating in LA's most romantic restaurant. You have any other family?"

"My mom and dad married because she was pregnant with me, but quickly realized that was a mistake. Instead of spending half her life with a man she didn't love, she asked for a divorce. Actually, she demanded it. He moved to South Africa to pursue some business opportunities. Remarried and started a whole new family there. Three kids I barely know." He shrugs. "He's okay. We're not super close, but I see him. We talk. Mama used to say she dodged a bullet, not because he was a bad man, but because he wasn't a great one."

"She was a spitfire, wasn't she?"

"She was. I've never met anyone who lived as freely as she did." He toys with the silverware wrapped in his napkin. "She had lovers and never tried to hide it from me. When we needed money, she didn't pretend everything was okay. Even when times were hard, she didn't take photography jobs she didn't like or believe in at least a little. She said, to survive, don't use your gift for shit you hate. Work in a grocery store, pump gas, pick up trash to get by before you corrupt your art."

"So she would not have approved of you directing 'Grind Up on Me, Girl'?" I tease.

"Probably not." His laugh comes quickly and goes as fast. "Artistic integrity was everything to her."

"Wow. So that's what it took to make a man like you." The words just slip out, and I immediately want to retract them. I sound like such a fangirl. I'm not starstruck. I admire him. Respect him.

Okay. Lust after him a little.

He doesn't smile or try to play off my words in the silence that elongates between us, but holds my stare with an intensity that makes my toes tingle. And as much as I wish I could take the words back, the ones that tell him too much, I don't look away either. If I'm glass, let him see. I'll figure out another day how to hide.

"Do we know what we want?" the server asks.

I'm so startled by her intrusion, I bump my water, but catch it before it spills.

Canon goes for the turkey dinner, and remembering Jill's suggestion about the fish, I order the salmon crepes.

He orders something dry and white to drink. I stick to water.

"I've never seen you drink," he says, sipping his. "Alcohol, I mean."

"I drink champagne occasionally, but I'm pretty strict with what I eat and have cut out alcohol for the most part. I have a skin and hair condition that I have to manage really carefully."

"Oh, nothing serious, I hope," he says with a frown.

Why did I even bring it up? It's irrelevant, as I knew it would be.

Takira's been vigilant about using natural products and monitoring my scalp for new spots. I've made sure to stay covered when I'm in the sun, avoid smoke, keep my diet clean, and meditate so my stress stays low. As low as possible under the circumstances, at least. As for exercise, Lucia and her choreography are the best personal trainers I've ever had.

"It won't affect the movie," I assure him. "It's under control."

"Neevah, I wasn't thinking about the movie." He shifts his gaze to the creek just beyond our gazebo. "I was thinking about you."

A small silence pools between us, rising like the water not far away until I think it's over my head and I can't breathe.

"So," he finally speaks into the tight quiet. "You're the last person I thought would be alone on Thanksgiving."

"Why do you say that?"

"Come on. You telling me half the cast didn't invite you over for dinner?"

"I guess I did have a few invitations, but…" I break off and laugh at his knowing look. "Okay. Yes. A lot of the cast invited me over when they heard I was staying in LA."

"You're one of those social people."

"And you're not?"

He lifts one *what do you think* brow before we both ease into light laughter.

"I needed some time alone," I tell him. "It's hard to explain, but I've never done a film before, and to start with something like *Dessi Blue*—to be the lead and have people constantly needing something, expecting something. The sheer physical demand—it's a lot. And we're coming up on some of the toughest scenes. I don't know all my lines for next week yet."

I give him a sheepish look because I probably shouldn't confess this to my boss.

"I won't tell," he teases, laughing when I roll my eyes. "Hey. I get it. I'm constantly pulled on, too. Someone asked Spielberg what's the hardest part of making a movie. He said getting out of the car. As soon as you arrive on set, everyone needs something."

"Well I don't have *that* kind of demand, but I really needed to focus and prepare. With Takira going home, it was a perfect opportunity."

"And your family? How'd they feel about you missing Thanksgiving?"

A bitter laugh leaks out before I can stop it. "It's not the first time, believe me."

"You and your family—you're not close?"

"We had a falling-out years ago, my sister and I. It drove a wedge between me and, well, everyone." I trace the rim of my plate with one finger. "Sorry. You don't want to hear this and I don't want to tell you."

"Tell me anyway."

Canon isn't an easy man to read, but he's never fake, and the curiosity, and yes, concern in his eyes right now, is sincere. It coaxes me to discuss something I've rarely told anyone.

"I got engaged my senior year in high school." I shake my head, wondering what that eighteen-year-old kid thought she knew about love and forever. "I know. It was stupid."

"Not with the right person, it wouldn't be. Jill and her husband were high school sweethearts."

"They were?"

"Yeah. They went off to college, never broke up, and got married their junior year. Twenty-five years and three kids later, they're still together, so I think it depends on the person."

"Well he was not the right person—at least not for me. My sister? Now they were apparently a perfect match."

"Wait." He leans forward, surprise alight in his dark eyes. "He cheated on you with your sister?"

"And my sister cheated on me with him. They might have gotten away with it had she not gotten pregnant."

"Damn, Neev. You had some *As the World Turns* shit going on."

"What you know 'bout *As the World Turns?*" I ask lightly, as much to shift the focus from me for a second as anything else.

"I watched my stories in the student union at college. Best way to pick up girls. They assumed I was sensitive."

"I bet that didn't last long."

"No, not for long." He laughs with a shrug of his broad shoulders. "I was very clear about what they were getting and not getting. That hasn't changed."

Lucia's warnings whisper in my ear.

Quickest way to get your heart stomped is to sleep with him and expect something he never gave a girl before.

Can't say he doesn't warn you.

"But we were discussing *your* soap opera. Your fiancé got your sister pregnant?"

"Yeah. And you know the crazy thing? I understand exactly what your mother meant about dodging a bullet. I almost gave up my scholarship for the Rutgers drama program and stayed in Clearview with him because he didn't want to leave and didn't want me to either. I was prepared to settle for whatever life he thought was big enough for me."

"His loss, our gain. You were made for the stage, for the movies, to perform. Anything that would've taken that from you couldn't have been right."

The hostess brings our food and drinks and we both dive into our meals, leaving my family drama behind, talking about the movie and politics and music between mouthfuls. My body revolts whenever I'm around him, all heart-pounding and weak-kneed, but when we talk, it's the best conversation. There's an ease underlaid with a steady hum of desire. I tried to convince myself that it was just me, that he didn't feel it, too, that I was delusional, but the heat in his eyes, the strike of lightning when our fingers brush accidentally at the bread basket, tells me the truth.

I think he wants me, too.

"So did you talk to your family today?" he asks, when we're almost done with our meals.

"To my mother briefly. It's awkward at home because they have a child together. They married. They have this whole life, and I don't envy it one bit. I would have been miserable as Brandon's wife, but the hurt doesn't go away. He's just as responsible for what happened, but she's my *sister*. It just hits different, that betrayal. His mother's family is in Virginia, and sometimes when they go there for the holidays, I'll go home."

I drag a fork through the remains of my mashed potatoes. "Otherwise it just causes tension for everyone because they're all used to it. My mother and aunts and cousins—they've seen Brandon and Terry build a life there. It's only when I come back around that everyone remembers how it all started. It makes *me* feel like the problem."

"Do you miss her? Were you and your sister close?"

I think of sitting in the Palace Theatre beside Terry, tears streaking down my face with Aida's song coursing through me. Gushing to my sister all the way home that I had discovered what I was made to do. I recall Sunday mornings in church, passing notes back and forth, giggling behind our hands when Mama pinched us. Remember us roller-skating through our neighborhood, braids and beads flying in the wind. Singing Brownstone's "If You Love Me" at the top of our lungs while washing dishes after supper, a whisk as our microphone.

Terry was my best friend.

"I miss what I thought we had," I finally say, surprised by the tears I have to blink away. "We couldn't have been what I thought we were for her to do that to me."

"Do they seem happy?"

"I haven't seen them very much, but they're still together, so I assume."

When the server comes to clear our plates, she hands us new menus and asks if we'd like dessert.

"Oh, no," I tell her, smiling at Canon. "I must have been at least a little homesick. I made my mother's apple cobbler. I'll have that when I get home."

"Apple cobbler is my favorite."

Those words, on their own, are completely innocent, but paired with the sparks firing between us, it's a dare I can't ignore. I won't.

"You could..." I falter, gulping down my nervousness and tossing caution out the window. "There's plenty. Cobbler, I mean. You could—you could come over."

While the invitation hangs over us, my breath seizes in my throat. My foot taps noiselessly beneath the table and I clutch my dress for dear life while I wait.

I can imagine his reasons for keeping things platonic between us. He doesn't have to articulate them. I'm not that obtuse, but I want to tell him I don't care. I don't care about the power dynamic. I don't care if people find out and think he gave me the part because we're sleeping together. What the *hell* do I care if the cast talk behind our backs or speculate that he's repeating his mistake by getting involved with another actress?

If I could say all of that, I would, but I don't think I have to. I pour it into my eyes and let the anticipation flow from every part of me. If he can read me as well as he claims, he'll know. If I'm glass to him, he'll see.

"So, dessert?" the server asks again.

"No." He hands the menu back to her, but doesn't look away from me. "We'll have dessert at home."

TWENTY-NINE

Canon

I thought I'd learned my lesson.

I promised myself and Evan I wouldn't get involved with one of the actresses again. Yet here I am at the door of Neevah's rented cottage under the pretense of cobbler. Light pours over her on the porch while she retrieves the keys from her purse, illuminating every reason I should follow her inside. When she opens the door and walks through, I hesitate, standing on the porch. Here's my chance to stop this. What are the odds of *not* fucking Neevah Saint if I go in?

Little to none.

It's not just the threshold of her house I'm crossing. It's the threshold of folly.

She turns back when she realizes I'm still outside, and the sight of her does something to me that used to feel foreign, but I've become accustomed to the effect. She takes my breath away. Not just the way her features are arranged into prettiness, or the dick-hardening slim-thick curves. When she looks at me, I feel like she *sees* me, and I'm not sure anyone ever really has.

Why her?

My curiosity rages as strong as my lust. This is the threshold to *why*—to answers. To satisfaction for the hunger the very sight of her arouses in me.

"Did you change your mind?" Disappointment sifts into her expression. "It won't take long to heat up, and I have ice cream."

There's something about the most fascinating woman I've ever met feeling like she has to put ice cream on top—to convince me—that destroys the last of my resistance. It's just cobbler, right? I have enough willpower to eat dessert and get out of here without anything happening.

Don't I?

I'm Canon Holt, renowned for my discipline and self-control.

And yet when she bends over and slides the cobbler into the oven, I'm like a horny teenager straining for a glimpse of her ass.

She straightens and tugs at the dress hugging her body. "Mind if I change? I just want to get comfortable."

"Sure." I settle onto the couch and try the only thing that's ever worked in my quest to resist Neevah. I don't look at her at all.

"You want coffee?"

I stare at my hands linked between my knees. "Nah. I won't be able to sleep tonight."

"K. I'll be right back."

She disappears down the short, arched hallway, her heels clicking on the flagstones. The Spanish-style cottage the studio is putting her up in boasts high ceilings and oversized picture windows. Even unlit, the dormant fireplace lends the room warmth and coziness. I assume both bedrooms, hers and Takira's, are down that hall. My mind wants to wander there, to her changing clothes, baring her skin inch by satiny inch. I've seen her nearly naked. We filmed a sex scene between Dessi and Tilda, but it was as calculated and choreographed as one of Lucia's dance numbers. Neevah wore a body stocking and everything was plotted, all the places she would touch and be touched mapped out and rehearsed. In front of ten people, they were repositioned several times to get the shots we wanted. There was an intimacy coach on set. It was a clinical thing.

It wouldn't be that way with us.

We would run wild through fire. I'd be mindless, my hands everywhere and our clothes flung to far corners. I'd trap her against a wall with my body and beg her to bite me, to break the skin.

"That's better," Neevah says, coming back into the room wearing a T-shirt that says *Ew, David* and a cotton skirt. She has dancer's legs, the muscles graceful and rippling under richly hued skin. Her feet are bare and toenails painted white.

"*Schitt's Creek?*" I ask, nodding to her shirt, hoping to distract myself from all the nasty shit running rampant through my thoughts about her legs wrapped around my waist or me licking the arch of her foot.

"Yes, Takira and I binge it in my trailer between scenes." She walks into the kitchen and opens the oven. "There's a lot less waiting in theater than in movies."

"Very true. How has the adjustment been?"

"You tell me," she says with a smile over one shoulder. "You're the director."

Don't remind me.

"I think you've done a great job." I smirk and lean deeper into the soft cushions. "Or you would have heard about it by now."

"Oh, I know. I was gesturing too much in the beginning and playing it too big, like I was onstage, not for a camera."

"The first day"—I grin, baring my amusement—"you were yelling at the camera."

She sends me a glare and walks into the living room with two bowls loaded with steaming cobbler.

"I'll never forget Kenneth's note." She hands one of the bowls to me and sits down at the other end of the couch. "Canon says to tell you *we're right here.*"

"That was the last time you yelled at me, though."

"Ya think?" She scoops up some of the dessert, chasing the ice cream around the bowl with her spoon. "I hope this is half as good as my mama's."

The first bite nearly crosses my eyes. "This is delicious. If your mama's is any better, I might marry her."

"She might have you."

I've heard about her sister and mother, but nothing about her father. "So is your dad still around?"

"No." Her smile withers and she lowers her eyes to the bowl in her hands. "He died. Heart attack."

"I'm sorry."

She lifts and drops one shoulder, her eyes sober when they meet mine.

"It actually made us closer—me, Mama, and Terry. That's why it hurt so much when Terry...when she did what she did."

She stands abruptly, her bowl still mostly full, and cuts down the emotion growing in her eyes. "Guess I didn't want dessert as much as I thought I did. I'm done."

"Hey." I take her wrist gently and pull her to stand between my knees, looking up, searching her face for lingering hurt. "You okay?"

She nods, glancing down her arm to where I clasp her wrist loosely. By the time she looks back, the hurt, the sadness, is gone. They've left behind a smoldering ember, an answer to the burning question ablaze in me. I should get out of here now. I've managed to keep the promise to myself. I'm ahead in this game and should cut my losses.

But do I?

Am I that smart?

Am I that strong?

Hell, no.

When she leans closer, aligning our faces, I don't pull back or push her away. Our noses touch and panting breaths wrestle between our lips. We're inches from the inevitable, and she's the only one who could stop us now. Desire clouds the clear brown, long-lashed eyes that bore into mine.

"I want to kiss you," she whispers over my lips. "Is that okay?"

I swallow deeply, wrestling with my own longings. If I say no, she'll step away. She'll go into the kitchen. I'll leave and return to my empty house. To my empty bed. To a life that, aside from the stories I tell, the movies I make, is pretty empty, too.

"It's not the best idea," I say, my voice low, raspy, nearly unrecognizable.

She carefully climbs onto the couch, over my knees. The short skirt rides up as she spreads her thighs to bracket mine.

"What would be a good idea?" she asks, so close now her lips skim the words over my mouth.

I take a deep breath that brushes my chest against the generous curves of her breasts, the contact robbing my brain of thoughts for a second. "I'm your boss, Neevah."

"What does that have to do with it?" She pulls back, concern knitting her thick, sleek brows. "You think I'll say you made me do it? I would never do that, Canon. If you think this is some kind of trap..."

She starts sliding off, but I can't let her do that. I don't want her to do that. Every inch separating us is excruciating. I hold her in place and draw her close again, my hands palming the tight, slim line of her back, rolling from her shoulder blades past the delicate cage of her ribs to the dramatic indent from waist to hip.

"I've dreamt of you touching me," she says, her breath scented with apples and spice and want. "Don't stop."

"Neevah—"

"Don't. Stop." She sets the bowls on the couch to our left and right, freeing her hands to reach back up and caress my nape, run her fingers over the coarse waves of hair I've let grow while we've been shooting. "I want to touch you, too."

She scrapes the neat crescents of her nails over my ears. I shudder, and she pauses smiling, repeating the simple caress. Her fingers wander to my jaw, scraping through the bristly beginnings of my beard.

"You are so beautiful," she says, leaning forward to rub her cheek against mine.

"I'm not." I keep my hands at her waist because if I touch her ass, it's over. My dick is already impossibly stiff, pressing into the warm cove between her legs where she straddles me.

"You know, at first I didn't think so either." She pulls back, the heat in her eyes tempered with a dangerous tenderness. "But then I saw you smile, and I could never think of you as anything but beautiful again."

And as much as I want more, there's a part of me that relishes just this. The eager discovering of first touches and near-kisses. We'll never have these again for the first time, and I've had enough things that weren't special to savor this thing that is.

"And as soon as I saw you onstage—"

"You saw your Dessi?" She lowers her lashes and toys with the buttons on my shirt.

"I saw a star, yes, but also the most generous performer I'd ever encountered. You gave the audience everything, and I wondered, is that for real? Does she hold nothing back?"

"Do you want to know?" She scoots an inch closer, her skirt rising higher and revealing the edge of her black panties. "If I would give you everything?"

She skates the tip of one finger over the bow of my lip, and I grit my teeth, gripping the last shreds of control with slippery palms. Her curious caress moves to my bottom lip, brushing back and forth until, on a pant, my mouth opens. Wasting no time, she grips my chin, leaning in, licking into me, searching, finding my tongue and drawing it into her mouth, sucking gently, softly. My control snaps like ropes holding back a beast, and it sets my hands free. I clutch the roundness of her ass, urging her even deeper into me until the place where I'm hardest touches the place where she is most soft and vulnerable and wet.

I groan into the kiss, pushing up, urging her hips into a deep wave over me. We build a rolling rhythm that collides our bodies over and over again, kindling for a fire. My hands slip under the T-shirt and find her skin, velvet and sleek stretched over her back. I hesitate at the clasp of her bra, not sure I should. Never breaking the contact of our kiss, she reaches behind and undoes the clasp herself. The freed weight of her breasts spills against my chest, and I push my tongue deeper into her mouth, so deep her breath catches like it might be too much. Like *I* might be too much, and I want that because she is too much for me to take in all at once. The vastness of her spirit and the urgency of her passion. I taste this night in the sweet recesses of her mouth, the dessert and the daring.

She breaks our kiss to tug the shirt over her head and ease her arms from the loops of her bra. My mouth waters at the sight of the dark nipples tipping her breasts like crown jewels.

"Touch me." There's begging in her voice I can't resist. I brush my thumb over her, watching her breast peak and tighten. She draws a sharp breath. "Taste."

I will.

My lips part, poised to accept the intimate invitation.

My phone rings, splitting the quiet.

Her eyes widen, find mine. I would ignore the call, but it's Evan's ringtone.

Shit.

Worst timing everrrrrr.

Not only did he ruin my vibe, but he reminded me of all the reasons this shouldn't happen—yet.

"I need to get this. It's Evan."

"Oh." She nods, grabbing the shirt and slipping it over her nakedness. "Alright."

She moves off me, glancing down at my dick tenting my jeans. She licks her lips and all I can imagine is that kiss-swollen mouth wrapped around my cock, and Evan can go to hell. Unthinking, I palm her hip and draw her back to me.

The ring comes again.

Dammit, Evan.

I pull the phone from my pocket and ease off the couch. She stands there a moment as if waiting for me to change my mind. If I don't walk away, I will, so I go to the fireplace and turn my back on her, resting my elbows on the mantel.

"What's up?" I ask Evan.

"Uh, Happy Thanksgiving to you, too. You still want to come over? Drink and dream some? My dad gave me these Cuban cigars at dinner today. My dude. I got one with your name on it. You on your way?"

Behind me, spoons clank in the bowls as Neevah walks to the kitchen, rinses the dishes, and slots them into the dishwasher. I look over my shoulder to find her turned away, hands gripping the edge of the sink, slim shoulders lifting and falling with deep breaths. She appears as discomposed as I feel, but she's younger, not just in years, but in experience. This is her first movie, and she gets into a relationship with the director? It's not wise. It could be a repeat mistake for me, yes, but one I could easily weather. There are passes I get because I'm a man, because I have power she doesn't. Because I tell stories that make people money. She doesn't have that track record yet. She has no idea that we could crush each other. That beyond this door and this feeling, her career, her whole life, could be jeopardized by what we do tonight.

But I know, and I won't let her risk it.

"Yeah, I'm on my way," I tell Evan, pulling the car keys from my pocket.

"Cool. By the pool. I'll light the fire pit and you can tell me all about your lonely turkey dinner."

"Bet." I let out a brief laugh and disconnect.

Neevah turns around, leaning against the sink, braless, her nipples still hard and round and high through the thin cotton T-shirt.

"You're leaving?"

I walk to the kitchen slowly, giving myself time to overcome the violent objections of my dick. When I reach the arched doorway, I stop. If I touch her, this blows up again, and I'm bending her over that sink, shoving that skirt up and pushing her panties to the side. I don't want our first time to be like that.

And I make a decision. There *will* be a first time for us, but not tonight.

"Yeah, I'm gonna go," I tell her, my voice still scratched and rough.

"Did I do something wrong?" She looks down, twists her fingers at her waist. "I'm embarrassed. I didn't mean to make you feel—"

"You didn't make me feel anything I wasn't already feeling." I walk forward, risking everything to reassure her. I lift her chin and make her meet my eyes. "It wasn't anything I didn't already want. That I still want."

"Then don't go." She reaches up, wrapping her hand around my forearm. "We can—"

"This is dangerous, Neevah, for me, yes, but even more for you. We should wait."

"But I don't..." She ventures a glance up at me. "Wait? For how long?"

"Until the film wraps."

I cup the tender curve of her cheek and jaw, searching her eyes for caution or hesitation. There is none. That openness that draws me to her is on full display, her desire unmasked.

"This is your first movie. Do you want everyone thinking you got the role because you were sleeping with the director?"

"I don't care what people think."

"You will. I've been in this business a long time. It's vicious. The rumors, scandal. Lots of truly talented people ruined their careers with bad personal decisions."

"You are not a bad decision, Canon."

"Maybe not, but I'm one you should wait to make." I bend to kiss her, giving my hands permission to slide down her arms, over her sides, and to her waist. She strains up on tiptoe, eating into our kiss, her lips soft and warm and eager. Neevah's sweetness hides a devouring kind of passion. When we happen, she will burn me inside out, and I can't wait.

But I will.

With my lips still clinging to hers, I force myself to step back. Not risking one more word or allowing one more touch, I leave.

THIRTY

Neevah

"Another inch." Linh Brody-Stone glances up from where she squats on the floor and pulls the measuring tape from my waist. "I'll have to take the costume in."

I let out a long, tired breath. "I'm sorry. I promise I'm eating."

"Yeah, but you're also doing the lindy hop and every other dance Lucia can think of for hours every day. Your body's burning calories faster than you can consume them."

"We're doing all the dance sequences at once. With this many dancers, production wants to get their parts out of the way so we can release them. Kind of clumping things together. Like all my songs are last because they require only me and a few musicians for the most part."

"Explains why I haven't seen Monk as much on set lately," she says.

Or Canon.

It's been three weeks since Thanksgiving, and if it weren't for my very real memories of that night, I might question that it ever happened. He ignores me and hasn't mentioned the kiss or our conversation—how much we wanted each other that night—and it's driving me crazy.

Linh walks over to a garment rack and flicks through the costumes we've used to create Dessi's character, ranging from deliberately drab to dazzling. A production of this magnitude requires a costuming team, which Linh leads. Some of the pieces she designs, and some they source. Everything is stored here, the shoes neatly on shelves, the clothes hanging on rolling racks, accessories tucked into clear boxes and cubbies. Ironing boards, irons, sewing machines, and steamers fill the compact space, Linh's domain.

She turns to grin at me, her feline-like features lit with rare excitement. She's such a steady boat, never rocked or swayed, that seeing her smile makes *me* smile despite my fatigue.

"Wanna see something incredible?" she asks.

"Sure!" I inject enthusiasm into my voice despite the pain in my muscles and aches in my joints.

The car service dropped me off on set at five a.m. for hair and makeup. We've been shooting all day. I could crash right here.

Linh disappears into one of the changing rooms and emerges, rolling out a covered mannequin.

"Behold!" she says, carefully lifting the cover to reveal one of the most gorgeous dresses I've ever seen. It's a vintage floor-length evening gown, as iridescent as a pearl, covered in sequins and with gossamer-thin spaghetti straps.

"It's modeled after one Josephine Baker wore for one of her Paris shows," Linh says. "I thought it'd be perfect for the scenes when Dessi and Cal tour Europe."

"This is... Linh, it's gorgeous. Where'd you find it?"

"Find it?" She laughs, adjusting the gown's bodice. "I made it."

"You made this? What the..." I knew Linh was talented, but this is haute couture level. The most sought-after designer would proudly send a dress like this down their runway. If anyone ever thought Linh landed this project because she's married to Law Stone, this dress and all the extraordinary work she has done should disabuse them of that notion.

In addition to being traffic-stop beautiful, she's been really sweet. Her concern about my weight loss goes beyond the work it causes her. It's personal. She's hung out with Takira and me in the trailer a few times when she was on set. Once her reserve cracks, she's funny and authentic.

I've met Law Stone a few times when "the suits" have come on set, and I'm not sure he deserves this woman. There's something about him. When he talks, his words are slick and smooth in his mouth like loaded dice.

"I'll have to take this one in a little, too," she says, practically petting the sparkling dress. "At the rate you're shedding pounds, I think I'll wait and alter it post-Christmas break. We aren't shooting those scenes until later."

"Right." I glance at my watch. "Crap! Livvie wanted to run lines before this next scene."

Linh shoos me toward the door, already opening accessory drawers and cubbies. "Go! But swing back before you start filming. One of the interns needs to do a continuity check on your wardrobe and make sure we haven't changed anything since we started this section."

"Will do." I rush from the wardrobe room, through the set, and out to the row of trailers. Olivia Ware, who plays Tilda, is only a few down from mine. I knock on the door and wait for her to invite me in.

"Sorry I'm late," I say, climbing the small set of steps. "I was in..."

The words dry up in my mouth when I see Canon sitting on the couch beside Livvie. They both look up from the script between them.

"I was in wardrobe," I finish. "Sorry to interrupt. I thought you wanted to run lines before—"

"I do," Livvie says. "I needed Canon to help ya girl get in touch with this next scene. It's tough, but I think I have it now."

"You got it. Don't worry." Canon stands, his head only a few inches shy of the ceiling in the compact trailer. "Let me know if you need anything else. I gotta go huddle with Jill before this next sequence."

He doesn't look at me, doesn't speak to me directly, but brushes past and walks out the door. I bite back a frustrated sigh. We have to wait. I get it, but does it have to be like this?

"Hey, Liv." I press my palms together in a slightly pleading pose. "I want to ask Canon something about this next scene, too. You mind if I catch him?"

"Nah, ask while you can." She unties her robe to reveal one of Tilda's day dresses. "Everybody always wants a piece of him."

"Right," I say, smiling stiffly. "Be right back."

I open the door and hustle down the steps just in time to see Canon heading back toward set. Miraculously, there aren't a dozen people teeming around the trailers.

"Canon," I call, rushing to catch up.

He turns back to face me, looking damn good in his gray USC Film School sweatshirt and dark jeans. That beard is getting thicker. How would it feel if he kissed me now?

He tugs at the headphones that are always draped around his neck, his eyes cautious as I approach. "Neevah, hey. You need something?"

"Yeah, I do. I, um..." I toy with the belt of the terrycloth robe tied over my costume, fixing my eyes on the production team's fake sidewalk. "I just wondered if I imagined Thanksgiving."

I keep my voice low, but he still looks left and right, no doubt checking to see if anyone is around to hear. Grabbing my hand, he pulls me into one of the New York alleys they fabricated for the set, a tight channel between the sides of two fake buildings. He leans against one wall and I face him, leaning against the other.

"No, you didn't imagine it," he finally says, his hands shoved into his pockets. "We just can't repeat it."

"Ever?" I squeak.

"What'd I tell you?" His smile is a slow-burning secret. "Not yet."

"You think you're being discreet by avoiding me, but I think it draws attention that you give everyone else their notes directly except me. All my notes come through Kenneth."

"I don't care if people speculate about that. That's not the only reason I don't want a lot of contact with you."

It stings, those words. Even knowing what's behind them, hearing him actually voice what I've suspected doesn't feel great.

"Then why?" I ask, keeping my chin and eyes level. I'm determined not to get emotional because that's the last thing he wants and that's not who I am. I never let personal stuff get in the way of a performance, of the work, but I've also never felt like this about someone I worked with.

"It's for me," he says, not looking away. "It's so I can focus. You distract me."

A huge grin spreads across my face.

"Don't." He chuckles and narrows his eyes. "Do not."

"I'm a distraction, huh?" I take the few steps separating us until only a heartbeat fits between our chests. The alley walls close in on us and I'm surrounded by the clean, masculine scent of him.

The humor fades from his expression, and he links our fingers at our sides. "We need to wait."

Disappointment pierces the lust and longing suffusing my senses. "Until we wrap?"

He bends to drop a kiss on my forehead, slides his lips down to briefly take mine, the beard a soft scrape against my cheek. I grip his elbows, not wanting him to pull away, to go back to ignoring me. Just beyond this fake alley and deep shadows is the set and the cast and the crew and the real world. And this…we…are not happening there yet. And I just want a few more seconds in *this* world where we are, even if the only real thing here is us.

"Did you really need help for this next scene?" he whispers in my ear, his wide palm running down my back and resting just above the curve of my ass.

"Yes. In this next scene, can you tell me…" I glance up mock-seriously through my lashes. "What's my motivation?"

He flashes that too-rare grin, white and wolfish, confident, bordering on cocky.

"You'll be fine." He squeezes my hip. "That's my girl."

And while I'm still relishing that, he turns and walks away.

THIRTY-ONE

Dessi Blue

INTERIOR - TILDA & DESSI'S APARTMENT - DAY

Dessi rushes around their bedroom, tossing clothes into a suitcase lying open on the bed. She grabs a pair of stockings drying on the radiator, checks them on her arms and fingers for runs, and folds them neatly into the suitcase, too. She opens a few drawers, looks in bags.

DESSI

Now where is my passport?

Keeps looking around the apartment, growing more panicked when she can't find it.

DESSI

Tilda, you seen my passport?

Dessi walks out to the fire escape where Tilda leans her elbows on the rail and blows smoke from a cigarette.

DESSI

My passport! You seen it? Cal will be here to get me soon. I coulda sworn I just had it.

TILDA

I still don't understand why you gotta go off to Europe anyway. The band's making perfectly good money playing clubs like Café Society. But no! That ain't good enough for high-and-mighty Cal. He gotta go overseas and prove something.

DESSI

It's a big opportunity, Til. We making perfectly good money, yeah, but in Paris, London, Rome—we can make great money. More to send home to Mama. More for you and me.

Dessi grabs Tilda's cigarette and takes a long draw.

DESSI

'Sides, I want to see the world.

Tilda snatches her cigarette back, stubbing it out on the rail with jerky movements.

TILDA

Thought I was your world.

DESSI (CARESSING TILDA'S FACE)

Aw, baby. You are. I'll send money back so soon you won't have to work at the Savoy no more. I'm doing this for us.

TILDA

Tell yourself that lie. You the one that want to be a star. This is for you, Dessi Johnson. Or should I say Dessi Blue since that's what Cal's calling you now?

DESSI

And if I do wanna be a star, what's wrong with that?

TILDA

You shooting too high is all. I don't want to see you fall.

DESSI

You could hope I'll fly. Could you just do that 'cause you love me?

Tilda nods reluctantly.

DESSI

And you'll wait for me? 'Cause I'll wait for you.

TILDA

Yes, just don't be gone too long. You know I hate waiting on hot fried chicken, much less waiting for your skinny ass.

They laugh and hug each other. Cal calls from the street below, waving in front of a parked car.

CAL

You ready to conquer the world, Dessi Blue?

Tilda rolls her eyes and Dessi laughs.

DESSI

Yeah, I just need to find my passport before...

She trails off when Tilda pulls the passport from the pocket of her dress and offers it begrudgingly.

DESSI

I know you don't want me to go.

TILDA (TEARS IN HER EYES)
It ain't gonna be the same if you leave, Dessi.
I feel it. Not ever again.

DESSI
It'll be better than ever. I know it will.

TILDA
You ain't got no crystal ball, Bama.

Cal honks from below.

CAL
I'll come up and help with your bags.

Dessi steps back into the apartment from the fire escape and closes her suitcase, grabs her purse, and shoves the passport inside.

DESSI
I gotta go. Tilda, you coming to see me off?

Tilda walks to the window and stops.

TILDA (WITH A SAD SMILE)
This is as far as I go.

Dessi walks to the window and kisses Tilda passionately, not caring who sees. With a choked cry, she grabs her suitcase, opens the apartment door, and leaves with Cal.

THIRTY-TWO

Canon

"You ain't slick."

I glance up to stare at Monk, lounging by the craft services table, not sure I even want to know what he's talking about.

I don't.

Without responding, I place a slice of smoked salmon on my plate.

"You hate fish," Monk says, now standing across from me. "Especially fish that ain't even cooked right."

"Monk, man, what the hell you talking about?"

"You over here pretending to eat smoked salmon when we both know why you slithered out of your video cave."

I stiffen.

"For the record." I point to the slimy pink fish-mass on my plate. "I love this stuff."

"Oh, you do?" He crosses his arms over his chest. "Let's see you eat it."

I make a scoffing noise, mostly as a delay tactic because I really do hate smoked salmon. Monk nods to the plate and lifts his brows. It's none of his damn business. I know that, but I can't let him win the point. I wish I wasn't so proud. And stubborn. And bullheaded.

I eat the salmon.

And literally gag into my napkin.

"Told your ass!"

"So I don't like it. Who cares?" I toss the plate into a trash can and grab a bottle of water from the corner of the table.

"My point was that you're not out here to eat." Monk looks over his shoulder where Trey and Neevah sit on a fabricated New York City stoop playing cards. One of the cameras malfunctioned and it's being worked on. A brief delay, but the actors took advantage of it and, as they always seem to, broke out a deck of cards.

"You're here to spy," Monk finishes with a gloating smile.

"You on some bullshit, man." I deliberately turn my back so I can't see the two of them throwing down cards, but I hear Neevah squeal, and it makes me grit my teeth.

"What are we talking about?" Jill asks, walking up to grab a protein bar from the table.

"How Canon likes Neevah," Monk says.

I turn on him. "Man, don't be saying that shit. Somebody might hear you."

"I mean, is that a secret?" Jill takes a bite of her bar. "Is he out here brooding over Trey and Neevah?"

"I do not brood," I reply. They exchange *if you say so* looks. "Okay, I brood, but not over them. Over that. Shit, I don't give a damn if they—"

Neevah lets out another peal of laughter that sails across the set.

What is so funny about some damn cards?

I resist the urge to turn around and look—to stomp over there and ask Nick at Nite myself.

"Should we tell him?" Jill asks Monk. "I feel like we should tell him."

"Tell me what?" I ask.

"No, definitely not." Monk laughs. "This is too much fun."

"Tell me what?" I repeat.

"But we could put him out of his misery," Jill says.

"Why would we do that?" Monk asks.

"Monk, motherfucker, you better tell me something."

"Trey has a girlfriend he's crazy about," Jill blurts.

"What?" That can't be true. I would have known. If that's true, I've been torturing myself for weeks thinking he was trying to get in Neevah's pants when he would have had no interest in her pants.

"They've been dating for about a year," Jill says, rolling her eyes.

"But at the party," I say to Monk. "You told me everyone thought they were already sleeping together."

"What can I say?" He shrugs. "I just like pulling your chain."

"Everyone knows. It's not some secret," Jill says. "You just don't pay attention to anything except your movies." She laughs and shoots an amused glance over my shoulder. "Oh, and now to her."

"Does everyone know?" I ask, my voice subdued, eyes fixed on my Air Force Ones.

"About Trey?" Monk asks. "Of course. You're the only one—"

"Not about Trey. About me." I tip my head back, gesturing behind me. "About her."

"No." Jill's voice and eyes hold sympathy and affection. "Monk and I have been with you for years. We know you, but no one else would suspect."

"Let's keep it that way." I split a warning look between the two of them. "I'm serious about that. We aren't... there's nothing going on between us."

"Yet," Jill says, squeezing her smile in at the corners.

"This is her first movie. She doesn't need what would come with us... She doesn't need that. She doesn't deserve it."

"Any idea if she..." Monk toggles his head back and forth. "Ya know. If she's feeling you, too?"

I don't answer with anything but a nod, but it's enough for them to exchange shit-eating grins.

"Why are you guys so giddy about this?" I demand, fighting a smile my-damn-self now.

"Because she's amazing and you deserve it," Jill says. "I've never seen you this way about anyone. I know the level of dedication it takes to tell the stories you do, and I'm glad you have your work, but we're your friends. We want more for you than that. We want to see you happy."

"Yeah, you need somebody in that lonely life of yours," Monk taunts.

"How *is* Verity, by the way?" Jill asks him.

Monk frowns down into his coffee, curses, and walks away.

"Why didn't I think of that?" I laugh.

"What can I say? I'm an expert button-pusher." Jill's expression sobers. "For real. All work. No play. You know the rest. If you want her—"

"It's not that simple. It's timing. While we're filming—"

"You're not filming over Christmas," she says, her grin mischievous and laced with trouble.

I knew there was a reason I kept her around.

THIRTY-THREE

Neevah

I need this break. Badly.

Our shooting schedule is demanding for everyone, but I'm in just about every scene. Most days I'm in makeup by five a.m., go straight to wardrobe, and am on set, ready to go with the sun barely up. The cast and crew have become like family the last few months, and I'll miss them for the two-week Christmas break, but I'm going to relish every day off.

"You sure you don't want to come home with me?" Takira asks from her bedroom across the hall. "I know you dread seeing your family."

I snap my suitcase closed and walk over to her bedroom, where she's still packing.

"I don't dread seeing them." I roll my eyes at her knowing look. "Okay, I don't enjoy seeing Terry and Brandon, but I miss my mama. My aunties and cousins. And I want all my mama's food."

"Oh, are we indulging for the holidays?"

"I still won't eat red meat or pork, but mac and cheese, stuffing, deviled eggs, yams, sweet potato pie, collard greens, corn bread? Babeeee, all them bets are off."

I sprawl on her bed, wallowing in the stillness I've had so seldom the last few months.

"Besides," I continue, "Terry and Brandon are going to visit his mama's people in Virginia. I doubt I'll see them much, if at all. I'm coming back for New Year's Eve."

"Aww." She turns from her closet and pokes her lip out. "It's my parents' fortieth anniversary, so we're giving them a party on New Year's Eve. You're welcome to join us in Texas. I don't want you ringing in the New Year alone."

"Girl, me, Ryan Seacrest, and that big ol' apple dropping will be just fine."

"You sure? 'Cause if you want to—"

"I promise I'll be okay."

My phone pings, and I reach into my back pocket for it to check the incoming text.

Livvie: Thank you again for the cookies! You're so sweet.

Me: No problem! It's not much, but I hope you enjoy them.

Livvie: They're so good! I already ate half of them and am hiding the rest from my boyfriend. LOL!

Me: I'm glad! Merry Christmas. See you after the break.

Livvie: Byeeeeee! Merry Christmas!

"That was Livvie," I tell Takira with a smile. "Thanking me for the Christmas cookies."

"Well I'm glad slaving over that hot stove making all those cookies paid off. Everybody seemed to love them."

"It was fun and easy." I shrug. "No big deal, and the crew especially work so hard. I wanted them to know how much we appreciate them."

The doorbell interrupts us, and I hop from the bed.

"I'll get it."

I shuffle down the hall, practically skipping at the prospect of days with no hair and makeup, no fittings or rehearsals or dance routines or dawn pickups. When I open the door without even checking the peephole, the man on the other side is the last person I expected to see.

"Canon?"

It goes without saying he looks bitable. His hair is longer than I'm used to seeing it. The cream-colored cable-knit sweater is stark against the mahogany of his skin. The sleeves are shoved up, exposing the corded muscles of his forearms.

"Hey." He peers over my shoulder into the house. "Can I come in?"

"Oh. Sure. Yeah."

I step back to let him in, suddenly self-conscious of my bare feet and shiny face; of the fact that I'm wearing no bra under my maxi dress. My hair is its own solar system, the big coils puffing in orbit around my head.

For a few seconds we simply stare at each other in the privacy of the foyer, but it doesn't feel awkward. It's a thirsty silence. We're drinking each other in, taking long gulps of one another when we've been alone so little.

"Oh!" I say, grasping for anything that resembles normal conversation. "I have something for you."

"You do?"

He follows me into the living room, and I bend to retrieve a festive tin from under our Christmas tree.

"I couldn't find you today when we broke," I explain, offering the cookies to him.

He pops the lid, peering down at what's inside and yielding a tiny curve of his lips. "Gingerbread."

"My mama's recipe." I laugh self-consciously. "Buttercream icing. I gave them to everyone, but I didn't see you today."

I never see you.

I don't have to say it for us to both know how little time, by design, we spend together. He closes the lid and frowns, tracing the raised pattern of the wreath decorating the tin.

"I didn't get you…shit. I guess I didn't get anyone anything. Some boss, huh?"

"I'm not tripping, and I know the rest of the cast and crew aren't either. We know you're busy."

"So are you." He tucks the cookies under his arm. "But you found the time. You always seem to find time for people. Thank you."

His eyes intent on my face, the admiration in his words, warms my cheeks.

"It's really nothing. It took…took no time." I laugh, needing to shift the attention. "So what brings you by?"

He glances around the living room and up the hall. "Are we here alone?"

"Um... Takira's in her room. We could talk outside?"

"That'd be great, yeah."

I lead him out back to my favorite part of this house. We step into the courtyard, the lush grass tickling my bare feet, licking between my toes. A lemon tree lends the air the invigorating scent of citrus.

"Nice," Canon says, sitting on the stone bench where I take a few moments to meditate some mornings.

"Yeah, we like it." I sit beside him, leaving a few inches and half a pound of cookies between us. "We didn't have lemon trees in our backyard in North Carolina, and we don't have yards in New York. LA is spoiling me."

"I'm sure you'll have more offers after this movie. Maybe you'll consider moving out here."

We stare at one another for a few seconds before I have to look away, the pent-up intensity straining my control.

"So did you need something?" I ask, knowing he must since there are no "just because" visits with us. I pull one knee up to my chest and swing the other leg, needing something to *do* with myself while I wait for his response.

"I was wondering what..." He clears his throat, stands, and walks over to the lemon tree, where he rubs a leaf between his fingers. "I was wondering if you have plans for New Year's Eve."

It's not what it sounds like. There's an explanation. It's a studio New Year's party. There's an event. The suits want to show the cast off. Something work-related.

"Um, I'm actually coming back to LA for New Year's."

He plucks a leaf from the tree and twirls it between his index finger and thumb. "Would you like to spend it with me?"

My foot slips off the bench and I almost fall, catching myself just in time. I grip the bench and let my bare toes dangle in the grass. "What do you mean? Like a party or—"

"More private." He glances up, a slow-burning fire in his eyes. "I was thinking just us for a few days."

If he had said we're boarding the next spaceship for Jupiter, I couldn't have been more surprised. Even though I know Takira can't hear us out here and that no one is listening, I walk over, standing close enough that he'll hear me whisper. "I thought you said we had to wait."

His usual inscrutable expression softens, opens to show me what he's thinking, that he's *feeling*.

"I thought I could." He pushes the hair away from my cheek, over my shoulder. "I was wrong."

There could be a dozen cameras out here right now and I wouldn't be able to stop myself. I tip up on my toes and link my hands behind his neck. "Yes."

"Don't you want to know—"

I press my finger to his lips. "I said yes."

He slides his hands down my back to rest at the curve of my hips, pulling me closer.

"What changed your mind?" I ask. "You've barely acknowledged my existence since Thanksgiving and you seemed to be clear we shouldn't... we shouldn't 'til after the movie wraps."

"I still feel that way, but I'm hoping we can be discreet. I need *something*." The way he looks at me brushes heat over my cheeks. "I want you."

He dips, takes my lips, and cups my ass. I strain up, opening my mouth under the hot, seeking slant of his. It's been weeks and I'm starved for this. His hunger circles mine and we're groaning and I'm grinding up against him, completely prepared to mount him under this lemon tree. He breaks the kiss, breathing as heavily as I am.

"We'll wait," he pants against my lips.

"Where?"

Antarctica?

Great this time of year.

The moon?

Who needs gravity?

Because wherever he says we can be together, even if only for a few days secreted away from everyone, that's where I'll be.

"I'd like it to be out of town," he says, "but we start shooting again in a few days, so I need it to be close. Easy. Ever been to Santa Barbara? There's this place I rent sometimes when I need to get away."

"That sounds great. I'll be back a few days before New Year's." A bitter laugh escapes me. "I'm going home for Christmas, but I don't exactly expect a relaxing time and I need to get into the right frame of mind before we start shooting again."

His big hands at my waist tighten and then caress my back. "You nervous about seeing your sister?"

"I don't know that I will. Maybe. They're spending Christmas in Virginia, and I'm only staying a few days. I have no idea what to expect."

"I hope it goes well."

"I'm most looking forward to spending some time with my mother. Somehow our relationship suffered, even though the split was between Terry and me." I shrug, not wanting to discuss my family right now. "Anyway, so I'll be back a couple of days before New Year's."

"I'm spending Christmas Day with my mom's people in Lemon Grove, but I'll be back in LA that night. When you return, we could drive up to Santa Barbara and come back to LA New Year's Day. Give us time to get ready for shooting to resume. How's that sound?"

As an answer, I nod and kiss him lightly, squeezing his dense muscles. I want to do cartwheels through the backyard, but I try to play it cool. He'll find out soon enough how not-cool I am when it comes to him. His hands tighten at my hips and he groans into our kiss, and then pulls back after a few seconds to drop his forehead against mine.

"I need to go," he says on a ragged breath. "Kenneth and I are meeting with the set design team one last time before we break for the holidays."

Taking my hand, he grabs his cookies from the bench and we walk back into the house. In the foyer, he leans against the door and pulls me close to kiss me again, like he can't help it. Like I'm against his better judgment, but he can't resist. I feel that. In his arms, risk weighs less than this necessary passion. And it does feel as necessary as breath. He's hard through the thin fabric of my dress and I have to stop myself from dropping to my knees right here and taking him down my throat.

It has been a long time, and he is the only man I've really wanted in ages. He breaks the kiss after a few drugging seconds, and when he pulls away, desire glazes the eyes that are usually so focused.

"I really have to go." He dips to kiss my forehead. "Thank you again for the cookies. Merry Christmas."

"Merry Christmas, Canon."

Once he's gone, I dance around in a circle.

I'm going to have him.

I'm going to have him.

I'm going to have him.

"So, question." Takira's pointed words break the spell, and I stop mid-circle, staring at her in surprise. I'd forgotten she was even in the house. "What was Canon Holt doing here, and why were you kissing him?"

"Uh, you saw that?" I squeak, unable to hold back a broad, delighted smile despite getting caught.

She crosses her arms, eyes bright with curiosity and anticipation. "Girl, you got some 'splaining to do."

THIRTY-FOUR

Neevah

A house is not a home.

Luther's lyric replays in my head as I pull up to the house where I grew up. A house may not always be a home, but this one used to be. In the years before my father died, this brick ranch-style house was filled with laughter and the four of us were happy.

When he passed away, grief drew Mama, Terry, and me closer. Love kept us tight.

It's hard to believe this patch of land, this street, this town, used to be the breadth of my existence. Not much has changed here. Oh, the Piggly Wiggly is gone and there's a new Taco Bell/KFC combo on Main Street, but Mama says Mrs. Shay still does a fish fry every Saturday and sells chitterlings dinners at Christmas.

I thank the Uber driver and drag my small rolling suitcase behind me under the car porch and to the door. My flight was delayed and Mama had to take one of the ladies from church to the doctor's office, so I told her I could find my way home.

"You still got your house key?" she had asked.

I pull out my key ring and select the one I haven't used in years. I wonder if the key, like me, no longer fits here, but it slides right in. I can only hope my homecoming goes as smoothly.

"I'm home," I tell the empty foyer, parking my suitcase at the foot of the stairs. I'm not quite ready to face the pink canopy bed and my wall poster gallery of Missy Elliott, Justin Timberlake, and Soulja Boy.

"Soulja Boy?" I grimace and laugh. "That was quick."

It's not my first time home in the twelve years since I left for college, but it's one of only a few, and the first time I've had this house and all its memories to myself. I wander down the hall into the living room and, like a shrine to what our family used to be, a lifetime of photos line the mantel. Each one chronicles a uniquely awkward phase of my life. Stockings decorated with candy canes hang over the fireplace, the same ones Mama used to stuff on Christmas Eve with our names on them. Now there's a new stocking.

Quianna.

The beautiful living indiscretion that demolished my illusions and tore my family at the seams. Mama was disappointed and angry with them, of course. She took my side, of course.

But Terry was pregnant and needed Mama more than I did.

Terry was a new mother and needed Mama more than I did.

Terry was here, and I was gone, so she got more of Mama than I did.

In a strange new city, I licked my wounds alone. Away from home for the first time and overwhelmed, I learned to stand on my own by necessity. I never stopped needing Mama, but I let her think I was fine, and to survive, I told myself the same lie. But lately with my life barreling ahead at breakneck speed, with a decade's worth of work harvesting rewards seemingly overnight, there's been a tiny hole in my happiness. An irritating tear like a sock in need of darning. A secret tucked inside my shoe, but it doesn't affect the way I walk, and I'm the only one who knows it's there.

Last I heard from Mama, Terry and Brandon were packed and ready to go to Virginia. Looks like we'll avoid each other again. I'm looking forward to some time with Mama, just us two. It's good that Terry and Brandon went to Virginia to see the other side of his family. After the strain of starring in my first movie, and one as huge as *Dessi Blue*, I need a break, not more stress.

This room hasn't changed much either. The couch is still here—the one Terry and Brandon sat on, side by side, building their little wall of solidarity with the mortar of deceit. Masons of betrayal.

An artificial Christmas tree stands in the corner. That's different. Growing up, we always had a live tree. Daddy insisted, and Mama continued the tradition when he was gone.

I haven't been here many Christmases. The holiday season is one of the busiest in theater, and it's hard to get off even for a few days. I often used that as an excuse to stay away, especially when I knew Terry and Brandon would be here. Touring or understudying, waiting in the wings, longing for home, I always pictured a live tree and imagined I could smell the pine.

Not this year.

This too-green thing sprinkled with cheap tinsel is odorless and stiff, with gaps and plug-by-the-number branches.

The alarm dings, signaling an open door. In New York, we keep a bat for protection when doors open unannounced, but the neighborhood watch is a formality here. Crime is not a thing.

I walk to the kitchen, eager to see Mama for the first time in nearly a year. "How was Mrs.—"

My words wither and die. Terry stands in the kitchen at the car porch entrance, toting grocery bags full of food. I can't remember the last time we were alone, but I know it was as awkward then as it is now.

"Oh." I lick my lips and grit my teeth. "I thought Mama was coming home."

"She took Mrs. Dobbs to—"

"I know. She told me. I didn't think you would…"

Be here.

We stare at each other with identical eyes, dark brown with gold-splashed centers. She was always the pretty one, but that wasn't enough for her. There was one boy in our whole school who preferred me, and she had to take him, too.

Brandon's betrayal doesn't even hurt anymore. He and I would have been driftwood and our marriage a shipwreck. But her? My sister and how she decided to hurt me—that I'm not sure when I'll get over. Not today.

"Brandon's Aunt Sharon has pneumonia." Terry lays a bushel of collard greens on the counter and pulls sweet potatoes from the grocery bag. "So they're not really doing much of a Christmas up there. We'll visit her soon, but decided last minute to stay here for the holidays."

"Oh."

That's the best I can do. It's been so many years, and I hope we can put this behind us, but I hadn't planned on confronting this particular demon for Christmas.

"Brandon's working at the garage," she adds, pulling out two-dozen eggs. "And I ran by Food Lion to pick up some stuff for Mama."

The least I can do is help. I pull out pepper and season salt from the grocery bag, instinctively opening the cabinet to the right of the stove, only to find stacks of plates.

"Spices over there now." Terry nods to the cabinet on the left.

It's a small thing, but not knowing where my mama keeps her spices feels like another thing Terry robbed me of. She betrayed me. She stole from me, but I've been the one in exile.

"Mama says you're starring in some big movie," she says, lifting her brows like she'll believe it when she sees it.

"I'm in a movie, yeah," I say, putting a pack of neck bones in the refrigerator.

"She's cooking those tonight," Terry says. "Leave the neck bones out."

I don't mean to slam the meat on the countertop, but it happens. I'm tired of her knowing all the things I want to know, too. She confiscated the man and the life I don't even want, but it was mine. And she didn't leave me any choice.

"Surprised you even came home." Terry twists her lips.

We've never discussed it, but of course she would know I've avoided coming because of her and Brandon.

"Assumed you thought you were too bougie for us now." Terry rolls her eyes and pulls out two bags of shredded cheese for Mama's famous macaroni.

"Wait." I lean against the counter and rewind what she just said. "What?"

"Yeah, all these years you been staying up in New York, and now you in Hollywood. Uppity and too big for your britches and—"

"You think I don't come home because I'm uppity? Bougie?"

"I mean, you were always bougie, thinking you were better than the rest of us. That you were gonna be a star. Go off and forget about your family. Hope you're happy now."

"Hold up. I didn't come home because of you."

"Because of me?" What looks like genuine surprise widens her eyes.

"Is that shocking? After what you did?"

"You can't be talking about the thing with Brandon."

"The *thing* with Brandon? I may have been young, and maybe it wouldn't have lasted. Who knows, but I was engaged and you cheated on me."

"There you go. Being dramatic." Terry sucks her teeth. "I guess that *is* your job."

"Did you bump your head and forget? Well, I didn't. You fucked my fiancé and got pregnant with his kid."

A gasp from the door leading to the car porch jerks both our heads around. Holding her phone, apparently mid-text, stands their daughter, Quianna. Horrified brown eyes with gold-splashed centers flick between her mother and me.

"Q," Terry says, her lips tight around the nickname. "Go back out to the car. Let me finish unloading Grandma's groceries."

"You were engaged to Daddy?" Quianna asks me, ignoring her mother.

I have no words. I can't confirm or deny. I just stare at her helplessly, this eleven-year-old girl who's too young to have her illusions stripped away. I may be mad as hell with my sister going on twelve years, but this is still my niece, and though I barely know her, I love her.

"You cheated?" she demands of Terry. "Oh, my God, Mom."

"Quianna," I start, not even sure what I'll say next.

"Is that why you're never around, Aunt Neevah?" She's volleying the questions between Terry and me, getting answers from neither, deducing the plain truth that neither of us can hide now.

"No wonder you and Daddy are such a mess," she spits, turning on her heel and going back the way she came.

The door slams behind her, leaving a silence swelling with shock and rage.

"Look what you did," Terry snaps. "What am I supposed to tell my daughter, Neevah?"

"I'll talk to her." I start for the door, but Terry steps in front of me.

"And say what? She don't know you. I need to be the one to explain."

"You mean tell her your version?"

"Ain't worth trying to hide the truth now that you've spilled it everywhere. Made a mess I gotta be the one to clean up."

For a second, I actually feel guilty. Yes, I wish Quianna hadn't heard it that way or even from me, but for Terry to shift the real blame of her actions to me for inadvertently exposing them?

It's too much.

"It's not my fault you have to explain the shady shit you did to me to your daughter."

"Oh, you're just loving this, aren't you? Terry got pregnant. Terry's stuck in this dead-end town. Terry's marriage is—" She breaks off and glares at me despite her bottom lip quivering. "You got it all, Neevah. You always had it all, didn't you?"

"I got it all? I always had it all? Seriously, you were the one everyone wanted."

"No, it's just that no one ever thought they could get you. You walked around like you were too good for everybody until Brandon."

"Like I was too good…" Beneath my indignation and rage, a small bud of hurt breaks through. I loved my sister best in the world back then, would have done anything for her, and this was how she saw me? How she truly felt?

"I can count on two hands with fingers to spare how many times I've been home in twelve years," I tell her, my voice trembling and tears filling my eyes. "Quianna wasn't just your child. She's Mama's grandchild. What was more important? That I be around? Or that she be around? But for years I couldn't look at you or Brandon without feeling sick. You didn't just take him. You took Mama. You took my home and you broke my heart."

I can't see my own eyes right now, but I imagine they look just like my sister's—brimming with tears, shaded by rage and regret. Her fists are balled at her sides. She glances at the door to the car porch, and I hear the car running in the driveway.

"I better go see about Quianna," she says, grabbing her purse from the kitchen counter and leaving without another word.

The door slams behind her and I grip the counter tight, my only support in the wake of that confrontation. I lower my head, letting hot tears spill over my cheeks. I knew this trip would be hard in some ways, but I'd thought they would be gone. I didn't think this would all burst, like an infected blister lanced and oozing everywhere. I have no idea how I'll face them tomorrow. Terry and Brandon and Quianna. I'm tempted to leave, but that's what I've done for twelve years—ceded the field, my home, for them. It's been too long. Tonight may have been awkward and even painful, but it's a step toward exposing the past and, hopefully, moving on to some kind of future. Maybe when I see them at Christmas dinner tomorrow, we'll figure it out.

But the next day Christmas comes, and they do not.

Their absence is glaring. It's so obvious they are missed.

The house is packed for Christmas dinner, as it was when we were growing up. Our natural family is not that large, but Mama has a way of collecting people. Strays. Friends. Folks who would be alone were it not for her "adopting" them. I've missed how she makes our home a community unto itself. It's loud and boisterous and much less trying than I'd thought it would be. Except when someone forgets and asks about Terry and Brandon. An awkward silence. A furtive glance my way. The last time many of them saw me, I was Brandon's fiancée. The girl who ran up north as soon as she graduated, rarely seen back in these parts.

And now I'm back, so Terry and Brandon aren't here for Christmas.

There are moments when I feel perfectly at home, and it's like one of our famous Mathis family reunions. And there are times I feel like an intruder, a sojourner in a strange land.

"You make this corn pudding?" my Aunt Alberta asks Mama. She seems virtually unchanged by time. A little more gray in her hair, brown skin still relatively smooth. She still walks around the house carrying her purse like she expects somebody to steal it.

"I made it, yeah." Mama scoops a generous portion of the corn pudding onto Alberta's plate.

"I bet it's not as good as Terry's," Alberta says teasingly. "That girl can throw down just like you."

When Alberta's eyes land on me while I'm waiting with my own plate, her smile freezes. I smile as naturally as I can, cut a slice of red velvet cake, and head for the kitchen. It's as crowded as the dining room, so I spread a wide smile around to everyone and keep walking to the back porch. Thank God no one is out here. I settle into one of the rocking chairs that have been here as long as I can remember. Mama and Daddy used to sit out here and watch Terry and me play in the backyard. They'd hold hands and talk while we played kickball or climbed one of the big oak trees that separated our yard from our neighbor's.

Tears gather in my eyes and emotion scorches my throat. Looking at the old tree, sitting in Daddy's chair, I miss him. It floods my heart with that ache that never fully leaves no matter how long someone has been gone. And I miss those days when we were a family and this house was full of our love and laughter. I've spackled the cracks in my heart with friends, but today, sitting on our back porch, I miss my family.

The screen door opens and I swipe at my eyes and, not even looking up to see who it is, take a bite of cake.

"I was wondering where you got to," Mama says, settling into the other rocking chair.

I smile and scrape at the white icing on my plate. "Just taking a minute for some quiet."

"I hear ya. It's a lot of folks in there." She spoons up some corn pudding. "Everybody's glad you came home."

I snort, not sure that's true, but smile and tap my fork against my mouth.

"We sure are proud of you on Broadway and getting this big movie." She pauses, licks her lips, and continues. "I hate I didn't make it up to New York to see you that week you got to be in the show. I had—"

"Knee surgery. I remember, Mama. It's fine. I know you would have come if you could have." I say it, but I'm not sure I believe it. It was hard for me to come back here after Terry and Brandon married and had Quianna. And Mama never seemed too pressed about coming to see me.

"You know I don't fly," Mama says, like she's reading my mind. "So it's hard to get up—"

"I know. It's fine."

An apology would feel so much better than an excuse. I've always thought that about Terry and Brandon, and I think it now as I hear Mama's reasons for not supporting me the way she could have. She's not the only one to blame for the space between us. I've used work and other things as an excuse not to come home. We've danced around this for more than a decade and things won't get better until we stop.

"Where did Terry and Brandon go?" I ask.

Mama's surprised eyes meet mine in the glow of the back porch light. "Um, one of his co-workers invited them over for dinner."

"Oh." I push the moist cake around my plate. "I'm surprised they went and didn't want to be with you and family on Christmas."

"I think they..." She blows out a tired sigh. "I guess they didn't want to make you uncomfortable."

"So it's my fault they aren't here."

"I didn't say that."

"Isn't that what everyone thinks?"

"This was never easy for any of us, Neevah."

"Oh, yeah. It was so hard for Brandon to sleep with Terry and get her pregnant when he was engaged to me. And poor Terry, having to cheat with my fiancé."

"It was hard for you, Neevah, I know that, but they were young. Terry was pregnant. They didn't have no money and—"

"They had you, Mama. What did I have? Who did I have?"

"Neevah, you were always self-sufficient. I knew you—"

"I was eighteen years old and had rarely left Clearview, much less moved by myself to another state. Living on my own for the first time."

"You could have come home. I tried to be there for both of you, but sometimes it felt like you didn't want anything to do with us anymore."

"You think I wanted to see her pregnant and them married and with a baby? To be reminded how they cheated and lied to me? I was angry. I was hurt, and yeah. I didn't want to be around them for years, but I wanted to be around *you*. It felt like you chose her over me."

"The body sends help to the part that needs it most. She had a rough pregnancy. She couldn't work for a while. They had no money. She was living here. I guess I thought you were happy chasing your dreams and Terry needed me more."

"I needed you, too." I sniff at the tears, now uncorked, slipping freely down my cheeks. "I still need you, Mama."

Mama reaches across to take my hand, bridging not only the space between these old chairs, but the space that has separated me from her for years.

"I'm here, now, Neev. I should have been there for you more before." She swallows, purses her lips, and lets her tears flow, too. "I'm sorry."

I was right. An apology does feel better than an excuse. The healing property of those two simple words salves my heart, broken and dented by the ones who should have loved me enough.

"It's not all on you, Mama," I say, squeezing her hand, squeezing my heart. "I could have done more. I'm sorry, too."

And the power of those words, said from her to me, said from me to her, pulls us out of the rocking chairs and up and into each other's arms. Not a hug in passing, but a tight one that grips and heals. We can't repair everything in one night, in one conversation, but these words and Mama's arms around me go a long way—go the *right* way. We are on our way back to each other. This new beginning with my mother is the greatest gift. It's restoration, or at least the start of one. I don't know how or when it will happen with Terry.

Or if it ever will.

Mama sniffs, pulling back to smile as I swipe at my wet cheeks, too.

"I think we have a lot to catch up on," she says, sitting back in her chair, setting it to a rocking rhythm. "How 'bout you start by telling me everything."

I tell her about the lean years during and after college when I needed so much, but didn't know how to ask for it. When I couldn't swallow my pride to call her because I resented how she was there for Terry, but in my eyes, wasn't there for me.

"That night on Broadway, I thought of you. You were the only thing missing," I whisper. "That was just one moment in a million I wanted to share with you. When I needed you."

"Neevah," Mama says, wiping at the corners of her eyes. "I thought you didn't want nothing to do with us. And I understood. After what Terry and Brandon did...well, I understood, but it did feel like I lost you, too. And now I know you felt like you lost me."

I hesitate over the next words, but decide I should say them. "Mama, I found out I have discoid lupus."

Mama's eyes go round and she reaches for my hand, holding it in both of hers. "Lupus? Like your Aunt Marian?"

"Not that kind of lupus. The kind she had was systemic and what I have is discoid. I have the rashes and some hair loss, but it's not life-threatening. When we were still figuring it all out, though," I say, blinking at fresh tears, "I wanted you. I wanted to ask about it, and even then just decided to try and figure it out on my own."

"Well, your Aunt Marian and I were never that close," Mama says, twisting her lips. "Nobody was good enough for her baby brother, but it was a long time before she even got her diagnosis. Things were different then. They didn't know as much."

She scans my face, and I make sure she'll find nothing to worry about in my expression.

"You sure you alright?"

"I'm sure, Mama. I just wanted you to know." I smile and squeeze her hand, wanting to shift to more exciting parts of my life. "Now, don't you want to hear about the movie I'm in?"

"Oh, yeah. Spill it all! And that director, that Canon Holt. He as fine up close as they say he is?" She leans over conspiratorially, her smile and her wink wicked. "You can tell your mama."

And for the first time in a long time, I do.

THIRTY-FIVE

Canon

Me: Merry Christmas. Well, Merry Post-Christmas.
Neevah: Merry Post-Christmas. How was yours?
Me: Great. Yours?
Neevah: Okay, I guess.
Me: Want to talk about it?
Neevah: With you?
Me: Yeah, with me. Unless there's someone else you'd rather talk to.

My phone rings right away.

"Everyone else was busy, huh?" I ask, stretching out on the lounge chair by my pool. Seventy-five degrees in December. Why would I ever leave Cali?

"Something like that." She laughs. "So what'd you do for Christmas? Lemon Grove with the fam?"

"I did. It was great seeing everyone. Drove up on Christmas morning. Came back to LA last night. How about you? How'd it go?"

"Rough." She breathes out a heavy sigh. "At least with my sister."

"Oh, so she *was* there? I thought they were going to Virginia."

"Good memory."

I could tell her I remember everything she says, but with me dragging her to Santa Barbara for New Year's, she probably already suspects how much I like her. "Like" is a tepid description for my burning curiosity about this woman. About how she thinks, what makes her laugh. How will she feel when I'm inside her? How will she look after I fuck her?

Questions.

"They *were* going to Virginia," Neevah continues, oblivious to the dirty track my mind is on. That's for the best. "They ended up staying. Terry and I had a run-in on Christmas Eve."

"You argued?" I ask, feeling protective of Neevah, even though I know she can hold her own.

"Epically." Her humorless laugh carries a note of sadness. "It was long overdue, but it was still…messy, and we didn't get anything resolved."

"I'm sorry."

"I am, too. Her daughter, my niece, Quianna, overheard us arguing. She apparently never knew I used to be engaged to her father, or that they cheated and she was the result. I mean, she's a kid. Why *would* she know? I feel awful that she heard it from me. It was very soap opera. College Canon would have loved it."

We both laugh at her attempt to lighten the mood. Family drama like this, though, you can only lighten so much.

"You said that was Christmas Eve. What about Christmas Day?"

"They didn't come to Mama's. They went somewhere else. I guess it would have made it more awkward for everyone, but it's that kind of thinking that kept me away so much the last decade. Sometimes shit has to get awkward before it gets right. I see that now."

"Will you reach out to her again?"

"I'm not ready. I know I should be, but she hurt me worse than anyone ever has, Canon. I don't have feelings for Brandon anymore. God, I was over him my freshman year in college. But what they did? What she did? It still hurts."

"I can imagine."

"And you know what hurts as much? She seems mad at me! Seems to resent me for…I don't know, pursuing my dreams? Finding some success? Getting out of our hometown?"

"I could see that."

"Well, I can't. I've been basically without my family since I was eighteen years old. It's like a divorce, and she got custody of everyone."

Neevah doesn't realize how fantastic she is. After *Dessi Blue* releases, there will be enough people letting her know. For now, I just listen, letting her unburden what she's obviously been holding in.

"At least Mama and I talked," she says.

"How was that?"

"Uncomfortable. Awkward. Needed. We cleared the air. She doesn't fly, but she'll try to get up to New York to see me when the movie wraps."

I don't like to think of Neevah returning to the East Coast. I have no hold on her, and I know New York is her home. There is a part of me, though, that hopes she'll decide to move to LA. I could find a dozen projects that would keep her here, but she would hate that. It would be a disservice to her. I'll make it clear if she needs anything from me, it's hers. We're still several steps away from that kind of discussion.

"I'm really excited about Santa Barbara," she says, her voice hushed, husky. "Are you?"

I answer first with a raspy chuckle. "What do you think?"

"Sometimes I don't know what to think. I understand your reasons for us not pursuing the…attraction between us until after the movie, but there are days when you are on set and I don't even see you, and Kenneth brings my notes and we have no contact, and I wonder if I'm dreaming it all."

"If you are," I tell her, my voice dropping lower with need and anticipation, "then we're having the same dream."

Usually when I'm shooting a movie, I'm completely consumed by that story. Nothing distracts me. The one time I strayed from that one-track mindedness, it bit me in the ass and ruined the story. Neevah has no idea how many of my rules I'm violating taking her away like this before *Dessi Blue* wraps, even if we are on a break.

"I want that—to be in a dream with you," she answers, sounding breathless—like maybe this thing between us that I've given up resisting she can't resist either.

THIRTY-SIX

Neevah

There's a feeling I get before a performance.

It vacillates between trepidation and almost unbearable excitement. I run the lines in my head and can barely sit still, I'm so ready to get on that stage, or lately, on set.

The time Canon and I will spend together over the next few days is not a performance. I know that, but I feel the same things. Breathless, like a moth got loose in my rib cage, the wings fluttering over my heart. I understand why Canon's been cautious, but I'm glad he wants this, too.

Now.

When my phone rings, I'm in the bathroom packing toiletries. He's due here soon, and I hope that's not him saying he'll be any earlier.

It's not.

"Hey, honey," Takira says.

"Hey. Let me put my headphones on so I can keep packing."

I slip on the headphones and return to the bathroom. "What's up, T? How's the break going?"

"Now, you know I did not call to talk about my boring Christmas break, though I did get some last night."

"Oh?" I stop to lean one hip against the bathroom counter. "With who? How was it?"

"Girl, this guy who works with my sister. We all met up for drinks, and one thing led to another."

One-night stands aren't usually Takira's bag, but we all do things out of character with the right dose of liquor.

"And?" I ask.

"Not worth it. He ain't halfway know what he was doing."

I reach under my sink for deodorant. "So it wasn't good?"

"I described him to my sister as if *please, God, make it stop* was a person."

I shake my head and chuckle, but keep it moving because Takira's disappointing sex will not make me late getting mine.

"Not like *make it stop* consent," she continues, "but like boredom. Like if I still wore a watch, I woulda been checking it. I mean, it's a clit. Not a Venn diagram."

"Oh, my God, T."

"And afterward he had the nerve to be all...so how was it? Negro, it was two stars. I got your Yelp review right here. Would not recommend and glad I packed my vibrator. Shiiiiiit."

"Why'd you even...well, you don't usually go for flash bangs with guys you don't know, so was he that fine? Or were you—"

"That desperate?" she cuts in, some of the humor fading from the other line. "The holidays are hell sometimes. I'm the only one in our family not married now, and you just *feel* it. Everybody's booed up and got their kids and family pics on Instagram, and running around all elated. I felt like an extra trapped in one of those Hallmark Christmas movies."

I pause, setting aside my packing and settling on the bed to really listen. Takira's the best friend I have in the world. I'm used to her swagger, her unfaltering confidence, but I'm glad she's trusting me with this, too.

"I just..." Takira stops and starts again. "...wanted some connection, I guess. Beyond the dick, I wanted to feel wanted and needed and all the things we dream about feeling, but don't get enough."

"I'm sorry it was such a letdown."

"To be expected. You don't walk in a bar, flirt with a frog, and think he'll be a prince by the time you get him home. Though, after that fourth shot, he *did* start looking like royalty."

She sounds more like herself, and we laugh, but I want to make sure she's alright. "T, if you need—"

"I said I didn't call to talk about me and I meant it. Now, is our esteemed director on his way?"

"Yeah." Reminded of the time, I scoot off the bed and get back to packing. "He'll be here soon. And don't forget, deep vault on this one. We aren't ready to go public until after the movie wraps. I mean, if there is a public to go after this. Who knows? We could have a bad Yelp review, too."

"Not likely. Canon has some serious big dick energy, and I have no doubt he'll back it up."

I actually don't either. Based on the chemistry we've had so far, I think we'll be fine in bed.

Correction.

I think we'll be *fire* in bed.

He's worried about the movie. What people will think, how they'll see me if they find out I slept with my director. I'm worried more about my heart. I've never met anyone like Canon, never felt anything like this. I know sex will only deepen this connection.

He thinks I can't afford the press. What I *can't* afford is heartbreak. Affairs like this in Hollywood don't exactly have the best track record, and he may be used to negotiating relationships like contracts, dealing with the fallout of a breakup in a public forum like he had to with Camille, but I'm not.

I suspect Camille lashed out because she lost him. If she hadn't been hurt, if her emotions hadn't been so invested, she wouldn't have sabotaged her movie that way. She got Canon fired and a movie that could have been great failed. Was it worth it? Was it just her wounded pride? I would never behave that way, but will I feel those things if Canon and I take this step and it doesn't work out? We still have two months of shooting left. This is my first big break.

Is this *wise?*

These questions circle the drain in my head, over and over, but I keep coming back to a resounding YES.

"Are you there?" Takira nearly shouts. "I mentioned Canon's big dick energy and you got mighty quiet. You better not be fantasizing about him with me on the phone. That's creepy as hell."

"Shut up." I laugh. "No, I just... it's a big step. You see how he is on set with me. Like he barely knows I'm alive."

"Real talk? I see a man who doesn't know what to do with what he's feeling. That night at the Halloween party, I saw you on the balcony with him. Saw him *laughing*. This is Canon we're talking about, whose smiles occur about as frequently as solar eclipses. I saw the way he looked at you. It's so obvious to me he's feeling you. I don't know how everyone *doesn't* see it. I don't know how you don't."

"I do. It just feels like a mirage sometimes. One minute it's there and it's clear, but after a few days of silence and no contact, it wavers. It disappears."

"Canon did not get where he is playing games on set and jeopardizing his paper. He is famous for his work ethic. For his obsessive focus. The fact that he's breaking that, even for a few days with *you*, tells me all I need to know."

"You think so?"

"Oh, me know so, guhl," she says, slipping effortlessly into the islands. "Now, let's talk logistics. You got condoms? Never rely on men, who barely remember to wash their hands after they pee, to handle *your* protection."

I stuff the shiny gold squares in my overnight bag. "Got 'em."

"Brazilian?"

"Waxed yesterday."

"Lube?"

"Yep."

"Star pupil," she says. "Okay. I guess you're set."

"I need to go. Warmest regards," I tell her, tapping into our *Schitt's Creek* vernacular.

"Warmest regards, honey. Have fun."

After we hang up, I finish packing and roll my overnight bag into the foyer with a few minutes to spare. When the doorbell rings, my heart skydives right into the pit of my stomach.

"Hey," Canon says when I open the door.

He looks *goooood*. Like *good good*.

Who knew pink Lacoste polo shirts were my kink? Contrasting with the rich hue of his dark skin, his biceps straining at the short sleeves. With his aviators pushed up, his "movie beard" well groomed, he has me immediately imagining how those bristles will scrape the inside of my thighs when he eats me out. I'm so ready for this.

"Hey," I say, my voice husky, like I just smoked a cigarette after the fantasy in my head.

I devour him with my eyes and he must feel the nip of my teeth. Must sense the *he can get it* coming off me in ho-waves. He steps in, closes the door, and presses me into the nearest wall. There's no preface to this kiss. No permission needed because my arms are already tangling around his neck and my tongue is aggressive, sparring with his. When his fingers brush over the skin at my waist, bared by my crop top, there's reverence and urgency in his touch. His hands skid down to my ass and squeeze. He groans against my mouth and I moan into his. Desperation rises up and overtakes us. His hand slips beneath the waistband of my sweatpants, his fingers searching and unerring in my panties, caressing my clit for the first time.

"Shit," I pant, breaking the kiss and dropping my head to his shoulder, sensation rocking me from the core. "Canon."

"I told myself I wouldn't let this happen." He sucks at the curve of my neck. "I don't want our first time to be in your foyer, but *fuuuuuck*, Neevah. I missed you. You look…"

He dips his head, disappearing beneath the cropped edge of my sweatshirt. His mouth opens over my breast and he takes me through the skimpy lace of my bra. His tongue is hot and wet and hungry on my nipple. He sucks hard, his teeth closing around the tight bud, sending a jolt through me that turns all the cartilage in my knees to mush. I reach between us and find his cock, hard, ready, huge in my palm. I tug once, twice, and again until he growls and straightens abruptly. He pulls my top down and into place, and much to my pussy's dismay, withdraws from my panties.

"No." He shoves his hands into his pockets. "I have plans."

"But I have a bed." I tip my head down the hall. "It's a long drive to Santa Barbara. We could just take the edge off."

"Neevah, no. I mean... yes. Hell, yes." He drops a kiss on my forehead, wraps his palm around my nape. "But I didn't wait this long for you to rush. I want this to be special."

He angles his head so our gazes hold. "You *are* special. You know that, right? I don't do this. Everyone talks so much about Camille, but in my whole career, she's the only actress I've ever dated."

"She was special, too, then, huh?" I ask, holding my breath. Not that if he says yes it changes anything between us. I'm not above jealousy, though.

"Sure," he says, nodding slowly. "But we weren't right for each other. When I realized that, we'd already started. I had to shut it down. It was only going to get messier and more involved."

"She loved you?"

His stare doesn't falter, honesty on display. "She thought she did, yeah."

"You thought you loved her?"

"I thought maybe I could, but I quickly realized I was wrong." He takes a step back, giving me room to breathe. "If you have any reservations about this, I understand. I want you. I'm tired of fighting how much I want you, but I will respect your wishes, and it won't affect anything in our working relationship. I promise you that."

How could he think I could walk away now? I'm still wet from his touch. My heart is still thudding, scurrying around its little chamber like a trapped rabbit. And I still want him, not just the sex. Yes, oh my, yes. I want that, but I also want the secrets behind his guarded eyes; the sentiments locked away in his heart. And if I didn't know before, I know now.

I'm willing to risk a lot to have it.

THIRTY-SEVEN

Canon

This is not how I saw this going.

We've been driving for twenty minutes, and I've been on the phone the entire time. Neevah knows I'm a workaholic, but I wanted to make an effort to focus on this, on us for a few days, and not think about *Dessi Blue*.

"You there, Canon?" Evan's voice comes from my car's dashboard.

"Yeah. I'm driving, on my way out of town, so you don't exactly have my undivided attention."

"We have to be back on set in three days. Where are you going?"

"Just to Santa Barbara for New Year's. I'll be back, obviously."

"My invitation get lost in the mail?"

"Private party. Just me."

It's not exactly the truth, but the last thing I need is one of Evan's "keep your hands off the actresses" lectures.

I glance over at Neevah in the passenger seat. She's poring over her script and doesn't seem to even hear me. So much for us leaving work behind.

"Could we wrap this up?" I ask. "I have just a few days before the holiday break is over. I'm trying to unplug."

"You have a plug? I would have pulled it years ago had I known."

"So the permit for that site fell through," I say, ignoring his jabs and returning to the reason for the call. We'll never get off the phone if I don't.

"Right. Henry sent over a few other possibilities," he says of our locations manager.

"Like what?"

"Westward Beach."

"Hell. We may as well film in my backyard. That would be less familiar. I don't want to sell Westward Beach as the French Riviera."

"We don't have much time. We want to be on location in a month. Don't shoot down every suggestion."

"I promise to only shoot down the ridiculous ones."

"You're getting in that mode when nothing's good enough."

"No, just bring me better options. Damn, Evan."

I feel Neevah's eyes on me now, and I don't want to have this conversation with her in the car. She's not just my...shit, what are we calling each other at this stage? But she's also an actor in this film. We try our best to shield our cast and crew from the behind-the-scenes madness producers deal with.

"Hey. Lemme get where we're going and I'll call you tomorrow."

"We? I thought you were alone."

"I'll call you tomorrow. Text Jill and ask her to send me three better options than damn Westward Beach. Bye."

I disconnect before he can virtually waterboard me about who is with me. Evan would cough up a lung if he knew I was with Neevah. If he knew I'd kissed her. If he suspected I was wrist-deep in her panties not even an hour ago.

If I don't want to drive the next hour with this hard dick under my seat belt, I'll find something to think about besides Neevah slick and wet under my hand. Plenty of time to think about that when we get to Santa Barbara.

"Something wrong?" Neevah asks.

Nah. I'm always this erect.

"Uh...what?" I ask, hoping she hasn't noticed.

"The call with Evan. It sounded like the location for next month has fallen through."

"Oh. That. Yeah. We'll figure it out." I nod to the script in her lap. "How's that going?"

"Pretty good. I guess. With so much focus on the musical numbers I had to get down, there's some dialogue I haven't memorized yet." She puts her finger to her lips. "Shhhh. Don't tell my boss. He's a hard ass."

"Funny." I shoot her a speculative glance. "Do the actors think I'm a hard ass?"

"You know they all think you walk on water, right? You're demanding, but not mean. They've all told me horror stories of directors chewing them out in front of everyone. Of directors coming on to them."

Like inviting them for a few days on a private getaway...

"This isn't that, Canon." Neevah reaches over to take my hand, resting our linked fingers on my leg. "I want this as much as you do. You know that. I was attracted to you before you even offered me the part."

"You were?"

"When you phoned about the audition that first time..." She laughs, covering her face with her free hand. "I thought you might be calling to ask me out. I kind of hoped you were."

"Were you disappointed?" I ask, grinning and keeping my eyes on I-5.

"No. I just reminded myself it would not be a good idea to crush on my director."

My grin fades. "It's *not* a good idea."

She tugs my hand until I tear my gaze away from the road long enough to look at her. "It's not a crush. I don't need this to advance my career. And this isn't some misplaced hero-worship actor-director complex. I like you. I respect you. I want to know you. I want to fuck you. Any questions?"

Her bold statement lands on the console between us in the front seat, waiting for me to address it. If I wait for my dick to go down, we'll be here all day, so I'll just have to learn to converse intelligibly while this hard. It's like chewing gum and walking, only much more arousing.

"I'm not gonna lie to you. If...when this gets out, it could be messy," I tell her.

"I already told you I don't care what people say."

"You say that because you've never been on the cover of every major tabloid, or had cameras camped outside your house, or been stalked every time you go to the grocery store or Starbucks. That's what happened when shit went down with Camille. It's not fun."

"I hear you. I just want you to know I don't have any hesitation about some reporter implying I got this job because of anything between us. I'll prove myself. Our work will speak for itself."

"It's also that attention like that, that kind of scrutiny, it ruins relationships. I've seen too many relationships barely get off the ground before they fizzle, wreck because of the pressure." I squeeze her hand, glance at her. "I don't want that for us."

"I don't either," she says, stroking my thumb with hers.

"I'm willing to chance it because everything you just said you want with me"—I pull her hand up to my lips—"I bet I want it more with you."

When I glance over, her eyes glow with anticipation, desire, and something so sweet I want to teleport the last hour of this trip. I want everything I see in her eyes right now.

"You want it more than I do?" She shakes her head, pulling our two hands back down to rest on her thigh. "We'll see about that, Mr. Holt."

THIRTY-EIGHT

Neevah

I turn a slow circle in the grand entrance of the house Canon rented for us, taking in the magnificent chandelier and the spiral staircase leading to the next floor. Marble floors, discreetly lit paintings and unique sculptures lend the entrance a cool elegance.

"It's gorgeous, Canon."

He walks up beside me, bringing in our luggage, and places his hand at the small of my back. "A guy I met at Cannes a few years ago told me about it, and I've come here each year at least once ever since. Usually alone, of course. I haven't brought anyone with me before."

"Never?" I turn to look at him.

He smiles and kisses the top of my hair. "Come on. I'll show you the rest."

The rest turns out to be a gourmet kitchen, fully equipped with every imaginable modern convenience, a living room with a fireplace big enough for me to hibernate in, luxurious bathrooms outfitted with sunken tubs and waterfall shower heads, and a balcony that juts out over an infinity pool and spa. The tour ends at the bedrooms, two directly across from each other, both the height of luxury.

"And there's two bedrooms," Canon tells me in the hall bisecting the floor.

I walk into what is obviously the main suite and sit on the bed, leaning back and letting him see that we could do this right now. "Well, that seems redundant."

He walks over and stands between my legs, nudging them wider, caressing the sides with his palms, moving to touch my inner thigh, stroking down to the curve of my knee. Even through the fabric of my pants, the contact burns. He could take me this second. I would like that very much, please and thank you. He must know by the way my breaths jerk, pushing my breasts into a rough rhythm. He's heavy-lidded, his full lips parting as he looks down at me. My crop top rides up, showing him my skin. He traces one index finger down the shallow valley running between the muscles of my stomach, which quiver under his touch. I gulp, trying to regulate my breathing.

"Canon."

He steps back abruptly, taking the heat, the provocative touch with him. "You want to shower? Did you bring a dress?"

The rapid change from sensual to pragmatic gives me whiplash. "Um, I have a dress, yeah."

"Wear it for me." He bends to take my lips in a much-too-brief kiss. I reach up to caress his neck, but he pulls away, his smile down at me a tantalizing taunt. "I'll go get dinner started."

"You're cooking?" I sit up, breathing a little easier without this big man standing between my legs.

"I'm full of surprises," he calls from the hall. "Come down when you're ready."

I'm tempted to masturbate in the shower because the desire is so keen, but I want to save it all for him. I'm surprised I don't sizzle as soon as the water hits my skin. I'm pretty sure this is the most turned on I've been in my life.

I'm still soaked between my legs from imagination and my nipples are so tight, they're stiff beneath the bright yellow sundress when it melts over my body. I don't bother with a bra, tying the halter dress behind my neck and letting my breasts peak beneath the silk. I also forego panties because that just seems like a waste of time. The dress is muslin-thin, clinging to my ass and hips. I sincerely hope he can see the shadow of my pussy in the right light. I *refuse* to be hornier than he is, dammit.

When I come down the steps, he's in the kitchen and dressed in a button-up and slacks.

"When did you change?" I ask, coming up behind him and slipping my arms around his waist.

He turns, leaning against the counter and splaying his hands low on my hips, brushing against my ass. He stiffens when there's obviously nothing beneath the dress. When he looks back to me, the glow of desire in his eyes is worth all the trouble I've taken not only with my appearance tonight, but yesterday's beauty triathlon. I've been waxed, scrubbed, and exfoliated more than a season's worth of Bacherlorettes. If he likes to lick toes, mine have been buffed and manicured. When he wants the cat, I'm slick as a Slip 'N Slide down there. And should he feel so inclined to eat ass, nary a hair survived that Brutal Brunhilda wax-a-thon I endured on all fours at the spa. I'm ready for *anything*. I've practically been in training for this.

"When did you change?" I repeat, since he seems to have lost his train of thought as soon as he saw my nipples headlighting and realized I'm wearing zero panties.

"Oh." He clears his throat, tightening his grip at my waist. "There's a shower down here, so I changed while I put the food on."

"I didn't know you could cook." I force myself to step out of his arms, though I could stay there all night, and look at the salad with its vividly colored vegetables on the counter.

"My mother would not send me out into the world unable to cook at least a li'l something. I know my way around a grill."

"Oh." It occurs to me that we have never talked much about food. "I don't eat red meat."

"I know. They always make sure to have an alternative for you with our crafts foods order."

"Oh. Yeah."

"That night on the roof, you got shrimp, and on Thanksgiving, you ordered fish." He looks over his shoulder to the patio and the grill. "I hope salmon is okay? You had the salmon crepes so..."

I'm awed that a man as busy as he is, working on the movie of a lifetime, would pay attention to such fine details and my preferences.

"Uh, salmon is great. Thank you."

"You hungry?"

I nod, and he takes my hand, leading me out to the balcony. The sun hasn't quite set, still deciding between day and night. We're at that golden hour—a photographer's dream.

"You've been busy down here," I say, smiling at the table on the balcony, set with beautiful china and glassware, lit by candles. Soft music pipes in from invisible speakers.

"It didn't take much." He pulls my chair out.

"What a gentleman," I say, glancing up at him over my shoulder when I sit.

"We'll see if you still think so by the end of the night," he says at my ear, kissing my neck where the dress is secured.

I catch his hand, hold him in place. "I'm not *that* hungry. We don't have to wait."

"I told you I have plans." He chuckles, pulling away and sitting across from me. "We'll get there."

I want to go all Willy Wonka Veruca Salt and tell him I want it now, but that didn't end so good for her. I can be a little patient a little while longer. I pick up my fork and slice into the food he prepared. Canon Holt cooked dinner for me.

Chewing, he points his fork at my face. "What's that smile about?"

"I was just thinking that I've never had a famous director cook for me." I take a bite of the salmon and groan. "And it's actually delicious."

"I am a man of many talents. Most of them behind a camera, but I can burn a little when pressed."

"And you were pressed?" I smile at him through the candlelight. "I'm actually pretty easy to please. You didn't have to go to all this trouble."

"I wanted tonight to be—"

"Special. I know."

The humor fades from his expression, and his face grows serious. "You have to be sure before we do this, Neevah. Even now, it's not too late to change your mind."

"We can skip dinner, as far as I'm concerned." I lay my fork down. "I'm not afraid of coming off as too eager, Canon. I *am* eager. You said you can read me easily anyway, so I can't hide that. You know I want you."

His stare doesn't waver, but darkens, the long lashes dropping as desire stirs behind his eyes.

"But I want more than sex," I confess. "I'm not saying it has to be serious, but I do want you to know this means something to me. You called me generous, and I am, onstage, when I perform, but I've never slept with anyone I worked for. I do hold myself back in this. I'm careful about who I share my body with, so when I do this with you, it will already be special to me."

Even through the soft beard, I see the muscle in his jaw flexing. His fists clench on the table by his plate. He looks like a man on the verge of losing control, and I want to push him over the edge. Before I can, the music changes and the low throb of bass ushers in Luther's opening lyrics of "If This World Were Mine," temporarily distracting me. Canon smiles, standing from the table and holding out his hand. Did he remember our conversation on the balcony? Arrange this?

"Is this a coincidence?" I ask, standing on shaky legs.

"I'm a director," he says, pulling me into his arms to sway with the languid chorus. "Things are rarely coincidental with me."

I laugh up at him, my heart a turnstile in my chest, and link my wrists behind his neck. The night has grown cooler, and I can't discern if the goose bumps splattering my arms are from the air or his hands moving on my bare skin, kneading the muscles into languor. Or the soft caress of him at my neck when he dips to breathe in the scent behind my ear. The sky has darkened, smudged into nightfall, lit by stars like lanterns. With the pool below glimmering like a jewel, these minutes in his arms, held close, are the most perfect I can remember.

I frame his face, the distinctive bone structure hard beneath my hands.

"And you say you're not a romantic," I whisper.

"I'm not. I just like *you*."

"Then I'm one lucky girl." I try to laugh, but what's happening tonight, now, means too much. I can't play it off or make it any less. It feels like the universe has come down to these seconds under a watching sky. It's come down to the contact between our bodies and our breaths, growing more ragged the longer we sway together. To our eyes, melded by passion and something subtly stronger.

He takes my chin between his thumb and forefinger and tugs until I open for him. The kiss, when it comes, starts tender with nibbles and brushes, but it soon consumes, our tongues sliding together, our hands searching, seeking, gripping, and squeezing.

"Upstairs," he gasps against the curve of my shoulder.

I nod, twining my fingers with his when he takes my hand, and he leads me up the steps. Lamps glow on either side of the bed, and the soft music has followed us, playing faintly in here, too.

He touches my face, running his knuckle over my cheekbone. "You're beautiful, Neevah. It wasn't the first thing I noticed about you, and it's not the most important, but I want you to know."

I reach up and brush my fingertips across the fullness of his lips. "And every time I make you smile, I feel like I've conquered the world."

His eyes, heated and hungry, slide over me, from the crown of my head to my open-toe shoes. "Then make me smile."

I've been waiting for this moment, but now that it's here, I'm unsure where to start.

Does she hold nothing back?

Canon said he asked himself that question when he saw me perform in *Splendor*, and I know. The first thing I'll do is give him everything.

My fingers find the tie of the halter at my neck, tugging until the top of the dress loosens and falls. The swell of my hips and ass anchors the dress on my body, but my torso—shoulders, stomach, breasts—is naked in the dim light.

With his bottom lip trapped between his teeth, Canon drags a finger across my collarbone, over the curve of my shoulder, down my arm to link our fingers. Tugging me closer, he looks down at me for long seconds. Not at my breasts, tight and heaving with anticipation, but into my eyes, and it makes me feel more exposed than the coolness of the air kissing my skin. I'm glass to him, he said, and he searches my eyes like he's peering into my head, turning my soul over in his hands. I don't even want to think about what he sees in my heart.

Just as I'm not sure I can bear the scrutiny anymore without his touch, he dips to kiss one nipple. My head drops back, exposing the line of my neck. He still holds one hand, and I tighten my grip on his fingers, needing the support to stand as his lips close around the tip, his teeth scraping gently. We are connected at only two points, our joined fingers and his mouth at my breast, but it feels like every inch of me is pressed to the length of him. My eyes are closed, but the air shifts in front of me when he drops to his knees. He releases my hand to grip my hips. I look down, and his eyes climb over me, starting with my belly button, skimming my stomach, and up my breasts until he reaches my face. His motions haven't been hurried, and his hands haven't been swift, so the wild hunger in his eyes startles me, and I realize he's controlling it. He's reined it in, and more than anything, I want to snap it like a twig.

I push at the silk puddled at my hips, coaxing the dress down my legs to pool around my shoes. I wind my fingers into the rough waves of his hair and subtly coax his head toward my bare pussy.

He breathes deeply and then rests his mouth against the lips, not opening me, or tasting.

"Jesus, Neev," he says, his whisper a caress over my sensitive skin.

I want to push him so far over the edge of his restraint, there is no going back. I step out of my shoes and slip trembling fingers between my legs, passing over my clit and through the wetness dripping down my inner thighs.

His breaths grow labored as he follows the motion of my fingers with his eyes. When I pull my hand away, the air cools my fingertips. With deliberate boldness, I hold his stare and glaze his lips with my fingers, adorning his mouth with my wetness. He growls against my pussy, the vibration of it playing over my nerves like a timpani.

"Spread your legs," he orders hoarsely.

I obey, widening my stance and waiting for his next move.

The breath stutters in my chest when his big fingers peel back the lips like petals, exposing the throbbing hood.

At first, he just licks it once.

I shudder, my knees almost failing me.

He pulls my whole clit into his mouth, sending an arrow of pleasure shooting through my body. His head bobs, his mouth moving against me with great force, with growing hunger. He cups my ass and nudges me back the few feet to the bed. With a gentle shove, I'm down, laid out on my back, completely nude while he is fully clothed, my legs dangling over the side of the bed, spread for him.

He wastes no time.

The sounds he makes when he feasts on my pussy will visit me in my dreams. Like a ravenous animal, he grunts and pants into the slick strip of nerves and flesh. He coaxes my legs up, sets my heels on the edge of the bed until my knees are bent and wide. His fingers push into me and I sit up on my elbows, unable to lay back any longer and desperate to see.

Three big fingers spear in and out, shiny with my wetness. He looks at me while he does it, and it is the most intimate act I've ever known. His beard gleams with my juices and he licks his lips, closing his eyes like the taste of me mesmerizes him. He shifts his hand, pushing his thumb inside and using all four fingers to squeeze and caress my clit, alternating the two touches until my breath huffs through my mouth. Spots appear before my eyes and I fall back again on the coolness of the comforter, helpless as the orgasm clenches the muscles in my legs and burns up my thighs until my pussy contracts around his fingers, gripping and flexing compulsively. I cover my eyes and scream, my release echoing in the room, slamming into the walls.

"Oh, God, Canon." It comes out as a broken sob, my body weeping for him in every way. Pouring out my desire like an offering, and wrenching tears from my eyes. His mouth slows, less urgent, licking, tasting, savoring.

When he stands, my knees are still bent, my legs pushed up. There's no dignity to it, and I don't give a damn. I ache for him. As my orgasm crests and falls, the emptiness where he should be yawns and yells.

"Canon, please," I whisper, careless of the tears slipping from the corners of my eyes. The ache is so strong, a creature demanding to be fed. "Right now."

He stands over me, still fully clothed, eyes blazing, nostrils flaring. I've never seen him like this. Canon has always been careful when and how he looks at me, reducing our contact to the minimum, so this unfiltered, unchecked force of his attention flies like sparks across my skin. There's something primitive and possessive in the stare that sweeps my body. The way he looms over me makes me feel small and powerful in the same breath.

I raise to my knees and reach for him. Lashes lowered, he watches me slide the buttons loose and spread the shirt open over his broad chest.

I feel, in some ways, like he was at an advantage. I've done sex scenes and been nearly nude on set. He's seen almost everything even before tonight, but I've only fantasized about the sculpted heat of his body. I tug at his belt, freeing it from the loops of his pants, and with deceptively steady fingers, unbutton and unzip, pushing them to the floor.

He's such a beautiful specimen and, under my hungry eyes, completely immobile. Still and waiting for my next move. It makes me feel even more powerful, this man, so completely in charge of everything all the time, at my mercy. Awaiting my pleasure and his. I slip my fingers beneath the waistband of his briefs and push them to the floor, too.

Big dick energy, indeed.

With one hand, I grip his neck, urge his head down, and crash our lips together. The kiss, spiced with my essence, spins my head and sends pinpricks of sensation through my body. While our tongues and breaths tangle, I reach between us and grip his cock, tugging at first tentatively and then with confidence. His breath grows ragged over my lips until our kiss dissolves altogether and his mouth opens on a groan.

My hand looks so small wrapped around him. I rub my thumb over the glistening head, spreading the slickness. I sit on the bed, wanting to take him into my mouth, but he stops me, his hand gripping my hair and holding my head back.

"Next time," he rasps.

Wordlessly, he climbs onto the bed, pulling me with him until his back rests against the headboard. Taking me by the hips, he guides me up and over his thighs until I'm straddling him. My pussy throbs with the promise of finally being filled, and I whimper at the delay when he reaches over to the bedside table, grabs a condom, and slides it over himself.

He runs his palms down my back, skimming my spine and spreading my ass.

"You okay?" he asks, searching my face in the warm light.

I nod. "I want this, Canon."

"Me too." He leans in to kiss me, and it's passionate, rough, and searching and demanding, his tongue plundering my mouth. All the while, he's shifting me forward until I'm poised over him. I spread my legs wider and guide him inside.

We gasp, pressing our foreheads together as our bodies break this seal. There is a little bit of a burning stretch as I become accustomed, but it feels right. It feels like my body was molded for this moment, for this man. With my knees on either side of his legs, I rock forward, driving him deeper, and his jaw clenches. His grip on my ass tightens, and he lifts me a little to reach my breast, pulling it into the cavern of his mouth. He reaches between us to the nexus of our bodies, and his finger slips over my clit, the rough pad caressing it with each roll of my hips. I've come once, but with his tongue and teeth at my nipple, his finger on my clit, and his hard dick filling me up, the orgasm builds again. He flips our positions, pressing me into the bed and pushing back inside before I can catch my breath.

"Canon," I pant into the sweat-slick crook of his neck, sliding my hands down his back to clutch his ass. "Fuck me."

He chokes out a laugh. "I am. Shit, Neevah."

He thrusts so deep, I stop breathing for a second and relish the shock of it. I wrap my arms around his neck and link my ankles behind his back as the pace of our lovemaking changes, shifting from long, deep, smooth strokes to a desperate cadence too frantic for me to control. Trying to is like riding the wind, like swimming in a tsunami. I'm tossed high and hard, helpless, weightless. When he comes with a deep growl, one hand clawed in my hair, the other gripping my thigh, I follow with a sob and a possessive kiss that marks him as mine as surely as I'm branded his however he wants me.

THIRTY-NINE

Canon

"We should leave the house today." I say this while we float naked in the swimming pool.

"Why?" Neevah asks, and with her breasts bobbing at the water's surface, her taut stomach and bare pussy visible in the water as she stands before me, I have to ask the same question.

"It's Santa Barbara," I say, only half-heartedly. "One of the most beautiful cities in the country. You should see something other than this place. And it's not LA. Less exposure, not that I have paparazzi trailing me or anything."

She swims the few feet over, her long, naked limbs slicing through the water. When she stands in front of me, her head only reaches my chin, and she tilts up, holds my gaze.

"But there's so much to do right here," she teases, her eyes growing sultry. Her hand moves between us and she takes my cock, pulling slowly, firmly.

"You're insatiable." I lift her so she can wrap her legs around me, and even though I don't enter, she rubs against me, the friction sweet and hot and glorious.

"You love that about me," she whispers into a kiss, her water-slick hands gripping my shoulders. "Fuck me again, Canon."

"We don't have a condom."

"Then at least make me come." She nips at my ear, running her palm over my nipple.

I slip my hand between our bodies, inching two fingers inside her.

"Oh my God." She rocks into the thrust of my fingers, tipping her head back until the sun glazes her face and neck, highlighting her clear skin, completely free of makeup.

I finger her and stroke her clit, suck on her nipples, until she shudders in my arms, rippling like the water around us.

Laughing at my neck, she pulls back to smile into my eyes. I return the smile and kiss her lightly on the lips. I can't remember a time in my life where I felt like this. This happy. This satisfied. This starved. This possessive. Every emotion seems to be exaggerated with Neevah.

I've always been obsessive about my work, about my art. For the first time, I think I've found something else, some*one* else, to inspire that kind of intensity. She's ruining me and I have no idea how to stop it. I'm not sure I want to.

It's scary as hell.

Because that gives her so much power, probably power she doesn't even realize she has. And I know she feels the same. I didn't lie when I said I could read her easily. She doesn't hide the emotion in her eyes when she comes. Doesn't pretend it's just fucking, or treat it lightly. I don't think she knows how to do that—to hold herself back. She is as generous in bed as she is on the stage or on camera. She scatters kisses over my face while the sweetest, dirtiest things spill from her lips into my ears. At the same time, there's a fearlessness about her, the same quality that makes her think it will all work out when people discover us. I hope she's right.

God help anyone who comes after her for wanting me—who tries to sabotage her career or dim her light. I can't protect her from all the pitfalls of Hollywood, but I'll shelter her from as much of the ugliness as I can.

Her eyelids are heavy in the wake of her orgasm, her body limp and boneless in my arms. I walk us out of the pool, uncaring that neither of us wears a stitch of clothing. This property is completely private and enclosed.

Instead of giving her a lounge chair of her own, I stretch out on one and lay her on top of me. She probably thinks I'm a stage-three clinger, but in a few days we'll go back to having very little contact. I want as much as I can get while I can have it.

"It's New Year's Eve," I tell her. "We should go out. Santa Barbara only does fireworks for the Fourth, not New Year's, but there will be parties on the waterfront. It'll be fun."

She cuddles into my side, making room for herself on the narrow lounge chair. "I don't want to go back tomorrow. I know we have to and I know we start shooting again, but I love this with you. I don't want to go back to *not* having it."

I don't either, but I know it will be best for my focus, her career, and our movie. I lift her chin, kiss her nose. "Only until the movie wraps."

"It'll fly by?"

I'm quiet because two months without this, even an hour, feels too long. I nod, laughing when she rolls her eyes at my subdued response. I slap her bare butt lightly and shift to stand.

"Get your pretty ass up." I extend my hand to pull her to her feet. "They don't call this the American Riviera for nothing."

"Did you guys consider Santa Barbara for the new location? If it's supposed to be America's French Riviera?"

It's such an obvious solution, I can't believe neither Evan nor I suggested it. I must be losing brain cells every time I come.

"Good idea. I'll mention that to Evan. Let's get inside so we can shower and get you out for New Year's Eve." I take her hand, and pause, noticing a small rash on her arm. "What's that? Sunburn or—"

"Dammit." She touches the rash and shakes her head. "It's that skin condition I told you about. I have to be really careful out in the sun. It wasn't that hot or bright when we first came out and I didn't realize how much sun I was taking in."

"Do you need some lotion or—"

"I have something from my dermatologist." She flashes a smile and rushes past me into the house. "I'm gonna shower and take care of this."

She dashes up the steps, and I call after her. "Leave in an hour?"

"Yup," she says over her shoulder, not looking back.

I've needed the last twenty-four hours. Not just the lovemaking, though it's the best on record. The conversation. Dream swapping. Being a director requires you to be a pragmatist who never stops dreaming. Last night in the huge master bathtub, we soaked together until the bubbles she poured in evaporated, along with all our reservations. With her back to my front, our legs and arms entwined, she told me her ambitions and I shared the stories I still want to tell. My life is a turntable in constant motion, and I can't remember the last time I slowed down this way. She makes me want to slow down so I don't miss a thing.

Dessi Blue has consumed most of my waking moments for the last two years, but I've barely thought about the movie since we arrived. I was right to hold out as long as I did, because if I'd felt this, had this with Neevah for the last few months, I wouldn't have been able to concentrate for shit. Not at the level I need to. Helming a film, especially one of this scope, requires an almost inhuman amount of focus, to the exclusion of nearly everything else.

We have two months of shooting left. I have to turn this off, this near-feral desire to have Neevah, to be with her, if I'm going to give the project the attention it deserves in this final stretch. After the movie wraps, we can discreetly pick up where we leave off here, and fuck anyone who has anything to say about it. There's not an acceptable scenario where we don't take this further—not after this time together.

I take the stairs two at a time and enter the bedroom. It's empty, but the shower is running. I step into the bathroom, but she's not in the shower yet. She's at the mirror, her hair lifted as she examines a tiny spot at the base of her nape using another mirror.

"Everything okay?"

She jumps and drops the mirror. It shatters on the floor.

"Hey, easy." I walk forward carefully, picking my way around the glass, and lift her up onto the bathroom counter. "I don't want you to cut your feet. Stay right there."

I walk back out to the bedroom, slip on my sneakers, and go downstairs to get a broom. I probably look ridiculous, running butt-naked wearing nothing but Jordans.

The mirror broke in big chunks, so it's easy to clean up. I sweep the area thoroughly, but still bring Neevah's flip-flops to her just in case. She hasn't moved or spoken throughout the whole process, and I tweak her toe. I've never seen this look in her eyes before. Worry or fear. I'm not sure what it is, but even the day she was so shaken shooting that difficult scene, she didn't look like this.

"Baby, you okay?" I reach up to touch the spot she was looking at in the mirror, but she jerks away.

"Don't," she says, her voice low and curt. She jumps off the counter and walks to the shower to test the water temperature with her fingertips before turning back to me.

"I'm sorry." Her throat moves with a deep swallow. "I didn't mean to be short. I'm frustrated with myself, not with you, because I stayed out in the sun too long and it can aggravate my skin."

"It's okay. God knows I've been abrupt a time or two."

She gives me a wry look.

"Alright, many times I've been abrupt." I laugh, but sober, struck by the concern she carefully smooths away from her expression.

She did tell me about her skin condition. I'm kicking myself for not thinking of it.

"You sure everything's okay?"

"It really is." She brightens, but I'm not sure I buy it yet. "Let's get dressed and bring in the New Year."

FORTY

Neevah

Downtown Santa Barbara did not come to play this New Year's Eve.

The massive crowd swarms the waterfront, moving to the DJ's music, reveling on the oceanside dance floor, and drinking enough liquor to float the *Titanic*.

"Just a friendly reminder," I yell in Canon's ear to be heard over the music. "We could be home fucking right now, but noooooo."

He tips his head back, laughing, his expression as open as I've ever seen it. Canon has a whole league of frowns I could spend hours categorizing. The distracted frown, indicating anything you say to him right now will be forgotten five seconds later. The *we can do better* frown, when he's looking at something that isn't quite up to his standards and trying to improve it. The *fuck off* frown when he cannot comprehend that you would actually bother him while he's doing something this important. The *no your ass did not* frown he reserves for actors who come unprepared or are (*gasp!*) late to his set. Fortunately, I've never been on the receiving end of that one.

"You not enjoying yourself?" His breath feathers over my ear. I shiver and press our bodies so close, not even the cooling night air intrudes between us.

"I am because you're here, but we're back in LA tomorrow, and then things return to normal."

"Do you want things to go back to normal?" The question in his eyes goes beyond the one he's asking, but he's my frosted glass, so I can only guess what that question could be.

"Don't they have to? I mean, since you don't want to go public." I hold up my hand to stem the flow of words I know is coming. "And I get all your reasons, but if there's a storm when and if this comes out, I'm ready to weather it."

"I think that may be the new ride or die." He chuckles, guiding us off the dance floor and toward a row of reserved tables at the water's edge. Canon actually dances and is pretty good. Surprised the hell outta me. Even though I teased him about this crowd, it's nice being out having fun and enjoying New Year's Eve like a typical couple. Canon wears a baseball cap just in case, but says he's not the brand of famous that people usually immediately recognize unless they're in the business or want to be. Since half the servers in New York and LA are aspiring actors, the chances are better. The cap tonight is an extra precaution.

"Soon you'll be the one recognized when we go out," he says, sitting at the table and pulling me onto his knee.

The announcement in *The Hollywood Reporter* that I landed the role didn't raise my profile much. My agent got a few nibbles, but beyond some curiosity, the industry is largely waiting to see how I do. Canon has been relatively tight-lipped about the movie, so while there is some anticipation, people don't really know what *Dessi Blue* is or what to expect. We've had a few entertainment shows come on set to get behind-the-scenes footage and cast interviews, but usually under the condition that the spots air closer to release.

"You know," I say, sitting on his lap and snuggling into the clean scent of him, "it's funny we're talking about being out together in the future since I could've sworn you didn't even like me in the beginning. You barely spoke to me and seemed irritated when you had to."

"Growing up, was there ever a boy who called you names, pulled your hair, and then tried to kiss you behind the sliding board on the playground?"

"Yeah, because it's never too early for toxic masculinity."

His face falls, and then he grins. "I was gonna say it's kinda like that, but never mind."

We laugh and eat bar food and drink, though I stick to water. Especially given the rash I found on my arms and legs, and the spots on my scalp, I'm staying away from alcohol. I get one glass of champagne to ring in the New Year, but that's it. I'll schedule a video call appointment with Dr. Ansford when we get back. I can't afford my body to start acting up now.

I shove those worries into my *not right now, can't you see I'm partying* box, and indulge in another hour of dancing, food, and the most stimulating conversation I've ever had. I've felt indifferent for so long, with no guy really holding my interest. Canon is like a supernova when you've been staring up at an empty, starless sky, and I cannot get enough of him. Even in the crowd, it feels intimate as we quiz each other with any and every question that comes to mind.

There's an anonymity in this partying press of bodies, and I take advantage of it, resting on Canon's chest, reaching up to caress his neck, kissing his chin. It's that much sweeter because I'm not sure when we'll get to be this open again. I pour my affection, my desire, into every look and every gesture for the next few hours, and Canon reciprocates, not holding back how much he wants me.

"At this rate," he says against my lips as we sway on the dance floor, "you won't even want to kiss at midnight."

We are lost in this writhing congregation of dancers, and I reach between us to grip his cock through his jeans. "This is where I want to kiss you at midnight."

I pull on him and slip my hand beneath his T-shirt, grazing my nails down his back. He shudders, the response reverberating into my chest, and clenches his eyes shut.

"You win," he says, resting his temple against mine. "Let's get out of here and go home. There are better ways to bring in the New Year."

He leads me off the dance floor and down to the water's edge. The house is about a mile up the shoreline, and I'm glad we walked.

We take off our shoes and venture close enough for the cool waves to lap at our feet. Several other couples shunned the waterfront party for the serenity of the beach, and we smile at them as we go, wishing each other a Happy New Year, even though we're still shy of midnight. It's an evening made of champagne, moonlight, and new beginnings.

"I know you need to get back tomorrow and start preparing to shoot," I tell him, squeezing his hand. "But—"

"I was thinking leisurely breakfast in bed." He stops on the beach, turning me into his arms and kissing the top of my head. "And take our time getting on the road."

"That sounds perfect." I grip his shoulders, nearly drunk on the ocean breeze and *him*. I don't care that we're still minutes from midnight. I want another kiss right now because life is short and fickle. I want to take life—to take him as my own at least for now. I fill my hands with this moment until it runs over, spilling into a desperate kiss with the ocean licking at our heels and the night still waiting.

"Canon?"

His name being called is like a scratch across a classic record, and so out of place in this alternate universe, that for a moment, neither of us moves.

"Canon?" a woman asks a second time.

Canon's head snaps around. We turn to greet the woman standing in our path, holding a man's hand on one side and a dog's leash on the other.

"I thought that was you earlier." Her smile widens. "Didn't I say it looked like Canon, Ralph?"

For his part, Ralph looks self-conscious, recognizing he's interrupted an intimate moment. His companion, however, is too obtuse or too rude to keep it moving.

"Well, it's dark," Ralph mumbles. "So I wasn't sure."

It is dark, but there are some lights on the beach, and the glow of moonlight reveals a middle-aged woman with silver hair. I can't make out the color of her eyes, but I know that as they flick between Canon and me, they are curious.

"Aren't you going to introduce us?" she asks Canon.

"Sure," Canon says, his voice terse. "Sylvia and Ralph Miller, this is Neevah Saint. Neevah, Ralph and Sylvia." He doesn't elaborate and beneath the beard, the angle of his jaw goes stony.

"Uh, hi."

I accept the hands they proffer, forcing a smile. I have no idea who they are, and running into anyone we know would be bad, but the tension their presence introduced tells me they are especially unwelcome.

"Oh, yes." Sylvia's eyes round and she looks like she just charted the route to Mars. "That's where I know you from. I saw the announcement. Canon, you'll have to share your new star with the world sooner or later, though I can see why you like keeping her to yourself."

"In due time," Canon says, his expression falling into familiar lines of inscrutability. "Enjoy the rest of your evening. We better get back."

"Staying nearby, are you?" she probes. "We love our place here. Such a great escape from LA."

"Right." Canon takes my hand and starts walking away. "Good seeing you."

It obviously was anything *but* good seeing them. Canon sighs heavily and shakes his head.

"Idiot," he mutters under his breath, looking out over the ocean.

"You better not be talking to me," I tease, tugging his hand. He doesn't quite smile, but he does pull me into the crook of his arm, into his side as we walk. "Who was that?"

"One of the biggest mouths in Hollywood," he says grimly. "Camille's publicist."

FORTY-ONE

Neevah

"Chile, you glowing, and I haven't even put on your makeup yet."

I meet Takira's eyes in the mirror and suppress a grin.

"I do drink a lot of water," I tell her, sipping from my ever-handy bottle. "That helps."

"Hmmm. I got your water right here. You been mighty quiet about that trip to Santa Barbara."

Even though we're alone in my trailer, I'm a little uncomfortable discussing our trip while I'm on set. Seeing Camille's publicist obviously irritated Canon and underscored the need for discretion.

"In my defense," I say, "you got back long after I was asleep and we were both nodding off in the back seat when the driver picked us up this morning, so we haven't really talked."

"True. That was a nice few days off, but I'm ready to get back at it. Hard to believe we only have two months left, and then we can go home."

I fiddle with a pile of hairpins in my lap. Two months before I put thousands of miles between Canon and me.

"You just did one of them woe-is-me sighs when I mentioned going home," Takira says, brushing my hair and prepping for the Dessi wig. "What's that all about?"

"No. I just…I don't have my next thing lined up yet. My agent has a new Broadway production she'd like me to audition for, but that would be committing to a show. And I might want to be more flexible." I hazard a glance up at her in the mirror. "Maybe even stay out here in LA for a few months to see what happens."

Takira lets her hands drop from my hair and puts them on her hips. "I knew it."

"Knew what?"

"That Canon. He inserted his dick directly into your heart, didn't he?"

I scrunch my expression. "Maybe a little bit?"

We both crack up laughing, and, leaning one hip against the vanity, she swivels my chair around to face her. "We got a few minutes to spare. Tell me how good it was."

"It was like Drake's the-best-you-ever-had sex. It was like Idris-on-a-cracker sex. It was like…if-your-favorite-vibrator-was-a-great-listener-and-sparkling-conversationalist-and-cooked-you-dinner-and-made-you-feel-like-the-only-girl-in-the-world…sex."

"Shut your mouth." Takira's eyes stretch wide. "Our grumpy director."

"Gets really ungrumpy, yeah, but shhhh. We're keeping it quiet until after the movie wraps."

Takira turns my chair back around and starts brushing my hair again. "Just be careful with that heart of yours. Remember the last time you were gonna make a career decision with a man in mind?"

"Ugh. Don't remind me."

"It's in my BFF job description to remind you." Her face softens, sympathy in her eyes. "I'm sorry it didn't go well over Christmas with your sister."

"It's alright." I force a smile. "I didn't expect all my problems with Terry to be solved just like that, but I also didn't expect it to be this hard. I guess we've waited too long and let it get too bad. I'm not sure what it'll take to repair things."

"Well, you know I'm here for you." She pats my shoulder and winks. "Whatever you need."

Takira and I tell each other everything, and I'm sure I'll be ready to talk more freely about Canon soon. It's not just our self-imposed muzzle order that keeps me reticent. The time we spent together, the steps we took forward, were precious to me. I want to keep it as just ours for a while.

I'd thought it would be hard not having contact with Canon, getting back to the set and pretending we aren't together while we're working. I underestimated Canon's near-obsessive focus.

And my own.

This is the role of a lifetime, and when I step on that set, I give it everything. Kenneth continues providing most of my notes, but on the rare occasion that Canon delivers feedback himself, it's with the same firm thoughtfulness he shows every other actor. Even though I miss him, we both do our jobs with the same professionalism we demonstrated before we went away together. I'm living off our few text messages and phone calls, but not much contact so far.

I don't know if I got soft or spoiled or what over the holiday break, but by the weekend our first week back, I'm done. I can barely move or keep my eyes open. When the car drops me off Saturday evening, everything aches. We adhere to a blended production schedule. French hours when possible, grind it out when necessary. We have five days of shooting and a day built in for rehearsals. That leaves Sunday as my only day off.

So I can't wait for Sunday, and I have every intention of sleeping until noon.

For this reason, I ignore my phone when it rings at eight o'clock in the a.m., and drift right back to sleep.

"Hey."

I bat one hand at something tickling my nose.

"Neevah, wake up."

Another tickle.

I crack one eye open and bring the object of my disruption into focus.

"Canon?" I croak, because you gotta croak at this ungodly hour.

"It's nine o'clock," he says. "Not ungodly."

"Am I talking in my sleep?"

"You're talking. I'm not sure if you're asleep. Your eyes are open."

"They are?"

"Do you see me?" he asks, amused indulgence in his voice.

I pull my pillow over my face. "Not now I don't. How'd you get in?"

"The usual way. Unlawful entry."

I poke my head out from under the pillow and stare at him.

"Takira let me in. You are in that deep sleep. I should let you rest." He stands. "I'll check in with you later."

"Wait." I sit up, the sight of him leaving jostling me from my near-catatonic state. "Why are you here? I thought we were...you know, not doing that."

He crosses back over to sit on the bed again. "I thought we could be extra careful and stealthy on our day off."

"Like, lay in bed and eat and make love for hours? 'Cause I'm very much down for that."

His raspy laughter awakens all my below-the-belt parts and makes me shiver. "I had other plans, but if that's what you want to do."

He leans over, sinewy forearms on either side of my head, and dips to take my lips possessively. I open my mouth, tangle our tongues, and then...

"Morning breath," I mumble against his lips, pushing at his shoulders.

"Don't care." He kisses down my neck, nudges the strap of my nightgown aside to lick my collarbone.

"I do." I laugh and shove him again. "I want to brush my teeth." I reach up to touch my silk sleep-scarf. "And do my hair and wash my face. We can't lose the mystery this early in our relationship."

"Who needs mystery when I can have stale breath and a drooly pillow?"

"I do not drool!" I bop my pillow over his head.

"Okay. Okay." He tosses the pillow to the floor, grabs my wrists, and pins them over my head, pressing me into the mattress with the weight of his chest, of his hard, warm body. "Do you want to hear about my stealthy plans or not?"

"Will there be food?"

"Definitely."

"Will there be hiking or any physical activity? Because I swear if I have to drag my body up anything today—"

"It's restful and low-key. Promise."

"Will there be kissing?"

His full lips twitch. "If you're a good girl."

"Good girls won't suck your dick the way I can."

Lust narrows his eyes and flares his pupils. "I think you're onto something with that staying-in-bed plan."

He looms over me again, his mouth descending. I giggle and push him away. Rolling off the bed and to my feet, I stride to the bathroom and look back at him stretched out, hands behind his head, watching me with embers in his eyes. His lazy smile blazes bright, even, and easy. Canon is so reserved, I didn't expect humor to take to his face this effortlessly, but it does, crinkling his eyes at the corners and slashing grooves into his lean, bearded cheeks. My heart pinches because I recognize the gift of seeing him this open when he only shows the world so much.

"Do I have time for a quick shower?" I ask, my voice coming out husky, which I hope he takes for Barry White morning voice instead of the unexpected emotion it is.

He glances at his watch. "Very quick. Dress comfortably."

He's wearing dark jeans, Jordans, and a long-sleeve *I'm Gonna Git You Sucka* T-shirt.

"I like that shirt," I say, going to start my shower.

"This movie's a classic. Do you need help with that shower?"

"No, lecher!" I yell, peeling off my short nightgown. "If you come in this bathroom when I'm naked, we'll never get out of here for our secret date."

"You've got a point."

Twenty minutes later, I'm ready, clad in dark jeans and a statement sweatshirt of my own.

"Zora Neale Hurston, huh?" He nods to the sketch on my chest of one of my favorite authors. "I like."

"I'm re-reading *Their Eyes Were Watching God* in all the spare time my boss leaves me."

"You have spare time?" He frowns. "I must not be doing it right. I'm obviously not working you guys hard enough."

"Tell that lie." I chuckle wryly. "I keep a book in my bag since we have so much stop and go on set."

"You finished *Schitt's Creek?*"

"We're saving the final season. I don't know what I'll do when it's done, so I'm reading instead."

Takira's door is closed, and when I poke my head in, she's gone back to sleep. I lock the front door behind me, glancing around the quiet neighborhood to make sure no one is watching us. We make our way up the driveway to the black Land Rover parked on the street. Buried in my script, I didn't think much about the car he drives when we went to Santa Barbara. Now, I take in the luxury as we climb in and buckle up.

"Nice ride," I tell him, running my hands along the supple leather seats.

"Thanks."

"Are you a car guy?"

He lifts one brow and glances over at me as we pull away from the curb. "You mean like do I have an underground garage with maybe ten sports cars? No."

"Just this one?"

"One other, but it's a classic. I don't spend a lot of money on cars."

"Clothes?"

"No. I mean, I like clothes, but I don't spend an inordinate amount of money on them."

"What then? What do you splurge on?"

"Honestly? Travel. As soon as I finish a project, I go somewhere I've never been or a place I love to go that has nothing to do with work."

"I didn't get to travel much growing up. My mother was afraid of flying." I smile, thinking of how adamant Mama was about it. "Even that family reunion I told you about in New York. Greyhound bus."

"Wow. So you haven't been out of the country much."

"Does a girls' trip to Mexico count?"

"Barely. We could drive to Mexico right now."

"After high school, I went straight to Rutgers. Then I did some regional theater, some touring, but it was all in the States."

"Now that's a shame. We gotta get you out."

"Where would you take me?" I turn in my seat a little, angling to see his face.

"Hmmm." He taps the steering wheel. "Paris first. Is that too cliché?"

"Won't hear me complaining. Where to next?"

"Johannesburg. My father's there, but we won't hold that against it." He flashes me a grin. "The City of Gold. It's gorgeous. There's several countries we need to hit in Africa."

"And?"

"Maybe Santorini. One of the Greek islands. It's stunning. The architecture is like an extension of the landscape. White houses, blue doors and windows. Like sky and the Aegean Sea. I've never seen anything like it."

"I'd love to see that," I say, my smile dissolving as I realize just how limited my view of the world has been until now.

"I'd love to take you." He reaches over to hold my hand, pulls it to his lips. "What do you say? After *Dessi* wraps?"

"Where?" I ask, leaning my head into the seat, watching his rugged profile.

"Wherever you want to go, but first I have somewhere for us to go *today*, and we're late."

"Late? You and your plans."

"You love them," he says, keeping his eyes on the road.

I don't answer, but I love everything about this puzzle of a man.

I'm surprised when we pull into the parking garage of The V.

"We could have stayed in my bed if you were just gonna bring me to a hotel."

"This is a date." He parks, gets out, and comes around to open my door. "We haven't really had those."

I stare at him for a second, letting that sink in, before taking his hand and getting out. He pulls me close and leans down to kiss me briefly, sweetly.

"I don't actually care what we're doing here," I murmur against his lips. "As long as we get to do more of this."

He walks us over to an elevator, pulls out a key, and turns it in the wall to summon the car.

"Fancy," I say, stepping in with him. The elevator keeps going until we reach the top.

"The roof?" I ask, my smile broadening.

"We'll have it all to ourselves."

Evan said Open Air was best when it was empty. Guess I'm about to find out.

When we step onto the roof, the city sprawls at our feet, and a vibrant fresco sky spreads out above, smeared with purple and pink-streaked clouds like a watercolor painting. It's LA, but it's still January, and I cross my arms over my chest, huddling into the sweatshirt a little more.

"Cold?" he asks.

"Not really. It's just brisk up here."

"Hungry?" He leads me toward a table set for two with silver dome covers and champagne flutes. Tulips grace the middle of the display.

"Hungry, yes." I sit in the chair he pulls out for me and lean forward to sniff the blooms. "This is all great, Canon."

He lifts the silver domes to reveal crepes and eggs and fruit. Bacon for him, none for me. I'll never take for granted how he takes care of the details.

"You sure nobody's coming up here to bust in on us?" I ask, shaking the linen napkin out over my lap and taking up my fork. "Blow our cover?"

"Ari said we have the place to ourselves for another two hours." Canon bites into his crepe. "The key I used unlocks the elevator. No one can come up here without one. The manager unlocks it around noon to prepare for opening."

"Did Ari…" I hesitate, sip my champagne-lite mimosa, and then press on. "Does she know about us? I mean, that it's me here with you this morning?"

"No, and it's killing her. She'll hound me for information all week. She knows I don't do this, so she has questions."

"Did you and Camille," I start and falter. "Do this? I mean, did you bring her here?"

His chewing slows like he's giving himself time to consider my question and its implications. What might lurk behind the innocuous query. "Never."

I cover my sigh of relief with another sip of the mimosa.

"It would be fine if you did," I say, taking a bite of my eggs. "I just wondered."

"Neevah." He waits until I stop busying myself with food and look at him. "Do you want to know what happened with Camille?"

"No, I—"

"Neevah." He reaches across the table to brush his thumb along my jaw. "I don't talk about this with anyone really, but I'll tell you if you want to know."

Do I want to hear about the first woman he broke his rules for? Hear how she seemed special enough to risk his career, his reputation? Was she worth it?

Resignedly, I gnaw at the corner of my mouth and nod.

His hand falls away and, resting his elbows on the table, he steeples his fingers at his chin.

"I'll start by saying it wasn't all her fault," he says quietly. "She thought we were headed somewhere I realized too late I couldn't go with her. I could have pretended, let things ride until the movie wrapped, but that wouldn't have been fair to either of us. As soon as I found out she wasn't who I thought she was, I knew I had to end it."

"She wasn't who you thought she was? What happened?"

"I first met Camille at a *Vanity Fair* party. I'd heard of her, of course, and she'd heard of me, of course. Hollywood isn't that big of a town. Black Hollywood? Even smaller. She was beautiful, obviously. Funny and warm and open. We spent the whole night in a corner talking, swapping horror stories about how phony things could get here. She seemed like me. Like she was tired of artifice—tired of the brittle beauty that people and this city are sometimes wrapped in."

"Wow," I say, my voice faint, my fingers tight on my fork. "Sounds like a fairy tale start."

He shrugs, his broad shoulders moving in a careless motion. "I didn't pursue anything with her because I was deep-diving into interviews and research for a documentary, which took me all over the world. The offer to direct *Primal* came as a surprise, but not an unpleasant one. It wasn't something I felt as much conviction around as I usually did my projects, but it was intriguing. I admit, when I heard Camille had already been attached to the project, it made it even more appealing."

I grab the carafe holding the mimosa and fill my glass to the rim.

"It didn't occur to me anything would actually happen between us while we were filming," Canon says. "I'd never done that, never gone there with an actress I was directing. We were attracted to each other. Evan saw it, warned me not to do it. All my instincts behooved me not to, but for once, I thought *why the hell not?*"

A self-mocking smile ghosts his lips. "Maybe I was lonely, tired of being solo, horny. All of the above? Who knows, but it happened."

"Indeed," I murmur, gulping my drink.

"She made the first move. I might have eventually, but when we were going over the script in her trailer, she kissed me. I kissed her back, and that's how it started. I can't say I loved her, and I never told her I did, but I liked her a lot. And we were great in and out of bed."

I choke on a grape, banging my chest and tearing up, wheezing to clear my air passage.

"You okay?" Canon asks, concern in his expression.

"Fine." I take a long draw of my drink and wave my hand for him to continue. "Just went down the wrong way. Go on."

"One night, I'd stayed over and was still in bed when I heard her on the phone with her agent."

Did I truly ask for this? It's torture hearing him talk about their intimacy, even in past tense, but I need to hear. I need to know, so I keep my face neutral while he goes on.

"She was lampooning another actress, another Black actress at that," Canon says, shaking his head. "And demanding the other woman, one I knew personally, be uninvited to an event where Camille was presenting.

For the next few minutes, I listened to her tear that woman apart and plot ways to slow her rise. Basically so she wouldn't outshine Camille. She needed to be the 'it' girl and saw someone else's success as a threat."

His frown, the rigid set of his mouth and jaw, hint at what he thought of that.

"I don't play that shit," he confirms. "When I confronted her about it, at first she tried to deny it, but then turned it on me like I was crazy for questioning her motives. Over the next few weeks, it was like scales had dropped from my eyes and I saw other cracks in her facade. As beautiful as she was, there was no light inside, and I never touched her again."

I should just be happy he says it stopped there, and I am, but the thought of Canon—*my Canon*—fucking that gorgeous woman…I swallow my jealousy and push out the necessary words. "So what happened next?"

"When I broke it off, she was furious. She claimed to love me."

"Hmmm." I practically hurl grapes down my gullet, barely pausing to chew. "And then?"

"Well, it wasn't love. It was pride. That was clear when she presented the studio with an ultimatum: her or me. They chose her. The rest is history, even though no one wants to let me live it down. I've never been in love, but I know that's not it."

He's never been in love?

How is that possible? Only as I think about it, neither have I. Can I count Brandon, my high school sweetheart who cheated with my sister, as love? The hurt of their betrayal, that lingered, but my feelings for him? Gone before freshman year ended.

"And when she got you fired?" I ask, pushing my plate away. "You confronted her about it?"

"She called. We argued." He turns the corners of his lips down. "And haven't spoken since."

"You can't just turn off feelings." I look down at my fingers, twisting in my lap. "Did it take you some time to get over her?"

He stands, crosses around to my side of the table, and pulls me to my feet. The cool morning air charges, heating, circulating in the small space separating our bodies. He eliminates even that, setting his hands at my hips, pulling me flush to him.

"Hey." With one finger, he lifts my chin, urging me to meet his eyes. I don't want to. As transparent as I am to him, I know he'll see all the ways I'm jealous. All the ways her very existence makes me question what we have. All the ways I'm insecure hearing how he wanted her.

All the parts of me that ask if he, even a little bit, still does?

"Can I tell you something?" he asks. Our bodies are so close, his words rumble into my chest, and for a moment, it feels like he's knocking on my heart. He can come in. As much as I've fought it from the moment we met, he's probably already inside.

"Yeah?" I ask, forcing my gaze to remain locked with his.

"I liked Camille a lot."

"I know," I say through the hot lump forming in my throat.

"Until she showed herself, and I could never unsee what was beneath that beautiful exterior." He takes my hand, lays the palm flat to his breastbone. "But you, I've seen since the first night we met, and I can't unsee your light. You have nothing to worry about, Neevah. You hear me?"

He cups my face, swipes his thumb across my lips until they open for him, inviting him to enter. With a deep sweep of his tongue, he does. We moan together, our hands in agreement, roaming over arms and faces and asses. He walks us backward to one of the VIP pods, and we step through the curtains into luxurious privacy. An oversized plum-colored couch dominates the space flanked by small tables on either side. The drawn curtains block the breeze, but allow in skeins of sunlight, revealing the desire in his eyes.

"Are we really doing this?" I whisper into our kiss, an illicit thrill zipping through my body at the thought of this intimacy with the whole city watching, yet oblivious.

Wordlessly, he tugs his belt loose, unsnaps his jeans, discarding them, his shirt and his briefs. He's fully erect. Extended. Hard. Long.

Readyyyyy.

I'll take that as a yes.

I tug the sweatshirt over my head, shuck off the jeans and shoes, standing only in a black sheer bra and panties. He deftly flicks open the front closure of my bra, and my breasts spill out like they're eager for his touch. He doesn't disappoint, cupping them, thumbing the nipples until they're hard, budded. He slides his hand into my panties and his fingers find me. The stroking, back-and-forth slide across my clit is shockingly erotic. It's only been a week since we made love in Santa Barbara, but my body is starving for this, and when he slides two fingers inside, my muscles clinch around him almost convulsively.

"Do you know how many times this week I thought about this pussy?" His breath mists my earlobe, inciting a shudder that skids down my nape and across my arms. With slow, deliberate, deep thrusts, he invades me. With each stroke, I go limper, my breath catching and releasing.

"Some days I couldn't concentrate." He pushes impatiently at the strip of lace ringing my hips, shoving the panties down to circle my ankles. "I walked around with a hard-on half the day."

I chuckle against the strong column of his neck, reaching between us to grip him, pull him, relishing the harshness of his breath in response to my touch.

"I was so turned on Wednesday," I tell him, capturing his eyes. "Watching you tug on your lips the way you do when you're trying to figure something out."

"I do?" he asks, absently, bending to take my nipple in his mouth.

"You do." My head drops back and I whimper at the warmth, at the tender tug of his lips wrapped around the sensitive tip. "And it was so damn sexy I went in my trailer on break and touched myself."

He goes statue-still, his hand tightening at my hip.

"I came so hard," I rasp into his ear.

"Turn around." It's a guttural command.

He bends me over the arm of the couch, and my hands hit the cushion for support, to steady myself. At the sound of the condom wrapper tearing, my inner muscles contract, bracing for him. He spreads my cheeks and, slipping his whole hand between my legs, cups the trembling flesh. I'm unprepared for the swipe of his tongue. For the subtle abrasion of his beard scraping the inner skin of my thighs. For the sound of him eating me. I push back against his face, helpless, no shame. Digging my nails into the cushions, I widen my legs to give me more, to take more for myself. He grips my thighs, holding me steady for his devouring mouth until, with a sob that sails over the rooftop, over the city, I contract around his delving tongue. The orgasm hits hard, tightening the muscles in my thighs and calves. With staccato breaths, I bury my face in the couch, biting my lip to the point of pain.

"Canon," I beg. "Stop teasing me and—"

He shoves in, and the words tumble back down my throat, recessing into the shock of this pleasure.

"Jesus." Need shreds my voice to ribbons.

He coasts his hand up my back, gently cuffs my neck. Ass in the air, I rise up on my toes, begging for breath, petitioning for more dick. He gives it to me, pushing impossibly deeper.

"So damn good," he grunts behind me.

I hope I never get over how perfect he feels inside me, like I was molded to his specifications. Shaped for his dimensions. I moan and reach my hand back to pull at one of my cheeks, widening the way for his cock. It feels like he goes where no dick has gone before, deeper, better. Somehow I feel each thrust in my heart. His every touch plays on my emotions, and tears sting my eyes. His hand tightens at my hip, and he slides the other hand up my arm, finds my hand on the couch and laces our fingers together. He sets a frenetic pace that sends the blood singing through my body again. The cushion absorbs my scream as I come, and I punish the soft cotton with clawing nails. With his voice strangled, his fingers fisted in my hair, he comes.

Collapsing against my back, a heavy, happy burden, his breath stilted and warm at my neck, he snakes one muscled arm around my middle, clutching me. After the urgent, feral coupling, it's a cherishing hold. I cross my arm over his at my waist and tangle our fingers. It's fragile and sweet, this moment, like flakes of sugar disintegrating on your tongue when you've barely had time to taste.

Leaving a kiss on my shoulder, he pulls out, and I miss him immediately. When he straightens, so do I, turning around to face him. Our still unsteady breaths brush our chests together, the tips of my breasts kissing his hard torso. He rubs a thumb along my areola, and I wonder if I could come again just from that touch and the look in his eyes.

He frowns at the redness surrounding the soft flesh.

"Beard burn," I tell him, smiling at the way his brows knit in chagrin.

"Does it bother you? The beard, I mean."

"And if it did?" I walk around him, bending to retrieve my underwear. "Would you cut it off?"

"If I didn't," he chuckles, tossing his condom into a small trash can and tying off the bag, "would you cut *me* off?"

"I think you already know the answer to that." I slide my arms into my bra, snapping the closure between my breasts. "Besides, growing the beard—it's your tradition."

His jeans are back on, but not the T-shirt, leaving his powerful chest still bare when he approaches me, cups my face. "You could be my new tradition."

The laughter dies on my lips, fades from his eyes, and we are trapped in a net of our own making. Thin as gossamer, it tightens around us, and I hold my breath, not wanting to disrupt these few seconds with even a heartbeat. Finally, I rise up on my bare toes to reach his cheek, leaving a kiss there.

"Keep the beard." I rake my nails through it and step back to put on my sweatshirt.

Once we leave the cabana, the moment dissipates, but the feeling lingers—that breathless contentment warmed by affection. We gather our things, and I study the debris of our breakfast, recall our conversation about Camille. I'll never like the fact that they were together. That's normal, and I am severely normal, but when Canon looks at me, when he holds me, there are no ghosts. No traces of her except in his regret. I don't know how long I get to have him, but as long as I do, he's only mine.

"You ready?" He assesses the patio, empty, but soon to be filled with people and music and food and gaiety. "They'll clean up when the staff comes in to get ready for tonight."

I nod, reluctant to leave the open-air intimacy of our rooftop.

He takes my hand and walks me to the elevator. Once on the road, he navigates the thickening traffic with one hand on the wheel, one hand holding mine on the console between us. We don't talk much, but he absently strokes the ink along my thumb. "In a Sentimental Mood" sighs through the speakers, Duke Ellington's keys and John Coltrane's collaborating notes filling the air. I can already sense Canon's mind slipping away into shadowed corners, probably for a clandestine meeting with his mistress, Dessi Blue.

"So I assume you have plans for the rest of the day?" I ask.

"What?" He glances over at me, that vague look in his eyes. I had all of him on that rooftop, but a man like Canon? His art is a demanding taskmaster, and I don't mind sharing.

"You have work to do?"

"Yeah." He nods. "I need to set up shots for tomorrow. Meeting Kenneth in an hour."

"Thank you for this morning," I say when we pull up in front of my place. "I enjoyed our secret Sunday."

I open the car door, knowing he'll probably pull off before the door is even closed, but he surprises me. He touches my arm and leans over to kiss me. It starts like butterfly wings, just brushes of our lips, and deepens, passion rising and overtaking. I slide my hand up his neck, cup the hard ridge of his jaw. I could kiss him all day, but he pulls back after a few seconds. Kisses my cheeks and nose.

"So next Sunday?" he asks, tucking my hair behind my ear. "It's a date?"

My big, cheesy grin holds nothing back because I don't know how where Canon is concerned, and I drop a quick kiss on his lips.

"Next Sunday. It's a date."

FORTY-TWO

Neevah

"Wardrobe took so long this morning," Takira mutters. "Now we rushing."

"Girl, it's my fault. My weight keeps fluctuating. Before Christmas, I was dropping weight, so they took the dresses in. Now I've gained some weight, and they had to take them back out. I think I'm retaining water."

I extend my leg, showing the slightly puffy ankles I noticed this morning.

"I might be 'retaining' Mama's macaroni and cheese, too," I joke, making us both laugh.

"Your body is probably so confused." Takira shakes her head, braiding my hair. "All this running around you doing. I can't wait 'til we're done so you can rest. Let me get this wig—"

She cuts herself off.

I look up to catch her wide eyes in the mirror.

"What is it, T?"

She gulps and holds out her palm to show me what took her by surprise.

A handful of my hair.

My heart hydroplanes in my chest, spinning with dread and fear. A rash on my arms after too much time in the sun.

Understandable.

A new spot or two on my scalp.

Not unexpected.

Whole clumps of my hair coming out in Takira's hands?

Alarming.

I swivel around to stare up at Takira, and her eyes reflect the worry building in me.

"Have you talked to Dr. Ansford?" she asks.

"Yeah, off and on, but not since the break. Everything's been going well."

I hesitate and then peel the sleeves of my bathrobe back, revealing the dark, dry patches on my arms. I hadn't paid much attention, but they've gotten a little worse since Santa Barbara. I've had them before, but there are a few more this time.

"You think this is the beginning of a serious flare-up?" Takira asks. She lifts my chin and scans my face. I know she's looking for the butterfly rash across my nose and cheeks I've had a few times before. "It's not on your face yet, but between these new patches and your hair, I think you need to be aggressive about getting in with Dr. Ansford."

I meant to call her after Santa Barbara, but things got so hectic when we started filming after Christmas break. To be honest, it wasn't a priority... until now.

"I'll call her today on my break." I turn back around, and grab Dessi's wig from the nearby mannequin head. I need to refocus for the upcoming scene. "Come on, T. I gotta be on set in fifteen minutes."

Takira stares at the wig for an extra few seconds. "What you *gotta* do is take this seriously."

"I am. I've been doing everything Dr. Ansford instructed. We've been filming for months with no real signs of trouble, and now that we have some symptoms, I'll address them."

"Stress feeds this, and what's more stressful than the situation you've been in? Dancing eight, nine hours a day? You're in almost every scene? It's a lot, Neev."

"And it's almost over. I don't need them to start doubting me now. I have to finish strong." I jiggle the wig. "Speaking of, make me Dessi?"

"Okay, but I'm not letting you off the hook. If you don't talk to Dr. Ansford today, I'll go to Canon myself."

"The hell you will. If there's a problem that will hinder my performance, I'll notify the producers. Until that time, let me decide what I'm capable of, okay? Canon's not just my..."

Lover?

Boyfriend?

My man?

"I'm not just involved with him," I settle on. "He's my boss. This is the movie of a lifetime, not just for me, but for him. For Evan. For all of us." I bite my lip and squeeze her hand. "Please, T? Just give me time to talk with Dr. Ansford at least."

Takira blows out a long, slow breath, nods, and takes the wig. She carefully tucks and pins my hair before slipping the cap over my braids and fitting the wig in place.

Within minutes, my makeup is done and I'm slipping into one of Linh's costumes. The woman staring back at me in the mirror is just as much Dessi as she is Neevah.

And we both have a job to do.

"This could get serious, Neevah."

Not the words I want to hear from Dr. Ansford when we chat on my break. She looks at me soberly from the video window on my iPad. I'd hoped, when I showed her the new rashes on my arms and legs and the additional bald spots, she would say it was just part of the disease. Nothing to worry about.

Except she does look worried.

"Any other symptoms?" she demands, leaning forward and probing with a sharp-eyed perusal.

"No."

"No fatigue? Muscle aches? Joint pain?"

"I spent the last few months dancing, acting ten, eleven, twelve hours a day. Some fatigue, muscle aches, and joint pain come with the territory."

"So you *could* have had unusual joint pain and fatigue that you chalked up to the rigorous dance numbers, but might actually have been signaling the onset of a flare-up."

"I mean..." A band tightens around my chest at the implication. "I guess, but I'm in the best shape of my life."

"Weight gain or loss?"

Linh's tape measure cinching my waist taunts me.

"I've lost weight. Again, dancing, but seem to be gaining some now. We're just coming out of the holidays. I ate too much."

"Swelling?"

I hesitate before answering honestly. "My ankles, some, yeah."

"We need to get bloodwork, urine test, metabolic panel."

"Okay. We're getting into one of the toughest stretches of shooting. In a few days I can—"

"Today, Neevah. The doctor I referred you to out there—I'll ask her to see you today and do a blood workup."

"You don't understand. I'm in every scene today. Our schedule is already set. If I don't show up, the whole day is thrown off. A hundred people don't work. I have to give them more notice than that. At least let me see if they can move some things around tomorrow so I can come in later and get the blood drawn then?"

Dr. Ansford bends her head, texting. After a moment, she looks back up, triumph all over her expression. "She can see you tomorrow morning first thing. Eight o'clock."

"I arrive on set at five. Maybe there's another time, because by eight I'll be—"

"Figure it out. This is your health, Neevah."

"I know, and this is my job. The opportunity of a lifetime. I need to be healthy, of course. All I want is to figure out both."

"Think of it this way: If you neglect your health, you might sabotage this opportunity."

Her sobering words still swirl in my head when I tie a bathrobe over my costume and head to video village. When I enter, Canon, Evan, Kenneth, and Jill are huddled around one laptop, all wearing heavy frowns. Four sets of eyes snap to me at the tent entrance.

"Neevah, hey," Kenneth says, clearing his expression to smile at me. "You need something?"

"Uh, yeah." I shove my hands into the deep pockets of my robe and force myself to focus on Kenneth and not look at Canon. "Could I talk to you for a second before this next scene?"

"Sure." He heads toward me, and I turn before anyone else asks or says anything. I feel Canon's stare on my back, and it's the closest I've come to his touch since Sunday.

For the last two weekends, we've stolen Sundays together. A few days ago, we donned caps and sunglasses, and strolled along the Venice canals. The arching pedestrian bridges and glimmering canals lined with beach houses completely charmed me. We rented a small boat, touring the sights by water, and found a secluded space for a picnic. This time when he took me home, he came inside. We made love and napped and laughed and talked and ate again, scavenging for food in my fridge.

That idyllic day feels distant as Dr. Ansford's warnings echo in my ears. Once outside the tent, I look up at Kenneth and try to put my emotions at ease. Canon says my face shows everything. Until I know what I'm dealing with, I want to keep this to myself.

"What's up?" he asks, sliding a pencil behind his ear.

"I know it's last minute, but I need to come in late tomorrow. I have a doctor's appointment."

"Is everything okay?" A frown puckers his salt-and-pepper brows. He's not much older than Canon, his unlined brown skin a paradox to his hair, which is completely, prematurely white.

"Yeah. I have a rash that needs looking at. It's something I've managed the last few years. Stress aggravates it, and I don't want it to get any worse. Then we'd have to disguise it with a lot of makeup, which might make it even worse. It's a whole thing. So I want to get ahead of it."

"Ah. Makes sense." He pulls a rolled-up script from his back pocket. I've rarely seen him without his copy and it's almost falling apart by now, littered with notes for all of us in the margins. "Obviously, you're in most of the scenes, but I'll look at what we might be able to move around and shoot for a few hours with you gone. May be able to use your double for some shots."

I ignore the guilt twisting my insides and nod. I don't want to cause problems. There's a part of me that wants to say, *Never mind, I'll work around the schedule and squeeze the doctor in later,* but I can't forget Dr. Ansford's grave expression.

"My appointment is scheduled for eight o'clock tomorrow morning. It's the earliest they had. I'm sorry—"

"Neevah, we can't afford to lose you for good." He chuckles, because it doesn't even occur to him that could happen. "So take care of it. We'll figure it out."

"Right." I force a smile. "Thanks."

I'm leaving a continuity check in wardrobe when I run into Canon, literally barreling into his chest as I round the corner.

"Sorry about that," I mutter.

He steadies me, and we both look down at his hands wrapped around my arms. All I can think about is how he touched me Sunday, like he couldn't believe I was real. Caressing me with reverence like he couldn't believe I was his.

But I am.

I look up at him and school my expression into normal person face. "Hey."

He doesn't answer, but takes my hand and pulls me into the false alley again. Once we're tucked away, shadowed, he leans against the wall and tugs me to stand between his legs. I toy with the buttons of his shirt and wait for him to make the next move in case the move I want to make is the wrong one.

"Kenneth says you have a doctor's appointment tomorrow?"

"Yeah." I grimace. "I'm sorry. I know it's a pain to shuffle the scenes, but I—"

"Hey." He lifts my chin, cups my neck, and dips to hold my gaze in the barely lit space between the building facades. "We'll figure that out. I want to make sure you're okay."

The chain tightened around my heart loosens at the concern evident in his eyes. And even though we're on set with cords and wires snaking over the floors, cameras all around and even some above, the cast and crew scurrying to prepare for the next scenes, the intimacy of his touch takes me back to my bed, the sheets rumpled by our passion. I put one hand over his caressing my neck.

"I'm fine. I just need to check into that rash."

He's seen me naked, obviously, and knows about the rash. It's still in just a few patches, though, so I'm hoping to keep it that way.

"Oh, yeah. That's good." He bends and brushes our lips together. "I miss you."

I take his bottom lip between mine, nodding and resting my elbows on his powerful shoulders. "Same."

"One month." His hands skate down my sides, mold to my waist, and settle low on my hips. "After Santa Barbara, we'll only have a month left."

"Like you don't immediately go into edit mode and all the post-production stuff once we wrap."

"I do, but it's a different level of concentration. We can—"

"Places!"

It comes from the real world just beyond our hiding place. Canon drops his forehead to mine and dusts kisses over my temple, my cheek, and finally, places one on my mouth. It's a possessive kiss fraught with longing and promise and hunger. I lean into it, answer it, open under it, inviting him in, but there's no time. There's never any time anymore. A flurry of footsteps freezes us both as everyone scrambles to get in place for the next scene. Canon blows out a resigned sigh, and then he's gone.

FORTY-THREE

Canon

"So we'll do thirty-five millimeters for the day exteriors," I say, tapping my pencil for emphasis and looking from Jill to Kenneth. "And digital for night exterior shots, yeah?"

"Yeah." Jill nods. "And I'm thinking the anamorphic for those huge outdoor shots. Like the sweeping ones."

Kenneth tilts his head, eyes the storyboard and our shot list. "We still using the drone for those aerial shots on day three?"

"Yup." Jill grins, her eyes alight with excitement. "Santa Barbara is gonna be our French Riviera, boys."

I toss the pencil onto the table and lean back to link my fingers behind my head. "The one advantage of Galaxy is they're paying for all this shit."

We laugh because shooting on film is expensive, and in the age of digital, a luxury most filmmakers don't experience often anymore. Guys like Scorsese, Tarantino, Christopher Nolan—standard bearers for the format who vehemently resist digital—they have the budgets and the clout to insist. We lose a lot of flexibility going with film and can't review it in real-time like we can with digital. Our dailies have to be sent off to a lab and come back later. It's slower and less precise. You're basically shooting onto dollar bills. More rehearsal. Fewer takes. A lot less room for error. Shooting parts of this movie on film will lend it the look I want and add layers of nostalgia, but it's costly, labor-intensive, and generally a pain in the ass.

And yet the three of us are like kids in a candy store at the prospect. We have the expertise, especially with Jill as our cinematographer, to vary our formats and really create something special, though it will require a different approach to shooting.

"We need to make sure the cast is ready for this shift," I say, directing the comment to Kenneth. "Everyone, of course, but especially Neevah and Trey. A lot of these scenes are just them and a whole bunch of background actors. We good on the extras?"

"I'll handle the extras." Kenneth hesitates and clears his throat. "But with so many of them to wrangle, I'll be less available for Neevah, and Trey, of course, so I guess you'll manage them on set."

Kenneth flips his phone in his hand, looking down at the screen instead of at me. Jill scribbles on her pad, pointedly fixing her eyes on the words as the silence stretches awkwardly between the three of us.

They know.

They can't know for sure that Neevah and I are together, but based on this shifty-eyed behavior, they know *something* is up. Obviously, based on our conversations, Jill has her suspicions and did her part to help things along, but I haven't even told her how things have developed. I grit my teeth, annoyed with myself for showing that much of my hand, but determined to make it clear it won't affect my work or this story.

"Sure." I stand and walk over to the model of the Lafayette Theatre for something to do. "That's no problem. I'll have to be out there more anyway since we can't watch the shots in real-time from the tent."

"Right." Kenneth pounces on this reasoning. "Works out perfectly. And I'll make sure all those extras are in place and ready."

"Sounds good." I split a look between them, my brows lifted. "Anything else?"

"Nope." Kenneth stands. "I'm meeting with the cast to go over logistics since tomorrow's our first day filming on location."

I grip his shoulder. "Thanks, man."

"You know it." Kenneth heads for the door, passing an unsmiling Evan as my production partner enters the tent.

"What is it?" I ask, sitting on the edge of the table. "Something with the permits? The housing in Santa Barbara?"

"The permits are fine," Evan says, his dark frown not lightening. "And we have cottages for the cast and crew at that resort Galaxy practically bought out for us."

"Good. Then why you look like somebody pissed in your cornflakes?"

"Jill, could you excuse us?" Evan asks, not acknowledging my joke.

"Uh, sure." Jill flashes a look that says *what have you done now*, but I have no clue.

Once it's just the two of us, I shrug. "Dude, what's up?"

"What's up is Camille Hensley telling the whole world on a podcast twenty minutes ago that you're fucking *another one of your actresses*."

He hurls the accusation—because it clearly is one—at me with narrowed eyes and hands shoved into his jeans.

Damn you, Sylvia Miller.

It was too much to hope Camille's publicist wouldn't recount seeing Neevah and me together, but why is Camille in my business? And so publicly?

"Nothing to say?" Evan asks, his voice tight. "I distinctly remember us agreeing you wouldn't do this again."

"Nothing is going on that will affect this movie, Evan."

"Whatever is going on already has. Camille's comments call Neevah's talent and ability into question before the world has seen one minute of this film."

A long, tired sigh jets between my lips. "What did she say, exactly?"

"The podcaster asked if there was a role she regretted turning down, and she said there was a role recently she wanted badly but wasn't even allowed to audition for."

I groan, sinking my head into my hands.

"Of course, since Camille can write her ticket in this town right now, they asked who would dare turn down the opportunity to work with her."

"And of course, she seized the chance to put my business in the streets."

"Why is there business, Canon? First of all, we agreed you'd keep your dick away from the actresses."

"Stop making me sound like some lecher taking advantage of my position to get some ass. You know I don't do that."

"In this current climate, no one takes that for granted, especially when the actress in question doesn't have one movie on IMDb. You're the one with all the power, and she'd be the one who wanted the big break and was willing to do whatever it took to get it."

"It's not like that." I slam my teeth shut on the words. "What else did Camille say?"

"That if you were just going to give the role to someone you're dating, she didn't understand why you wouldn't at least give her a chance. And that she heard Galaxy had serious concerns about an unknown carrying a blockbuster biopic like this, but that you overrode their concerns, threatening to walk away if they didn't cave and cast your new girlfriend."

There's just enough truth in there to render the reality insignificant.

"Law Stone from Galaxy called, of course," Evan says, his stare boring a hole in my face.

"And?"

"And he wants you to address it."

"What? Go on some late-night show and apologize for something that's nobody's business but the two consenting adults involved? Nope. The hell if I'll be their dancing monkey out there saying I'm sorry for something I shouldn't have to apologize for. I don't owe them shit."

"And me? You don't owe me shit? We're supposed to be partners. Friends. In this together."

"You know we are."

"But you let me get blindsided by this. Egg on my fucking face, caught flat-footed with that moron Stone calling me, demanding explanations."

"He wants explanations so bad, why didn't he call me himself?"

Evan rolls his eyes. We both know Lawson Stone couldn't *buy* the balls to roll up on me like that. He knows what he'd get.

"That's what I thought," I say, slumping into a chair and tugging at my mouth, trying to figure this out.

"Maybe you don't go on late-night shows, but—"

"No 'maybe' to it. That's not happening."

"But we've had a closed set, with few exceptions. Maybe we allow a few entertainment reporters on set. Do a few cast interviews. Leak some behind-the-scenes footage of the cast laughing together. Some shots of us filming and them seeing Neevah work like anyone else."

"She doesn't work like anyone else. She works harder than everyone else, and you know it. New or not, she is carrying this film. She was the right choice."

"Agreed. I think she's gonna blow everyone away. That's what I want to protect, so can we at least consider some on-set stuff? Just behind the scenes, seeing them in costume, some B roll of dance numbers. Nothing too specific, but giving glimpses of how big this is gonna be, and drop some hints of just how good Neevah is. Why she earned this with her talent. Not addressing it directly, but retaking control of the narrative."

I blow out a breath and, after a few tense seconds, nod.

"When did this happen?" he asks. "Can you at least tell me that?"

"When did what happen?"

His look is wry and knowing.

"I've been attracted to her since the beginning," I admit grudgingly. "But kept my distance as much as I could. Over Thanksgiving we ended up in the same restaurant for dinner, and just connected."

"So that's when the affair started?"

"Stop making it sound seedy, and no. New Year's, we went away to Santa Barbara."

"So when I talked to you on your way up there, she was with you?"

I nod and he aims one accusing finger at me. "So you lied."

"Can we do this later? The cast and crew know all of this yet? Heard the podcast?"

"It's making its way through the grapevine now. Of course, the actors leave their phones in their trailers, but now that we've wrapped for the day, I'm sure they all know or will soon."

Neevah, baby, I'm so sorry.

"I need to see her." I stand abruptly. "Everyone will be acting weird and speculating. Shit."

"Where are you going?"

"To try to catch her before she leaves. Kenneth's meeting with them about the new protocols for shooting on location."

"I'll work on connecting with a few of the entertainment shows."

"I need to sign off on anyone who's coming to my set. I'm not playing, Evan. This foolishness is not messing with the chemistry we have or anything we've spent so much time building."

"Got it," he says, his expression finally yielding just a little bit. "And hey. In the grand scheme of things, this is just a PR speed bump. We'll be fine."

But is Neevah?

FORTY-FOUR

Neevah

We hold our production meetings in Café Society—at least in the replica our property master and his team built of the historic establishment. The Greenwich Village hot spot was the first completely racially integrated nightclub in the country. The specters of greats like Ethel Waters, Lena Horne, Sarah Vaughan, Hazel Scott, and Pete Johnson wait in the wings, sit around the tables, and eventually take the stage. You can practically smell the cigarette smoke wafting in the air. This may not be the actual club, but sometimes when I enter, I can almost feel the reverberations of shock rippling through the crowd the night Billie Holiday sang "Strange Fruit" for the first time anywhere ever; she shook up the world with a song.

With all that history playing in my head, Kenneth's production meeting could feel mundane, but he's reviewing the schedule for tomorrow and highlighting how working on film will affect how we shoot so I'm tuned in. Then people start looking at their phones instead of at Kenneth.

And then they start looking at *me*.

At least I think they are. I'm too busy eating every word falling from Kenneth's mouth like some baby bird because shooting on film sounds crucial. Like fewer takes and less room for error when I'm in every scene and have more dialogue to memorize than everyone else. Whatever is on their phones has *their* attention. Kenneth has mine.

"Everyone understand?" Kenneth asks, wrapping up the meeting. "So in Santa Barbara, we all need to be sharp and prepared."

"Or Canon will tear us a new one," Livvie says, sliding a glance over to me. "Well, *some* of us. He may be nicer to others."

An awkward silence follows her comment and I'm seriously not sure what is going on. Even though we break, the cast lingers, decompressing and chatting after a tough day of shooting. The work distracted me from waiting for my test results. I know we just did the bloodwork yesterday, but I want the assurance that everything is okay, and I would love to know before we leave for Santa Barbara. Not likely. In the meantime, I walk over to Kenneth, script in hand, to ask him about an upcoming scene.

"Kenneth, got a sec?"

His face lights up, his eyes kind. "For you, always. What's up?"

We're talking through the scene when phone alerts start going off around the room, followed by whispers and covert glances.

"What's up?" I ask Kenneth. "Am I imagining that something is… off?"

"I have no idea." Kenneth glances around with a frown.

Takira approaches, her face set, and grabs my arm. "We need to talk."

"Um, Kenneth and I were—"

"It's fine." Kenneth flicks a glance between Takira and me. "Don't hesitate to ask if you still have questions."

"T, what's up?" I demand as soon as Kenneth walks away. "I was just—"

"You need to see this." She thrusts her phone into my hand.

I can't even believe what I'm reading. It's a post online about a podcast and Camille Hensley and me and Canon and the movie. It's all these disparate parts that shouldn't have anything to do with each other but have somehow landed in the same place. All of Canon's concerns, the things he warned me about, are splashed on a digital page for any and everyone to see.

I glance up and all eyes are on me before being quickly averted.

"Oh, my God," I whisper to Takira. "They think—"

"Right. Yeah."

Embarrassment clenches my throat, and I can barely swallow. A knot tightens in my belly. If these people, my cast, look at me like that—like I didn't earn this after seeing me bust my butt the last three months—what will people who don't know me at all think? But on the heels of embarrassment comes indignation. They *have* seen me putting in work to do my best. Seriously? Some vindictive bitch who couldn't get her way makes a few comments and they look at me like they're not sure?

And then I just feel…alone. Even with Takira standing beside me, Canon isn't. I don't blame him. No doubt he's in some production meeting, exactly where he should be, but he's not here. And I have to face the speculation and judgment I sense from my colleagues by myself. He probably doesn't even know this is going on.

"Oh, shit," Takira says, looking over my shoulder.

I turn my head to see what has her cussing, and draw a sharp breath when Canon walks in. He's a few feet away, several people between us.

"Hey," he says to the room, issuing a general greeting. "Great job today, everybody."

They mumble and nod and stutter, almost like he caught them in the act of something. I don't know where to look. Don't know what to do or how to behave. I don't want to make this worse, but everyone keeps looking from him to me and from me to him like we're onstage and they're waiting for our next lines.

I have no script for this.

"Neevah," he calls, his voice carrying clearly across the room.

I force myself to look at him and not focus on the invisible bullseye covering my whole body.

"You want a ride home?" he asks.

In front of everyone.

What is he doing?

Everyone knows a driver brings me to and picks me up from set every day. I blink at him stupidly, and the whole room seems to be holding its breath, waiting for my answer.

"Um…yeah? Sure?"

"Come on."

He extends his hand. *His hand!* Like he means for me to take it. I'm superglued in place, but Takira nudges me forward, and I stumble a little before righting myself and taking the few steps to reach him. He immediately links our fingers and leaves the room, tugging me after him. I hold my tongue for as long as possible, conscious of all the eyes on our departure. As soon as we are out of eyeshot and reach the parking lot, I turn on him.

"What the hell was that?" I ask. "You decided taking me home, holding my hand, and confirming everyone's suspicions was the best idea?"

"Yeah, because rumors, gossip, and speculation disrupt chemistry and, if left unchecked, can compromise performances." He leans against his car and folds his arms across his chest. "I don't plan to address it directly, but there's no reason to hide when it's been exposed."

"We could deny it."

"Denying it, hiding it once something like this comes out, is counterproductive. I'm not wasting energy maintaining a lie when they're looking for it now. Digging for any sign that it may be true. That's distracting, and I cannot afford a distracted, gossiping cast and crew."

With a shrug, he glances at me from beneath an arch of dark brows. "Besides, maybe Camille did us a favor." He reaches for my hand, twining our fingers. "I don't particularly like hiding it. I guess I should have checked with you first."

A smile toys with the corners of my mouth and I step closer. "I guess I'm fine with everyone knowing you're into me." I laugh when he rolls his eyes but grins. "So now what?"

"Now I've confirmed we're together, and if they know what's best for them, they deal with it and keep doing their jobs."

"It sounds simple, and maybe it will be for you because you won't have to put up with your colleagues thinking you didn't get your job on merit."

"Hey." He lifts my chin, his gaze traveling down nearly a foot to meet mine. "What happened to 'If they find out, I'll prove myself'? 'I'll show them I can do the job.'"

A wry grin tips one side of my mouth. "I thought I was so big and bad. Everyone was staring at me tonight."

"They were staring because they were wondering. We don't make them wonder. I'm not saying we flaunt it, but we don't hide anymore. It'll be old hat soon and they'll think of us like any other couple who—"

"Are we?" A feather tickles the lining of my belly. "A couple, I mean?"

He caresses the ink along my thumb. "What'd you think this was?"

We haven't put much language to what's been going on between us. For me, I don't care what we call it. I'm just glad it's happening.

"Well, you did practically drag me out of the production team meeting by the hair," I say, allowing a teasing note into my voice.

"I didn't."

"I mean . . . it was a little growly, mine, claim-y."

"Do you want to be someone else's?" he asks softly, drawing me to him in inches until the tips of our toes touch and I'm too close to see or smell or consider anyone but the man in front of me.

"No." I don't smile or make light of it or try to hide the certainty in my eyes. I want this. I want him, and if I have to endure some speculation, well, dammit, I'll do what I said. I'll prove I deserve this job. I'll keep earning their trust.

"Good," he says, opening the passenger door of his car. "Then let's get you home."

FORTY-FIVE

Canon

It never ends.

The list of things that needs to be done marches through my head, an infinite line of tasks and meetings as we prepare to shoot on location. This drama with Camille today? Last damn thing I needed. Everything I thought would happen if I got involved with Neevah is happening exactly as I predicted.

And yet…

Glancing over at her, curled up and asleep in my passenger seat on the way to her place, I don't regret it. I don't regret kissing her on Thanksgiving. I don't regret our time away in Santa Barbara. I don't regret starting a relationship with her, because it's like nothing I've had before. I hate the chaos Camille's interview could potentially create, but Neevah is the best thing to happen to me in a long time. Today, when faced with the consequences of our actions, I had to admit that to myself. In spite of all the trouble this could cause, I can't regret *her.*

Of course, my phone has been ringing nonstop. Neevah nodded off almost immediately and has been that way for the forty-minute drive to her rental in Studio City. It's not far from the lot, but this is LA, so everywhere you go becomes a hump. I have one more call to make before I can rest for an hour or so. Maybe we can have a quick meal before I go home and prepare for tomorrow.

I use one earphone to make this last call so the speakerphone won't disturb Neevah's sleep.

"Canon, hey," Verity answers on the first ring. "I wasn't sure if our call was still on."

"Why wouldn't it be? I told you I'd call to talk through the script revisions. They're minor, but I want to give the cast plenty of time to learn the new lines before we reach those scenes."

"Yeah, but you've had quite the eventful day, breaking the internet and whatnot," Verity says, her voice curious and cautious.

"I didn't break the Internet. Camille did, and every day for the last three months has been eventful," I answer stiffly. "We're shooting one of the biggest biopics of the last decade, so things get busy. You got a point?"

"Don't get defensive with me, Canon. You know how much I like and respect Neevah. The interview was everywhere today, and I'm sure that was disruptive. Not trying to be all up in your shit. Just trying to be sensitive."

"I don't need you to be sensitive. I need those revisions, like, yesterday."

"Why you gotta be a dick?" A bit of laughter eases the bite of her words.

"Occupational hazard," I say, allowing myself to relax the smallest bit.

"Can I just say I'm happy for you?"

I don't discuss my personal life freely. I haven't known Verity long and I don't know her as well as I do Jill or Kenneth or Evan, who have worked with me for years. Verity, though, is good people. I'm not sure what went down with her and Monk, but for some reason, I think I can trust her.

"Thank you."

"She's amazing."

"I'm aware," I say, an unstoppable grin taking over my mouth.

"Much too good for you."

"Also, very aware of that fact and agreed. Now can we please talk through these line edits so I can check you off my list and maybe have half an hour to eat uninterrupted with my girlfriend?"

The word lands between us like a rock for a moment before it starts to float. It's the first time I've called Neevah that even to myself, much less aloud to someone I work with. I expect it to feel like a shirt that's one size too small—tight, restrictive, choking at the collar. Instead, it's the opposite. It feels the way *she* feels—tailor-made for me.

"Girlfriend, huh?" Verity chuckles. "Alright. I see you, Canon. All booed up."

"The edits," I remind her. "We need to tweak that dialogue with Cal and Dessi in France after she receives Tilda's letter."

That refocuses her, and we talk through how she might approach retooling some of that scene. After promising to send revisions before morning, she disconnects. Perfect timing because I pull up to Neevah's place. She hasn't stirred the whole drive home, and without the heavy makeup, the shadows under her eyes are much more evident. She's wearing one of the head wraps she often puts on when she sheds Dessi's wig for the day. The tempting fullness of her lips is unpainted, unadorned. Her arms are folded at her waist. Is that rash she had in Santa Barbara worse?

"Why are you frowning at me?" she asks, her voice drowsy.

I glance from her arm to her bleary-eyed expression. "Your arm. The rash seems to be getting worse."

"Oh." She rubs the discolorations, looking down and clearing her throat. "Yeah, we should get the results of all the tests they ran any day now. I think it'll be fine."

She reaches for the door handle. "I'm exhausted and starving. You coming in or you need to go?"

"I have some stuff to sort through before we leave tomorrow, and I still have to pack."

"Okay." Her smile looks a little forced, and like most of the emotions that cross her face, I can easily read the disappointment. "I understand. I'll see you in Santa Barbara, then."

When she gets out, so do I, alarming the car and following her to the front door.

"Oh." She turns to face me, her gaze flitting from me to my car parked on the street. "I thought you had things to do."

"I do, but a man's gotta eat."

She grins and retrieves her keys, opening the front door. "Well, I hope you don't expect *me* to cook. I'm ordering takeout and calling it a night."

"Sounds great, but let the record show I *did* cook for you."

"Not after a twelve-hour workday you didn't."

The house is dark and quiet, and as soon as the door closes behind us, the stress drains from my shoulders. She walks ahead, but I catch her from behind by her waist, pulling her into me.

"Hi," I say, dusting kisses along the curve of her neck.

She tilts her head, offering me more of her satiny skin like a cat who wants to be stroked. "Hi."

"Today was crazy." I turn her to face me, trying to read her expression in the half-dark. "You okay?"

"I am if you are."

"What's that mean?"

"At first, with everyone looking at me and all the phones going off and...it kind of caught me off guard."

"And then?"

"Well, with some time to think about it," she says, grinning, "and to nap on it, I feel the way I did before. Let 'em talk. Let them believe what they want to believe. We will show them. *Dessi Blue* is brilliant, Canon. I dare anyone not to be moved by this story. It's music and art and history. It's restorative. Redemptive. And I'm proud to be a part of it."

She reaches up to skim her thumb across my bottom lip and then the top one, tracing the bow and trailing over my beard. "And I'm proud to be with you. How could I be ashamed of this? Of us? I'm not."

"I'm not," I echo back to her. She put into words what I felt when I was talking to Verity. The way forward is open. "I told Verity you were my girlfriend."

Her eyes widen and her mouth pops open, shock projected onto her face. "You what?"

"I think it's kind of anticlimactic after Camille's stunt."

"But you haven't even asked me."

Well, ain't this some shit? I don't call a woman my girlfriend for... years, and when I do, she responds like this?

"So...you don't want to be my girlfriend?"

"Oh my God! You should see your face." She points at me and laughs. "Of course, I want to be your girlfriend. What do you think I am? Crazy?"

She snatches the phone from my hand, waggling it in the air. "And in my *boyfriend's* best interest, I'm taking this. No work for a few minutes."

I try to grab the phone, try to grab her, but she dances out of reach, running up the hall. I'm so damn tired, but do I literally run after her like a horny teenager?

Yes. Yes, I do.

She dashes into one of the bedrooms and I follow her in. She locks the door as soon as it's closed.

"You fell for that?" She grins, plucking at the buttons running down the front of her sundress. "Now I have you."

Our lovemaking has been restricted to Sundays for the last month. Having her during the week? No longer needing to keep this a secret?

I push the dress away from her shoulders and sigh at the delicious sight of her.

"Now you have me."

FORTY-SIX

Neevah

A storm in repose.

Genius at rest.

Canon asleep in my bed.

I should wake him because I know he has things to do before tomorrow's first day on location, but he's exhausted. And as much as I'd like to think it's the potency of this pussy that put him out…it's more than that. The man's been working sixteen- to eighteen-hour days for months. I don't want to touch him in case he wakes, but with my gaze I trace the powerful lines of his shoulders and the defined muscles of his torso and abs. He's dark and rich in my sheets, like chocolate left on my pillow. I could eat him up.

I did.

Canon's pleasure fed mine. The taste of him, the blissful agony on his face when his control broke, the rough tug of his fingers in my hair.

I'm lucky he didn't pull out a chunk of it. This is no time for jokes, but it's better than fear and uncertainty while I wait for my test results. And if bad jokes don't distract me, these lines I need to nail down will. I grab the script from my nightstand and try to absorb the words swimming before my tired eyes.

A yawn from Canon's side of the bed tears my attention from the page.

He props his head in one hand. "I wouldn't get too attached to that."

Now that he's awake, I can touch him, so I run one finger over his high cheekbone and brush across his incongruously long lashes. "Don't get attached to what?"

"That version of the script." He kisses my finger and drags himself to sit up against my headboard, swallowing all the space with the breadth of his shoulders. "Verity is doing rewrites."

"No. I just learned these lines." I slap the script against my forehead and let it fall to the bed. "Are you kidding me?"

"It won't be that significant. It needed more emotional pull. The stakes didn't feel high enough the way it was written originally."

"And by originally you mean the way I just learned it?"

"Sorry. Them's the breaks. The script sometimes evolves once we get into it." He must see the dismay on my face. "We know you'll be getting new lines. We'll be patient."

I look at him disbelievingly. *Patient?*

"Okay. I'll try." He laughs, linking our fingers on the sheets. "But we do slow things down a lot when we shoot on film instead of digital. There will be more rehearsals. More time to nail it because it's so much more expensive. We can't afford a lot of throwaway takes."

I know he meant that to reassure me, but a screw turns in my chest tighter at the thought of less room for error.

"How long did you let me sleep?" Canon reaches for his phone, which goes off just as he grabs it. "You set my alarm?"

"You said you still have things to do, but I also thought it wouldn't hurt to nap for ten minutes."

"You wore me out." He pulls me from my side of the bed to his lap, and I'm completely unresistant, looping my arms around his neck. He palms my hip through the sheet.

"You complaining?" I nip his earlobe with my teeth.

"What do you think?" He tilts his head to capture my lips, deepening the kiss, drawing my tongue into his mouth. The script forgotten, I turn until my legs are spread over him and I'm pressing him into the headboard. The sheet wrapped around my breasts falls away, revealing that they are naked and tight and ready for his attention again.

He kisses down my throat and takes the tip of one breast into his mouth. A jolt of pleasure steals my breath, and my knees tighten at his hips. I slide my fingers into his hair. He groans at my shoulder, traces my spine, and kisses my collarbone before pulling back.

"I need to go," he says, gently setting me off his lap and swinging his long legs over the side of the bed.

I stare at the broad expanse of his back, tapering down to the narrow waist and tight ass. I wish I was a painter and could skillfully commit him to canvas. Or a sculptor like Linh's father, molding his muscles into clay or chiseled stone. Or even a musician like Monk and could set this feeling to music.

Stay.

It whispers through my head, and I'm so close to asking him, but I don't want to be the clingy girlfriend who distracts him from work.

Girlfriend.

I'll have to unpack my giddy feelings about him using that word later.

"I ordered Thai," I say, watching him slip his jeans on.

He looks over one naked shoulder, a dark brow lifted. "When did you have time? Between the blow job and the climax?"

"Silly rabbit." I pull the sheets around my breasts and walk on my knees to the edge of the bed, leaning up to kiss his nose. "I ordered as soon as you fell asleep. It should be here in like ten minutes."

"Ten minutes?"

I nod, even though it might be closer to fifteen. His phone pings, and he grabs it, reading the screen.

"Verity just sent over some rewrites. I may be able to give you the new lines before I leave."

"That would be awesome. I guess it does pay to date the director."

His expression sobers and he steps closer, resting his hands low on my hips. He presses his forehead to mine. "I don't know if I actually said it, but I'm sorry it happened like this. I wanted to shield you from this kind of shit so early in your career."

"I don't get stronger when you shield me from things, but I can draw strength from you if you walk with me through them. The way you came into the meeting today and claimed us; not acting like it was something to be ashamed of, or I was something to hide; how you showed them you were fine if they know we're together? That made me feel like I wasn't in this alone."

"You're not alone. I want this, Neevah." He sighs, tightening his grip on me possessively, comfortingly. "I don't want outside forces wrecking us before we even get off the ground."

"Oh, we are off the ground, Mr. Holt. After how you put it down tonight," I say, laughing and throwing my head back, "I'm way off the ground on cloud nine."

He shakes his head and grins, rolling his eyes. The doorbell rings and he pulls on his T-shirt.

"I got it. That's probably the food." He tosses me his phone. "Meanwhile, you wanna look at these new lines?"

I dive for the phone like a baby seal performing tricks. I want as much of a head start as I can get learning any new material. Tomorrow is a travel day, even though Santa Barbara is less than two hours away, so the crew will have to get us set up. We'll rehearse the upcoming scenes, but not actually film anything. I'm nervous, though, because with all the dance numbers behind me, this will be my first scene singing. We're saving the lion's share of vocal performances for the very last part of production since they mostly only affect me, Trey, and the musicians. Those scenes will be filmed primarily on our studio back lots, but this one needs to be captured on our French Riviera set.

Monk arrives tomorrow and we'll start working on the song while production gets everything set up. It's an original he wrote for the time Dessi and the band spent touring Europe, doing a residency at a hotel in the French Riviera. Monk sent the song to me a few weeks ago, and I've practiced on my own. I want to do it justice.

Which means this voice needs to rest.

My vocal coach sent a regimen in preparation for this song and the more vocal-intensive portion of the end of production. She shared the recipe for an elixir she concocted that's "guaranteed" to get your voice ready for anything. I'll be sipping on that for the next few days and getting plenty of vocal rest.

"Food's here," Canon yells from the living room.

I'll have to kick him out as soon as he eats. How am I supposed to concentrate with him here?

When I pad barefoot out of my bedroom and up the hall, he has our food and two place settings in the small dining room. He looks distracted half the time, like his mind is somewhere else. Like you don't have all of him, and the part you have wishes it were somewhere else.

Not right now.

With a hectic two weeks ahead of us on location, with rewrites burning a hole in his email, with a dozen things on his list I bet he needs to do before he sleeps, his eyes, when he looks up, are fully set on me. He's all there…for me. I hold his undivided attention, even if only for the next hour, and it is like stretching out under the sun at its highest. It is warm and illuminating.

There aren't candles on the table like there were our first night making love in Santa Barbara, but we make our own glow. Today Camille tried to steal it, to ruin it with her antics. The world tried to pick it apart, to mock it, to figure out what's real and what is true. *This* is real—eating, laughing with him right now. Talking with the ease of summer breezes until we have to tear ourselves away from each other. Stealing the last kisses of the day and having to push him out the door because we both want him to stay, but know he has to go. *This* is true. And leaning against the door after he leaves, my heart aches and swells with the unexpected sweetness of it.

FORTY-SEVEN

Canon

It's hard not to spend the whole night with Neevah; to stay and have her again; try to slake this quenchless thirst. Not only for sex, but for her closeness and the intimacy when my body relinquishes hers and we talk, our heads on one pillow. Our fingers linked on my chest. Laughing and touching in the dark where we don't hide anything from each other. Even in this, the most hectic stretch of our shooting schedule, I want that. Bad. Ignoring her answering desire and the hands reluctant to let me go, I leave her at the door. I need to make a call.

Camille.

I can't let what she did go unaddressed. I haven't bothered to deal directly with her animosity before, and if she hadn't involved Neevah, I probably wouldn't bother now.

But she did.

My fingers flex and grip the steering wheel in the struggle to control my anger, which has crouched like a tiger ever since Evan dropped his bombshell news. I strategized with him. I made sure Neevah was okay. I even checked in with Kenneth and Jill to confirm we're ready for tomorrow. With all of those things handled, now I can deal with Camille.

This was low.

Even for her, the woman who got me fired, not based on my inability, but out of spite and, yes, hurt. I know that. I could have pretended, let things ride until the movie wrapped, but that wouldn't have been fair to either of us.

Headed home, I pull onto the interstate and select her contact. After half a ring, she answers like she was expecting my call.

"Canon." Her voice fills the car, but she doesn't say anything else. She's almost as good as I am at hiding her feelings. It makes me appreciate Neevah's openness and generosity even more.

"We need to talk," I say.

"You could come over." Her husky voice suggests wicked things. "I still keep Macallan...just in case."

She thinks because she knows what I like to drink she knows *me*, like that's intimacy. She has no idea how to burrow into my thoughts, into my system so deeply I couldn't stop her if I wanted to. Neevah did that. What Camille and I had? It's a shadow of the real thing.

"What you did today was uncalled for," I say without acknowledging her offer. "Bitchy, even for you."

"I merely expressed my desire to work with you again and my disappointment at not even being given a chance over some novice. Did you *not* want people to know you're fucking yet another actress from one of your movies?"

"I don't have time for games or to rehash the past. I won't mislead you that there's a future for us."

"Don't flatter yourself."

"You obviously wanted my attention." I shrug, even though she can't see it. "You got it. Now what?"

"I actually think we could put all this behind us and try again," she says. "It was good. I know you remember." Her words are a sultry promise, but my dick doesn't even twitch.

"Now who's flattering herself?" I scoff.

"You're saying it wasn't?"

"I'm saying it wasn't enough."

"Oh, and your little piece of ass is?"

My jaw clenches and I force my breaths to flow in even and slow, refusing to reveal my tumultuous emotions. "I called to ask for a truce," I say. "To ask nicely."

"And if I don't?"

"It will be better if we both agree to let this go. To put this behind us.

I'll stay out of your way." I pause, pouring ice over the small silence. "And you'll stay the hell away from Neevah Saint."

"Oh, now we get down to it," she says, her words like the slash of a knife. "You know what I can't wait for? I can't wait for this movie to tank and everyone to know, including your studio and Evan, that you could have had me and you passed. That you could have had a star guarantee this movie succeeded, and you chose some unknown basic bitch with a tight pussy."

"Tank? You mean the way *Primal* tanked without me?"

My retort dulls her blade and she goes quiet.

"Leave her alone, Camille."

"How lucky she is to have a champion, someone who gave her a shot when literally no one in their right mind would."

"Neevah is more talented on an off day than you are on your best," I say, my voice not raising. "Is that what you want me to tell you? She's the best thing about this movie, and there are a million great things about *Dessi Blue*. It's the role of a lifetime, and I understand why you resent not getting a shot at it, but it wasn't a fit for you."

"No. If you had let me—"

"I tell her things that I tell no one else," I continue softly, injecting the words with truth so she can hear that I'm not lying. "I want to be with her all the time. It has been torture pretending I don't want her and hiding that we're together. I'm proud of her, and because of what you did today, now everyone knows."

"Son of a bitch," she hisses, but the hurt slips through. I hear it. What she did was low, but what I just said, though honest, was low in its own way, because when it comes down to it, I know why Camille got me fired. I know why she lashed out publicly. I know why she threw her tantrum today.

Hurt people holler, Mama used to say.

When something hurts, you scream.

"Look," I say, switching lanes on the interstate to exit as carefully as I'm changing the tone of this conversation. "Things ended badly between us, and we never really talked about it."

"Oh, you talked about it. You eavesdropped on one phone call and decided I'm a bitch and you couldn't be with me." She pauses, draws a shaky breath. "That wasn't fair, Canon."

I heard what I heard and I know what I know. Anyone who would do what I overheard Camille doing, saying, is not for me, but that is not the point to make right now.

"I'm sorry I hurt you."

I could have said it—sincerely said it—when we broke up, but maybe I didn't understand the power of acknowledging someone else's pain. Not that I would take her back, do it differently, or choose her over Neevah if given the chance, because hell naw. But Camille was emotionally involved, and I knew the break would hurt. Still, I never had *this* conversation with her. If I had, maybe we could have avoided all the subsequent shit that soured things so badly, so publicly between us.

"You did hurt me," she says, her voice less sure, less hard. "I thought we..."

I know what she thought.

"I'm sorry," I tell her again.

There's a part of me that doesn't want to apologize at all. Of course, there is. She hurt me, too. Tried to publicly embarrass me. Tried to damage my reputation. She was in the wrong. At this point, though, I'm more concerned about making things right than I am about being right.

"Are you..." She inhales sharply like someone does before they take an icy plunge. "Are you serious? About her, I mean?"

"Yes." Lying won't help. "I care about her a lot."

"So that shit you said, about telling her things you don't tell anyone else, you weren't saying it just to get at me? You've opened up to her?"

"I have. I do."

"I always wondered what that would look like," she says, her voice softening around the edges some, almost wistful. "Canon Holt, open."

"Do you remember what it was like when you first started, Mille? Before things got this big and before you felt like you were living in a den of vipers. That feeling of just loving the work and being grateful for a shot?"

"Yeah, I remember. It's been a long time, but I remember."

"I don't want to fight with you, and I don't want her caught in the middle. She shouldn't be. Your problem, your real problem, was with me, and I'm saying I'm sorry."

"Because of her you're saying you're sorry."

"No, because of you I'm saying I'm sorry. Yes, I want this to stop, but also, I hurt you and I'm sorry."

"So I guess now I'm supposed to apologize, too?" We used to make each other laugh, and some of that humor shows in her words.

"I won't hold my breath." I chuckle. "But know that when I say it, I mean it."

"Yeah, well..." She sighs, her voice soft if not humble. "I'm sorry, too."

"Thank you," I tell her as I arrive at my house and pull into the garage. I park and wait for her next move because I'm out of them.

"So a truce, huh?" she asks.

"I'd like that, yeah."

"Alright, whatever," she says, her voice going brisk. "Truce."

FORTY-EIGHT

Dessi Blue

June 1939 - THE FRENCH RIVIERA - HOTEL DU CAP

EXTERIOR - BEACH - DAY

The shore is crowded with people sunbathing and swimming. Dessi and Cal lounge on the sand beneath a large umbrella, both in swimwear typical of the 1930s. Sheet music is spread on the blanket between them, along with a basket of fruit, cheese, and wine.

DESSI

Why you gotta write all these sad songs, Cal?

CAL (LAUGHING)

Now you know you lying. Look at this one. It's happy.

Cal offers her a sheet of music and Dessi rolls her eyes.

DESSI

Gon' have them poor folks tonight crying in their champagne. This hotel is mighty fine. I'm glad we're here for a little while.

CAL

We're lucky. The Hot Club, those students from Paris, want to promote Negro jazz. The band seems to love it here, too, so far.

DESSI (LAUGHING AND HOLDING UP ANOTHER PIECE OF SHEET MUSIC)
The band gon' get as tired of playing these sad old songs as I am singing 'em. Like this one. "Walk Away"? What made you want to write a song this sad?

CAL (SOBERING)
"Walk Away" is about a girl who finds somebody else to love. She tells the boy to just walk away or she will.

DESSI (WATCHING CAL'S EXPRESSION)
And was that boy you?

CAL
I don't want to talk about it, Dess. You're right. We need to sing some happy songs for the people tonight. We're in France on a beach and got nothing to be sad about. Look at all these white folks. Back home, they wouldn't be caught dead on the beach with us. I wish every Negro could come here. Could see how it feels to be treated like you a human being.

DESSI
You still writing that travel column for *The Chicago Defender*?

CAL
Yes, I am, and the people back home love hearing about what we up to here traveling all over Europe.

DESSI

Galivanting is what Mama would call it. Galivanting all over Europe. It was reading *The Defender* that made Daddy want to move to New York. That and our cousins having to buy their own farm three times. Not to mention the lynching.

CAL

They got war brewing here in Europe. We got war at home right there in the South, and who's fighting for us? In my last column I wrote that the only discrimination I've experienced here has been from Americans.

DESSI

Like them Texas boys we saw on the train from Florence. Tried to make us get up like we got their seats. Hmmmph.

CAL

Difference is here, they couldn't make us get up. I'll never go back South. I was born in North Carolina, but we moved to Chicago when I was a pup. I'm a city boy, Bama. Ain't that what Tilda calls you?

DESSI

Yeah. She crazy.

CAL

You still haven't heard from her?

DESSI

Nah, and I'm a little worried 'cause it's been a long time since her last letter. When we were traveling from city to city, it was hard to get mail, but she knows we're here at the hotel for a while. I've written to her, but she . . . I don't know.

CAL

You two are so close. The best of friends.

DESSI (LOOKING A LITTLE UNCOMFORTABLE)

We are, yeah.

CAL

Dessi, it's okay, ya know?

DESSI

What's okay?

CAL

That you love Tilda.

DESSI (STARES AT HIM)

Yeah?

CAL

Yeah.

DESSI (LOOKS AT HER WATCH AND RUBS HER ARMS)

Well, we been out here long enough. My black is burning.

CAL (LAUGHING AND PACKING THE FOOD AND MUSIC)

I heard that. Let's go find the band so we can rehearse.

INTERIOR - HOTEL DU CAP - DAY

Dessi and Cal enter the hotel still carrying their beach bag and dressed in swimwear. Concierge at the front desk flags them down.

CONCIERGE
Miss Blue, you have mail.

DESSI (SMILES BRIGHTLY AND TEARS THE LETTER OPEN)
Cal, you done talked her up. It's from Tilda.

CAL
Oh, good. She alright? What's she say?

Dessi's smile falls and she grips the edge of the hotel front desk for support. A newspaper clipping floats from the letter and lands on the floor. Camera zooms close to show Tilda and a nightclub owner pictured in a wedding announcement. Scribbled at the bottom of the picture are the words *I had to. Forgive me.*

CAL
Oh, Dessi.

Dessi swipes at a few tears, shoving the letter and the newspaper clipping into her beach bag.

DESSI
It's alright. I'm alright. Dessi Blue always gon' be alright.

CAL
You want to rest for a bit? I can tell the boys we'll do the same songs. No need to rehearse and give you some time to—

DESSI

No. I don't need no time.

Dessi digs through the pile of music in the basket until she finds the song she's looking for.

DESSI (SHOVES THE SONG AT HIM)

We doing this one.

CLOSE ON SHEET MUSIC: Song is "Walk Away"

INTERIOR - HOTEL DU CAP DINING ROOM - NIGHT

Dessi wears an evening gown and stands in a spotlight on the small stage in a roomful of patrons eating and listening. The band plays behind her—piano, saxophone, drums, and Cal on trumpet. With tears in her eyes, she sings "Walk Away."

FORTY-NINE

Neevah

"I need you to go grab that C up top, Neevah."

I swear. If Monk tells me to go "grab" one more damn note. We've been rehearsing for hours, and he more than lives up to his reputation as a perfectionist.

"Okay," I say, shifting beside him on the piano bench in the hotel ballroom. Galaxy Studios bought a set of rooms for the cast and crew's accommodations, and has also blocked off portions of the hotel for rehearsals and shooting.

"Walk Away," the tune Monk wrote for the French Riviera scene, will be on repeat in my head long after we're done. The opening strains float from the piano as we start the song again. It's lush and heartbreaking and haunting. A song about a love betrayed, a lover abandoned. I close my eyes, blocking out the empty ballroom and Monk on the piano and every other distraction. I fall into the heartbreak of the lyrics—crack my heart open to let Dessi's pain over losing Tilda flood in.

When I first started this movie, Dessi was some distant figure trapped in the pages of the past. She was history, but now I feel her present with me every day. I thought she was here to serve me, a means to the end of my big break. Now, I realize I'm here to serve *her*—to make sure a voice this rich and true, swallowed by the years and by injustice, is finally heard.

The closing notes hang in the air before evaporating into silence. I almost can't bear to open my eyes, I'm so lost in the feeling this song perfectly conveys. I wipe the tears from my cheeks and force myself to look around, surprised to see several cast and crew members now gathered around the piano, some of them with wet cheeks and shiny eyes, too.

Some of them snap their appreciation, some clap approvingly, and others offer smiles. I let my gaze lovingly drift over their faces. In only a few months, you can become pretty tight, and we have.

After the initial shock of Camille's interview, no one has said anything snide to me or made me feel weird about my relationship with Canon. We've only been on location two days, and I've barely seen him, so there hasn't been much opportunity for awkwardness, but I can already tell most of them are fine with it. A few of them even teased me, asking how I tamed the beast.

Of course, I haven't.

"Now that's a song," Trey says, leaning his elbows on the top of the piano. "You wrote that specifically for the movie, Monk?"

"I did." Monk's fingers skate across the keys in a brighter-sounding flourish. "I used the script to write some of the original songs. I won't score the film until after I see the final cut."

"It's a fantastic script," Livvie says.

"Thank you." That comes from the ballroom entrance where Verity stands, watching us all, but her eyes invariably returning to Monk. His eyes always invariably return to her.

"You know," Monk says, "there was a song that was perfect for that scene when Dessi realizes Tilda was unfaithful. That she cheated and couldn't be trusted."

He looks directly at Verity, his fingers coaxing a few haunting notes from the instrument.

"It's called 'Don't Explain,'" he continues, eyes still locked with Verity's. "Billie Holiday wrote it when she discovered her husband's infidelity. When she found out he wasn't who she thought he was. Or maybe he was exactly who she thought he was, and she had lied to herself. Either way, he was a cheat."

I glance at Verity. Several of us do, the discomfort filling the room the longer they stare each other down. Her lips tighten and her eyes slit with anger behind black-rimmed reading glasses.

"That would have been musically anachronistic, though, since this scene took place in 1939 and she didn't write the song until 1946." Monk presses his fingers into a dark extended note and then slams the piano lid down. "So too late."

His harsh words seem to break a spell, and the people around me start laughing and talking, most of them about how long the day of rehearsal has been and how hungry they are. I concur, except I've been feeling a little nauseous. Even if I were hungry, I probably wouldn't eat much. This sick feeling has persisted. Probably just nerves, but I've pushed it aside to get through today. We shoot this tomorrow, and I don't want to be the reason things slow down.

I can't be.

"I came to tell you guys dinner is ready and down on the beach tonight," Verity says, looking pointedly away from Monk. "They're doing a bonfire for us."

"Oooh, fun," Livvie says, gathering her bag and script, which we all seem to carry, with all the new lines we've been getting.

"You sound amazing, Neevah," Monk says, standing from the piano and walking with me toward the ballroom exit.

"Gosh, it feels like it took all day to get it right."

"You weren't that far off anyway. I'm just a demanding dude who's hard to satisfy."

"Between you and Canon, I don't know how any of us survive."

"So you and our esteemed director, huh?" Monk asks, the smile he slants down to me teasing and kind.

My cheeks burn, but I don't look away. "Guess everyone knows now."

"I mean, I already knew."

"He told you?"

"No way. We don't sit around talking about that kind of shit." He laughs and takes my elbow as we negotiate a steep set of steps leading down to the beach where the cast and crew have already started forming a line at an outdoor buffet. "I knew because he's never been like this before about anyone else."

"Thanks, Monk." I smile gratefully, but shut the conversation down as we approach the watching eyes and listening ears of the cast and crew. They may be fine with Canon and me, but that doesn't mean they aren't rabidly curious. And I have no intention of giving them any food for thought.

"I see Takira over there," I tell him. "Thanks again for today. The song sounds a hundred times better."

"You were already good, but you sound even better."

I'm still glowing with the pleasure of that when I reach Takira. She and I have separate rooms, which I didn't expect. She, like most of the crew, has a room in the hotel. I, along with other "above the line" cast and crew, am staying in one of the luxurious cottages along the shoreline. Not a bad view to wake up to. The only thing that would make it better is waking up with Canon. He, Jill, and Kenneth have worked tirelessly with the production team these first two days to prepare the sets and the equipment, plan the shots, review the line edits, confirm the costumes—everything to ensure things on location go as efficiently as possible. I've barely seen him, much less slept with him. He did text from a production meeting last night that went on well after midnight. He knew I had an early start and said we'd see each other today.

But alas...

"How's it been going for you guys?" I ask Takira as we load up our plates. I'm pleased to see lots of fish, leafy greens, and fruit.

"All these damn extras! They may be in the background most of the time, but they all need costumes, hair, and makeup."

Takira doesn't just do my hair and makeup, but helps wherever she is needed.

"How was your day?" She looks at me searchingly. "You feeling okay?"

"Good." I don't mention the nausea, which even now stirs at the smell of the mahi mahi on my plate. I'm sure it's just stress and working too hard. "Monk's song is great, and we spent most of the day getting it just right for tomorrow's shoot."

"Any word from the doc on your blood tests yet?"

"Nope. They sent them off to the lab, and should have them back maybe tomorrow."

We sit at one of the long tables dotted along the shore, and soon, with the evening breeze, the setting sun, and the great conversation, I've forgotten the unsettled feeling in my stomach and am having a great time.

"Hey," Canon says an hour or so into dinner, standing beside my table. He's holding a plate loaded with chicken and salad. "Mind if I squeeze in?"

The girl beside me, one of the grips, hastily scoots over to make room for Canon. I feel all eyes on us, but I don't give a damn. I can't suppress the grin that widens when he settles in at my side. It's quiet around us for a few seconds, like everyone's not sure if they should carry on with the boss at the table. One by one, the crew resume their conversations, and Canon shoots me a wink and a grin.

"How was your day?" I ask when there's a break for us to talk, keeping my voice low.

"Long. Getting ready to start shooting, but Verity is also tweaking the London scene in the tube during The Blitz."

"I'm licking my chops for that scene. It's already fantastic. Can't wait to see how she makes it even better."

"If anyone can, it's Verity. And how was *your* day?"

"Long." I laugh. "Monk is as bad as you are."

"I try to tell people, but they don't believe me. He fools them with the smile."

"Whereas you don't bother with a smile?"

He flashes an exaggerated caricature of a grin, which looks so odd on him, I snort.

"Was that a snuckle?" he asks, taking a bite of his chicken.

I lean my shoulder into his, laughing. "I can't believe you remember that. I was so nervous around you that night."

"And now?" he asks, his voice husky, his eyes smoldering. "Do I still make you nervous?"

I don't answer, just shake my head. Someone across the table asks him a question, and Takira pulls me into a debate about some love at first sight or arranged marriage reality show. Canon and I go our separate ways conversationally, both being drawn in different directions, but he anchors us by holding my hand under the table, and it's so sweet it makes my heart ache.

He calls me his girlfriend.

He seeks me out in front of everyone.

He holds my hand.

I'm not starstruck by Canon anymore. That's not where this surreal feeling comes from. You don't really know a person when you're starstruck. You're awed by the idea of them and your idea of them is filtered through a public lens. What has me tripping is that Canon is so much more, so much better in private, when we're alone. And he's so guarded that most of the people at this table are still a little in awe of his talent and his reputation. Starstruck.

Me? I've kissed the star. I've felt its burn and held it close.

And when Canon squeezes my hand under the table, stealing a look that is private even at a dinner for a hundred people, I feel like, as improbable as it seems, this star belongs to me.

When they light the bonfire, everyone gathers around, singing songs and getting a little drunk.

"You wanna go for a walk?" Canon asks.

I nod, gripping his hand as he leads us away from the large circle of people rimming the fire.

"This brings back memories," Canon says, taking off his shoes and holding them in the hand not holding mine.

I slip off my shoes and do the same. "You mean of New Year's?"

"Yeah. That was such a great time." He slides me a hot, teasing glance. "Though we barely left the house. We only walked on the beach once."

"And got caught! Canon, is that *you?*" I imitate Sylvia Miller's fake surprised tone.

"We can laugh about it now, but that shit pisses me off." The smile fades from his face, and in the moonlight, his expression hardens. "Camille didn't just come after me. She wanted to sabotage you. Not cool."

I step closer and he slips an arm around my waist. For minutes, neither of us speaks. I don't know if Canon is lost in the myriad things he must have to do before we start shooting tomorrow, but I'm not. My mind is clear of everything but him and this moment with the stars as our chaperones. When he finally speaks, his words surprise me.

"Mama loved photographing at night, too." He stares up at the sky. "She thought the darkness, the stars, were almost as beautiful as the sunset. You know what an aspect ratio is, I assume. The ratio of an image's width to its height. Well, she used to look up at the sky and say aspect ratio infinity: immeasurable."

"I wish I could have met her," I whisper, squeezing his hand.

"She would have loved you."

And all of a sudden, the question, the one I've promised myself I will not ask, enters my head, even though I've banned it from my thoughts.

And could you love me?

It's still so early, too early for me to put much stock in whatever he would say.

But if I'm honest with myself about what I feel for him…I can't be. Not yet. My feelings are like a priceless carpet, unrolled little by little until it fills the room. And we are really just getting started.

I thought our walk was as aimless as our conversation, which meandered from our childhoods, to our heroes, to the scenes we'll shoot tomorrow, but there was some direction. He was guiding and I didn't even notice until we arrive at my cottage door.

He looks down at me under the light of the small porch.

"Come inside," I whisper, glancing around, searching for prying eyes.

"I will, but only to kiss you because these folks don't get that for free."

We laugh and I fumble to get the door open. As soon as we're inside, I'm in his arms. Our mouths fuse with immediate passion, lust that has lain low and waited to strike. Walking me back the few steps to my bedroom, he doesn't bother turning on the light, and gives me a gentle push to the bed. He feathers kisses over my cheeks, down my neck, lingering at my breasts to pull my dress away so he can suck hard, worshiping each nipple with lips and teeth for long moments. My legs spread beneath him, and I grind up against the steel of his cock. His fingers find me, stroking along the seam of my pussy, filling the aching, empty, waiting void with three fingers and then four and it's still not as much as he would be. I cannot get his belt off, his jeans undone fast enough.

"Neev," he whispers into my neck. "Damn, I missed you."

It's only been three days. Three days multiplied by interminable.

"Fuck me, Canon," I beg, sliding my own panties down my legs as far as I can get them, down to my knees.

"I don't have a condom."

"I took my insurance physical for the movie." I blink up at him, panting and starved. "I'm clean and on the pill. I haven't been with anyone but you since then."

"Same." He pulls back a little, his eyes burning and intent. "Are you saying we can—"

"Yeah." I flip onto all fours on my bed, panties still ringing my knees, and pull up my sundress, offering him my bare ass.

"Damn," he mutters, positioning himself behind me, the jangle of his buckle, the susurrus of the ocean the only sounds in the room. "I've never done this before."

"What?" I laugh and pull one cheek, spreading myself for him. "Now I know for a fact you've hit it from the back."

His answering chuckle is husky, but there's a note of…something. I look over my shoulder. "What's wrong? You don't want to?"

"It's the first time I've ever done this raw, with nothing. You're the only one."

It strikes me that Canon won at Sundance when he was twenty-one years old. He's been swimming in the shark-infested waters of entertainment nearly half his life. A man like that would have had to, by necessity, approach every encounter, sexual or romantic, as a potential snare. As a possible trap, or at the very least, as an ill-motivated act. He'd have to vet a woman before even considering this kind of vulnerability. The trust this must require of him.

I sit up and face him, letting my dress fall back around my hips and legs. I cup one side of his face. "If you're not comfortable, we can—"

He silences me with a kiss—a craving, intense thing that sends subcutaneous shivers burrowing beneath my skin to skitter over my bones. A tender thing that disarms all my anxieties, my worries. He breaks our kiss long enough to pull the dress over my head and toss it aside. We tug at his clothes until they fall in a heap by the bed, and there's nothing between us. We're skin to skin. Our heartbeats strain for each other through our chests. My hands travel over him in claiming sweeps. He is suede and silk and leather, smooth and hard and rough, a decadence of textures between my sheets.

Staring into my eyes and tangling our fingers on the bed beside my head, he enters me on one deep thrust. The slick, hot entry, with nothing separating us, is startlingly good. He clutches my thigh, pulling it up and sinking deeper, his eyes blazing into mine. A harmony of gasps and sighs are accompanied by the pounding rhythm that thumps the headboard against the wall. A voracious hunger builds between us, and we grip, our hands tight on each other like we might slip away, might lose this if we don't cling. It's like riding a rocket, the propulsive force of it beyond our control, and its destination a place our minds can't even conceive. When I unspool inside, I turn my face into the pillow, bury my scream of release. When my body jerks beneath him, it triggers an answering response, a matching release. This is the moment I treasure most, when he comes apart in my arms. When all the rigid discipline fails him in the face of our passion, and he drops his head to the curve of my neck, his breaths coming harshly, holding on to me like we are indeed in outer space and I'm the only solid thing in his universe.

Zero gravity.

Celestial. Astral.

Infinity: immeasurable.

FIFTY

Canon

"What are we waiting for?" I ask Kenneth.

It appears that everything is finally in place. And I say finally because this morning can kiss my black ass. Working with film presents enough challenges without the power going out and lights not working. At least we have a backup generator until we figure out what the hell is going on. If I hear one more person yell *we're working on it* from the equipment truck, I can't be held responsible.

"Uh, so... we're missing someone," Kenneth says.

"Missing someone?" I gesture to the beach and what seems like an army of extras. "Seems like the gang's all here. We've had enough delays. Let's get started."

"We're waiting on one cast member." Kenneth adjusts his glasses and averts his eyes.

"I know you're not saying an actor is late to my set. That can't be what you're saying."

"Well, late may not be the right word," Kenneth hedges. And I know he's hedging because I've known him for a long-ass time. "Delayed."

"Delayed is late if I can't start shooting. Who is it?"

"Neevah."

Right. So now the uncomfortable silence and shifty stares make sense. No one is late to my set. I've been known to track tardy actors down and deal with them myself. Everyone knows Neevah and I are together and are watching to see how I'll handle it when my girlfriend is late.

I didn't spend the night with her. I forced myself out of bed, left her asleep, and went back to my own cottage to prepare for today. A lot of good that did me since the day feels shot to hell before we've even gotten started.

"Did she report for hair and makeup?" I demand, sitting forward in my director's chair.

"Yeah, Takira—"

"Where is Takira?"

"I'm here," Takira says from a few feet away.

I walk over and ask her in as low a voice as I can manage when I'm this annoyed. "Where is she?"

"She got hair and makeup over an hour ago," Takira says. "And she was headed for wardrobe. Maybe she—"

"Where's wardrobe?" With it being a new set on location, I don't actually know where everything is situated.

"This way," Takira says, starting to walk. "But she probably isn't—"

"Do I look like I have time for probably? We're wasting money and time. Believe me, the first union break will come before you know it."

I stride past craft services and through a jungle of equipment and crew to a white hard-topped tent marked *wardrobe*. When I walk in, the large space is divided into smaller sections, separated by privacy dividers and populated with hanging wardrobe bars. Linh glances up from a table where she's seated in front of a sewing machine. Her eyes flick, filled with curiosity, between Takira and me.

"Is there a problem?" she asks.

"We're looking for Neevah," I say. "She came to wardrobe?"

"Of course." Linh frowns. "But that was like an hour ago. She was headed for set."

"Well, she hasn't made it to set and I need to get started." I turn on Takira. "Did you check her room?"

"I knocked, but there was no answer, and I didn't actually expect her to be there because she's been here." Consternation pinches Takira's expression. "I can go check again."

"No, I will."

I certainly know the way after last night, and I have a key.

I'm an idiot.

I lowered my guard. I can't afford to be lax on this—the biggest project of my career. And instead of nailing down shot lists and making sure I was ready for the first day of shooting, where was I?

With my girlfriend.

Even irritated, I can't dismiss what we had last night. It shook me. Being inside her raw was…

Am I seriously getting hard in the middle of a crisis?

I don't regret one minute of it, but this is what I get. The more I think about it on the way to Neevah's room, the more annoyed I become. With myself and with her. We'll have to be smarter than this, better than this if we expect our relationship to work, on set and off. And if we expect other people to respect it.

I reach her room and don't bother knocking, but use the key she gave me last night.

"Neevah!" I yell as soon as I enter the cottage.

No response.

I walk down the short hall to her bedroom. Wearing her white terry-cloth bathrobe over her costume, she's asleep on the bed.

"Really?" I say harshly, but shake her shoulder gently. "Neevah, wake up."

Her lashes flutter, and I steel myself against the big brown eyes that come into focus. She smiles sleepily at me and reaches up to touch my beard. "Hey, you."

I jerk my head back. "Neevah, what the fuck? The whole crew is waiting for you."

She frowns, tilting her head like she's not sure what I could be talking about, but then she glances down at her bathrobe, reaches up to touch her wig.

"Crap!" she says, scrambling from the bed.

"Rule number one. Never be late to my set."

"I wasn't late." She rushes to the mirror to check her makeup and the wig. "I was on time. I just came back here because with the power out, we couldn't do anything. I was feeling so…I'm sorry."

"I can't put sorry on film. Don't be sorry. Be on time. Be where you're supposed to be. Be prepared, dammit."

"Are you kidding right now?" She whirls from the mirror to face me, indignation splashed across her expression. "I miss one call time in four months and you light into me like this?"

"What should I do when one of my actors is late? Give you a gold star for every time you weren't?"

"You're being a dick."

"I'm being the director, Neevah. I can't play favorites."

"Favorites? Who's asking you to?"

"You've put me in a position where my crew is wondering if I'll go easy on you because we're—"

"Fucking? Is that what you were gonna say?"

The word torpedoes between us, sounding coarse in this room where we made love last night. When it was lusty and tender and perfect. All the things I don't have time to consider when I'm burning money having a damn lover's quarrel.

"Don't do this shit with me, Neevah. Not today. Of all days, not today. I don't have time for it. We're behind, and we're gonna fuck around and lose my light."

"Ever think there might be something more important than your damn light?"

"No, because that's my job to think there is nothing more important than my damn light, and it's your job to be ready when I have it." I leave the room and yell over my shoulder, "Cameras roll in two minutes."

FIFTY-ONE

Dessi Blue

EXTERIOR - LONDON - NIGHT

Dessi and Cal walk swiftly through Central London, both looking around as if unsure where they are. Both carry gas masks. Cal also totes his trumpet case. The streets have steady traffic with a few people milling about.

DESSI

It's Surrey Street, you said?

CAL

Yeah. I don't see—oh, wait. I think it's... here's The Strand.

DESSI

We the blind leading the blind. Why we have to do this tonight?

CAL

We need to meet this cat, see if he can play. A band with no drummer—what's that?

DESSI

I hate you had to fire Bird. He's been with us since the beginning.

CAL

Bird is on that hop and not even trying to get off that ride. Not showing up for gigs, missing cues, falling asleep onstage—he gotta get clean before he can be in my band.

DESSI

I know. At least he's going home.

CAL

What's so great about home? Why you think Langston Hughes, James Baldwin, and all them come over here? America don't love us.

DESSI

Sometimes home ain't great, but it's still home. I miss my mama. You know the last time I saw my mama? Had her fried chicken?

A group of uniformed British soldiers walks by. Dessi turns her head to follow their progress before turning back to Cal.

DESSI

Been five years since Mama moved back to Alabama. At least there ain't war at home. We running outta France to escape the Germans. Now we running underground in London, hiding from the Germans. Bombs dropping.

Dessi holds up her gas mask.

DESSI

Gotta wear these just to stay alive.

CAL

You know what we are? Working. Making music and seeing the world. You get tired of that, let me know, and you can catch the next boat with Bird back to the States. I don't miss America and it don't feel like home. Where I can make money with this horn right here and don't have to fear for my life just for looking at a white woman? That feels like home.

DESSI (TEASING, TRYING TO LIGHTEN THE TENSION)

You want a white woman, Cal? You can get you one over here and nobody'll even blink twice.

CAL

I don't want no white woman.

DESSI

Well, who you want? In all this time, all these cities, I ain't ever seen you with nobody.

CAL (LOOKS AT HER INTENSELY)

Oh, there's somebody I want, but just ain't sure she'd ever want me.

Before Dessi can respond, an air raid siren goes off, a mournful, eerie sound that rises and falls, signaling that bombs will be dropping soon. The people walking around begin scrambling, heading for a building with red-glazed terra-cotta blocks: Aldwych tube station.

CAL (GRABS DESSI'S HAND)

Come on! We gotta find shelter.

Dessi and Cal follow the streams of people underground.

CLOSE SHOT ON SIGNS ON THE TUBE STATION WALLS THAT READ:

Shelter's bedding
The practice of shaking bedding over the platforms, tracks, and in the subways is strictly forbidden.

In air raids
If you are in a train during an air raid or when an alert is sounded: Do not leave the train between stations unless so requested by a railway official.

Should a gas attack be suspected:
Close all windows and ventilators. Refrain from smoking. Do not touch any outside part of a car.

Always have your gas mask with you.

The escalators are still. People crowd the tracks with makeshift bedding. Some cluster at the corners of the escalators. Some are bedding down on benches. Children huddle with their parents, looking afraid.

CAL (POINTING TO AN EMPTY SPACE AGAINST THE WALL)
This'll do.

The sounds of the night's first bombs drop above.

DESSI
How long we gotta be down here?

CAL
Better down here than out there. A lot safer.

TIME LAPSE/MONTAGE

Sounds of the bombs. Those taking shelter demonstrate an array of emotions and ways to pass the time. Some look startled and frightened. Others go on playing cards, reading, ducking under blankets, and lying down to go to sleep.

CLOSE SHOT ON A LITTLE GIRL STARTING TO CRY

BRITISH GIRL
Mummy, I'm scared.

MOTHER
It'll be alright.

Bombs drop above and walls shake. Little girl huddles into her mother's shoulder and starts to cry. Dessi scoots over the few feet to sit beside them and starts to sing "Look for the Silver Lining."

DESSI (SINGING)
Look for the silver lining,
Whenever a cloud appears in the blue,
Remember, somewhere the sun is shining,
And so the right thing to do is make it shine
for you

A heart, full of joy and gladness,
Will always banish sadness and strife,
So always look for the silver lining,
And try to find the sunny side of life

A heart, full of joy and gladness,
Will always banish sadness and strife,
So always look for the silver lining,
And try to find the sunny side of life

The little girl peeks out from her mother's dress and watches Dessi with wide eyes, thumb in her mouth. When the song ends, someone sitting on a blanket at the base of the quiet escalator calls out.

MAN AT ESCALATOR
Sing us another one!

Cal takes out his trumpet and accompanies Dessi on two more tunes, "Them There Eyes" and "Easy Living." When they finish, those around clap. Dessi and Cal scoot back against the wall. Dessi huddles into her coat trying to stay warm. The man from the escalator, who asked them to sing another, brings them a blanket.

Cal and Dessi snuggle together under the blanket while bombs continue blasting above ground. Dessi loops her arm through Cal's elbow and lowers her head to his shoulder.

DESSI
That right there, what we just did,
making music and making people smile—that
feels like home. Maybe music means I can be
at home anywhere in the world.

CAL
You're amazing, Dess.

DESSI (BUMPS HIS SHOULDER)
Go on with you.

CAL
You remember you asked me who I want?

Dessi lifts and turns her head to look at him.

DESSI
Well, yeah.

CAL
The girl I want is you, Dessi Blue.

She stares at him for a few seconds, her expression softening, before leaning in to cup his face and kiss him.

The all-clear signal sounds, a long single whine, telling them it's safe to leave, but most don't move. Cal and Dessi stay where they are for the night.

FIFTY-TWO

Neevah

If I thought the dance numbers were grueling, today gave them a run for their money. We rehearsed the scenes over and over before committing them to film, and made sure to get a few takes because mistakes on film are usually harder to fix in post than they are in digital.

Not to mention how mentally taxing today proved to be. At a time when I need to be sharper than I have ever been, I feel like I'm moving underwater, my brain as weighed down as my arms and legs. The script revisions didn't help. I had more content to learn in less time than I've had before. I've never dropped as many lines as I did today, and I couldn't help but wonder if anyone in the cast is thinking my inexperience is showing.

Hell, *I'm* wondering if my inexperience is showing. If maybe the last four months were some extended beginner's luck, and now, in the final stretch of filming, my luck is running out.

I fled that set as soon as Kenneth said it was a wrap for the day. I didn't look for Canon, and I'm sure he's not looking for me. Our fight this morning didn't help my concentration. I was hurt by his harshness, but I was also frustrated with myself, with my body. I only came to lie down for a quick second because I was so exhausted, lying down seemed a better use of the time we spent waiting for them to fix the power than standing around. I never oversleep that way. I snapped at him as much out of misplaced embarrassment as anything else.

I told Takira to go eat with the rest of the crew and I'd see her tomorrow. I still don't have much appetite and fought nausea most of the day—yet another thing to distract me. I was a mess on set. Trey, Kenneth, Linh—all asked if I was feeling okay. Not Canon, though. He and I barely spoke, besides the notes he delivered himself instead of through Kenneth. No one observing us would think our relationship tempts him to favor me. He was the same with me as with everyone else. Maybe even more indifferent. The intimacy of last night feels light-years away right now.

I drag my weary body to the bedroom. I don't even make it to the shower. I'm more tired right this very second than I have ever been in my entire life. And today was a relatively easy schedule compared to nine-hour dance rehearsals. I know this isn't normal, this level of fatigue. No amount of rest seems able to penetrate it.

"I'm so close," I whisper, staring up at the ceiling. "Only three weeks left. Just please let me finish."

I don't know if I'm asking God or my body, begging it to hold out long enough to finish strong, but I choke down a sob. It feels like some internal clock is ticking, and I'm racing against it.

After a few seconds, I stand, strip, shower, and get into my lounge pants and tank top. All I want is my bed. Five o'clock will be here before you know it, and I need tomorrow to go better than today. It's not that we didn't get what we needed. If we hadn't, we'd still be there. Canon wouldn't settle for less than that, but it just took so much. And most of the time it was my fault. Even with new content, I'm usually sharper than this.

"Ugh." I tap my head as if that might clear it.

I'll never get rest if I replay all my mistakes over and over on this loop. I pull back the comforter and climb in, but notice my phone plugged in by the bed. A ringing phone on set will get you chewed out as fast as being late will, so I usually leave mine here.

I have missed calls and messages.

"Neevah, hi. It's Dr. Ansford. I know you're on set, but call me first thing tomorrow. We need to talk. Your tests came back. Your antinuclear antibodies are elevated. Low red and white blood count. ESR indicates inflammation. Most concerning is your high creatinine levels."

I've barely absorbed all she's saying in the pause she takes to breathe when she launches another attack on my peace of mind. "I'm coordinating with your doctor out there. We're calling in a prescription for prednisone.

You should be able to get it tomorrow. I'm sorry, Neevah. I know you like to manage things naturally, but all signs indicate you're experiencing a flare-up—a very serious one. We have to get that under control. Based on those elevated creatinine levels, we need to biopsy your kidney."

I press a trembling hand to my temple and draw a shaky breath, listening to the rest of the message through ringing ears and with a dozen questions winnowing through my head.

I have discoid lupus. She hasn't even mentioned the rash or my hair falling out. Why are they looking at my kidneys? I want to hurl the phone into the wall because I can't ask her my questions and it's almost midnight in New York.

"I don't want to alarm you," she continues in the message.

Too late.

"But things can go south with kidneys very quickly and with fewer symptoms than you might think. We want to see what we're dealing with as soon as possible, but you take a lot of supplements. Stop taking those right away. We need them out of your system before the procedure. So it'll be a few days before we can get the biopsy done, but we can at least get you on the prednisone. Call me first thing and try not to worry. Stress will only exacerbate things, and we're going to figure this out, okay? Good night."

I sit on my bed for a few minutes after Dr. Ansford's message. Shock and worry and dread swim through my thoughts as I process what she said.

Biopsy.

That word…

This isn't something I need to keep to myself. I won't be able to. We're so close to wrapping, with less than a month left. I was hoping I would make it to the end without dragging the producers into it.

The producers means Canon, but it also means Evan. Call me a coward, but I think the conversation with Evan will be easier. He's my boss, too.

My phone rings, and it's the person I want to talk to the most and the least in the world.

"Canon, hey."

"Hey. I didn't want the day to end with things the way they were with us. I know I was a jerk."

"And I was late," I reply, my voice soft and restrained because I don't want to spill everything in a rush of emotion. He opens my floodgates, makes me want to give him everything at once, even the crappy parts. "And I was so distracted today on set. I forgot lines and—"

"It's okay. We all have off days. I can't remember you even having one in the last four months, so you're due. Just get some rest. You seemed tired."

"Yeah, I really am." But my fatigue and all the possible reasons for it are the last things I want to discuss. "Where are you?"

"Home Depot. Don't ask."

I snort, glad I can find even the smallest humor in this shit day, and glad it came from him.

"Look, Jill and Kenneth and I have a long night ahead. We need to go through the shot list and change some things. We're here with the prop guys. I just wanted you to know…"

He draws and expels a sharp breath. "I just wanted you to know I'm sorry for this morning and that I don't want work to mess up…things."

"Things, huh?" I lean back on my pillow and cross my ankles. "You just don't want me to cut off your supply."

His low chuckle from the other end is dupioni silk, smooth on one side, rougher on the other. "Cutting off mine means cutting off yours, so I think I'll be a'ight."

"You're right." I close my eyes and let his rich voice wash over me, soothe my nerves. "You have nothing to worry about."

There's a pause on the other end before he says the words like air being released from a tire. "I miss you, Neevah. I know I just saw you, but I miss last night. Holding you and…I messed up this morning, huh?"

"We both did, but you're too mean for me to fight with. Let's not do that again."

"I'm sorry." Someone calls his name. "Okay. I gotta go. Jill and Kenneth are side-eyeing me hard."

"Hey! Is Evan with you guys?"

"Evan? Nah. Get some rest. See you first thing."

"Yeah, first thing."

Once he disconnects, I fire off a quick text before I change my mind.

Me: Hey. I need to talk to you about something.

Evan: Tonight?

Me: Yeah. Now?

Evan: Where are you?

Me: At my cottage.

Evan: I'm on my way.

FIFTY-THREE

Canon

"So let's save those scenes for later," Jill says the next morning, "because the sun will be highest. I think that'll be our best light."

Kenneth and I nod. When it comes to cinematography, light, and composition, I defer to Jill. There aren't many people I defer to on...well, anything, but Jill knows her craft in the way you'd be crazy not to trust her.

Evan walks into the cottage we've designated as our command station of sorts. Lines of strain bracket his mouth, which is not unusual when we're in the final stretch of a movie, but he shoots me a wary look that makes me wonder what's up.

"Hey, guys," he says, pulling up a chair and joining us at the table. "We need to talk before the day starts."

"Okay." I lean back and link my hands over my stomach. "Shoot."

"It's about Neevah."

The air tightens in the room instantly, for obvious reasons.

One.

She's the star of this movie and in just about every scene. When something goes wrong with Neevah, it affects the entire production.

Two.

She's my girl. And if there's something going on with Neevah, shouldn't I already know about it?

"What about Neevah?" Kenneth asks, as if number two is not a consideration.

"She texted me wanting to talk last night," Evan says, leaning forward.

"What time?" I demand, because I talked to Neevah last night, if only for a few minutes.

"I don't remember. Maybe nine? Does it matter?"

Hell, yeah, it does.

"No," I say. "So what's up?"

"You know a few days ago she had to get some bloodwork done for her dermatologist," he continues. "Well, when she got back to her room last night, the doctor had left a message for her with the results."

My teeth clamp together to the point of discomfort. My jaw must be about to shatter. This cannot be good, and I'm bracing myself not to explode all over my team when Evan says whatever the hell he's taking forever to tell us.

"The skin condition Neevah has is discoid lupus," Evan says, looking up when Jill gasps. "Discoid lupus isn't life-threatening. You're probably thinking of systemic lupus, like I did at first. Neevah had to explain the difference to me."

"Oh." Jill touches her chest, closing her eyes. "Thank God."

"But," Evan says, shifting his eyes to me, "they're concerned that Neevah may be in the middle of or approaching a flare-up."

"What the hell does that mean?" I demand, my voice sounding like it's being strained by a cheese grater.

"Apparently, her levels—don't ask me for all the acronyms she gave me. ANA, WBC, all kinds of letters and tests—are all off. They're especially concerned about her elevated creatinine levels."

"And that indicates what?" Kenneth asks.

"Um, maybe not much. She starts a new prescription today, which they hope will level things out, but I guess the combination of what they saw across the panel has them concerned about her kidneys. They want to biopsy her kidney as soon as possible."

Biopsy her kidney.

Lupus.

Life-threatening.

Even though he said discoid lupus is *not* life-threatening, it's apparent the doctor doesn't like the direction this is headed.

"This shouldn't affect production today," Evan continues. "But in a few days, when she goes in for the biopsy—"

I stand abruptly, the action scraping the chair across the hardwood floor and cutting Evan off.

"Fuck you," I tell him, my eyes narrowed. "You find this out and you don't tell me? And then you speed right past this information like I'm supposed to—"

"I knew you were on a run with the props team and—"

"And so you just neglected to tell me at the absolute earliest moment that my girlfriend has lupus and needs a biopsy on her kidneys?"

"If you check your phone, you'll see I tried calling you," he says in that even tone I hate, like he's reasoning with me when I'm being unreasonable. "You didn't answer, and I got caught up taking care of some issues this morning before we had a chance to talk."

He runs an agitated hand through his hair. "Maybe the real problem you have," Evan grinds out, "is that she didn't tell you, and that is something you'll have to take up with your *girlfriend* later. My job is to make sure this disrupts the movie we've spent two years and millions of dollars on as little as possible, which is why she came to me and not you. *She* understands that."

"Well, I don't understand," I fire back, heading toward the door. "Guys, I think we were just about done anyway. As Evan has so effectively reported, Neevah's medical condition shouldn't affect shooting today. We'll figure out tomorrow."

"And where are you going?" Evan asks, his tone sharp as a new blade.

"Motherfucker, where you think I'm going?"

I stomp out of the room and take a few paces before realizing I am *stomping* and probably scowling, based on the concerned looks of the cast and crew. My steps slow and then stop, right in the middle of our 1930s French Riviera. I let all the information I just heard sink in. My fists are clenched at my sides. My chest heaves from the effort of walking and breathing. I hate being in the dark and I hate being out of control, and this shit with Neevah is too much of both.

I need to know *everything*.

I start with hair and makeup, but she's not in the tent they've set up for the crew. Takira is, though, trimming a wig on a mannequin. She looks up, smiling when she sees me approaching. She must not know, or she doesn't want me to know. I don't care to figure out why she's smiling. After hearing Evan tell me about Neevah, I need to hear it from her and no one else.

"Where is she?" I ask, unable to summon manners.

Takira's smile slips, but a teasing glint enters her eye, like we have a secret. We do *not* have a secret. Everyone knows I'm sprung for Neevah. I've failed at concealing that fact.

"Wardrobe," Takira answers. " 'Bout five minutes ago."

"Thanks," I mutter tersely, heading for the hard-topped tent I searched yesterday. This time, I find her. She's standing in a floor-length gold dress embellished with sequined orchids. It molds to her upper body, faithfully follows the curves of her breasts and waist and hips. It shimmers across the rich hue of her skin like gold dust, and she's laughing down at Linh, who's on her knees with pins in her mouth, grinning while she adjusts something on the costume. Joy—there's no other way to describe it—lights Neevah's face. Her laugh rings out like a chime and her head is thrown back, like she's giving herself completely over to the moment she's in right now. Like besides doing what she loves most, she doesn't have a care in the world.

But I do.

And as much as I've given this movie, as much as I care about it, right now, all I care about is her.

I enter the tent and her smile falters. Our eyes hold, and we're both searching. For someone who can usually read her as easily as the alphabet, I have no idea what she's thinking. And I need to.

"Linh," I say. "Could you excuse us for a second?"

Linh glances over her shoulder, seeing me for the first time, and rises gracefully. She carries herself with such dignity and a quiet strength. What is she doing married to a guy like Law Stone?

"I'll be back to check this," Linh says, "before the first scene."

"It's gorgeous," Neevah tells her. "I'm honored to wear it."

Linh's expression, typically impassive, reveals uncharacteristic enthusiasm and pride. "I think it's my favorite dress I've ever designed."

"It looks incredible," I add, smiling at her. "Great job."

She inclines her head indicating her thanks, and then leaves Neevah and me alone.

Simply seeing her takes some of the edge off my frustration and anger. She has fighter's eyes. The force of her personality, that undimming light, was one of the first things I noticed about her.

"Where is everybody?" I ask, walking deeper into the space. "Isn't it usually kinda crazy in here with so many extras?"

"Uh, yeah. They're down on the beach already. There's so many background actors for these scenes, it's easier for Linh's team to do some things on set instead of cramming everyone in here." She looks at me squarely, almost defiantly. "I suppose Evan told you."

When I reach her, I take her hands, stroke the line of script along her thumb.

"Gotta admit," I say with a chuckle, void of humor, "I was kinda thinking I should have known before Evan did."

"I get that." She slips her finger out to mirror my caress, running her fingertip along my thumb, too. "But when the rest of the cast has issues that would affect filming, they don't usually start with the director. They start with Evan, and—"

"I'm not dating the rest of the cast." My words fall between us, and her fingers tighten on mine.

"We have to maintain some professional distance," she says, looking down, lashes wispy against her cheeks.

I grip her hips and pull her into me, aligning our bodies, shaping her curves to my hardness. I lay my forehead to hers. "This is all the distance you get."

"Canon," she whispers, bracketing my face, running her thumb over my mouth. "I don't want to mess this up."

"Mess us up? You won't. I just need you to be honest with me. Hearing this from Evan? Not cool."

She laughs, her breath misting my lips. "I meant mess up your movie."

"Of course I care about the movie, but I'm a lot more concerned about you right now. Lupus, baby?"

"I didn't want to use that word in the beginning because people don't know enough about it, and they make assumptions, make judgments. Yes, I get rashes and have hair loss, but I've been managing this naturally. It's never affected my work."

"But Evan says you may be having a flare-up? And they're concerned about your kidneys? That sounds more serious."

She licks her lips and nods. "It could be. My doctor prescribed prednisone, which I've been able to do without until now. It's a steroid that suppresses the immune system's response. One of the PAs is picking it up for me from the pharmacist. I'll start taking it today."

"And that will fix whatever's going on?"

"I don't…I don't know. The biopsy…" She closes her eyes, drops her head to my chest. "We'll know more after the biopsy. I get that in a few days. Evan said you guys can work around it and shoot other stuff, or shoot rear shots with my stand-in." A wry smile tips one corner of her mouth. "I'm still not used to having a stand-in after being someone else's for so long."

"Don't worry about us. We'll figure out the filming. Worry about you, about this." I hesitate over the next question, lifting her chin so I can read those beautiful eyes. "Are you scared?"

She loops her arms behind my neck and burrows into my shoulder. After a few seconds, she nods. I walk us over to one of the couches, sit down, and pull her onto my lap, stroking her back as she takes deep breaths in my arms.

"We don't have time for this," she says unevenly. "We need to—"

"I'm making time." I pull back to peer into her face. Her eyes are dry, but wide and uncertain. "I'm the boss, remember?"

She laughs and leans against me again, splaying her hand over my chest.

"So, this biopsy—do you want me to go with you?"

"No. Takira will, besides you're needed here."

"Neevah, come on."

"No, it's fine. It's just a biopsy. Not that big a deal." She stands, reaching down to pull me up from the couch. "Now can we get to work? We got a long day ahead."

"You sure you're okay?"

"I'm doing the job I love with the man I..." She bites her lip and blows out a short laugh. "The amazing man I'm dating."

The man I love.

I wanted her to say it. I wanted her to put words to this thing that was planted in me the first night I saw her onstage and has grown little by little ever since until now it's full-blown. Those aren't words I ever thought I would want to hear from a woman, much less consider saying them myself. But I find that I do. Not when two hundred people are waiting for us. Not when we have biopsies hanging over our heads. Not when things are this crazy.

But when the time is right, I do want to hear it from her.

And I do want to say it.

FIFTY-FOUR

Neevah

Almost there.

Almost there.

Almost there.

I've been reciting that to myself all morning, but my body doesn't seem to care or want to cooperate. I've thrown up three times between scenes, fortunately each time on a break. There's an awful taste in my mouth, and no matter how much water I drink or how many mints I eat, it won't go away.

A miasma fills my head, fogging my thoughts and clouding my concentration. I struggle to follow every word as it leaves Trey's mouth when he delivers his lines. I know I'm next. I go to say the line…and nothing. There's nothing there. My mind is a galactic void of nothingness. I open my mouth, hoping the words will tumble out on their own without me having to think about it, but there's only silence while the entire cast and crew wait for me to find myself in this scene.

But I can't.

Whatever holds my body, my mind hostage, overpowers my will. It stirs in my stomach and makes my head throb and spin.

"Cut!" Canon yells.

Trey touches my shoulder, concern etched on his movie-star-handsome face. "Neevah, you okay?"

I nod, though I'm sure by now it's apparent I'm not. It's not only the lines I've lost. It seems I can't say anything. I open my mouth to try again, and another wave of nausea rises in my throat.

"Oh, God," I mumble into my hand. I try to run, hoping to make it to the bathroom, but I can't. I haven't been able to eat much the last few days, but what is in my stomach is violently ejected out and all over Linh's perfect costume.

I lean against a pole. Tears roll down my cheeks as people rush over to me. I'm a mess. Vomit all over the dress. My wig slips. The entire set is a Tilt-A-Whirl. The floor slides from beneath my feet. Trey catches me and yells for help.

And then the world goes dark.

"Her blood pressure is alarmingly high," someone says.

I try to pry my eyes open, but it's too bright and everything hurts. I can't lift my head, can't make my limbs work, can't speak. I'm in some half-state of consciousness.

"Should we call nine-one-one?" someone asks.

"No hospital," I manage to croak, fumbling to get the tight band off my arm. "I need to... to finish."

"You will not finish," Canon says. That harsh voice I would recognize anywhere.

Other bits of sensory information slowly filter in. The coolness of the ocean air drifts over my face. The waves roar in my ears, and I remember we were in one of the French Riviera scenes on the beach. Over the scent of salt is an awful, pungent smell. Linh's precious costume she spent weeks sewing. I've ruined it.

"Change," I mumble, forcing my eyes open. "I want to change clothes."

Canon's face is the first thing I see. I'm on one of the lounge chairs, and he's on his knees beside me, his expression bent into a heavy frown. I reach up to touch his face.

"Beautiful," I whisper, trying to smile. He swallows hard, his Adam's apple moving with the effort.

"Neevah, baby, listen to me," he says. "Your blood pressure is really high. We have to get you to the hospital. You—"

"Please let me change clothes. I threw... I threw..."

I dissolve into tears because I'm so tired and every part of me aches and I can't imagine walking, but so many people are standing around watching me in this vomit-covered dress. I just want to sleep.

"It doesn't matter," Canon says. "You can change when you get—"

"Please. I think I'm going to be sick again if you make me keep this on."

His scowl deepens, but he stands and picks me up from the lounge chair.

"Canon, I don't want to get it on you." I'm even more embarrassed for him to hold me this close. To see me, to smell this, to *be here* when this is happening to me. He strides through the set, and I tuck my face into his shoulder, as much from exhaustion as not wanting to meet the curious eyes of the cast and crew. I would prefer to go to my cottage, but wardrobe is closer so he dips into the tent, sets me down gently on one of the tables, and pulls a privacy divider between us and the door. He starts unbuttoning the dress, but his fingers are shaking. "Shit," he curses under his breath, slowing down to pull the tiny buttons loose one by one.

The quiet is suffocating and I finally clear my throat to speak.

"Canon, I—"

"Don't, Neevah." He peels the dress away from my shoulders, lifts me so I can kick it off completely. "No, you cannot finish filming. Yes, you're going to the hospital. And no, you will not come back to this set until the doctor clears you to."

He meets my eyes, the muscle in his jaw clenched. You could easily mistake his fierce scowl and tight lips for anger, but I see it for what it really is. For once, he's not opaque. I see right through him.

I see his fear.

All my protests die on my lips and I nod, my heart clenching with the knowledge that he's as scared as I am. He grabs the T-shirt and shorts I discarded this morning, puts them on me. He peels off his sweatshirt, which I'm sure I've stained, revealing a T-shirt beneath. He picks me up again.

"I can walk," I mumble, though it may not be true. I can barely keep my eyes open, much less make my legs work. "This is hella dramatic."

He doesn't acknowledge the comment, but walks me off set to the parking lot. My feet never touch the ground, and I go from his arms to the back seat of his car. Takira runs up, her face streaked with worry.

"Oh, my God, Neevah," she says. "I just heard what happened. Are you okay?"

"No, she's not okay," Canon answers, climbing into the driver's seat and slamming the door. "I'm taking her to the emergency room."

"Can I come?" she asks.

"If you can get in right now. I'm not waiting."

She climbs into the passenger seat and Canon doesn't even wait for her to close the door or fasten her seat belt, but lurches out of the parking lot with a squeal of tires. His hands tighten on the steering wheel, knuckles straining against the tight skin. Takira gasps and clutches the dashboard as he runs one light and then another. I can't muster the energy or stir my voice to caution Canon he should slow down. Judging by the implacable lines of his profile, he wouldn't listen anyway. I glance through the rearview window, down the road to the set, and envision our replica of the French Riviera.

When will I be back?

Will I be back?

I want to commit the sight of the big equipment trucks and the cameras and wardrobe tent—every detail—to vivid memory, except I'm so tired I barely know my name, and despite my efforts, I fall right to sleep.

FIFTY-FIVE

Canon

I'm trying to be patient.

They took Neevah back an hour and a half ago, and no word. I've started pacing because apparently that's supposed to help.

"Pacing won't help," Takira says, not lifting her eyes from the *ESSENCE* magazine she's reading.

"I know that."

Still pacing.

"Then stop."

Shit.

"Is this what they do?" I demand of her…and the empty waiting room. "They just leave people out here wondering for hours if their loved ones are okay?"

The magazine lowers and her eyes set on me, sharp and alert. "Love?"

Shit again.

I haven't even said that to Neevah. I'll be damned if Takira hears it before she does.

"Loved *ones.*" I stop pacing. "Friends. Relatives. You know what I mean."

"Oh, I do." She gives me another one of those stupid secret grins. "I see you, Canon."

"Speaking of relatives, should we call her mom? Or…"

Her sister?

I know things haven't been great between Neevah and her family, but they would want to know this, right? But does Neevah want them involved?

"I think we wait on that." Takira sets *ESSENCE* aside. "As strained as things have been with her sister, I don't think we can assume anything."

"She mentioned she and her mom had a good talk at Christmas."

"Yeah, but it's all been weird for so many years, I think we let Neevah decide when she brings them in."

Takira's phone rings, and she frowns down at the screen, rolling her eyes. "Somebody from set. I had to drop what I was doing to leave. Lemme get this. I'll be right back."

She answers and walks up the hall, disappearing around the corner.

A long sigh exits my body, and it feels like my first full breath I've expelled since I saw Neevah fall. My hands ache from being clenched so tightly. First around the wheel driving here. And ever since they took her away. But when I open my fists...

I hold my hands out, watching the fingers' tremor, a reflection of the quake happening inside me. I had to drive here. I could not let the ambulance take her. No one else knows because no one else was there the night they took my mother for the last time in a wail of sirens and a specter of flashing lights. Her palliative nurse had left for the evening. I was home for the weekend from school.

Bacterial pneumonia.

In the end, that's what took her—a complication of the disease she had fought so valiantly that snuck through the back door.

I'll never forget the sound of her gasping for air, fighting until the end for every breath.

The idea of seeing, hearing, Neevah taken away in an ambulance the way they took Mama...in the moment, I couldn't withstand it, so I prayed to God and chased the devil to drive her here in record time.

Slowly, deliberately, I curl my shaking fingers back into fists. It's a time for control. Not to indulge emotions or to be plagued by fears. Neevah needs me to be strong. To be here, which means I can't walk out, fleeing the warring scents of disinfectant and disease and the eerie, careful quiet of a waiting room.

I have to stay.

And despite all of that, there's nowhere else I'd rather be.

I can't believe how little thought I've given to what's happening on set or how this will impact production. Best believe Evan and the rest of the cast and crew are thinking about it. Not to mention Law Stone, once he finds out. No doubt I have some difficult conversations ahead of me tonight, but for now, I don't give a damn about any of it.

Just her.

One small woman has turned my world upside down, capsized all my priorities. And not knowing how she's doing, I'm adrift.

A young nurse in pink scrubs walks into the waiting room holding a clipboard. "Are you here for Neevah Mathis?"

"Yeah, we are," Takira answers, speeding up the hall just as the nurse appears.

Did I really not even know my girl's government name? I've fallen in love with Neevah Saint, and it's a stage name?

"You can see her now," she says, smiling and turning for us to follow.

When we reach the room, Takira rushes over to the bed and hugs Neevah. Her eyelids droop and there are circles beneath her eyes. Even in just a few hours, there seems to be a darker cast to her skin. She smiles weakly at me over Takira's shoulder and extends her hand, which I take, and move to the opposite side facing Takira.

"I'm sorry about all this." She flops back on the pillow, lines of exhaustion sketched around her mouth. "I'll get back on set as soon as possible."

"Don't even think about that right now." I frown and rub my thumb over the back of her hand. "That'll all get figured out."

Before I can reassure Neevah any more, a tall man with salt-and-pepper hair walks in.

"Ms. Mathis?" he asks, glancing from the chart he's holding to Neevah. "I'm Dr. Baines."

"Hi." Neevah looks a little wary, but smiles. "Did they tell you I have a rheumatologist in New York and one who's been consulting locally since I've been here? I told them when I came in that I have discoid lupus and gave them my doctor's information."

"Yes, I've seen your records and spoken with both rheumatologists." He hangs the chart on a hook at the foot of the bed. "You're on top of it."

"I think we can safely say," Neevah offers with a wry grin and waves a hand over her hospital bed, "that it is on top of me."

"I need to discuss what we're seeing in your case so far." He glances at Takira and me. "So if we need some privacy—"

"Oh, no." Neevah squeezes my hand again and smiles at Takira. "They're fine. They know as much as I do so far, and it's okay if they hear."

"Alright." Dr. Baines nods and adjusts his glasses. "I've seen the notes from both your doctors. I've seen the blood, urine, and antibodies test results, which prompted them, very wisely, to order a kidney biopsy. You haven't had that yet, correct?"

"Correct," Neevah says, a frown knitting her brows. "They wanted to get some of the supplements I take out of my system first."

"I understand. Your blood pressure was extremely elevated. You were complaining of a headache. You've been nauseous."

"Yes." Neevah laughs nervously. "Why do I feel like you're building a case, Doctor?"

His smile is faint and kind. "I'm not building the case. Your body is."

"What does that mean?" I ask, unable to stay quiet.

"Neevah," Dr. Baines says. "We won't know for sure until we get the results from the biopsy, but you're obviously in the midst of a flare-up. Been under a lot of stress lately?"

Guilt tightens a hand around my throat as I consider what the movie has demanded of her. God, just yesterday I chewed her out for being late.

"Maybe some." Neevah looks down at the hospital sheet.

"She's been starring in a movie," I interject. "For the last four months it's been rigorous dancing, late nights, a very demanding schedule."

"You wanna get kicked out?" Neevah asks, the look she shoots me only half-joking.

"He does need the full picture," Takira says. "So they can know exactly what we're dealing with."

Neevah heaves an exasperated sigh. "So maybe there was *some* stress, yeah, but nothing I couldn't handle."

"I'm sure you're aware stress is one of the main triggers for flare-ups,"

Dr. Baines says. "In talking with your rheumatologists, we suspect your lupus diagnosis has evolved and we may need to broaden the original assessment of what we're dealing with."

The corners of Neevah's eyes tighten. "What does that mean?"

"We won't know for sure until we see the results of the biopsy," Dr. Baines says, hesitation obvious in his voice. "Neevah, all signs indicate you're not just dealing with discoid lupus, but possibly nephritis. Probably systemic lupus, but again, I don't feel comfortable confirming that until we get the biopsy results."

Neevah draws a sharp breath, and her fingers tighten around mine, but I don't give any indication I see her fear. I stroke along the ink decorating her thumb, hoping I can offer some measure of comfort even silently. I'm trying to remain as calm as possible, but inwardly, panic takes off like a runner, sprinting past reason. Evan's voice echoes in my head and I hear him telling us just this morning that systemic lupus is the life-threatening one, and what a relief that's not what Neevah has. I'd never heard someone use the phrase *systemic lupus* until today, and they're suddenly the most important words in the world.

"No." Neevah shakes her head, her wig going a little more askew. "Dr. Ansford said...she told me it was discoid."

"And based on the information your body presented to her a few years ago, even four months ago, that diagnosis was appropriate," Dr. Baines says. "But a lot has happened over the last four months, and things can escalate very quickly. We can't say for sure until after the biopsy, so let's go ahead and get it done so we can see what comes back."

"Okay." Neevah stares at the bed with wide, unfocused eyes, like she's looking at something none of us can see, and I guess she is. Takira and I are here for her, but it's her body.

It shocks me that I would literally put myself in her place if it meant sparing her the possible road ahead, but the truth of it hits me standing by her bed and watching the fear soak into her eyes. I felt this way with my mom over and over. Watching MS steal so much from her, feeling helpless, but wanting to be strong for her. I don't know what those test results will tell us, but I do know what it's like to walk a hard road with someone you love.

I've done it before. I can do it again.

FIFTY-SIX

Neevah

There's a heaviness in the room even before the three doctors say one word. Two of them I know, Dr. Ansford from New York via video conference, and Dr. Baines, the doctor who talked with me a few days ago. I don't know the third doctor, which instantly puts me a little on the defensive. I've been here three days and never seen her. I've started the prednisone, the drug I spent the last few years of my life avoiding, and I have to admit, it seems to be helping. My blood pressure is down. I have much more energy and feel somewhat better, but Dr. Baines wanted to keep me for observation until the kidney biopsy results came back.

Takira is on set helping with the extras and crowd shots. They're shooting everything they can while I'm out, but at a certain point they'll run out of scenes they can do without me. That's why I'm eager to get this news, figure out what needs to be done, and get back to set.

Canon insisted on being here, which makes me feel even more guilty. He says Kenneth is the best AD in the business and can handle a few crowd shots on his own.

"You okay?" he asks, sitting on the edge of the hospital bed beside me, his voice low and concerned.

"Yeah." I smile and nod to reassure him and hope that everything *will* be okay.

But this new doctor doesn't help.

If you can have an air of competence, this woman carries it. Her eyes are steady, framed by a faint network of laugh lines stenciled into her smooth brown skin. With her long dreadlocks pulled into a stylish updo, she emits a confidence that probably puts most patients at ease right away.

I feel nervous because she's here and has never been before, indicating a new bend in the road on my journey with this disease.

"Neevah," Dr. Baines says, "I'd like to introduce you to Dr. Okafor. She's a very well-respected nephrologist who we've asked to consult on your case."

Nephrologist?

I tighten my fingers on Canon's and try to control my breathing.

"I personally requested Dr. Okafor, Neevah," Dr. Ansford says from the screen. "She's the best there is in cases like yours."

"Cases like mine?" I ask, watching Dr. Okafor warily. "What kind of case is that, exactly?"

"May I explain?" she asks Dr. Baines. At his nod, she walks closer to the hospital bed, those steady eyes never leaving mine. "Neevah, when we biopsied your kidneys, we found significant scarring."

"What does that mean?" Canon asks.

She flicks a questioning glance from him to me, silently asking if he gets to speak. If I weren't so anxious, it would be funny to see someone question Canon, even if silently.

"It's fine," I tell her. "He's my boyfriend."

Canon glances at me, a pleased look in his eyes even in the midst of this, and I realize that's the first time I've referred to him that way. This situation seems to have ripped the training wheels off our relationship. In so many ways, we're already at full speed.

"Yes, well," Dr. Okafor says, "the scarring on your kidneys, coupled with what we've seen in your blood, urine, and ANA tests, indicate that your original diagnosis of discoid lupus should be expanded to systemic lupus."

I'm already lying down, but I think I've fallen. There is a thud in my ears as if I've hit the floor. The breath whooshes from my chest on impact. Canon slips an arm around my shoulder, and I clutch his hand for dear life. Literally for life and health I've always taken for granted that now seems imperiled.

"I...I don't understand." I shake my head, look to Dr. Ansford onscreen. "We said it was just discoid and not…no. Can you run more tests?"

"Initially," Dr. Ansford says solemnly, "your symptoms presented very narrowly, but during this flare-up, it's apparent we're dealing with a broader diagnosis."

"And we could waste time running more tests," Dr. Okafor says, "or we can start treating this now for the best results. I know it's a lot to process, but can I tell you what we're dealing with?"

I square my shoulders and nod.

"The scarring on your kidneys is irreversible." Dr. Okafor's stare doesn't waver. "And the damage is significant."

"No." I bark out a disbelieving laugh. "My kidneys? It couldn't have happened that fast?"

"It can. It does. It did," Dr. Okafor says. "Kidney failure can be quite insidious and hard to detect until the damage has been done. And it can be accelerated if you have an aggressive autoimmune event like what you have, most likely triggered by extreme conditions."

"You mean stress," Canon says, his jaw sharply-edged with restraint.

"Yes." Dr. Okafor flicks her gaze to him. "Your immune system makes antibodies to fight foreign substances, bacteria, viruses, etcetera. When your body produces antinuclear antibodies, they attack the nucleus of your healthy cells."

"Because your disease had presented so narrowly in the past," Dr. Ansford interjects, "and you were in conditions that could have caused similar symptoms like muscle soreness and achy joints, those signals may have been disguised until they were severe enough to present as things you hadn't experienced in the past."

"Like the nausea and high blood pressure you came in with," Dr. Baines adds.

"Regardless of how we got here," Dr. Okafor says, "we are here now. The autoantibodies have affected your kidneys to the point of failure."

"Failure?" I ask numbly.

"I know it feels sudden to you, but it has been happening quietly in your body the last few months." Dr. Okafor slides her hands into the pockets of her white lab coat. "And now it's getting loud."

"How loud?" Canon asks. "What do you mean?"

"We put kidney disease into five different stages," Dr. Okafor says. "We've determined you're in stage four. Patients in this stage will most likely require dialysis for life or will need a kidney transplant. As I said, the damage, once done, is irreversible."

I shake my head and toss my legs over the side of the bed. I need to walk, to move. I can't bear just lying here and taking this. *Accepting* this, when it cannot be right. I can dance nine hours a day. I do yoga. I eat right. I barely drink alcohol. I'm healthy.

"I know this is a lot to take in, Neevah," Dr. Okafor says.

"Take in?" I shout, my voice loud and outraged and desperate. "It's not a lot to take in. It's impossible. I can't be..." My words splinter into the doctors' practiced silence. That silence, that space they make for patients to accept the news. The world tilts. I'm wavering. I stagger and Canon is there, grabbing my elbow and pulling me into his chest. I stand there, sheltered in his arms, on the outside, completely still, but inside, *reeling*.

Vertiginous.

Spinning and falling into a deadly new reality that I'm not sure I'm ready to face. I feel Canon's kiss in my hair, and I cling to him like he's the only thing keeping me afloat in this storm.

"You mentioned dialysis or a transplant," Canon says, his voice low and level. "What is your recommendation?"

I turn in Canon's arms, resting my back against the wide, warm chest, my gaze intent on Dr. Okafor.

"Well, she's on the prednisone," Dr. Okafor says. "That and other drugs will help manage some of the symptoms. We *can* put you on dialysis. Some are on it for life, but I think our best option is a preemptive kidney transplant."

"What's that?" I ask.

"As I'm sure you know, with dialysis," Dr. Okafor says, "a machine filters out the toxins, cleans your blood because your kidneys can no longer effectively do that. You could go that route, but it would be for the rest of your life."

"No." I shake my head, adamant. "I'm an actor. A performer. I need to be active. I don't want that."

"I figured you would feel that way." Dr. Okafor gives me an assessing glance. "The preemptive transplant gets you a new kidney."

"Aren't there long waiting lists?" Canon asks, his deep voice a comforting rumble at my back.

"There are for deceased-donor organs," Dr. Okafor agrees. "But we also start hunting everywhere for a living donor. Friends, family, your community."

"A living donor?" Canon asks, sounding like he's pouncing on it. "How do you determine if someone is a match?"

"That is a long, involved process," Dr. Okafor says. "We start with blood type and go from there in a series of tests to determine compatibility."

"We have a huge cast and crew," Canon says. "I can put out the call for anyone who might want to test to see if they're a match. Can you test me today?"

"Canon." I look over my shoulder, staring at him. "You can't just...give me a kidney. And you can't volunteer the cast and crew."

"I can do whatever the hell I want if my kidney is a match. And I would never pressure any of them, but when they hear you need a kidney, a lot of them will want to at least check."

"He's right," Dr. Okafor says. "We check everywhere and anyone who is willing. Our best shot, though, would be a family member. Especially a sibling. A brother or a sister."

A sister.

I used to have one of those.

But not anymore.

And all of a sudden, it may be my kidneys that are failing, but it's my heart that hurts. Aches that with my life on the line, I can't wrap my mind around asking Terry for anything, much less an organ. Why would she give it? Why would I take anything from her? I know I'll have to set our differences aside to ask, but God, I don't want to.

"This is good." Canon starts pacing and tugs at his bottom lip the way he does when a scene isn't going the way he thinks it should. He's in full director mode. "Dr. Okafor, you start with the transplant list. I'll get the word out to the cast and crew and my network, which is pretty broad. Neevah, baby, I know you don't want to, but you'll have to ask your mom and sister."

"Um, thank you for the marching orders," Dr. Okafor says dryly. "But I'll take it from here, General."

Unbelievably, in the midst of the worst news I've ever received, I snort. Chuckle. Snuckle.

Canon looks at me, his eyes softening with the tiniest glint of humor, and I know he's thinking the same thing—of our first conversation, a chilly autumn night on a New York sidewalk. In the relatively brief time we've been together, we've made our own history. I don't have the aerial view to see where and how it ends, but right now we are in the thick of it, and it feels good. Somehow, even in the muck of my life right now, having him still feels good.

"Sorry for his bossiness," I say, walking over to sit on the bed because that bone-deep exhaustion is no joke. "He's a director."

"He's right. We'll have to take swift action," Dr. Okafor says. "We already started the prednisone, which should help some, but you've got a long road ahead. We have other drugs that can help do the work your kidneys aren't right now. If that doesn't work, we may have to do dialysis until we find a donor."

"Wait. I can't get on dialysis." I arrow a look between the three doctors. "I have another month left on my movie."

"The hell you do," Canon says harshly. "You're not coming back on my set until she says so."

"Canon." I gulp back tears. "You know the whole production shuts down if I'm not there."

"You think I give a damn about that?" His scowl deepens. "This is your life we're talking about, Neev. Nothing...there's nothing more important than that."

"I don't think Galaxy Studios will agree."

"You let me handle Galaxy and anyone else who tries to give us shit. Here's what you're missing," he says, grabbing my hand. "I'm the boss. Galaxy may have funded this movie, but it's mine, and I hold all the cards, and they'll do whatever the fuck I want."

He glances at Dr. Okafor. "You were telling us about the dialysis."

"It may not come to that," she says. "We may be able to manage this with good eating habits, exercise, and pharmaceuticals until we find a kidney."

I glance at Dr. Ansford onscreen, who winks, knowing I balk at any kind of drugs, but at this point, don't have much choice.

"You said exercise." I lean back into the pillows. "I can still work and be active?"

"We encourage patients to remain active. It only helps, but I'll be frank." Dr. Okafor sits on the bed, meeting my eyes. "You have lupus for life, Neevah. Even giving you a new kidney won't change that. And stress will always be a possible trigger for a flare. You may need to reassess how you do what you do. Not that you can't be a performer, but this disease will exploit every weakness and go after your organs the first chance it gets. Sometimes that is unavoidable, but there are lifestyle adjustments you can make to give your body the best shot."

I nod, processing everything and looking for any silver lining I can find.

"We'll work on getting you stabilized so you can resume some of your normal routines while we search for a viable kidney," Dr. Okafor says. "But let me be clear. When I say you can go back to work, that's when you go. Not a minute before."

"Agreed," Canon says. "I may be the director, but Neevah's health is my priority, too."

"You know, he *is* bossy," she tells me, offering her first wide smile since she came bearing this awful news, "but I like him."

I take in the contrasting hollows beneath his cheekbones. The fiery eyes that dare me to challenge him on this. The full lips pulled into a tight, level line. He is formidable, and right now, the doctor may like him, but I do not.

But I think I love him.

And how two such opposite moments—realizing I have a life-threatening illness and realizing I'm in love—can exist in the same hour, in the same room, is beyond me, but stranger things have happened. Or maybe it was always supposed to be this way. Maybe my love and this threat have been on a collision course since the beginning. Since the day a woman in a wheelchair on a rotting pier in the last rays of a dying sun stared the camera down, asking if we would live, or just wait to die. That day I only saw the words she was gifting me as inspiration to make the most out of life. Something to scribble on a sticky note and pin to my wall. Now, as Canon watches Dr. Okafor intently, noting everything that must be done over the next few months, things I'm too numb to even absorb right now, I realize there was a greater gift she was leaving me.

Her son.

But is it a gift I should refuse?

This isn't what Canon expected. Hell, it's not what I expected, but I have no choice. He does have a choice, or at least he should. After what he went through and witnessed with his mother, he should have a choice about going down this road again. What if he doesn't feel he can step away from me now, even if this is too much? I couldn't handle it if he stayed with me out of some misplaced sense of nobility or loyalty. That would be an insult to what we've been. An insult, in the future I can't even see right now, to what we could be.

FIFTY-SEVEN

Canon

"We can't afford to sit around and wait like this," Lawson snaps, his brows furrowed. "How did this happen?"

"We aren't sitting around and waiting," Evan says, sipping the drink the hotel restaurant's server placed at his elbow. "I mean, yes, production is shut down today because we've done as much as we can until Neevah comes back."

"And I'm paying for this hotel and the rooms and the cast and the crew," Lawson says, red crawling up his neck and over his cheeks, "while Neevah's laid up somewhere? When will she be back?"

"If by *laid up*," I interject, leaning forward and locking eyes with the idiot, "you mean in a hospital being monitored by her medical team because of kidney failure, then, yeah. That's where she is. And to answer your question, she'll be back on set as soon as her doctor clears her to be and not one damn minute sooner."

"You did this." He points his finger at me. "You cast a novice, an unknown."

"That's not fair," Evan says. "Neevah has killed this role. You know it. You've said it. Everyone at Galaxy has been blown away by her performance."

"But did she lie to us?" he demands. "If we had known she had lupus, we could have—"

"Discriminated against her?" I ask, the anger barely checked beneath my low tone. "Based on her medical condition?"

"Uh, no." He clears his throat, hearing what he *didn't* say voiced out loud. "Of course not."

"The fact is," Evan says, "Neevah passed the insurance company's medical exam with no red flags. We've obtained a letter from her doctor that states at the time she began our movie, her official diagnosis was discoid lupus, a condition that is not considered life-threatening and primarily affects skin and hair."

"When she negotiated her personal hairstylist into her contract," I add, "she disclosed a hair and skin condition, though she didn't call it lupus. There was no reason or requirement for her to. If you're looking for some legal loophole to save you money and vilify Neevah, you won't find one, and you'll have me to deal with."

"Oh, I'll have you to deal with?" he sneers. "The elephant in the room is that you're fucking the lead actress... again. Maybe if you knew how to keep your dick separate from your work, you could objectively see that this is bad for business."

"What will be bad for business," I say, my voice rolling out wrapped in barbed wire, "is when I punch you in the face and Galaxy has to choose between me, the director who's going to make them lots of money and give them the ultimate movie to check all their fucking DEI boxes, or the privileged asshole who tried to weaponize his power against a young woman fighting for her life."

I sit back in my chair, reining my rage by a string, but determined I won't give this son of a bitch the satisfaction of seeing it.

"I don't see public opinion favoring you in that scenario, Stone," Evan adds.

"Public," Lawson mutters. "None of this has to go public. I mean, at Galaxy, we're a family. Of course, we want to accommodate whatever needs to be done so Neevah can be well. If you misconstrued anything I said—"

"Get up," I say through gritted teeth. "Get off my set right now, Stone. Take your ass home to LA. If I catch you on my lot when we get back, I promise I'll find a way to take that job from you and make your name shit in this town."

"I think—"

"You heard him," Evan interrupts Lawson. "Get your ass up. Get off the set. And don't even stop to see your wife, who you don't deserve, by the way. You can see her when she gets home."

Lawson stands, his expression and posture stiff, and leaves the hotel dining room without another word.

"That last part about his wife was pretty cold-blooded," I tell Evan. "Don't even stop to see your wife on the way out? Dayuuuum, Evan."

"That was my favorite part, actually."

We share a smile across the table and sigh in unison. The reality is, we may have called Lawson out and stripped his ass of some bravado, but we are losing money, and this is hard.

"You know he could still cause trouble for us," I say, some of my hubris draining away with the adrenaline. "Maybe blackball me."

The irony of making *Dessi Blue* is that so much has changed since then, but some things remain the same. The reality is that in this town, there are barriers harder for me to clear than others. A powerful man like Lawson Stone can do a lot of damage in ways I might not even be able to foresee.

"He can try," Evan scoffs. "We may not be those young, scrappy kids anymore, but they knew how to get shit done. Knew how to find money when it was scarce, and managed to make great movies without studio backing. We'll do it again if it comes to that, but I don't think it will. Not if he's smart."

"Thanks for having my back, by the way." I meet Evan's eyes cautiously. "I know you didn't approve of me getting involved with Neevah."

"It was clear from day one that Neevah was perfect for this role, and it's just as clear that this is not just you wanting to get in some actress's pants. You love her."

I lift one querying brow. "Do I? How you know that?"

"I've known you almost twenty years, Holt. That's a lot of years and a lot of women, and I've never seen you like this."

I've never felt like this.

"So enough of the mushy stuff," Evan says abruptly. "I've prepped Kenneth and Jill and the team about Neevah's situation and the implications, but I thought you might want to address the cast and crew."

I don't want to be here. I want to be at the hospital with Neevah, and I will be, but first, I have a responsibility to my team. I feel like a wishbone being pulled from two sides, tensile, but also easy to break.

"Yeah, I'll talk to them." I hesitate and then push forward. "I'm going to tell them Neevah needs a kidney in case there's anyone who wants to be tested. You okay with that?"

"We can give them the info. No pressure to do anything with it. That's what they said you should do, right? Put the call out to everyone you know so we can get Neevah a new kidney as soon as possible."

"Yeah." I drum my fingers on the table, the restlessness due only in part to not shooting the last few days. "She still needs to talk to her family about it."

Surprise raises Evan's brows. "They don't already know?"

"It's...awkward. They haven't been close in years, and...anyway. She can't put it off much longer."

"Speaking of awkward," Evan says, standing from the table. "Let's go ask for a kidney."

We walk across the hall to the large ballroom where the cast and crew are assembled, waiting. Their expressions range from curious to concerned. When you lose the star of a movie, depending on what stage, it could mean in the worst-case scenarios, the movie never sees the light of day and a production falls apart. Or it could mean reshooting. Or making do and cobbling together whatever you can without the actor. This project has put a lot of people to work, and I know they're glad to get paid, but I believe they all share my passion for the stories and contributions that slipped through history's cracks. The Black people who deserved better from this country. They're not sure what will become of *Dessi Blue*. My job, right now, is to reassure them.

"Hey, guys," I say, sitting on the lip of the small stage at the front of the room. "Hope you enjoyed your day off. You're welcome, and don't get used to it."

Their faint laughter breaks some of the tension.

"So, you all know Neevah was sick on set a few days ago and has been in the hospital. We have a little more information now, so I wanted to update you on her condition and how that will affect production."

Jill, Kenneth, and Monk are seated at a table up front, only a few feet away, and Jill meets my eyes with a sad smile.

"Neevah has lupus," I say, cutting to the heart of it.

A few people in the room gasp. Sounds of dismay and concern drift through the crowd.

"I know everyone has different ideas about what lupus is, what it can do, and what it means, but Neevah is a fighter and is getting the best care we could ask for. Her doctor is working hard to get her back on set as soon as possible."

"Thank God," someone says.

"As you know," I say, "we've only got about three weeks left in production. Most of you will be done shooting once we leave Santa Barbara. A few scenes on the back lots, and we'll be done. The majority of what's left only affects Neevah, Trey, and the musicians from the cast. We'll do the musical numbers back in LA. Neevah should be returning in the next day or so to wrap up our Riviera shots."

"Such good news," Livvie says, relief evident in her smile.

"Getting Neevah well enough to return to work *isn't* enough," I say. "She needs a kidney."

The room goes completely silent. Disbelief and horror mark their faces as I scan the room.

"She's talking to her family, because that's her best..." I squeeze the bridge of my nose and clench my teeth, holding on to my composure. "...her best shot, but the medical team encouraged her to put the call out as far as possible. Family, friends, the community. There is absolutely no pressure to do this, but if anyone wants to check if they're a match, Graham has the information. I already tried." I heave a sigh and spread a rueful grin around the room. "Unfortunately, I'm not the right blood type, but we'll keep looking."

Evan stands and comes to sit on the edge of the stage beside me. "Are there any questions, concerns, anything, about how we move forward and finish this movie strong?"

"I have a question," Livvie says. "Um, will we have notice before Neevah comes back?"

"Like a day, probably," I say. "Plenty of time to prepare to shoot."

"I wasn't thinking about shooting," she says. "I mean, of course that, but I thought it might be kinda cool to have a cake or something. Just to welcome her back and let her know we love her."

The image of Neevah's bright smile, her stuttering explanation when she gave me gingerbread cookies for Christmas, pounces my heart in my chest. She baked cookies for the whole cast and crew.

God, she's sweet, and if anything happens to her...

"That's a great idea, Livvie," Jill adds, her eyes bright with tears and eagerness.

"She loves red velvet." Takira, who's been quiet the whole time, swipes at the corner of one eye. "And I think she'd really appreciate that."

Seeing how this team has bonded around this story, and now how they're rallying around Neevah, moves something in me. Emotion climbs up my throat, and I don't know if it's the cumulative effect of all Neevah is facing and the emotional roller coaster of the last few days, or what. The compassion, the concern, the love they have for her, it washes over me, and I just want to get out of here before I lose it.

The group disperses, some clustering around Evan a few feet away, probably to ask questions they didn't want to ask me. Jill takes the spot where Evan sat beside me onstage.

"You sure you're okay?" she asks.

Shit. Don't ask me that. This is one of those things where you're fine until somebody asks how you're doing.

My eyes burn, and I knot my hands into fists. No way I'm breaking down in front of my team. I'm their leader. They need to see confidence now.

"I'm fine," I answer, my tone terse. I stand and take the first step away, but she grabs my wrist.

"You have people who care about you," she says, her voice so low only I can hear. Her green eyes, swimming with tears, are locked on mine. "We're here." She squeezes my hand. "*I'm* here, okay?"

I brush a hand over my eyes, impatient with the dampness on my lashes. The people in this room always see me strong, but I can't remember ever feeling this weak. This job, this movie—for the last two years, they've been everything, and now, in a matter of a few days, I can barely concentrate because I can't stop thinking about the possibility of losing her.

"Her aunt died of this, you know?" I ask. "What if she—"

"She won't. She'll be okay."

"You can't know that. You can never know that, which is why I didn't want this."

"Didn't want what?"

I look down at the floor, conscious of all the eyes and ears in the room. "To love her," I admit softly. "To love anyone like this again, because I know how it feels when you lose it."

"Canon, look at me," she says. Reluctantly, I do. "You have so much to offer, and you've poured it into your work ever since I've known you, which was fine, but if there was someone you could share your life with, I hoped you'd find her because you deserve that."

She reaches for me, hugs me, and whispers in my ear, "There's no one better prepared to walk through this with her than you."

She's right. If there's one thing my mother taught me, it's how to love through hard times. I thought I had forgotten, or hoped I'd never have to again.

I pride myself on control, on restraint, but ever since Neevah sang her way into my life that first night, the guard I've kept over my heart, over my whole life, has been falling away in layers. I *feel* more. It's almost too much. *Everything* is almost too much.

When Mama died, I think I retired certain parts of myself. Her extended illness and when she passed away—they battered me. Stripped me of faith and illusions and, in many ways, hope. Hope lures you from safety, makes you dream again of things you thought impossible. It coaxes you out of your fears. Forget mercury or arsenic. Hope is the most dangerous element in the world.

But that is exactly what I'll need if I'm going to be there for Neevah. I honestly don't know what will be left when all these protective layers fall away, but whatever *is* left, it's hers.

FIFTY-EIGHT

Neevah

"How do I get tested?" Mama asks.

Her voice, the question, seems to come from much farther away than Clearview, North Carolina. After all these years making do without her, I need her now more than I ever have. I want one of those hugs only mothers can give that make you feel, even if only for a few moments, like everything will be okay. I've spent the last hour discussing lupus and the kidney transplant and the need for a donor, but what I want most right now is her.

"I'll send you all the info." I try to smile, hoping she'll hear it in my voice.

"You should have told me as soon as this all happened."

"I know. The meds they put me on actually made me feel a little better, though they warned it's not a long-term solution. I guess I just dove right back into my routine and..."

The excuse probably sounds as lame in her ears as it does in mine.

"You're right," I say. "I was putting off asking. I'm sorry."

Her sigh is weary and the slightest bit disapproving. "You still trying to do it all on your own, baby. I want to be there for you. You gonna let me?"

I clear my throat, not sure how to fix some of the things that remain broken between my family and me. Old habits die hard, but I need to try.

"Yes, ma'am," I whisper, feeling like the little girl she used to chastise. "I'll try."

"Good, 'cause this is serious. Your Aunt Marian—"

"Aunt Marian was a long time ago. They know a lot more and can do a lot more now. I'm not saying this is easy. It's not. It won't be, and even the transplant won't be an end-all solution, but it's the next thing we do, and then we hope for the best."

"A transplant sounds expensive. All of this does. You got insurance?"

"I do, yeah. Through the stage union."

"How are you feeling?"

Exhausted. Depressed. Overwhelmed.

"I'm fine."

She's right. Even now, I find myself sheltering my mother from the full extent of what's going on with me. Why do I do that? Why can't I just unburden myself to her? All my life I've seen her shoulder other people's troubles, help them when they needed it, but when I need her, I always hold back. Maybe on some level I still feel she chose Terry over me, and I'm not sure if when I really need her, she'll be there.

"Have you talked to Terry yet?"

I knew she would ask, but something inside still startles at the mention of my sister. Most of the cast and crew are being tested, and I've only known them four months. Yet the hardest person to ask when it's life or death is my own sister.

"I will. I'm just busy trying to wrap this movie."

"You're still working?" Mama's volume rises with her disbelief. "Shouldn't you be in the hospital or on dialysis or...something? You need a kidney, for God's sake."

"I'm on lots of medicine, Mama. The prednisone makes me feel like I can conquer the world, until it doesn't. I'm actually really tired, like, can barely keep my eyes open."

"You need to get some rest."

"I will. We've been on location the last couple of weeks, but we're back in LA now. I don't have many scenes left to shoot, and believe me, Canon makes sure I do as little as possible."

"How are things with your director?" Mama's teasing makes this feel more like a normal conversation, and not one in which I ask for organs.

"Canon has been amazing and supportive."

As much as I appreciate it, I keep asking myself if he really wants to be here? Still? We were just getting off the ground, just really started dating, and then *this*. These are higher stakes than he saw coming. What if he feels trapped?

"I want to meet him," Mama says.

"You'll love him. Everyone loves him even if they don't want to."

"He sounds like a real character, but then, he'd have to be to handle you," Mama says, a note of pride in her voice I don't think I've ever recognized before. She's missed so much over the years that at times, it felt like she didn't notice me pursuing my dreams.

"He's..." I pause, unsure how to describe Canon in a way that would make Mama understand why he's so special. "He's one of a kind. Hopefully you'll get to meet him soon."

"Well, I'm glad he makes you rest."

I set my small suitcase on the bed so I can finish packing. I'm waiting for Canon to pick me up. I've tried to subtly give him space, pleading fatigue every time he's wanted to see me this week after we finished shooting. He insisted we spend this weekend together.

"Mama, I need to go."

"Okay. I'll look at the information to get tested. Promise me you'll talk to Terry soon. It feels strange, me knowing all this and not saying anything."

"I want to talk to her myself." *Want* is the wrong word, but I don't need Mama asking for me.

"Then talk to her, Neevah. This thing with the two of you has gone on long enough. I want my girls to be sisters again."

"Well, I don't think a kidney will fix all our problems, Mama."

"No, but maybe it'll make you face them."

When your mama drops the mic...

"Okay. Give me until tomorrow."

"Tomorrow. I love you, Neev."

"Love you, too, Mama."

Takira walks across the hall to my room, slipping something into the suitcase open at the end of my bed. "How's your mom?"

"Worried. What did you put in my suitcase?"

"Lube," she says with a grin. "You're lucky I didn't yell out, 'I'm packing this lube for you' while your mama was on the phone."

"My mom has no clue about lube."

Takira falls onto my bed and chuckles. "Girl, I bet your mama knows all about lube. Your daddy passed a long time ago. Now you know your mama got her some at some point in the last twenty years."

"Ewwww, David!" I scream, pulling from our *Schitt's Creek* vernacular.

"We need to binge the last season, and you will thank me for that lube later."

"I'm taking your lube because I want to normalize women carrying their own lube," I say, but give her a wicked glance. "But we've never needed it."

"Ewwww, David!" She pretends to gag. "You will refrain from telling me how wet you get. Ma'am, boundaries."

We laugh and I fall onto the bed beside her, forgetting for a few moments that I'm sick and just enjoying being alive. It feels like a regular day with my best friend. Except my suitcase is not just packed with lube, but with a battalion of bottles, meds to stabilize me until I can get a kidney.

"You know, if we don't find a kidney soon," I say, staring up at the ceiling, "I may have to go on dialysis."

"I know." Takira reaches for my hand. "If that happens, we'll get through it. Whatever. I got you, Neev."

"I know you do."

I've been holding it together. Going through the motions of my life. Distracting myself with the work I've always dreamt of doing, but as soon as it all stops, the life-altering reality comes crashing back in on me. I'm racing against the clock in some ways, but will manage this condition in some shape, form, or fashion, forever.

Tears prick my eyes and leak from the corners. I swipe at them quickly because if I start now, I won't stop. I'm at my emotional tipping point. In a matter of four months, I've starred in my first movie, fallen in love, and been diagnosed with a chronic illness that requires an organ transplant. I'm reeling. It's a lot for me to process. I can only imagine how Canon is actually doing.

"This isn't what Canon signed on for," I say. "It's one thing if this happens to your long-time girlfriend or fiancée or wife, but we haven't been together long. This has to be the last thing he wants to go through after what he saw with his mom."

"Is that why you've been avoiding him this week?"

"I haven't been avoiding him," I lie. "We've both been busy."

"Neevah."

"I need to finish packing." I slide off the bed and, I hope, out of the conversation.

"Imma let you get away with it for now, young lady, but you need to discuss this with Canon. I already know he doesn't feel trapped or—"

"T, please." I grab a dress from the closet and toss it into the suitcase. "Can we talk about something else?"

"You talked to your sister about getting tested?"

Not quite what I had in mind.

"Not yet. Tomorrow."

"You have to. She may be your sister, but so am I. I can't lose you."

I stare at the rows of dresses in my closet, grasping for my composure. I can't think of anything to say that doesn't end up with me in a puddle Takira has to mop up before Canon comes.

The doorbell rings, and Takira says, "Your love has arrived."

"Who said I love him?" I walk to the mirror to adjust my floral-patterned headscarf.

"Since when do you have to tell me something for me to know it?" she asks. "And leave that scarf alone. Your hair is fine."

The cornucopia of meds has eased my nausea and helped with fatigue, though sometimes both return, but it hasn't stopped the hair loss. Lately, if I'm not wearing one of Dessi's wigs, I wear a head wrap to hide the gaps which, even with hair as thick as mine, are noticeable now. My stage makeup still camouflages the butterfly-shaped rash that has spread its wings over my nose and cheeks, but there's no disguising how my face has started to swell. The hollows beneath my cheeks that used to sharpen my bone structure have filled into a puffiness no amount of dieting can reduce. This is one way the powerful steroid I'm taking is wreaking havoc on my physical appearance. I don't want to think about the invisible toll the drugs may take on my body.

"I look okay?" I ask, meeting Takira's compassion in the mirror.

"You look beautiful," she assures me as the doorbell rings again. "He'll think so, too. Now go get him before he busts that door down."

I kiss her cheek, grab my suitcase, and answer the door. On the front porch, Canon wears the perma-frown he can only shake for so long until the movie wraps. It clears, though, as soon as he sees me.

"You ready?" he asks.

I miss my chance to answer when Takira screams from the back, "Don't forget the lube!"

Canon and I lock eyes for half a second before we both laugh. It feels like forever since we laughed together. He pulls me into him, and I let myself go limp in his arms.

I let go.

For the space of a few heartbeats, I let go. The sound of his humor vibrates through his chest and reaches all the parts of me hungry for hope, for joy.

And yes, for love.

I haven't even told him, and I'm not sure I should. If he does somehow feel he can't walk away from the sick girl, won't me telling him how I feel, how much I've come to love and need him in even just a few months, only make it worse? He's always said he can read my every emotion. I'm glass, an open window.

For the first time since I've known him, I want to pull the shade.

FIFTY-NINE

Canon

"Neevah, we're here."

I say it softly, and she doesn't wake, her head drooped against the passenger side window. On the short drive from her place to mine, she fell asleep almost immediately. I'm in no rush so I sit back with the car parked in the driveway and watch her sleep. She still wears the heavy makeup from being on set today, and not for the first time, I hope she isn't overdoing it. Dr. Okafor wouldn't have cleared her to come back if she wasn't stabilized and able to work. Fortunately, most of what we have left is musical numbers, just her singing, so not as demanding as the last few months.

I wrestle with guilt constantly. I cast her in the movie that stressed her out so badly it triggered this flare. I push hard to get what I want from my actors. Did I push her too much? Is there anything I could have done differently? Did I overlook the signs that she was getting sicker? That day she was so exhausted, she fell asleep in her room. We argued. I blasted her for being late, when she was...

Dammit.

She shifts, slightly dislodging the headscarf covering her hair. Right above her ear there's a hairless spot, and my heart pinches. Not because I give a damn about her losing hair, but because she has glorious hair, and she's worked so hard to keep it.

I've done this before—walked with someone I love through a tough disease. When Mama died of complications from MS, it had eaten its way through her life, and bearing witness fundamentally changed me. It's how I learned to compartmentalize—to shelve my grief and deepest emotions so I could get through life. When *The Magic Hour* broke out, I was still grieving

Mama's passing. I learned how to smile for cameras and to get through press junkets with a heart torn to shreds. And to a degree, I put my heart in a deep freezer box so I could do what I needed to do, and it worked.

Until Neevah.

She found that box when she wasn't even looking, stumbled upon it and right into my heart. It's hard to compartmentalize—to focus on this one thing and not worry about this other thing when this "other thing" is the woman I love navigating a life-threatening illness.

Dr. Okafor keeps saying they've come so far in lupus research and, with the huge pool of people willing to be tested, she's hopeful Neevah will find a donor soon. But I lie awake at night doing what I always do—running through all the worst-case scenarios and troubleshooting how I could fix them.

And I can't.

There isn't a damn thing I can do to control or to fix it. And this helpless feeling, the one that hounded me to every pier my mother wanted to visit, that dimmed every sunset—it's back. The one woman who reaches my heart could shatter it the same way my mother did when I lost her. I don't let myself think that way often because it would drive me crazy and I'd roll Neevah in bubble wrap and hold Dr. Okafor hostage twenty-four hours a day to make sure my girl is okay.

And that would be extreme.

Or would it?

I mean…I would keep them comfortable.

"Why didn't you wake me up?" Neevah asks, yawning and stretching.

"You made that sleep look so good." I reach across to cup her face. "I didn't want to disturb you."

She smiles, then reaches up to touch her headscarf like she's making sure it's still there. When she finds it askew, her wide eyes zip to meet mine. I keep my face impassive like I don't know what's bothering her—what she's afraid I've seen.

"Um, well, I'm awake now." She opens the car door and starts toward the house.

I grab her suitcase from the trunk and wheel it up my driveway. My house isn't as big as Evan's. That feels like more space than I need for just me, but it's one of those houses I grew up seeing, thinking I could never have. Lots of glass and dark wood floors and soaring ceilings and a king's view of the city.

"Your house is beautiful," Neevah says. "I can't believe this is the first time I'm here."

Ours has been an unusual courtship, played out on location and in back lots, on secret Sunday dates, and in between takes. There's nothing normal about this phase of our relationship either—finishing a movie while waiting for a kidney transplant.

Mama used to say, *Who wants normal? Extraordinary wants no parts of normal.*

And that's Neevah. I should have known being with her would wreak havoc on my heart. I wouldn't have it any other way. Wouldn't have *her* any other way, but as she tugs at her scarf again, I wonder if she believes that. If she thinks I would choose something or someone different had I known this was the deal. I wouldn't have. I want her however she comes. She's worth all of the gambles with no guarantees.

"Can I get the grand tour later?" she asks, glancing around the foyer. "I barely had time to pack when I got home from set. I want a bath, a meal, and a bed in that order."

"Sure. We can order something." I gesture to the floating stairs leading up to the next floor. "Bed and bath this way."

She looks so tired, I want to scoop her up and take the stairs for her, but I already know she would say I'm being dramatic and overprotective. When we reach my bedroom, she flops onto the California king and closes her eyes.

"Wake me up next week." She cracks one eye open and grins at me. "I promise not to be a drag tonight. I just need a second wind."

"Babe, you can sleep. Eat when the food comes and turn in. We don't have to..."

She must know I don't need sex. I mean, do I *want* sex? With her, all the time, but I'm a grown man and I love her. I'm not that selfish.

"Um, I want to get this makeup off." She looks toward the bathroom, the door standing open. "And maybe take that bath?"

"Sure."

I show her through to the bathroom and she closes the door, leaving a small crack, which I immediately exploit. I'm starved for the sight of her after spending so little time together this week. We were in each other's vicinity on set, and I gave her a few notes, but we're firmly in Monk's territory now with the musical numbers. Most of my notes center on how we're capturing her and the band onstage.

From where I sit on the bed, I catch quick glimpses of her at my sink washing her face. She bends to rinse the cleanser away, and when she rises and pats her face dry, in the mirror I see the faint rash across her nose and cheeks the makeup hid. She unzips her sundress, letting it fall into a floral pool around her feet. At the sight of her only in panties, my cock screams for release. It's been me and my hand for the last couple of weeks, and I'm fine if that doesn't change tonight, but damn. Seeing her again—the intimacy of her bare skin and toned curves—I'll settle for this reminder of what we've had before and will have again whenever she's ready. I'll be content to hold her, and won't pressure her for anything else, but I have to acknowledge at least to myself how much I want her.

"Um, this bathtub should come with a manual," she calls out, amusement tinting her voice. "How do I get the hot water to work?"

"Oh, right." I open the door wider, entering, but being careful not to look since she's scrambling to cover herself, clutching a floor-length bathrobe like a shield. I could remind her I've probably seen and licked every inch of her body, but I resist that temptation, along with all the others she presents.

It's a freestanding tub, big enough for the two of us if she wanted that. I want that.

"I rarely use it." I twist the knobs until hot water flows. "I always shower. This temperature okay?"

She nods, testing the water with one hand and gripping the collar of the bathrobe with the other.

"Can I stay?" I ask, watching her face for signs of welcome or rejection. "So we can talk?"

Something close to distress flares in her expression. Everything in me wants to growl that she is mine and I am hers, and I won't tolerate closed doors and bathrobes between us, but I don't want to misstep. I miss her. I miss us together.

"Sorry. I'll leave." I start toward the door. "I don't want to make you uncomfortable by—"

"You can stay." She perches on the edge of the tub, sprinkling something white and powdery into the water.

"Are you sure?" I ask, even though I have no intention of leaving if she's fine with me being here. I lean against the wall, fold my arms across my chest, and watch her with hungry eyes.

"I hope you plan to eat," she says, a slight smile playing on her lips. "Something other than me, I mean."

I laugh self-deprecatingly, defusing some of the tension I don't even understand that has crept up between us. "I'm hovering, huh?"

"You are. You don't have to worry that I'll pass out in the tub and drown." She says it like I'm some nursemaid instead of her man who can barely restrain himself from fucking her in that bathtub.

"I've just missed you," I say. "And it feels like you…have you been avoiding me?"

The laughter fades and she lowers her eyes to the marble floor. "No, of course not. We've been busy."

"Not that busy."

"I've been tired." She raises defiant eyes like she's daring me to question if she's been too tired to spend time with me. Of course, I can't.

"Then I'm glad we have this weekend," I say, instead of calling her out on what I suspect is an excuse. I just can't figure out *why* she's been avoiding me.

"Me too." She glances at me surreptitiously before dropping the bathrobe and nearly diving into the tub before I can see much. She's a blur of coppery legs and berry-tipped breasts. If I'd blinked, I would have missed it, but it was enough to make my dick hard. I shift, crossing my legs at the ankles in hopes she'll overlook how arousing I find this whole bath situation. She's submerged in frothy bubbles, her pretty face and the colorful headscarf the only things visible.

I can't stay away, so I walk over to the tub and sit on the edge, running my hand through the water.

She stiffens, her eyes glued to my hand clearing a path through the bubbles. I notice the razor on the small table by the tub.

I pick it up and turn it, smiling. "Shaving your legs?"

"Uh, yeah." She clears her throat. "I plan to."

"Can I help?"

I've never wanted to shave any part of a woman's body, but it suddenly seems like the safest erotic thing I could do. Our gazes lock, and just beneath the reserve I've met more than once the last week, heat stirs.

I can work with heat.

"You don't have to," she says, her voice barely audible in the quiet bathroom.

"I want to." I pick up the pink canister of shaving cream. "Use this?"

She nods, her eyes flicking between the razor and my face. I've never done this, but how hard can it be? How different from shaving a jaw and chin and cheeks?

I lift one long, lean leg from the water and immediately recognize that this is very different.

"I don't see any hair," I tease. "What am I supposed to be shaving?"

"I like to shave before the hair shows," she says, her expression loosening into a smile.

"That doesn't make sense."

"Gimme that." She laughs, reaching for the razor. "You're gonna cut me."

I gently push her shoulder until her back rests against the lip of the tub.

"I can do this." I squeeze a dollop of the cream into my palm, spread it slowly over the curve of her knee and down the muscle of her calf. All humor is snuffed, because I'm touching her more intimately than I have since we last made love in Santa Barbara. In tandem, our breathing hitches, hurries. I run the razor down the length of her leg, clearing a path in the foamy shaving cream. She goes still, our stare unbroken, her chest heaving with labored breaths, while I repeat the action until her leg is smooth and soapless.

"One down," I say, unable to look away from the elegant lines of her throat and collarbone. "One to go."

I wait for her to extend the other leg, and begin again. I'm smoothing on the shaving cream when I notice the same rash on her arm a few weeks ago on her calf and knee.

"Does it hurt or itch?" I ask, frowning, unsure if I should put shaving cream on the affected areas.

The simmering passion stirring in her eyes extinguishes, and she jerks away, dropping her leg back into the water.

"I'll finish later. You can…I can do this. Thanks anyway."

First the uncharacteristic modesty and now this. Neevah's incredibly comfortable with her body and has never been shy with me. So her hiding and withdrawing this way—it's not her.

"What's wrong?" I ask, trying to keep my voice low and reasonable when I want to yell. Want to demand why she's been avoiding me. Why she acts like I haven't seen her naked before. Haven't touched her. Haven't fucked her in every position I've ever fantasized about. I have. I remember the slide of our sweat-slick skin—recall the mingled scents of our bodies. I know how tightly she contracts around me when she comes.

So what is this?

"Baby, please talk to me." I dip my hand into the water, find her fingers, and link them with mine, watching her face for those feelings she usually can't hide. "I've been with you. I have seen you."

"You haven't seen me like this," she whispers, her bottom lip trembling. "You don't want to see me like this."

"Or *you* don't want me to see you like this?"

"Does it make a difference?"

"Yeah, because one implies that I don't want you unconditionally, and the other implies you don't trust me to."

My words linger in the silent bathroom, echoing off the walls. Neither of us looks away from the other, but for once I'm not sure what I'm seeing. She has frosted the glass, and I have no idea how to read her, how to reach her like this.

"Ya know," she says, sitting forward so her breasts push through the suds, "if this is the setup for a pity fuck, I'll pass. Is this the part where you pat yourself on the back for sticking around? Where you tell yourself how noble you are for not leaving? Because you can go."

"You'd like that, wouldn't you?" I ask, tilting my head and peering past her anger and bravado to what I suspect is beneath. "If I left so you could do this on your own and I wouldn't have to see you any way but perfect?"

"I've never been perfect."

"You are for me, and it has nothing to do with how smooth your skin is." I gesture to her headscarf. "Or if you lose hair or need a kidney or whatever the hell this disease has in store."

"Lemme guess." She barks a sardonic laugh. "Because you're in it for the long haul, right?"

"Is this some kick-him-out-before-he-has-the-chance-to-leave shit? Because if so, try something else. I will not be disposed of. You hear me?"

She stands so abruptly the water sloshes over the side and splashes my clothes.

"Then have a look." She throws her arms out at her sides. The rash, scalier now, before contained to just a few patches on her forearms, has spread to her biceps, and sprinkled across her belly, the tops of her thighs, and a few patches on her calves. She turns so I can see it all over her back and along her nape.

"And while we're at it," she says, her voice breaking, "you may as well see this."

She snatches off the headscarf, and though her hair is neatly braided, there are large areas where chunks of it are missing. I see it. I see the discolored patches on her arms, legs, stomach. I see the spots where there is no hair. I note the rash on her face that the makeup hid. I know what she thinks I see, but all I really see is light. The same light that shone blindingly bright that first night on a Broadway stage, it's still there. If anything, this fight she's in, what it requires of her, is the filament to make her shine even brighter.

"Why do you think I'm here?" I ask harshly, standing, stepping so close my shirt turns wet against her bare breasts.

She drops her head, shaking it, closing her eyes. Shutting me out.

I lift her chin, force her to meet my gaze. "You don't know?"

"I don't want you to stay out of obligation, or because it's the noble thing to do, or because you can't figure out how to walk away from the sick girl without looking like an asshole."

I rear back, shocked that she would be that misguided. Here I am, literally about to come in my pants at the sight of her naked, and she thinks I don't want her? That I'm here out of misplaced guilt? That I'm making a fool of myself to get a glimpse of a leg, a breast, anything to be *noble*?

I grab her hand and press it to my cock, rigid and swollen behind my zipper.

"Is that noble?" I snarl, pressing my nose to hers. "Does that feel like guilt to you?"

She squeezes and I flinch, it feels so good, lowering my head until our temples kiss. I reach blindly between us, finding the juncture of her thighs and sliding two fingers over her seam between the lips, caressing her slick clit in a rubbing rhythm, holding my breath so it's quiet enough for me to hear how wet she sounds—to hear her breath hitch.

"Oh," I whisper into her hair, sliding two fingers inside the hot, tight channel that clenches and contracts. "I see you're feeling guilty, too."

Her breasts heave, lids lowering over the smoky passion in her eyes. I pull back far enough to catch and hold her gaze.

"Do you want me?" I ask, searching her face for the truth.

She grinds her hips against my hand and nods, her eyes drifting closed.

"And did you ask Dr. Okafor if we can?" I press.

She licks her lips and doesn't respond.

"You did, didn't you? Because I can feel how bad you want this dick, so I know you asked. And what did she say?"

"She said…" She moans when I hook my fingers inside, finding that spot that always sets her off. "She said as long as I feel up to it."

"And do you feel up to it?" I ask seriously, because I could be as horny as a mustang in heat and I wouldn't do anything to hurt her.

Instead of answering with words, she tips up on her toes, grabs my jaw, pulls my mouth open, and dives in, commanding the kiss. It feels like I've been holding my breath since I last had this. I go deeper, exploring the hot, sweet interior of her mouth. Our heads bob as we try to get more of each other. Teeth colliding, tongues slipping and slurping. It's a wet, hot, heart-racing mess, and I've missed it. Missed her so damn much. Skimming my hands down the wet satin of her back, I dip to slide my arms beneath her ass, and my hands are full of naked woman. I lift her from the tub and she wraps her legs around my waist, dampening my shirt and jeans. I rush to the bed and lay her down gently, staring at her for a few seconds. Self-consciousness spreads over her in the hand she reaches for her hair, and the way she crosses one leg over the other, trying to hide the lesions.

"Don't," I tell her, the one word ragged on my lips. "Don't you dare think I see you as any less beautiful than I ever have or that I want you less."

"Canon." She closes her eyes. "If I thought you stayed out of guilt or—"

"I *can't* leave because there's nowhere else to go. So it won't do you any good to drive me away, though I can see you tried tonight."

"Not very effectively," she says, looking at me with a teary smile.

"I'm not going anywhere."

I traverse her thigh, knee, calf, with the back of my hand, tracing the dry places on her skin with the same reverence I do the smooth. I take her foot, kissing the arch. When my breath dusts the sensitive sole, her toes twitch.

"It tickles," she says, her laugh husky. Our gazes catch and cling, amusement evaporating like steam the longer we stare at one another. Looking into her eyes, the glass becomes clear again, the frost swiped completely until I see all her emotions. The desire, the fear, the self-consciousness.

The love.

And the glass is suddenly a mirror, reflecting back to me something I should have told her weeks ago.

"I love you, Neevah Saint." I chuckle, emotion crowding my throat. "Or Mathis—whatever your damn name is. I love you."

She's wet, naked, with rashes and all the things she's afraid I'll reject her for on full display, but I'm the one holding my breath. Exposed. Waiting. My future in her hands. And while I wait, watch, a single tear skates over the rash covering her cheek.

"I love you back."

Her words, spoken softly in a wobbling voice, with a steady stare, land like a boulder. They crush my control and steal my breath. The fact that I love her is a secret I've been keeping from her for weeks.

I want you to find someone you love more than your art.

Mama said the magic hour was waiting on a miracle you knew would come. I've waited all my life to want someone, to love someone the way I do Neevah, but I didn't actually believe it would happen.

She sits up, widening her legs so I'm standing between them, and tips her head back to meet my eyes through a spray of long lashes. When she reaches for my belt, her throat—smooth and burnished and brown—moves as she swallows and licks her lips. Every part of my body clenches when she undoes my jeans. Her cool fingers dust the muscles of my stomach as she urges the shirt up. I yank it by the collar over my head, my chest heaving as I wait for what she wants next. She pushes my pants down and then my briefs. Predictably, my cock is at full stand, begging for her attention. She obliges, leaning forward, letting her breath mist the wet tip before sneaking her tongue out for one torturous swipe.

Fuck.

My teeth grit around a collection of expletives. Her grin is all salacious mischief. She opens her mouth, sliding over me while her eyes penetrate mine. My breath hiccups at the brush of her tongue, the sweet grip of her mouth around me. She cups my balls, and the muscles in my legs go rigid. Instinctively, I cup her head and push her farther down on my cock.

Her head. Her hair.

I open my eyes, concerned that I've ruined this for us before it's gotten started, but she's not bothered, her eyes closed, full lips wrapped around me, head bobbing as she sucks me off.

"Shit," I hiss, gripping her neck, feeding more of it down her throat. She clutches my thigh with one hand, caresses my balls with the other, and my whole body is a nerve she sets on fire with her lips and tongue and the barest scrape of her teeth—with the wonder of her hands. And I'm coming like a motherfucker, spilling down her throat and roaring like something set free. She moans around me, the hum of it extending my pleasure into impossibility—into the range of almost unbearable. I grip her shoulders, my head flung back, as she takes all of me, her nails digging in my ass possessively, her mouth moving over my cock like she owns it.

Damn, she does.

Even when I'm spent, she persists, licking at every drop like a thirsty cat. I'm her saucer, her milk, her treat. I don't give a fuck. The room goes hazy around me, and only she is in focus. Her beautiful face, berry nipples, and the splay of her long legs, shamelessly showing me how wet she is, how ready.

"Lay back," I mutter, still seeing stars, my head spinning.

She complies, licking at the traces of me on her lips. After lifting her leg, bending her knee, and resting her heel on the edge of the bed, I run my palm up and down the inside of her thigh, with each pass moving closer to where she wants to be touched most. To where I want to touch her.

"Canon, just..." She watches me with passion-glazed eyes.

"Just what?" I maintain the simple, steady strokes, kneading the firm muscle of her thigh, working my fingers down to the private space just shy of her pussy. She moans, widening her legs as if to tempt me, to force my hand.

"You know," she whispers.

I do.

Skimming my hand over the taut muscles of her stomach and the valley between her breasts, I pluck her nipple in time with the taunting touch along her thigh. In slow inches, I slide two fingers inside, searching for that elusive spot that sends her to bliss. When I find it, she gasps, her neck arched, nails clawing the sheets. A frantic pulse batters beneath the vellum skin at the base of her throat. Lifting her foot, I kiss the delicate arch, run my nose over the fragile bone of her ankle, and lead a procession of kisses down the curve of her calf, behind the delicate bend of her knee. I grip the backs of her thighs and drag her to the edge of the bed, sinking to the floor, my mouth watering at the rising scent of her. Spreading her, I close my mouth around her clit, sucking, eating her like sun-ripened fruit. A peach, the flesh slick and sweet and wet, juices dripping down my chin. I'm a pauper at a feast, so lost in pleasure, I almost forget it's hers, too, until her sobs and whimpers float over my head.

I draw deep breaths, struggling to subdue my most primitive instincts. I know Dr. Okafor gave the greenlight for us to do this, but she probably doesn't expect me to fuck like a wild boar after only two weeks of celibacy. If I were to hurt Neevah…I can't even contemplate that transgression. I'd never forgive myself.

I stand and crawl onto the bed, gently turning her to her side. Leaving her left leg on the bed, I straddle it and bring her other leg up to my chest, resting it on my shoulder. She watches me, her eyes curious, excited.

"We've never done it this way," she says.

"Is it okay? Are you sure us doing this is okay?"

"I won't break, Canon." She frowns. "It feels like I'm losing everything. Don't take this from me, too."

I will make this good for her, for us both, but this position leaves her completely receiving and exerting no effort except to come. I enter in one quick thrust, and we both gasp at the fit—a large fist in a tight glove. I take up a rhythm, slowly building, delving deeper. She's spread for me, one leg on the bed, the other on my shoulder. With one fingertip, I caress her clit, never letting up the pumping pace.

"Jesus," she gasps, eyes wide and fixed on the ceiling like a stargazer. Our bodies move in sensual unison—a hypnotic rhythm that we can't break, but that only builds. With one small hand, she cups her breast and thumbs the nipple until it peaks. I wrestle with the beast inside who laughs at my restraint, a pitiful thing weakening every second I'm inside her. I grip her leg to me, turning my head to kiss her calf, biting into the sleek muscle. She tilts her head back, her eyes shutting tightly, the orgasm shuddering through her. Ecstasy seizes my muscles, rolling through my legs and the taut muscles of my shoulders. I drop my head back, my voice exploding in the room like full-throated thunder. She skitters her hand over the sheet until she finds mine, joining our fingers and meeting my gaze in the dying storm.

"Tell me again," she whispers.

I don't have to ask what she means. She wants the same words I want to hear.

"I love you."

A contented smile lights her eyes, christens her lips. "And I love you back."

SIXTY

Neevah

Canon loves me.

It's my first thought, and absolute joy and a sated body coax my lips into an irrepressible smile. The previous night plays out in full panoramic color projected onto the walls of my memory. It was measured not in hours or minutes, but in kisses and whispers. At first, we had urgent, impatient, frenzied fucking. Then languid, lazy, we've-got-all-night loving. We ordered food. We climbed into Canon's oversized tub, my back against his chest, and talked until my fingers and toes wrinkled, and the water grew cold. He shared his dreams with me, bright and unfinished like uncut diamonds kept in a bag no one else has seen. I shared my aspirations with him, which have been revised since the diagnosis. They've gone from winning a Tony to living to see my next birthday.

It's funny how we speak of the future like it's promised. Now, I feel less and less like I can assume anything, even tomorrow. It does lend life a certain preciousness it's easy to take for granted. It's a different perspective that forces you to change your lens. I do believe I'll beat this. If Canon has to scour the whole country, we'll find a kidney for me, but facing something like this changes you.

I roll over in the rumpled sheets, breathing in the coupled scents of our bodies. I'm alone, and I wriggle over to Canon's side, fitting my head into the dip in his pillow.

"You got it so bad, girl." I laugh at myself ruefully. It's true, but at least so does he.

He told me so last night.

The best and worst of life make strange bedfellows. I've worked so hard for years to have an opportunity as big as *Dessi Blue*, and I've gone years never feeling for anyone even an ounce of what I feel for Canon. I should be high on possibility, and yet the future is as uncertain in many ways as it is bright.

I sit up, tucking the sheets under my arms.

What time is it?

I grab my phone from the bedside table, shocked to see it's after noon.

"Good grief," I mutter, swinging my legs over the side of the large bed. "I've slept half the day away."

The production schedule has slowed significantly—partly because we only have music to finish, and partly because I need it to be slower, and it's still a lot. I could literally lie right down in the bed and go back to sleep.

When I stand, I stagger and sink back down into the soft mattress for a second before trying again. A tiny hammer taps behind my eyes and at my temples. My ankles and feet are swollen. So are my hands. This is part of the disease, I know that, but it's a cruel reminder that despite the drugs that manage these symptoms so I can get through each day, my kidneys are still failing. Toxins that should be filtered from my body aren't leaving efficiently. And every day without a new kidney, it will only get worse.

I have to call Terry. Mama promised to give me today and I'm taking it. I'm facing enough crap without thinking about the most awkward conversation in the history of awkward conversations.

I know we've been beefing the last twelve years, but could I have your kidney?

No more awkward than *I fucked your fiancé and I'm having his baby, sis.*

And who's to say she'll even be a match? We won't know until we try, and I know we need to try. Sighing, I grab underwear from my suitcase, but ignore my clothes, instead opting for one of Canon's USC hoodies slung over a chair. For a bachelor, Canon keeps his house very orderly. I'm sure someone helps with that, but still, his closet is as big as my tiny apartment in New York. One whole wall for shelves of shoes. A segment of his closet is dedicated to suits, and I remember how incredible he looked that night on the rooftop. His collection of sweatshirts, jeans, button-ups—they're all color-coordinated and neatly arranged.

My body protests, begging me to crawl back into bed, but I push myself to venture downstairs. The house looks even more impressive now that I'm not distracted by hunger and nerves. I wander through expensively decorated rooms, each screaming *interior design*. There's no way Canon would slow down long enough to shop and create this beautiful space.

"Where are you?" I ask the empty room. Nowhere on this floor.

Spotting a door ajar beneath the floating stairs, I hear the rumble of voices. Tiptoeing down the steps, I peek around the corner. A huge home theater takes up most of this floor, outfitted with four rows of movie-theater seats and a huge screen dominating an entire wall. Canon is slumped in a seat in the front row, a pad on his knee, his eyes fixed to the screen. His laptop rests at his bare feet, open and frozen on what I recognize as one of the French Riviera scenes.

"Looking good?" I ask, walking across the plush rug to stand beside him.

He drops the pad and pulls me down to sit on his knee. I snuggle into his strong arms and hard chest.

"It looks amazing," he says. "It's not perfect, but we'll get there."

He takes my hand, frowning at my swollen fingers and wrists. His glance slides lower to the puffy ankles and feet. I tense, not needing him to tell me this isn't good, but sure he'll ask.

"Did you take your meds?"

"Of course. I know it's a little bit of swelling."

"Any other symptoms?"

Extreme exhaustion. A touch of nausea and a headache that's playing ping-pong behind my eyes.

"I'm fine," I assure him.

"When do you see Dr. Okafor again?"

"I have a checkup Monday."

"And have you called your sister about getting tested to see if she's a match?"

"Not yet. I'll do it today."

"Neevah," he says, shaking his head disapprovingly. "I don't care about whatever shit you and Terry have going on. She has the highest likelihood of being a match. You have to ask her."

"Does this place have popcorn, too?" I stand to get away from the conversation. I've already decided I'll call Terry. I don't want to be nagged about it. I sound like a spoiled child, but between work and what my body's been putting me through, I just want to turn off for a second.

"You're hungry?" he asks. "I can cook something."

I'm actually nauseous and cannot imagine food right now, but I nod so we can shift from the unpleasant task of begging my sister for a vital organ. He grabs the remote to turn off the video, but pauses, staring at the screen.

"Wait." He pulls me to stand in front of him and links his arms around my middle, tucking his head into the crook of my shoulder. "Watch this."

The onscreen image rolls into a different file. Digital, not film. It's one of the musical numbers at the Savoy we recorded early on. Days, weeks in the making, relentless hours of hard work, and the scene comes and goes in a matter of minutes. Lucia's meticulous attention to detail and her exacting demands are evident in every step. The dance is precisely executed, but there is a wild joy on my face, in the abandon of my limbs when I'm tossed and when I glide and when I kick and swing. The spirit of the Savoy inhabits every inch of the screen. The excellence and the pride and creativity that swept through Harlem and reverberated around the world—they're all there. Even now, standing here in the circle of Canon's arms, I'm an echo of those artists—their talent and persistence in the face of prejudice or war or poverty or any flaming darts the world threw at them. Instead of burning them to death, adversity lit a fire under them to make something the world had never seen. Innovating with their bodies and minds and voices. The chaos and necessity of imagination. And this is their legacy. *I* am their legacy.

Tears blur the beauty onscreen and I grip Canon's forearms, sinking into the hardness of his chest.

"It's fantastic," I whisper, moved almost beyond words at the privilege of being in this film. "You've made something…Canon, this is so magnificent."

"It is," he agrees, excitement woven into the dark fabric of his voice. "You are. Everyone who sees this movie will see what I saw in you." He turns me around to face him, his big hands resting at the curve of my hips.

"Which was what?" I ask, placing my palms flat against his chest.

"Light." He cups my face, his eyes intent and unwavering. "I get it now—my mother's fascination with light. She chased it for years, committing it to memory and film with every sunset. She taught me what to look for, and when I saw it in you, I recognized it. I didn't fully understand what it would mean for me, who you would be to me, but I saw that light and wanted it." He nods to the screen. "I wanted it for *Dessi Blue*, and though I wouldn't admit it, I wanted it for myself."

"It was a crazy thing to do." I chuckle, cupping the hard angle of his jaw. "Trusting some girl nobody knows with a movie this big."

"I always know what I'm doing," he says immodestly, grinning when I roll my eyes. "Enough about my brilliance. I mean, for now. We can revisit it later. Let's get you some food."

My stomach roils and I swallow another wave of nausea, but I smile and follow him back up the stairs.

We're on our way to the kitchen when he stops and detours to a room through an archway down the hall. "Let me show you something."

It's a studio of sorts with a wide skylight, inviting light into every corner. A cushioned seat is built into one nook. The walls are filled, mere slivers of space separating the photos and shelves. Photographs of sunsets, ocean scenes, buildings, Canon at various ages, self-portraits of Remy Holt—her work takes up all the space on two walls. The other two walls hold shelves with more cameras than I've ever seen.

"Wow." I walk over to inspect a vintage-looking Nikon. "This is some collection."

"Hers," he says, inspecting a selection of Polaroids showing Canon and his mother at the beach. "She was obsessed."

I'm afraid to touch the cameras. It's obvious they're in excellent condition. They aren't dusty, but shine and are neatly arranged.

"They still work?" I ask.

He picks up the Nikon and aims it at me. "Let's see."

The click of the camera startles me. "Canon! Don't."

One hand flies to my hair, covered by the silk scarf I slept in last night.

Lowering the camera, he offers a slight smile. "We don't have any pictures together."

"Is that true?"

"Someone may have snapped one of us on set or something, but I don't have any." He walks over to an old-fashioned camera on a stand. "Let me take a few."

I don't want him to. Call it vanity or fear, I'm not sure what, but something inside me recoils at the idea of documenting this time of my life. In the film, I have makeup and wigs and costumes and a character to hide behind. But here in the unforgiving light of day, there's nowhere to hide. It's just me and my battle scars and bald spots. He's asking to memorialize it when I just want it to be over.

"A few," I relent.

His triumphant grin makes me regret my acquiescence immediately because give Canon an inch and he takes a road trip. In a few minutes, he makes quick work of fiddling with the buttons and setting the timer.

"Look into the camera?" I ask, nervous for some reason.

"Look at me," he says, bending, taking my lips between his, sucking gently. I lose myself in the kiss.

The camera goes off and I pull away, looking from his face to his lens.

"So just a picture of us kissing?"

"Can I take a few more?" he asks, walking over to grab the Polaroid camera.

"Okay."

He extends his arm away from us, aiming at our faces pressed together. He captures us kissing, crossing our eyes, laughing. The camera spits each photo out and Canon lets them fall to the ground, not bothering to stop until several photos litter the floor, scattered at our feet. He collects them, opens a drawer with clothespins, and clips the photos of us to a line that stretches between walls.

"This one," he says, picking up another camera, "was one of her favorites. It's an EOS DCS 3. Expensive at the time and a little unwieldly, but she used it a lot. In Greek mythology, Eos was the goddess of the dawn who rose each morning from the edge of the ocean. What do you say?" He aims the camera at me. "Just a few?"

No rests on the tip of my tongue. It somehow feels different than when he took pictures of us together. Me standing alone in the light, no makeup or a persona I can don and doff, feels more exposed, vulnerable.

I nod permission, but give him nothing to work with. I stand in a pool of light and stare back at his camera. He doesn't do that photographer thing—coax me, direct me, encourage me to pose or "give" him anything. He just clicks, changes the angle of her camera, of his head, the camera's eye never leaving me.

"You done?" I ask.

"Not unless you want me to be." He lowers the camera. "I'd like to take more."

"Why?"

"Because I want to remember you exactly as you are right now."

I scoff and shoot him a sour look. "Right now? Like this?"

He nods, his expression sober. "Exactly like this."

There is such love in his eyes, such...I don't know...adoration...that for a moment, I don't know how to respond. It is a look, a love that reaches in and fills me up. I'm about to yield because that look could get this man anything he wants, when a wave of nausea overwhelms me. I rush from the studio, zigzagging from unfamiliar room to unfamiliar room until I stumble into a bathroom just in time to vomit. I haven't eaten anything, so it's a violent, fruitless expelling, but I hug the bowl tightly, my tears running into the toilet. I've tried to ignore the persistent pain battering the inside of my skull since I woke, but the heaving worsens the agony, and I close my eyes against light that has suddenly become unbearable. Slumping on the cold tiles, I let my body go limp, praying for oblivion.

"Dammit," Canon curses, rushing in and scooping me up off the floor.

I want to tell him I can walk, but I honestly don't know that I can. My head flops onto his shoulder.

"Neevah, baby." I've never heard his voice this way. Desperate, panicked. Frightened. "I'm taking you to the emergency room."

I open my mouth to tell him that's unnecessary, but a sob comes out instead. It's a wretched sound, and I resent my body for making it. I taste tears and grip his shirt with one weak fist.

"Mama. I want my mama."

Most times when I've really needed her in the past, I've had to make do on my own. As I give in to the debilitating fatigue, I don't believe this time could be any different, but I have to ask.

SIXTY-ONE

Canon

"Mrs. Saint…uh, Mathis, it's Canon Holt."

There's a loaded pause on the other end of the line.

"Neevah's director?"

"Yes, but I'm also…" I should have asked Neevah what she told her mother about us. Fuck it. "We're also seeing each other. I'm not sure if she mentioned—"

"She did. In so many words. Is she…is she okay? Is something wrong?"

"I know she's spoken with you about her lupus diagnosis and the kidney trouble."

"Yes, I'm being tested, but they think I may be too old. Sixty is not old," she says with indignant pride. "But they want a younger kidney."

"Her sister still doesn't know, right?" An edge creeps into my words.

"I told Neevah to ask her because it's killing me, not being able to tell Terry. Has something happened?"

"Neevah's in the hospital." I glance up the hall that leads to her room. "She's resting, but her blood pressure spiked again. They want to keep her here to monitor for at least a few days. They said some patients with kidney failure have been known to have strokes or heart problems."

I draw a sharp breath that does jack shit to calm my rioting emotions. "The medications they've been using to manage her kidney function just aren't doing a good enough job. She's been trying to avoid dialysis, but her doctor thinks temporary dialysis is the best thing until we find a kidney."

"Oh, my God," Mrs. Mathis gasps. "What…what can I do?"

"She asked for you. Can you come?"

"I...I'm afraid to fly," she says, and I hear the shame and frustration in her voice. "I know it's silly, but—"

"Galaxy, the studio producing the movie Neevah's in, has a private plane. Would you be willing to come, to try, if I could arrange that? It's more comfortable than flying commercial, and it might be easier for you."

"Could I bring someone with me?"

"Of course." I don't hesitate because she could bring Attila the Hun, far as I care.

"Terry?" Mrs. Mathis asks tentatively. "Could I bring Neevah's sister? I think I could fly if she's with me."

I already know Neevah won't be happy, but I don't know how to balance everything she wants with what she needs. She needs a kidney but doesn't want to ask her sister, who is her best shot. She wants her mother but wouldn't want her sister to come. I love her enough to deal with the fallout if I make the wrong moves.

"Just come," I say with a heavy sigh. "Can you come tonight if I make the arrangements?"

She agrees and we disconnect. I immediately dial Evan and brace myself for another conversation I'd rather not have.

"Hey, what's up?" Evan asks. "Have you seen that last batch of film from the labs? It looks fantastic."

"Yeah, I watched some earlier today. I need—"

"You should be able to start editing soon, right? I mean, I know we still have a few scenes with Neevah and the band, but Monk says we should wrap this week. We can get at least close to back on track."

"I don't think that's gonna happen, man." I sit in one of the waiting room chairs. "Neevah's back in the hospital."

"What? Is she...what's going on?"

"Basically, the meds they have her on aren't doing a good enough job." I pass a hand over my eyes and rest my elbows on my knees. "Dr. Okafor wants to put her on dialysis."

"Dialysis? Wow. That's..."

I know Evan too well not to anticipate how torn he is. He feels for

Neevah, and by extension, for me, but his wheels are also turning to work out how we can salvage this production. I never thought I'd say it, but *Dessi Blue* is the least of my worries right now.

"You have my permission," I tell him with grim humor.

"What do you mean?"

"To put on your producer hat because I'll be damned if I can right now, and I guess somebody has to."

"Galaxy is gonna ride us on this. They don't want to be all *am I the asshole,* and they're concerned for Neevah's health, obviously—"

"Obviously."

"But they'll want a timeline. Trey has another project that begins shooting next month. Jill is booked for another film soon after. So is Kenneth. If we shut this production down now, it could compromise the last scenes."

"No, it won't."

"And how do you guarantee that?"

"Because I'll still be involved and I'll make sure we get what we need once Neevah's able to resume shooting."

Tension pulls the line taut between us.

"Canon, but what if she—"

"Don't you say it, Evan."

"God, I don't want to, but we have an unfinished movie with a huge budget on our hands. You're the one who just told me to be the producer here, so I am."

"What do you want me to do?" I explode, springing to my feet, prowling the waiting room. "I can't think about that with Neevah sick. I just can't care about this damn movie until she's better."

Story must be protected, at all costs. Sometimes at personal cost.

My words from the night of the New York film festival, the night I met Neevah, come back to haunt me. Damn, I was arrogant. It was so easy to say story must be protected at all costs, at personal cost when I had so little to lose. Now the only thing I care about protecting is Neevah, and there is no cost higher than losing her.

"Canon, I know," Evan says, his voice sober. "I get it. You focus on her.

I'll buy us some time with Galaxy. They've been understanding with the slower schedule to accommodate her illness."

"Well, I need them to understand that it's doctor's orders that she stop production immediately until further notice. Dr. Okafor wants her to start dialysis this week. That's four hours a day, three days a week."

"Shit."

"Lots of people on dialysis can work and lead relatively normal lives. They do the dialysis and then go about their regular routines. Some even do it from home, but that takes weeks of training. Dr. Okafor hopes we'll find a match for a kidney soon and not have to go that route, which brings me to the reason for my call."

"There's more?" Evan asks, injecting the tiniest bit of humor into the question.

"Can we see if Galaxy could bring Neevah's mom here? She's afraid of flying, and I think the private route might be better for her, and maybe get her here quicker."

"I don't see why that would be a problem. They'll probably want to do anything that could move this along."

"Right. I honestly don't care about their motivation. I just want to give Neevah *something*. I feel pretty useless right now."

"You're where you should be, doing what you should do. Now I'm going to go do what I should do. Let me talk with Trey's agent and the rest of the production team. Update them and talk through some possible solutions."

"Thanks, man." I glance up to see Dr. Okafor approaching. "I gotta go. Keep me posted and I'll circle back."

Dr. Okafor's usual impassive expression is tinged with concern.

"How is she?" I demand, slipping my phone in my jeans back pocket.

"She wants to see you. I'm glad you got her here when you did. This could have been a lot worse. She could have had a stroke, Canon."

My heart palpitates. Skips several beats and the bottom drops out of my belly. I grip the back of my neck and have to sit down.

"Did you tell her about the dialysis?" I ask, my voice wobbling and scratchy.

"Yes." Dr. Okafor's brows dip into a frown. "She's not happy about it, and I tried to reassure her it's a temporary measure, but...she's not taking any of it well, especially when I advised that she stop production for now."

"Well, obviously she's not going back to work until she's better."

"She feels an inordinate amount of pressure that the movie is on her shoulders. Honestly, I think that pressure has contributed to the aggressiveness of this flare—of her disease progressing this rapidly. Flares are a part of this condition, and most people have to learn to adjust their lifestyles to make this work. She's no different."

Guilt gnaws at my gut hearing Dr. Okafor voice what I've been wrestling with. Doing this movie triggered all of this.

"Can I see her now?"

"Yes."

"Her mother may be flying in." I hesitate. "I might be speaking out of turn, but I don't really care. I'll deal with Neevah being pissed later. Her sister may be coming, too. How much testing could we get done if she's here a few days?"

Dr. Okafor's eyes light up. "You know a sibling is our best shot. Only a twin is a higher likelihood. Beyond blood, there is extensive testing. It's not fast, which is why Neevah has to go on dialysis while we wait."

"How many tests are we talking? How long?"

"There's a general medical history and physical exam before we start the more invasive tests, but blood and tissue tests like the ones you took. Beyond that, a long laundry list of labs, EKG, chest exam to test lungs, a psych eval."

"Good grief."

"For women, gynecological and mammograms and—"

"Okay. A lot of damn tests. And how long does all this take?"

"Usually weeks. Is her sister coming prepared to at least begin the process?"

"Uh...her sister didn't know Neevah needs a kidney as of ten minutes ago, but their mother is talking to her and hopefully bringing her here."

"Neevah hasn't even..." Dr. Okafor chops the sentence off and presses her lips together. "You want to see her now?"

"Please."

As soon as we enter Neevah's hospital room, her disappointment burdens the air. Her skin looks darker even in the few hours since I brought her in. Her face seems a little swollen, like her ankles. The rash across her nose and cheeks, more prominent. I should have grabbed her headscarf when it fell as we rushed out of the house. I was so freaked out, I just put her in the car and drove like a madman. Now, though, she reaches up to touch the spots where her hair has fallen out, and I wish I'd thought of it. Not because it bothers me, but because I know it bothers her. I'll text Takira and ask her to bring some.

"Hey." I sit on the edge of the bed and take her hand. "How are you feeling?"

Her lips quiver, even though she presses them tightly together, as if she's fighting for control of the emotions spilling out. "Did Dr. Okafor tell you about the dialysis?"

"Yeah, she did. It's only temporary, baby."

"I wanted...she says I have to stop shooting, too. Did she tell you that?"

"She did, and I'm in complete agreement."

"Canon, come on. I know you. I know this movie means everything to you and I'm messing up...I'm sorry."

"You're wrong. It's not this movie that means everything to me." I run the back of my hand over her cheek. "That'd be you."

I can't say I wish I'd never cast her because then I might not have met her or loved her, and I cannot imagine life without her now.

"Don't think about the movie right now," I tell her.

"And you aren't?"

"I'm not. I'm letting Evan and the team worry about that." I lean in, kissing her forehead and cheek. "I'm only worried about you."

I go to pull back, but she doesn't let me, gripping my arm and tugging me up.

"Will you hold me?" she whispers. I'm so used to her confidence, her fearlessness, that I almost miss her fear.

"Yeah. Of course." It's probably breaking some hospital rule, but I don't give a damn, climbing up into the bed, squeezing into the tight space and tucking her head into the crook of my neck. After a few seconds, she starts sniffing quietly and her tears wet my shirt. God, hearing her cry is ripping me apart inside.

"Baby." I stroke her arm and back. "It'll be alright. We got this. We'll fight this."

"Can you just..." She pauses, her voice breaking on a sob. "Can you just let me be sad? Can you just let it hurt? I don't need you to tell me why it shouldn't, or that it will be okay. I just want to *not* fight for a minute. Can you be here for me, with me, while I stop fighting and let myself feel this? I promise I'll get back up, but for just a minute, let me fall."

She doesn't need words from me right now, and anything I say will only sound like I'm trying to make it better, so I simply nod and kiss the top of her head while my shirt absorbs her tears. And for the space of a few minutes, I don't think of Galaxy, or Neevah's mother and sister, or anything beyond this room and the two of us in this bed. For a few minutes, she wants to fall. My only thought is to hold her and be here when she gets back up.

SIXTY-TWO

Neevah

"This must be the worst food I've ever tasted," I complain, pushing the tasteless cabbage and cauliflower around on my plate. Even the salmon, which I usually enjoy, has little flavor.

Dr. Okafor said a renal diet avoids foods with too much sodium, phosphorus, and potassium. Blueberries, apples, pineapple, cranberries—all my new best friends.

"Eat," Canon says, from the small table he's set up in the corner, not lifting his gaze from his computer.

"If they gave me food instead of cardboard, I would."

He shoots a wry look over the edge of his laptop. "It's not that bad."

"Oh." I lift a forkful of the bland morsels. "Then come see for yourself."

He rolls his eyes, but walks over to the bed and leans forward, mouth open. I shove the fork inside and watch his face closely. He grimaces before catching himself and humming approvingly. "Delicious."

"Liar."

He grins and bends down to kiss my lips lightly. I reach up and grip his neck, holding him, kissing him deeper. I'm in no shape for anything more, but just the closeness, the intimacy of his tongue exploring my mouth, gives me something to look forward to.

"I love you," he whispers into our kiss.

"I love you back. You've been so good to me, Canon."

"You can thank me later." He catches my eyes, wicked humor lurking beneath the surface of his smile. "I think a week's worth of blow jobs should suffice."

"Only a week?"

"I'm easy to please."

"The whole world, especially your cast and crew, would disagree."

"Shiiiit. If they know what's good—"

Someone clears their throat at the door, and Canon and I both turn to see who's there.

"Mama?" My voice emerges strangled and disbelieving and hopeful.

She looks exhausted and slightly disheveled, her dress wrinkled and her eyes weary, but she's here. Tears immediately leak over my cheeks, and Mama comes over, reaching down to me in the bed to hug me. I grip her neck and run my hands over her shoulders, not sure she's real. With our faces pressed together, the tears mingle on our cheeks, and I can't even find the words to ask how she's here.

"Mama..." I touch her face and laugh. "You don't fly."

"I finally did," she says, smiling over at Canon. "Thanks to Mr. Holt here."

Fresh tears clog my throat at his thoughtfulness. So many times I've needed her and she wasn't there, and this time she is. Canon made sure of that.

"Thank you," I say tearfully, taking and squeezing his hand.

He drops a kiss at my temple.

"Mama, you actually got on a plane for me. I can't believe it."

"Well, Canon got me a private jet, so how could I refuse?"

"Galaxy's," Canon answers my querying look. "They flew her in. I thought it might be a little easier."

"I'm spoiled now." Mama laughs, but it fades, and she looks over her shoulder at the door. "There's something you should know. I didn't come alone. I—"

"I'm here," Terry says from the door.

All the joy that surged inside me stalls at the sight of my sister. She's dressed simply in jeans and a T-shirt, her natural hair surrounding her face in thick coils. I should speak, but I can't find the words.

"Needed the bathroom after that long ride," she mutters, her expression growing stiffer and more uncertain the longer we stare at each other.

"Your…your sister," Mama says haltingly. "She flew with me. I don't think I could have come if she hadn't."

I lower my eyes to the starkness of the white hospital bedding, not sure how to process all this good and all this awkward at once.

"So you just weren't gonna tell me you needed a kidney?" Terry asks.

My gaze snaps to her and then to Mama and Canon.

"You hadn't asked her," Mama says, shrugging defensively. "And I needed to get here. I had to tell her something."

"*You* should have told me." Terry walks farther into the room, stopping at the end of my hospital bed. "I'm your best shot."

"Oh, you just love saying that, don't you?" I bark out a raw laugh that scratches my throat. "And you wonder why I hadn't told you."

"Yeah, I wonder why," she fires back. "Letting your pride endanger your life."

"You haven't been a part of my life in a long time, Terry. Why start now?"

"Because you might not have a life if you don't get a kidney."

"You're misinformed."

"And you're stubborn, but then, I knew that based on the way you've behaved this long."

"The way I behaved? You fuck my fiancé, have his baby, drive a wedge between me and my entire family—"

"I didn't put that wedge there, sis. You did that with your siditty ways."

"Siditty? Me? What the hell are you talking about?"

"Going off to New York."

"To get away from you and Brandon."

"And never coming home."

"To avoid you and Brandon. Look, you made your choices and I made mine. You got some nerve—"

"I'm gonna shut this shit down right now," Canon interrupts, his expression thunderous. "Terry, if you aren't here to help, you can jump on the next plane leaving LAX. I don't give a damn about you or your husband or this feud. Stress was a trigger for this flare-up, and if you're gonna make things worse, go. If you want to help, get tested to see if we can use your kidney. Those are your options."

"Who is this?" Terry sneers, hands on hips.

"This is Canon Holt," Mama says hastily. "He arranged for us to fly here. He's Neevah's director and—"

"And I said what I said," Canon inserts, narrowing his eyes. "You will not stress Neevah out any more than she already is. Believe me, her doctor will kick you out before I get the chance if she walks in and finds you yelling at the woman who literally is about to begin dialysis waiting for a kidney."

"Dialysis?" Terry asks faintly, glancing at me and frowning.

"This isn't a game," Canon continues. "That's what I'm telling you. We don't have time to argue. You guys can dive into some serious family therapy later, but right now, I need you to start the testing process, if you're willing."

"Of course I'm willing," Terry says, swallowing. "She's my sister."

"Even though I'm siditty, uppity, stubborn?" I ask, a sob clogging my throat.

"Exactly all that." Some of the fire reignites in Terry's stare. "But you're still my little sister. When shit hits the fan, family should be there for each other. I know we have a lot to work out, but let me at least try to help."

"That sounds like a great idea," Dr. Okafor says from the open hospital door. "You're Neevah's sister, I assume? I see the resemblance."

Is there? I study Terry's beautiful face. She was always the pretty one when we were growing up, so I didn't try to compare us. I knew she'd win the face race, but it didn't really matter. I loved my sister with an affection so deep it bordered on hero worship. When she betrayed that, the only way I could deal with it and the consequences was to cut her off completely. With our strident words still echoing in my ears, it's apparent there's just as much hurt and resentment in this room as there was in our living room over a decade ago.

"I'm glad to hear you want to help," Dr. Okafor continues. "Can I ask how long you're here?"

"I have three days before I have to get back to work," Terry says. "And my daughter needs me. Her daddy..." Her wide eyes meet mine at the mention of Brandon.

"We can talk about testing. We can't get it all done in three days," Dr. Okafor says. "We can coordinate with labs and doctors in your home state, too, which is?"

"North Carolina," Terry says.

"Good then," Dr. Okafor says, a smile lighting her dark eyes. "Well, let's get started."

SIXTY-THREE

Neevah

"You sure you'll be okay while I'm gone?" Canon asks.

"Are you sure *you'll* be okay while you're gone? You've barely left this room since I checked in. Kenneth and Jill need you. The movie needs you. Go."

"I'll be here," Mama reassures him. "By the time you get back, she'll be done."

Done with dialysis. Hooked up to this machine for hours at a time motivates me even more to find a match. I know this is how some people manage kidney disease, but this doesn't fit how I see my life as a performer, dancer, actor. I don't want to be chained to this machine. I can't be.

"Okay." Canon wears his hesitation in every line of his face. "I won't be long."

"Tell everyone I said hello." I want to be on set so badly and I hate how things have stalled because of this.

Canon kisses my forehead and then my lips in a touch that lingers but, with my mama watching, doesn't deepen. I want it to.

"I love you," he whispers, pulling back to search my eyes.

"Love you back." I give him a gentle shove. "Now go."

"I'll be back."

"You mentioned that." I laugh. "But first you have to *go* to come *back*."

Shaking his head, he grabs his bag, waves at my mother, and strides from the room as purposefully as he goes everywhere.

"Now *that* is a man," Mama breathes.

"He sure is."

I smile faintly, losing some of my shine now that Canon is gone. I'm actually exhausted and slightly miserable, but Canon is already hovering and here pretty much around the clock. He may not be thinking about *Dessi Blue*, but I am. It's my break. It will be one of the biggest movies of the year. It's potentially Canon's most significant work. It's Evan and Kenneth and Jill and Trey and Monk and Verity and Linh and all the cast and crew who worked and sweat and sacrificed to make this important piece of not just entertainment, but history. Lost, discarded history. We have the chance to restore, to amplify people and events that have too long been overlooked, and my damn kidneys are not going to ruin that because the director cannot focus on anything other than his sick girlfriend.

But now that he's gone, I slump into the pillows and watch the machine cleaning my blood and sending it back into my body since my kidneys have abdicated their duties.

The hospital door eases open and Terry walks in carrying an armful of magazines, which she passes to Mama, and a bag overflowing with colorful balls of yarn. She settles into a chair near the door and pulls out needles and yarn.

"You knit?" I ask skeptically. It doesn't really fit my image of her as the temptress who lured my fiancé into a scandalous affair.

"Yeah." She shrugs, not glancing up from her yarn. "It's soothing."

"There's a whole group of us at church who do it," Mama pipes up, reaching into Terry's bag for another set of needles and some yarn.

"Oh, you go to church, too?" I ask with raised brows, because Terry left church as soon as Mama could no longer make her go. I, however, was still singing in the choir until I left for college.

"Terry's the choir director," Mama says, pride evident in her voice.

"Nothing compared to Broadway, obviously," Terry says, roughly thrusting a needle into the innocent pile of yarn. "Or a big-time movie."

"At least Mama's seen you in the choir." I close my eyes and lean back into the pile of pillows. "More than I can say."

"I came and saw you that time, Neevah," Mama says.

"That one time in twelve years." I open my eyes and laugh. "Not that I've been in that many shows. Canon plucked me out of relative obscurity."

"You just have to rub that in our faces, too, huh?" Terry says, dropping the needles in her lap. "That you're dating Canon Holt and he's crazy about you. We get it, Neevah. Your life is perfect."

"Perfect?" I choke out an incredulous laugh. "In case you hadn't noticed, I'm hooked up to a machine that is cleaning my blood, and have to beg for a kidney from the sister who can't stand me. Also, the big break I have for this movie? Not going so good since the whole production is shut down until I'm well enough to go back to work. What's so perfect about that?"

"You got out of Clearview, for one."

"You could have, too, if you'd wanted."

"Not with a baby on the way and no income."

"Well, you screwed Brandon in that bed, T. Wasn't nobody gonna lay in it for you."

"Bitch," Terry snarls, standing, her fists balled at her sides. "You think just because you're sick you can say anything you want to me and get away with it?"

"No, I think I can say anything I want to you and get away with it because you're a cheat who hasn't earned my respect."

"Well, you respect this kidney, though, don't you?"

"Take your kidney!" I shout, sitting up in the bed. "You and your kidney can catch the next flight back to Clearview, far as I'm concerned. I'll get a kidney from someone I can actually stand."

"Stop it!" Mama stands in the space separating Terry and me like a referee in a boxing ring. "Do you hear yourselves? You're supposed to be sisters."

"Sisters don't do what she did," I clip out, drained by the shouting match and falling limp on the pillows.

"I did you a favor and you know it," Terry says. "Like you would have lasted in Clearview with that scholarship letter burning a hole in your drawer. You would have broken it off with him anyway."

"Maybe that's true. Who knows? But you slept with him a year before the scholarship and walked around all that time letting me believe he loved me."

"He did love you." Terry's bitter laugh sounds like it hurts. "Everyone did."

"So you decided to take everyone away from me? Or was that just an added bonus?"

"Nobody told your ass not to come home."

"And look at you with him? Look at Quianna, knowing she was the result of you betraying me? The first time I saw her, I had to lock myself in my old room I was crying so hard. Not because she was a reminder, but because she was so beautiful."

Tears spring to my eyes and I bite my lip to keep it from trembling. "She looked just like you, and I was angry I couldn't just love her, just be her auntie without all of this between us."

"You can," Terry says more softly. "She barely knows you, but she wants to be just like you. She's in every school play. Sings like she breathes."

"Reminds us all of you," Mama adds, smiling and sitting back down to pick up her knitting.

"She does?" I ask weakly.

"I told her I was coming out here about your kidney and she wanted to come, but she has exams," Terry says. "We, um, haven't been getting along lately. Not since she found out why you never come home."

I recall her stricken expression, her anger in the kitchen when she overheard us arguing.

"I'm sorry she had to find out that way," I say. "So she never knew about Brandon and me?"

"What was I supposed to say? I stole your daddy? I almost got rid of you because I didn't want to lose my sis…" She doesn't finish the thought, but I can see how saying even part of it affects her. Her lips tremble and her fingers clench around the knitting needles.

"Don't say that, Terry," Mama reprimands.

"Well, it's true." She lifts her chin defiantly. "Thank God I didn't go through with it, but I was scared. I had no money and I knew it was shady, what Brand and me did. I was terrified of losing Neevah once she found out, and I did."

"You didn't even seem that sorry," I tell her. "It felt like you had won something and I didn't even know we were competing."

"There was a small, petty part of me deep inside that felt like, *finally, I have something she wants. I'm the best at something this one time.*"

"The best at my boyfriend?" I ask in harsh disbelief. "You were the prettiest girl at our school. In the whole town, T. You could have had anyone you wanted, and you chose the one who should have been off-limits."

"I was young and stupid. I paid for it."

"It's not so bad, Terry," Mama says, her voice low and gentle. "You have a husband who loves you and an amazing daughter. A great job. A great life that most folks would envy. Learn to be content."

"I am satisfied." Terry casts me a baleful look. "Until she comes around, and I think of all the things I don't have. What I gave up."

"I bet you were glad I couldn't bring myself home to face you, weren't you?"

"I really didn't want to hurt you," Terry says. "But on some level, I did want you to know how it felt not to have what you wanted. For someone else to have it, because it felt like you had it all. Ironically, I drove you out of town and on to all the things I always suspected you'd have and I wouldn't."

"What exactly did you think I had?" I ask, puzzled. "You were the popular one. The prettiest one. The one everybody wanted."

"I wasn't the one Brand wanted," she said softly. "I'm ashamed to say it now, but I went after him to prove I could do it. And once I had him, he hated me. Do you know how it feels to be married to someone who's in love with someone else? Who loves your sister and resents you for ruining that?"

"Are you saying that he still—"

"Not anymore." Terry chuckles, a wry grin playing at the corners of her mouth. "I think he finally accepted he was stuck with me and decided he may as well get on with loving me since we had no choice. At first, though, yeah. So I didn't want you around, no."

"Quianna mentioned some trouble between you two," I venture. "Are you—"

"We working on it." Her lips tighten and she fiddles with the pile of yarn in her lap. "Marriage is hard, but we trying like everybody else."

"I'm... well, I'm glad."

Dr. Okafor enters, carrying a clipboard and her usual air of efficiency.

"Terry," she says, a bright smile on her face. "If you'll come with me, we'll start the first battery of tests."

Terry sets her knitting aside and stands to follow Dr. Okafor. I can't let her go like this. We just spent the last ten minutes talking about things we should have been discussing the last twelve years.

"Terry," I say, not sure what should come next.

She turns at the door, her expression guarded again—braced for the resentment, the anger that has characterized our relationship.

"Yeah?" she asks warily.

"Just... thank you."

She doesn't smile exactly, but relief flickers in her eyes and maybe the first kindling of hope. She's my sister. Used to be my best friend. Has been my enemy. Bad blood has been between us for years—maybe we can finally find our way to a clean start. I'm literally hooked up to a machine taking all my bad blood and making it clean. Making it new. Surely, somehow, she and I can do the same.

SIXTY-FOUR

Neevah

"I've missed this," Takira says, sitting down with her popcorn on the massive leather sectional in Canon's living room. "Our girl time."

"Me too." I cradle my bowl of blueberries and snuggle into Takira's side. "I've missed you."

"Canon needs to learn the rules of girl gang. You do not roll up and steal my best friend in a time of crisis. Does he realize you *do* have a place here in LA? And a roommate who is perfectly capable of making sure you take your meds and follow the doctor's orders?"

"This is one of the few times over the last three weeks Canon has not been glued to my side. If he didn't have this meeting with Galaxy he can't miss, he'd be right here. I think if I told him I wanted to go home, he'd be like, 'Sure. Gimme a minute so I can pack my bag.'"

"He got it bad, girl. That man is in love with you."

"He is." I can't hold back a sigh. "And it is definitely a two-way street. I've never felt this way about anyone before. I'm just as gone over him."

"Oh, that is evident." Takira laughs when I punch her arm. "It is! I saw it the night we met him."

"You did?"

"Girl, you could barely keep your eyes off that man. I thought you were gonna jump him at the table, po thang."

"I was not that bad!" I close my eyes and crack one open. "Was I?"

"And remember when he called that first time and you almost maimed yourself?"

"You are literally cackling over this. I have no shame about it. My massive crush is now the love of my life, so everything is perfect." My smile slips. "I mean, besides the part where I've been in the hospital for approximately a quarter of our relationship and I need a kidney if I want to live to see our first anniversary... things are perfect."

"Hey." Takira loops her arm around my shoulders and pulls me close. "It's gonna work out. Terry's still making her way through all the tests, right?"

"Yeah, she and Mama had to go back, but Dr. Okafor is coordinating with labs there in North Carolina for the rest of the process. If she's a match, there's a transplant center not far from Clearview."

"You'd fly there?"

"Yeah. The transplant is actually much harder on the donor than the recipient. If Terry's a match, she won't be able to travel right after the transplant. She'll be out of work for up to six weeks. It'll be better for her to be at home near her family. And she has Quianna to take care of, so getting stuck out here wouldn't be great."

"How were things between you guys when she was here?"

"It was... off and on. One minute I'd feel like we were making some progress, and the next we'd be at each other's throats. There's a lot we should have sorted through before now. It's like a leg that should have healed a long time ago, and now it's all rotty, but you can't cut it off, so you still have to save it."

"You *do* see me trying to eat, right?" Takira points to her popcorn. "And all this rotten limb talk ain't helping."

"Well, you get my point," I say, laughing and scooping up a handful of blueberries. "As much as I hate that I had to go on dialysis, even if just temporarily, I'm glad they came to see me in the hospital. We need to sort through some of this before her kidney is inside me."

"You guys considering counseling?"

"We actually are, which is something we should have done a long time ago, but counseling is part of the screening process before you donate. Usually just to make sure the donor is certain about giving up an organ and understands the risks, but for us, considering that we've been estranged, Dr. Okafor recommends we have at least a few sessions together."

"And that's if she's a match, right?"

"Well, the counseling I think we need to do even if she isn't. I'm open to that and think it's overdue. I want to connect with my family again without this between us. I mean, that happened. We can't undo what they did, and there's a child, so there's no forgetting, but you have to remember something before you can forgive it. Forgiving is harder than forgetting. Forgetting would be the oblivion of never knowing how you hurt me. Forgiving is accepting you hurt me, deciding that I'm going to keep loving you anyway."

"And trust that you won't do it again," Takira murmurs. "Will you ever trust your sister?"

"I hope I can. We were soooo young, and both of us had emotions we didn't know how to handle. You're just a loaded weapon at that age. Old enough to drive and have sex and get into a bunch of shit that's legal to do without a fully developed frontal lobe."

"Where's Brandon in all this?"

"I don't care about him. I know that sounds bad, but he was a teenage crush I probably would have grown out of anyway. He got caught in the crossfire, but this is less about him than about restoring a relationship with my sister, and I hope, establishing one with my niece. If that can happen, it will be one good thing that comes out of this fiasco."

"Speaking of fiasco, I'm here for this *Housewives* reunion show." She points the remote at the television, frowning when nothing happens. "Damn this sophisticated technology. How are we supposed to know how to operate all this stuff?"

I take the remote and press the on button, bringing the screen to life. "That's step one."

"I hate you."

"And yet, here you are. Now where do we find this debacle for the culture?" I start flipping through channels, pausing on a shampoo commercial featuring a stunning woman.

Camille Hensley.

She looks into the camera, her tawny brown eyes coy and flirty, and flicks a fall of long, shining, highlighted hair over one smooth, golden shoulder. She looks like every shampoo fantasy come to life.

"You know that's a weave," Takira says waspishly. "I mean, I make my living off extensions, so I ain't trying to hate, but she walk around like she—"

"Shhhh! I want to hear."

The commercial is actually almost over, so we only catch the tail end of what she has to say.

"And I'm so honored to offer this all-natural product for *us*," she says. "Designed with black hair in mind. Give it a try and in no time…" She twirls, the long hair fanning out in a shimmering arc. "Beautiful."

The commercial changes into another for dishwashing liquid, but I can't stop seeing all that beautiful hair. That flawless skin. Involuntarily, I reach up to touch the headscarf I'm rarely without lately. I've lost so much hair, I don't even want to look most days. I've lost hair before and it's always grown back, but never this much. And the rash has spread everywhere. I find myself hiding my body from Canon, and I hate it.

I've never thought of myself as vain. I work in an industry where physical appearance and image are important. I've always taken care of myself, exercised because I wanted to be healthy, but also because my job requires it. With my body under attack—a cellular sedition where my own antibodies are the enemy—my skin, hair, and confidence are the casualties. In a relationship with one of Hollywood's critical darlings, I can't help but feel exposed and in some ways…wanting.

He had Camille.

He was with her.

She wanted him enough to pitch a foolish hissy fit when he walked away.

Does he ever look at me and wish…

I have to stop this vicious cycle of self-doubt. It's as harmful as the disease itself.

"Gimme that remote," Takira says. "Lemme find the reunion."

She pauses on one of those entertainment channels. We both gasp when my face comes onscreen.

"Ahhhhh!" Takira squeals. "Look at you, Neev!"

I remember this crew coming on set. There's a clip of us recording one of the dance sequences. The camera closes in on me flying through the air, gliding across the floor, doing the lindy hop.

"Oh, my God." I cover my mouth, stunned and disoriented to see myself this way. The enormity of this opportunity hasn't sunk in until right now. I know it's a huge break, of course, but we've been grinding for months. I'm not famous. I've spent most of my time in LA on set, working ten to twelve hours a day. And the little bit I've done venturing into the city has been undisturbed by paparazzi or fans because…who am I? No one really knows me yet. Seeing myself this way, on television, feels like an out-of-body experience.

"Canon Holt found Neevah Saint when she was an understudy on Broadway," the entertainment reporter says. "It's not clear when their relationship turned romantic, but we found out about it a few weeks ago when Camille Hensley, A-lister and Holt's former girlfriend, revealed she had been denied the chance to audition for *Dessi Blue*, Holt's latest biopic, which has been years in the making. According to reports, production has been shut down indefinitely because of an undisclosed illness Ms. Saint has been hospitalized for. We wish her the best and hope this film still makes it to screen. It would be a shame if it doesn't."

"Still makes it to screen?" Takira huffs. "Of course it will still make it to screen. There are only a few scenes left to shoot. They need to check their sources. That's not even in question."

"I bet the Galaxy executives are asking Canon those very same questions right now," I say ruefully. "Camille said they never wanted me for the part, which…of course, they wouldn't. They'd want a big name, not a no-name. And now it looks like Canon cast his girlfriend and it's all gone south. Ugh. This is a mess."

"It's a mess in your head, but the reality is we have a spectacular movie almost completed, and when everyone sees what you did as Dessi Blue, there will be no question Canon made the right call casting you."

I manage a flimsy smile. "You think so?"

"I know so." She aims the remote and keeps flipping. "Now you 'bout to make me miss my *Housewives.* I need my ratchet fix, so hush."

I eat my blueberries and drink my water and, midway, get up to take my evening dose of medications. Is this the rest of my life? Pills and labs and flares and hospital stays?

Every day that ends with me still breathing has ended well.

Remy Holt's words from *The Magic Hour* bounce around in my thoughts even after Takira leaves and goes home. Alone in Canon's big, empty house, I wander into the studio. Running my fingers carefully across her Nikons and Kodaks and Canons, I feel her spirit so strongly I wish I could ask her advice—wish I could have just a few minutes of her time.

And then I remember that I can.

Canon's full documentary is online now, so I pull it up and watch it from beginning to end, ninety minutes of wisdom and fearlessness. Knowing her son is the one holding the camera makes the way Remy looks into its lens—with so much love and pride—that much more meaningful. Over the course of the documentary, she goes from standing on her own two feet and running to the edge of the pier, to wheeling herself, holding her camera with increasingly shaky hands. But she never fades. The fire, the fight, the zest for life, never vacate the dark eyes that seem, even years later, to see right through me.

"Tomorrow," she says from the screen, from a wheelchair precipitously close to the edge of a pier, "is the most presumptuous word in the world, because who knows if you even get that. Yesterday, spilled milk and old news. You can't do nothing about how you messed up or fell short or didn't do yesterday. Even when you mess up and make it right, it has to be done today."

She flashes a wide smile, so much like Canon's an invisible hand squeezes my heart.

"Whoo, child, today we can work with. It's all I have and this thing." She bangs the wheel of her chair and then bangs her chest. "And this thing, this body, won't take away today. The only thing you can do with today is make it count, because soon it will be tomorrow. And I already told you about them tomorrows. Better todays make better tomorrows, and if you don't get tomorrow, at least you had today."

For the entire documentary she has been all smiles and sunsets, but it's near the end. *She's* near the end, and tears fill her eyes.

"This body is a shell," she says, her voice sober. "No matter how beautiful or what size or how healthy, every single body inevitably returns to dust. It is not your legacy. It is not what you leave behind."

Her eyes shift just above the lens, to the man holding it, and her smile returns. "I love you, Canon," she says, addressing him directly by name for the first and only time during the documentary.

And you can see it in her eyes, the pride, the assurance that *he* is what she has done. *He* is what she leaves behind. *He* is the best part of her legacy.

"That's enough for today," she says, turning away from his camera and lifting her own to the sun disappearing into the ocean. "I'm getting tired."

It's the final sunset. A montage of home videos and photos follows, revealing her life beyond the piers. We see Canon at birthday parties and first days of school and graduations, and his mother is there in every frame. Watching the documentary, seeing her obsession with sunsets and chasing magic hours, one could be fooled into thinking her art was all she had. Canon's choice to include the rest pulls out the camera for a wider shot of her life beyond her art. Her life with him.

Hers was a race that had already been decided, a race against time, but the beauty was in how she ran. And I think that's the point. Every single one of us is in that race, and a race against time is one you'll never win.

But how will you run?

It's not an existential question of immortality, of living forever, but a challenge of numbered days and what we do with what we have. It's not a string of todays that become yesterdays and aspire to tomorrow, but living like there is no guarantee. Living with an urgency to say what needs to be said, do what needs to be done. To no matter what, live with what you'll leave behind in mind.

I want to reach through the screen and touch her in hopes that her zeal, her assuredness of life in the face of a diminishing future, would rub off on me. I wish I could turn back the clock, find them on one of their piers as the sun dipped into the ocean to thank her for all she sowed into the remarkable man her son has become.

Some days I feel like that powerful, vibrant girl, the painted butterfly who flitted through the Savoy Ballroom, the wind of trumpets beneath her wings. And some days I'm that broken ballerina from Dessi's jewelry box, my twists and turns a lurching revolution to a song composed from dust and regret. One thing I'm sure of. On any given day, the look in Canon's eyes never changes. It's as constant as the refrain of rising and setting suns.

I'm still sitting in the middle of the studio floor, staring up at the Polaroids of us he pinned to the line, when he comes home.

"Hey." He leans against the doorjamb, hands in the pockets of his dark jeans. "How are you feeling?"

"Better." I smile, gesturing to my laptop on the floor in front of me. "I was just watching your mom."

"My mom?" He walks over, sits on the floor beside me, and peers at my screen. "Oh. Wow. I haven't looked at this in years."

His eyes soften and a smile crooks one corner of the stern line of his mouth.

"She was something else," I tell him. "I see so much of her in you. It's funny. When I was diagnosed, I only thought about the fear of dying, of living a life that was somehow less than what other people lived. Your mother embodied the opposite. She seems to become more fearless. The more the disease tries to change her, the more she becomes completely herself."

"That's it exactly. I think my mother was one of the earliest examples I had of looking beyond the surface. When we would go out sometimes, as her disease progressed, I would catch people looking at her with something like pity. And I would just think, you have no idea who she is. That she gets stronger every day."

"Is that why you look at me the same way no matter how my appearance changes?"

He studies me for long, silent seconds. "No, baby." He caresses my cheek with his thumb, smiling into my eyes. "That's just love."

His words, spoken with such surety, untie the last knots of anxiety and self-doubt tangled in my thoughts. He's right. When you love someone, you truly see who they are beyond the surface. And whether I look like the headshot I proudly passed all over New York when I auditioned, or I look the way I do right now, I have to see and love myself beyond the high gloss. That first taste of unconditional love and acceptance—we should feed it to our own souls.

I reach up to pull the headscarf away, and then I peel off the sweatshirt covering the silk camisole I wear instead of a bra. For a moment, the air kisses my skin, cools the heated plane of my self-consciousness, and then, under the heat of his stare—an equal, unwavering mix of love and desire—I grow warm. I lean back on my palms and stretch my legs in front of me. I am battered. This body is a battlefield, and my limbs, once flawless, carry the scars. I trust, I hope, that they will fade in time, but I must accept who and how I am right now.

Today.

"You said before that you'd like to photograph me," I say.

"Whenever you like," he replies, his voice soft, subdued.

I connect my eyes and his by a single thread of *no turning back* and nod to the cameras displayed on the wall. "How about right now?"

SIXTY-FIVE

Canon

"It's a match."

I look up from the desk in my home office. Neevah stands in the doorway, cautious excitement in her expression.

"What'd you say?" I slam my laptop shut and focus on her.

"Terry finished all her tests, and she's a match." She covers her mouth, catching a tiny sob/laugh, then rushing over and throwing herself in my lap. We hold each other and I absorb the sigh of relief that shudders through her. I don't know if it's hers or mine, but our bodies share it. I pull back to rain kisses on her cheeks and nose and lips, resting my forehead against hers for a few seconds to let this sink in.

Neevah has a kidney.

She'll always have to manage this disease, but getting a new kidney should drastically improve things for her.

She cups my face and smiles down at me. "I can finish the movie."

"Whoa, whoa, whoa. Let's get through the transplant first. And then Dr. Okafor will say when."

"But, Canon, everyone is going their separate ways soon. Trey has another project, and I know Jill does, too."

"Let me worry about that. It's my job to figure all that out, and I don't want you thinking about it."

"Of course I'm thinking about it. It's my fault."

"It's not your fault. It's your health. It's your life, and I don't give a damn about *Dessi Blue* if you're not well."

Saying it aloud is liberating. Mama would be pleased. Her wish for me—that I would find someone to love more than my work, than my art—has come true with a vengeance. This thing that threatened Neevah's life and our future together shifted my priorities. Changed my lens and brought everything into focus. There is no question what—*who*—is most important in my life.

Neevah.

Dessi Blue may be the best movie I've ever made—may be the best I'll *ever* make. That remains to be seen, but I know it means more to me than everything I've done besides *The Magic Hour.* And still it stands pale and insignificant beside my love for Neevah. I've known it, have conducted myself that way in every meeting when Galaxy demanded a timeline for the finished product. When will Neevah be back? When can we start editing? I've made it very clear that she is the priority, not just because she's my girlfriend, but because that is human decency. That's the way we should approach it. I hope I would feel that way for any actor who trusted themselves to me for a performance, but I know I feel that way for Neevah. Anyone who pressures her to come back a day sooner than she's ready has to go through me.

That includes Neevah herself.

"We'll talk more about the movie later. What's the next step for the transplant?"

"The counselor still needs to talk to Terry and make sure she understands the risks and really grasps what this means. She'll only have one kidney for the rest of her life." Neevah presses her lips together, shakes her head. "It's so much to ask of someone, especially when you've been at odds with them for this long."

"It is, but she's your sister. Something like this has a way of cutting through all the bullshit that comes between us and keeps us apart. You would do the same for her."

"I would." Her mouth trembles and tears shimmer in her dark eyes. "She wouldn't even have to ask."

"If you think about it, neither did you. She flew out here before you even got a chance to tell her you needed her."

"You're right." Realization dawns on her face. "Wow, she did. It's like Dessi says when she and Cal leave Paris and go home to Alabama. When family needs you, you go even if they don't call."

I know it's still a lot for Neevah to wrap her head around—that her sister, with whom she has had so little relationship her entire adult life, is willing to make this sacrifice—but I just want her to start healing. I want her off dialysis and with a fresh start. She and her sister can work out any remaining differences in their own time.

I've tried to hide it from Neevah as much as possible because I didn't want to add to her anxiety, but I haven't had a good night's sleep since we found out she needed a kidney. I realized I loved her just before I realized I could lose her, and that has tortured me. I've known the pain of losing the person you love most in the world. That is the risk of love, what makes it a radical act. You pour everything into another person who is bound by fragile humanity. You could lose them at any time, but you can't reason with your heart.

All these years, I managed to convince myself I would never do anything that foolhardy. Why would you open yourself up to that potential pain again? And then someone walks onstage, into the light, and you realize you want to let them in, but they bring with them not only the best of life, but the risk of loss.

And at some point, your heart decides it's worth it.

Sometimes attraction is the body's way of keeping a secret from your heart until you're ready to hear it. Maybe my heart recognized immediately who Neevah was to me—my light, the part that would fit with me like we were crafted for one another—but disguised it as admiration, lust, desire, need. Emotions I could accept, giving me time to fall in love. Inevitably. Irrevocably.

"So what's next?" I ask, reminding us both that we need to make plans. "When is this happening?"

"Dr. Okafor is coordinating with the transplant center," Neevah says. "But it could be as soon as the end of next week. I'll fly to North Carolina for the surgery. I'll be in ICU for probably a week and then they may keep me a little longer, but after that, I go home."

"Home... meaning where?"

"Once I'm released from the hospital, I still may not be quite ready to fly, so I'll stay at Mama's for a little bit, but then I should be ready to come back to LA."

"*We'll* fly back to LA. I hope your mama doesn't mind a houseguest. I can stay at a hotel while you're in the hospital, but once you leave, I'm not letting you out of my sight."

"I don't want to be out of your sight," she whispers, running her fingers through the beard that will be Gandalf-esque if I follow my tradition of not shaving until a movie wraps.

"How do you feel now that this is happening?" I ask.

"Relieved. Scared. Guilty for putting Terry through this, but also happy that it brought us back together so we can at least start to become sisters again. There is a lot going on in my heart." She leans close, her eyes glowing with confidence and love. "*You* are going on in my heart, Mr. Holt."

The laughter fades from her expression and she dips to press her lips to mine, deepening the kiss, stirring a passion I've checked the last few weeks. My hands tighten possessively at her waist, and I pull away, breathing hard.

"You want me." She reaches between us to palm my cock.

"Shit," I groan. "Of course, I do. You're not helping."

"You haven't been…I don't know." She shrugs. "I wasn't sure if you were turned off or…"

"Turned off? What the…I thought we'd been through this."

"I know you love me, but I wasn't sure if—"

"Baby, loving you and wanting to fuck you all the time are inextricably tied together."

"Then why haven't you—"

"You have been really sick, Neevah. I know you don't like to acknowledge that, but I've had to. In how I managed our workload and how I managed my own desires. I wanted to be careful. I *still* want to be careful. I know you'll think I'm crazy, but I prefer to wait."

"You may be the first man to ever say that to me." She laughs.

"If anything went wrong because we…I wouldn't forgive myself. Just let me suffer until you're completely healed."

She sets her pretty lips in a pout. "That means I suffer, too."

"Then we are in this together." I kiss her fingers. "And now we don't have long to wait."

SIXTY-SIX

Dessi Blue

INTERIOR - PARIS - NIGHT — 1956

In their Paris apartment, Cal is dressing for the evening, tying his tie in the mirror. Dessi sits on their bed wearing only a slip and stockings, hair and makeup done, a sequined evening gown laid out on the bed beside her. She's reading a letter, and a diamond wedding ring glints on her ring finger. A young girl rushes into the room and crawls into Dessi's lap.

DESSI (STROKING HER DAUGHTER'S HAIR)
Hey, kitty-cat. Shouldn't you be in bed?

KATHERINE
I wanted a glass of water, and Madame Charbonnet said I could say good night before you and Papa leave. Where are you singing tonight, *Maman?*

DESSI
The band's playing at Le Caveau de la Huchette. Go drink your water and then bed, you hear me, little girl? We'll be home when you wake up in the morning.

KATHERINE
Oui, Maman.

DESSI (PATS HER BOTTOM)

Tell Papa good night and go to bed.

Katherine walks over to Cal at the mirror and he scoops her up, tickling her and making her laugh. A plump, dark-haired woman comes to the door.

MADAME CHARBONNET (WITH A HEAVY FRENCH ACCENT)

Katherine, *ma cherie*. Leave your parents to dress. They must depart soon.

Cal kisses Katherine's hair and sets her on the floor.

KATHERINE

Bon soir.

Madame Charbonnet and Katherine leave the room. Dessi picks the letter up again and starts to read.

CAL

That little girl don't know if she coming in French or going in English. Dessi, you can read that letter later. The band'll be waiting.

Dessi lays the letter on the bed, but doesn't move to put her dress on.

DESSI

Mama's sick, Cal.

Cal pauses in pomading his hair.

CAL (LOOKING AT DESSI IN THE MIRROR)

What kind of sick?

DESSI

The letter is from my cousin Dorothy. It's cancer. Mama wasn't gonna tell me.

Cal walks over to sit beside her on the bed and picks up the letter.

CAL

She need help with medical bills? We can send more money.

DESSI (HESITANTLY)

What would you say if I said I want to go home?

He gestures around the beautifully appointed bedroom.

CAL

I would say we *are* home. Look at where we live. *How* we live, Dess. Sold out crowds every night. More money than we can count. Respect. I get treated like a man here in France. Not there. They treat dogs better than they treat Negroes, and that's the God's honest truth.

DESSI

Cal, I've barely seen my mama at all for the last fifteen years, and now she's sick. She needs me.

CAL

Ain't nothing in the States for us, Dess. Sidney Bechet is here in France with the world at his feet. One of the greatest to ever pick up a horn, and you know what he was doing in America before he came here? He was a tailor. Last time Josephine Baker went home, the Stork Club wouldn't even serve her. The toast of Paris. One of the most famous women in the world refused service in her home country. Why would we go back?

DESSI

Because my mama needs me. She may be dying, Cal.

Dessi stands up and puts on the dress as they continue the discussion.

DESSI

We could just go until she gets better or... until she...

Dessi sniffs and wipes away a tear. Cal walks over and takes her in his arms.

CAL

Don't cry, baby. You know I can't deny you a thing when you cry.

DESSI (SMILING TEARFULLY)

I'm counting on it.

CAL

I just got a bad feeling about it. Like if we leave, we won't ever come back. We live a good life here, don't we?

DESSI

Of course, we do. When we left Harlem, I couldn't have even dreamt half the stuff we've done. The places we been. But I miss my family. When your people need you, you go.

I know we have our music, but is it really home if you don't have the people you love?

CAL
I love you and Kitty.

DESSI
You and Katherine are my whole world. You know that, but we can't just hide here when people we love are suffering. In her last letter, Mama told me all about the Montgomery bus boycott, but didn't even mention that she was sick.

CAL
It's only getting worse there, but it's gonna get much worse before it gets better, especially in the South. At least Negroes are standing up for themselves.

DESSI (SMILING WRYLY)
Or in Rosa Parks's case, sitting down.

CAL
I was talking with the editorial staff at *The Defender*. They love my expat report from Paris. If we did go home to see your mama in Alabama, maybe I could send them some photos and stories on the boycott.

DESSI
That would be so good, Cal. Who knows how we could help while we're there?

Cal turns and holds Dessi, kissing her cheek.

CAL

When your people need you, you go. Maybe you're right, but can we talk about it after tonight's show? We 'bout to be late.

DESSI

That's all I ask.

CAL (CHUCKLING)

All you ask, my foot. You always asking for the world, Odessa.

DESSI

And you the man who gives it to me.

SIXTY-SEVEN

Neevah

I walk up the hall to my sister's hospital room with a divided heart. On one hand, I'm elated. I'm getting a new kidney, and potentially, a new lease on life. I can't even adequately express my gratitude to Terry for this sacrifice, but there are things that remain unsaid between us. I fully anticipate that we'll both be fine. Our surgeries are straightforward, but not without potential complications and risks. We've done a few family counseling sessions by video, and we've made progress repairing the breach. Things are getting better between us than they've been in years, but I can't say we've forgiven each other. And I won't go under until I've at least told her she has that from me.

I poke my head in, glad to find her alone in the room. Soon all the preparations will begin. Her surgery occurs first, obviously, to remove her kidney, and then they'll transplant it into me. Any minute, the nurses and doctors will come. I have to get back to my room up the hall for preparation, too, but this won't take long.

"Hey." I fix a smile on my face, which feels unnatural because there have been too few smiles between us since I left home.

She glances up, and I see myself in her. In the heart-shaped face and the coppery skin. The tilt of our eyes. I recognize the fear, too. As much of a blessing as this is, it's scary for us both.

"Hey," she says, her smile looking as forced as mine feels. "They let you out?"

I nod, stepping all the way in, letting the door close behind me, and approach the bed.

"One of the ladies from church called," she says. "So Mama stepped out to take it. She'll be back, if you're looking for her."

"I came to see you," I say, holding her guarded gaze. "I only have a few minutes. I'm sure my warden will be looking for me soon."

"You mean your nurse or your man? Because I think this is the first time I've seen you without Canon glued to your side."

I chuckle, my forced smile easing into the real thing. "He's intense and concerned. He's in one of the waiting rooms finishing a call with the studio and wanted to get it over with before the surgery starts."

"He loves you and it's obvious you got it bad for him."

"I do." I nod, my insides melting at the thought of how supportive and protective and unwavering Canon has been. "I had no idea he would be… who he is. I guess you never know where your heart will lead you."

"Brand and Quianna ran down to grab something to eat," she says abruptly, the softened lines of her face stiffening to wax. "If you want to avoid him, you should make this quick."

"I don't need to avoid him. This does have to be quick, but only because we both need to prepare." I haul in a deep breath and dive in. "I couldn't go into surgery, let you do this without—"

"Let me just stop you right there, Neev." A deep swallow moves her throat and she bites her bottom lip, glancing down at the hands in her lap. "You don't have to thank me or whatever this is. I should have been the one walking up the hall. I've been thinking about it all morning, knowing you were down there. I've been…" She closes her eyes and a single tear streaks down her cheek. "I've been ashamed of what I did, of what we did, since that day in the living room all those years ago. I was young and stupid and insecure and jealous."

She huffs a rough laugh, a wry grin tipping her mouth. "I did like him, you know."

I take a few steps closer until my hip butts up against the hospital bed. "Brandon?"

"I liked him as soon as I saw him in freshman orientation, but he was the only boy in our class who wasn't after me. That's probably why I wanted him, because he wasn't interested." She looks up, the last dregs of resentment there. "And then you came. A freshman, and you were the one he wanted. I hated that. I guess I hated you a little. One more thing you hadn't even tried to get and got anyway."

"You could have told me you liked him, T. I wouldn't have given him the time of day if I'd known."

"I was too proud to admit the boy I wanted didn't want me back. When you told me that he wanted to have sex and that you weren't ready... well, I know how boys are, and I saw my chance."

After all these years, after all we've been through and who we've become, knowing now what real love is, I can't even muster anger anymore for what Terry and Brandon destroyed. What I had with him was love in effigy, a crude imitation worthy of only being burned. If Brandon had betrayed me with anyone other than the person I held dearest, I would have moved on, never looking back. But it had been with Terry. And there was a child, the beautiful, breathing evidence of not how much his betrayal hurt, but of hers.

"Can you forgive me?" Terry asks, her voice breaking over the plea, her eyes overflowing. "I know what I did—"

"Yes." I lean forward and wrap my arms around her. It is our first hug in almost thirteen years, and she feels the same. Not the dimensions of her body, but the comfort of her; the tight squeeze of her arms. "I forgive you, T. And I'm sorry it took so long. I wish..."

I don't have words for all the wishes, only tears, and they pour out of me. Tears for every missed birthday and Christmas. For all the times I had something to celebrate and wished I could share it with her, but was unable to forget or forgive. For every gut-busting laugh we haven't had, and for all the hard times we haven't walked through together.

For my niece. Not knowing her because of our pride and our foolishness.

All the stone encasing my heart against Terry shatters, and I don't feel the hate or anger or bitterness. I feel *her*, and I am overwhelmed by the rightness of my sister in my arms again. We are both prodigals, wandered far from one another, now home again. Every test the doctors ran proved that we were matched by God. Bone, tissue, flesh, blood. We were made for today—for a moment when my sister would save me. We weep together, a release long coming. A flood of broken cries and half-words and gasps of relief.

"Oh!"

The sound from the door has Terry and me turning our heads. Mama stands there, hand to her mouth, tears streaking her face, too.

"It's about time," she says with a shaky, tearful laugh.

Crossing the room, she adds her arms to ours, her happy laughter joining ours to fill the sterile hospital room.

"I love you, Neev," Terry whispers, kissing my temple. "I'm so sorry and I'm so glad I can do this for you."

I'm too moved to speak and just nod, tightening my arms around them, my family.

"And I love both my girls." Mama splits a smile between us. "I thought today I would just be scared, but this right here feels as important as the surgery itself."

A movement at the door catches our attention. Quianna stands there, wide eyes flitting from her mother to me. With no hesitation, I extend one arm, breaking the circle of our hug long enough to invite her in. She rushes over, a bright smile on her face. She buries her head in my neck and closes the circle again. We stay like that for long moments until the nurse comes in.

"I'm sorry," the nurse says. "But we need to start preparations for surgery. And, Ms. Mathis, you need to go back to your room so they can prepare you, too."

I stand, ready to follow orders, but Mama sets a staying hand on my arm.

"Can you give us just a minute to pray?" she asks the nurse, who, after a quick hesitation, nods and steps back to the wall, giving us some space, but not leaving the room. The four of us hold hands and bow our heads, but before Mama begins, I glance up and see Brandon hovering in the hall, his worried eyes on my sister.

He does love her.

And she loves him.

Maybe it wasn't the best start, and I know they're still working some things out, but they have love and they have Quianna.

And after all these years and all this pain, they have my blessing.

"You should come pray with us," I say to him, tilting my head toward our circle.

Terry's hand tightens around mine and she smiles tentatively. "Come on in, Brand."

I once thought he was the finest man I'd ever seen. Now, whatever once drew me to him, I can't detect any sign of, which is as it should be. He's my sister's husband and I feel nothing but hope that he is good to her. I sincerely hope they are more faithful to one another than they were to me. Forgiveness has cleared the way in my heart to truly wish them only the best. Brandon walks over to stand between his daughter and his wife, and bows his head.

"Amen," Mama says at the end of the prayer. "God got both of my girls. I don't have any doubt."

"Ms. Mathis," the nurse says. "You need to go to your room. Mrs. Olson, we need to begin the preparation."

Terry and I look at each other, and I see a measure of the fear return. I feel it, too, now that we are really about to do this. Her recovery will be harder, but my surgery is more invasive. Through laparoscopic surgery, they will remove her kidney from an incision just below her belly button. During mine, which also should take about three hours, they'll enter through my lower abdomen, and my kidneys will actually be left in place, and nearby blood vessels used to attach her kidney to one of mine.

Three hours, and my life will be changed.

"You ready?" Terry asks, smiling tremulously.

I nod, the reality of what we are about to do landing on me like a house. "Thank you, T."

"I'll see you on the other side." She laughs, her voice shaking.

The nurse shoos me out and down the hall to my hospital room where a team waits, ready to prepare me for my surgery.

"I'm here," Canon says, coming to the door, looking more flustered than I've ever seen him. "Sorry I cut it close. Galaxy had a million questions and didn't want to let me off the phone."

"We're about to start preparations," the nurse says sternly. "You'll have to leave, Mr. Holt."

"Please," I beg from the hospital bed. "Just one minute."

"One minute," she relents. "We need to get in your IV and get you prepped."

Canon flashes her a grateful smile and walks over to the bed, sitting down and taking my hand.

"How'd it go talking to your sister?" he asks, his voice low and concerned.

"It was good." I laugh ruefully. "I hate it took me needing an organ to bring us back together, and I'm sure we still have issues to work through, but I needed to go into this with a clear heart. And now I can."

"I'm glad." His eyes sober, his full lips flattening into a line. "Are you scared?"

"Are you?" I counter with a smile.

"Yeah. I know you'll be fine, but I just..." A frown disrupts the smooth arch of his brows. "You've become the most important part of my life. I want this over. I want your body to accept the kidney. For us to know it won't reject it. For you to start healing."

"You want a lot."

"Just you." His smile is tender and warm, and something I never would have thought I'd see from the man who intimidated me the first night we met. "I—"

Before he can say it, I say it first this time. "I love you, Canon."

He swallows, blinks, and kisses my forehead, lingering like he's having to drag himself away. "I love you back."

SIXTY-EIGHT

Canon

Neevah's laughter floats down to me from upstairs when I walk in the front door. Thoughts of all it will take to finish *Dessi Blue*—shoot the last few scenes, go into post-production, editing, not to mention promotion and the work Monk still needs to do on the score—crowd my mind. A lot of time has passed since the day on Highway 31 I found that little green sign footnoting Dessi's life. There have been a series of delays, stops and starts, but the fire to tell her story, which is the story of so many Black performers from that era, is no less bright than the day I found her. Once Neevah is cleared to finish, and not a minute before, we will get it done. I didn't just find one amazing woman when I saw that sign. I found two. The other one is upstairs, filling my house, which used to be so empty; hell, *lonely*, with the sound of her happiness. I want to see that sound on her face, so I set aside all the to-dos that came out of our meeting with Galaxy, and quietly make my way up the stairs.

I pause in the door, watching her on the bed. She's lying on her stomach, her legs bent and swinging back and forth as she grins at her iPad screen. Her niece, Quianna, who I think looks as much like Neevah as she does Terry, laughs, displaying her new braces.

"So you think Canon will be okay if I come visit for a few weeks this summer?" Quianna asks.

"I think he will be," I speak up, walking farther into the room and into the camera's view.

"Hey, Canon!" The young girl's pretty face brightens. "I won't stay long, and I won't break anything."

"You have to ask your parents first," Neevah says, her chin resting in her palm.

"Oh, you know she already did," Terry says, walking into the frame. "Think I'll turn down some time where I'm not worrying about this child? Shoot, I'll be what? Unbothered."

"We'll make a plan," Neevah says, smiling. "Maybe you can convince your grandmother to fly out to Cali again."

"You spoiled Mama, Canon." Terry laughs. "You'll have to charter her another private plane for that."

"I'll see what we can do," I tell her.

"Quianna, come on," Terry says. "Wrap it up. You gonna be late for dance."

"I'll talk to you later, Aunt Neevah," Quianna says, "and we'll make plans."

"Definitely." Neevah waves. "Love you guys. Bye."

Once they sign off, Neevah flips onto her back and stares up at the ceiling. "Never could have seen that conversation happening a few months ago."

I lie down beside her on my back. "I think recovering from the surgery in North Carolina was smart."

"I mean, at the time I didn't have any choice."

"You could have come back to Cali after the first week or so, once they cleared you to fly, but you stayed there to heal. Not just your body, but your relationship with them." I link our fingers between us on the bed. "I love that you did that. It's paid off."

"Seems to have." She turns onto her side, looking at my profile. "I have some good news, by the way."

I turn my head to look at her and have to smile. The malar, or butterfly rash, that splayed its wings across her nose and cheeks has faded now that we've got that flare under control. With a functioning kidney, the healthy tone of her coppery skin has been restored and most of the lesions and rashes on her arms and legs have faded. She lost so much hair, she decided to cut it off, leaving a short cap of natural curls. There are still a few spots growing back in, but her scalp seems to be recovering, along with the rest of her.

"Sooooooo," she says, sitting up on one elbow to peer down at me. "I had an appointment with Dr. Okafor today."

"Good. I bet she's tired of you by now."

"Not as tired as I am of her. We've seen each other, like, every week for the last two months."

I tense, but keep my expression unchanged. I haven't wanted to pressure Neevah at all about finishing the last scenes of *Dessi Blue*. The flare was so bad and so obviously triggered by the stress of filming. Dr. Okafor wouldn't even entertain Neevah going back until we saw clear signs things were turning around for the better, in addition to making sure her body didn't reject the kidney and that she was recovering from the surgery well. I completely agreed and have been the loudest voice making sure Neevah follows every one of the doctor's instructions.

My tension comes from my own fear that something will go unexpectedly wrong. I'll never forget carrying Neevah off the set, terrified about what would happen to her. I've actually been talking through my fears with my therapist, especially since I've lived through chronic and, in Mama's case, terminal illness with a loved one before.

And Neevah is so loved.

"So what did the good doctor say?"

"I asked if I can go back to work." Neevah glances up at me through long lashes.

"And?"

"And yes!"

"I need to talk to her for myself."

"Canon! You don't trust me?"

"I do, but I want to hear any parameters or restrictions from the doctor with my own ears. I'm responsible for the actors in my movies. I'd want something clearly stated in writing with anyone, not just you."

"And would you ask the doctor if any of your other actors were cleared for sexual activity?"

"I'm sure I—"

I stare up at her, taking in the mischievous gleam in her eyes and the siren's smile.

"Don't play with me, Neevah."

"I'm not." She leans down, aligning our faces, looking deeply into my eyes. "I'm all cleared for takeoff."

"Oh yeah?" I don't want to pounce on her, which is what my dick tells me to do, that hard slab of steel in my pants.

"Yes." She traces the bow of my mouth. "I love your lips."

"Hmmm." I settle for a grunt because anything else that comes out of my mouth would be the nastiest shit ever. I'm trying not to be *that* dude, whose girlfriend recently had surgery, but who might break her the first time we have sex if not very careful.

"Let's make love," she whispers, her breath misting my lips, her eyes boring into mine with an intensity that goes straight for my cock.

"Are you sure?" I ask hoarsely. "Did Dr. Okafor—"

I choke on the question when she grabs me through my jeans.

"What you're not gonna do," Neevah says, squeezing, pulling, "is fuck me like I might break."

For the last few months, it has felt as if she *could* break, and I don't trust my hands on her. I lay back, letting her strip me, touch me, explore the muscles of my chest, my abs, trace my cheekbones and lips, but I don't move to reciprocate. She leans down, sealing her lips over mine, slipping her tongue inside and going deep with sweeping licks, searching for and finding my reciprocal hunger. She frames my face in her hands and pulls my lip between her teeth. Bites hard. She's provoking me. I know it, but my hands knot into fists at my sides.

"Are you sure?" My breath comes out heavy, stunted between our lips.

She stands, tugging at buttons until the panels of her sundress fall away, revealing a transparent bra and panties, sprigged with lace flowers. With her smoldering eyes snaring mine, she reaches behind her to unfasten the bra. My mouth goes dry at the sight of her breasts, the areolae a dark halo crowning their fullness. She skims her fingers over her stomach, teases the silk at her hips, and slides the underwear over the legs of a dancer. They slip down her calves and pool around her bare feet. She stands waiting at the edge of the bed.

"How do you want me, Canon?" she asks, her words an open invitation to fantasy.

My eyes rove greedily over the expanse of satiny skin. The taut muscles of her stomach and the slope of her shoulders; the elegant line of her collarbone. Her breasts are ripe and round and tipped with nipples like blackberries.

I notice her scar immediately. I've seen it so many times since the transplant. It sprouts from her belly button and grows around her back like a vine. I sit up and trace it with reverent fingers, awed that this smooth strip of raised skin is the reminder of how I could lose her. Evidence of how she was saved.

There was a time when she would have shied away from my touch, from my eyes, but we're well past that. True intimacy, laced with trust, curls around us like tendrils of smoke.

I pull her to the bed and press her naked shoulders into the down of our comforter, permitting my fingers to trace her lips, the delicate construction of her face. I lavish kisses behind her ears, opening my mouth over her throat, worshiping her breasts, drawing her nipples between my lips, first one and then the other. My name tumbles from her lips, carried on heaving breaths and ragged sighs. She grips behind my neck to keep me against her, her hands and hold imperative. My appetite for her is a barely checked thing on a straining leash.

I want to make slow love to her, sweet and stretched out like taffy. A dish peppered with we've-got-all-night kisses. But we can't convince our hands, our lips, or tongues, that there is time. The urgency of banked passion blows across the flame, and we are clothed in fire. Naked skin hot to the touch. Our hearts are talking drums through our chests, saying all the words when desperation steals our voices.

I bracket my knees on either side of her thighs, and she is naked beneath me. I push one knee up and then the other until her legs are open and she is wet and exposed. Breasts, thighs, pussy—she is a table set for me, and I dip my head to lick her from top to bottom. She jerks, her breath catching and her hands gripping the sheets. I spread her lips and suck on her clit like a cherry, delving my tongue inside until her desire flows and I'm drowning in her essence.

"I'm coming," she says, her back bowing, her knees collapsing, pressing into my head. Her hands claw my hair, urging me deeper into the cleft of her body.

It is all I've wanted, but been afraid to have in case I couldn't control it. There's still a part of me that wants her to set the pace—control it until we are sure of her body's limits.

I lie down, positioning her on top of me, her knees spread over mine.

"I know why you're doing this." She grins, her eyes dilated and her lips kiss-puffy. "And I'll let you get away with it this first time, but next time no holding back."

"I promise you'll have no complaints."

"Hard as I just came, I already have nothing to complain about." She takes me in her hand, the firm grip riding up and down my stiffened cock. Seeing the most vulnerable part of me in her small hand affects me deeply.

Only that's not right. The most vulnerable part of me is my heart, and it is in her hands as surely as my cock is. She holds it just as tightly, her eyes caressing my face as surely as her hands run over my body. The long seconds of our eyes locked, seeing each other, conjures an inescapable intimacy. A spell we can't break that lures her body to mine. She takes me inside, the hot, tight oneness suspending my heartbeats.

She starts to move. At first, it's a tight undulation of her hips, rolling over me in measured motion. It's unbearably erotic, the way I feel her all around me like a vise. I thrust up, needing to take some control, and I plunge so deep she goes still, contracting her muscles around me, dragging me past pleasure to delirium. She plants her palm on my chest for leverage, raises her body and lets it fall, lets it rock, each time tightening the rope that binds me to her. Her breasts bounce and her eyes glaze over as she tips her head back, baring her throat and torso to me.

This is everything I've missed, and my body laps at it like a starved stray, taking not one drop for granted. I slip my thumb between her legs, stroking the nub of nerves every time she rocks and rolls, takes me deeper into her body.

We pound out a rhythm of *you are mine* and *I am yours.*

And mine and mine and mine and mine.

And yours and yours and yours and yours.

Our bodies don't let go, wet and wondrous and welded by sweat and lust and desperation.

"Oh, God," she cries out, linking her hands behind her neck and riding me harder, her face twisting in ecstasy. I'm not far behind, spilling into her, my voice broken, harsh, hoarse, nothing but strips of sound. I come so hard it's bright behind my eyes, and we are incandescent. The dying rays of sunlight—the last breath of day.

Golden.

Magic.

Light.

I sit up while she's still astride, while I'm still inside, and press my palms to her back. Through the smooth skin and through the latticework of her bones, her heart bellows. Somehow this union, more than the transplant, more than the last two months of healing, confirms that she is alive—that she is safe—and it moves me. I'm not sure if I've held it back on purpose, or if this reuniting of soul and flesh razes my defenses, but I taste tears. Mine, hers, relief, joy, mingling on our cheeks.

"I love you," she sobs, clenching her knees at my waist, folding her elbows around my neck, holding me so tightly I can't breathe and I don't care.

"And I..." My voice fails. The moment palpitates with the unevenness of my breaths and I give up on controlling anything. This is a free fall and I surrender. "I love you back."

We stay that way, her head tucked into the curve of my neck. For a few moments, the scent and feel of her comprise my entire universe. When she finally rolls off and falls to her side on the bed, her fingers find mine immediately. I lie down, too, drawing her into me, kissing the top of her head. I pull back a little so I can study her face, commit every curve and line to memory. I wish I had my camera to capture not just her beautiful body, which still bears the scars of her fight, but to capture my life molded into flesh and bone—formed into a person. To capture the picture of my contentment, mixed into her molecules and layered in her skin and bones.

And then I remember that we *have* captured it.

"Hey," I tell her, cupping her cheek. "I want to show you something."

SIXTY-NINE

Neevah

I'm still halfway to Mars after we make love, and it's hard to come back to earth, but I clean up, slip on Canon's *I'm Gonna Git You Sucka* T-shirt, and follow him downstairs. He grins over his shoulder and opens the door to the theater.

"So I had an idea," he says, leading me down the steps.

"Always dangerous," I laugh.

He sits down in the front row and pulls me onto his lap. "We have all this footage now of your journey with lupus."

"Yeah," I reply, smiling at the thought of my initial reticence to even have my picture taken while I was in the thick of the flare-up. Canon took so many photos of me that day in the studio after I re-watched *The Magic Hour*. Then he turned on his video camera, and I started talking. Everything that was happening inside came pouring out, a deluge of emotions and reflections. We haven't looked back since, capturing all my thoughts and milestones along the way. It's been cathartic, maybe as much for him as for me. Another thing we've bonded around.

"I thought about doing a documentary," he says, caressing my hand.

I turn my head to peer at him in the dim light of the theater. "Really? Wow that could be...that could be amazing."

"I'm glad you think so." He stands, depositing me in the seat and walking to the back of the theater. "Because I want to show you a little something I've been working on."

"Working on? In all your spare time?"

"We weren't shooting," he says, shrugging. "I had a *little* time on my hands. Actually once I started, I couldn't stop."

"Couldn't stop what?"

"This."

He dims the lights and the screen comes to life. My *words* come to life.

"I have lupus. It does not have me."

I watch myself—that version of myself from a few months ago—onscreen, staring into the camera and saying the words that changed my life. Those words and that perspective, so much a part of me now, were new to me then. The fear still lingered in my eyes that day after I watched Remy's final sunset. Hell, sometimes that fear returns, roaring back to taunt me, but sitting on the floor of Canon's studio that day, I kept it at bay. For the first time, I held the reality of my disease in one hand and the necessity of my will to fight in the other. Not only to fight its effects on my body, but on my soul. On my very sense of self.

Canon slips back into the seat beside me. I don't take my eyes from the screen because I'm riveted by this slice of my life he's captured, but I take his hand and squeeze.

"Lupus will not go away," the onscreen version of me continues. "For the rest of my days, it will roam my body, searching for weaknesses. It will watch my life, waiting for anything it can use to cause a flare—to do me harm."

I was in the fight of my life the day Canon started documenting my epiphany, and I looked like it. A scaly rash crawling over much of my skin was revealed as I spoke to the camera wearing only my cami and underwear. My hair was a winter garden ravaged by the elements, my scalp exposed and picked clean in large patches. My face was fuller, unnaturally rounder. I don't even look like myself onscreen, and yet that is the moment when I became *most* myself. More sure of who I was in my damaged skin than I had ever been when it was flawless.

"Lupus goes after my self-esteem," I tell the camera. "It wants my confidence, and there have been times it won—when it stole those things simply by taking my hair and marking my skin—but I fought back."

I swallow scorching emotion recalling this battle: the fatigue and aching joints, the soaring blood pressure, and the could-have-been-fatal close calls. The kidney transplant that gave me more than an organ—it restored my sister to me.

"I'm not in this fight alone," I continue. "About five million people worldwide are living with lupus. Ninety percent of them women. The overwhelming majority of them women of color."

The footage tracks my spells in the hospital. Seeing myself hooked up to the dialysis machine brings the uncertainty of those days rushing back—when I didn't know if or when I would find a kidney. Quianna recorded the appointment when Terry found out she was my match—that she could give me her kidney. There is no fear or reluctance on her face. Only relief. Only love. And I'm moved anew by her sacrifice—by her willingness to give me so much even at a time when there was so little between us.

The camera follows me into surgery until the doors close and Canon retreats, slumping into a chair against a wall of the hospital waiting room. He turns the lens around on himself.

"I don't want to tell you what I'm feeling now," he says, his expression grim. "But I'll try because Neevah wants me to. She wants to document this. There's a part of me that resists because it reminds me of..."

A haunted look possesses his eyes. A twinge of guilt squeezes my heart because I know exactly what it brings to his mind—how he documented his mother's last days.

"It's not the same," he says, almost like he's trying to convince himself as much as he is the invisible audience. "But it's the same feeling. It's like carrying priceless china that falls from your hands and shatters on the floor. Something so precious, broken beyond repair. Gone. When you're given porcelain again, something you can't even put a value to it means so much, you want to wrap it up and lock it away and protect it in case it falls. In case it shatters."

He glances up from his clasped hands, allowing the lens's scrutiny. "Every day since I found out Neevah has lupus, I've felt like she might shatter beyond repair. They wheeled her away a few minutes ago, and I know she'll be fine and that this transplant is exactly what needs to happen, but it feels like everything could go wrong without warning because it has before, and that's my nightmare."

Canon offers a hollow laugh, accompanied by half a grin. "The irony is that in the middle of all this shit, I've never been happier."

He shrugs, the helpless movement at odds with the powerful shoulders making it. "I love her and it feels like the strongest thing I've ever had. At the same time, it feels like the most fragile."

His words, so vulnerable and fear-tinged, steal my breath. As open as we are with each other, I've never heard this from him. Not this way. I was in surgery when he said these things, oblivious that he would confess these private moments, the intimacy of his struggle and doubts. It's hard to believe the enigmatic man I met the night of my Broadway debut is this open, is sharing this much. Our love has transformed us both. I know it's changed me, deepening my trust and giving me even more to live and fight for.

A photo comes onscreen, and I gasp. Literally gasp and cover my mouth, tears immediately stinging my eyes. It's a photo of Terry and me. Right before they started her surgery, they wheeled me down to her room. We look high, our eyes glassy with the drugs they've given us, but also shining with a joy so strong it eclipses our fear. Our hair is tucked beneath the surgical caps. IVs pierce our arms, but we're holding hands.

And I see it.

For maybe the first time I really see the resemblance, the sameness nature stamped into our DNA. The very sameness that saved my life.

That saved our sisterhood.

I don't even try to check the tears as they skate over my cheeks and into the corners of my mouth. I lay my head on Canon's shoulder, turning into him and letting the quiet sobs shake me. He cups my head, kisses my hair, and strokes the ink scrawled on my thumb, the message from a play that has remained with me since I was eighteen years old, *Our Town.*

Do any human beings ever realize life while they live it? Every, every minute?

Saints and poets maybe.

And that's what I'd like to call this documentary when it's done. It's the lesson of seizing this existence with both hands; of not letting anything stand in your way; of living with as few regrets as possible. Of loving even when it might hurt because loss is as much a part of life as what we gain. The beautiful man sitting beside me in this darkened theater is proof of that. This poignant art testifies that he's taken as much care telling my story as he took telling Remy's. It's a labor of love.

"I thought maybe once we finish it," Canon says after I've cried all my tears, "we could screen it at Cannes next year."

I lift my head to stare at him, dumbfounded by the idea. Delighted.

"Oh, my God!" I laugh, swiping at my wet cheeks. "That would be… seriously?"

"And we could take the whole family. Get your mom on somebody's private jet. Take Terry and Quianna." He smirks. "Even Brandon could come."

"That would be… wow."

"I know we said you'd start with Paris, but maybe we can do Cannes first."

Cannes, with its curving coastline, the beaches sanded like grains of sugar, the azure waters and boulevards dotted with palm trees, the palatial villas.

I want to see the world.

Dessi's words, delivered to Tilda with the fearlessness of youth, drift back to my mind on a warm Mediterranean breeze.

How will that view, the French Riviera, have changed since she stood there, surveying its lush landscape, Cal at her side, her first love behind her? Did she ever regret leaving Harlem? From what we gathered, she never returned. Did she ever wonder how different her life would have been had she never struck out in search of stardom? Or did she ever sit on her little porch in Alabama after she returned home to take care of her dying mother, wondering how vast her life, her legacy, could have grown had she stayed in Europe? What bends her road could have taken had she remained, brushing up against the greatness of luminaries like Bud

Powell, Thelonious Monk, Miles Davis? They all fled racism in America and sought their fortunes, their fame, in Paris, in a country and among a people who appreciated their genius before looking at their skin. Despite her modest ending, I don't think Dessi wallowed in could-have-beens.

Canon once asked if I ever regretted doing the movie since the stress of it probably caused the flare-up that sent me into a darker phase of this disease. I understood his question and the guilt behind it, but I reassured him immediately that I didn't. Have never. I can't live like that. Life is indiscriminately seasoned, usually not sweet without some bitter. Usually not sun without some rain. I'm in a support group, and one lady's lupus was triggered while she carried her first child. Does she regret her baby, a miracle who brings her joy because her body paid the toll? She says unequivocally no. And I can't resent the movie that gave me Canon, the love of my life. Can't regret the role that gave me Dessi, because even once the movie wraps, I will carry a part of her always.

As crazy as it sounds, I think she carried me. And Canon and Monk and Verity and all the storytellers, musicians, and artists who benefit from the path she forged. From the way she and so many others made for us during untenable circumstances, in adversity and against impossible odds. She carried me and I carry her, and somehow, we are knitted together in a way that reaches across generations, across years, binding our hearts.

"It's nowhere near done, yet," Canon says, a rare uncertainty in my confident man's voice. "I just started putting some stuff together, but we can look at it. You like it so far?"

"I love it so far."

I feel his heart in the look he gives me. Ours is a love so much richer and deeper than anything I could have dreamt or imagined, girded with trust and burning with passion. That forever kind of love that doesn't waver when times get tough and things go bad. That *come what may* kind of love, and every time he looks at me, I see it.

"I love it when you look at me like that," I whisper.

"How do I look at you?" He pulls me to him, fitting our bodies together, locking in our love.

This disease could kill me, but it hasn't, and I'll do everything every day to make sure I do what Remy did—live every second with the urgency of time slipping away, and savor every moment, making this life taste like eternity. I can't always put the depth of our love into words, but in this moment, I know exactly how to describe it.

"You look at me the way your mom looked at sunsets."

If possible, the emotion in his eyes deepens. His arms around me tighten, like he's found something precious he'll never let go.

"Mama always said waiting for sunsets was like waiting for a miracle you knew would come," he says, his voice graveled with the emotion in his eyes. "How happy she must be to know I finally found mine."

EPILOGUE

2004—Dessi Blue

Birthplace of Dessi Blue

The small green roadside sign is as unassuming as I am these days. Break the speed limit and you'll miss it, but the law-abiding citizens will catch this tribute to my life the city planted along Highway 31. And what a life it's been. When Mama and Daddy left Alabama for New York City, I had no idea what was in store for me.

You ain't got no crystal ball, Bama.

Tilda's voice teases me even over the applause of the crowd gathered around the sign. Even over the mayor's kind words. That girl was something else. Despite how we ended, I always smile to think of her.

I never saw her again, except in black-and-white newsprint. The clippings of her wedding announcement and obituary are tucked away with the letters she sent me all those years ago. My little secret. Oh, never from Cal. He always knew there was a tiny sliver of my heart that stayed behind in Harlem. I gave him everything else, and he said it was more than enough. More than he could handle sometimes, bless his heart.

I caress the ring on my finger, the one he placed there on our wedding day in London. That seems like another life. We left behind the glamour of Paris for the call of home. Mama lost her battle with cancer, but we had two years together, and I took care of her like she took care of me. Good daughters do that, don't they?

I guess we could have returned to Europe after Mama passed, but by then we had answered another call, Cal and me. Alabama during the civil rights movement was a perilous place, but we chose to stay. We *had* to stay. Nothing wrong with fame and fortune in Europe. We did it, but when we saw this fight our people were in, we wanted to be soldiers, not civilians. This state was, in many ways, the epicenter of the war against racial injustice. Boycotts, bombings, the march from Selma to Montgomery—we found ourselves in the thick of it. Overseas, we counted the world's talented elite among our friends—James Baldwin, Josephine Baker, Richard Wright, Sidney Bechet. All fled this country to thrive in France, but ultimately we returned to fight.

If I were white, I could capture the world.

When Dorothy Dandridge said that, I almost cried because I knew exactly what she meant. Felt it in my bones. We lived in a time of limits and barriers young folks now can't even comprehend. Ceilings there were no ladders tall enough to ever reach. Oh, there's still work to do and a ways to go, but what we endured? The way they tried to hold us back and deny us, blunt and dull us? It was always one step forward, start all over again. You couldn't get far here, and for those who *did* break through, we held them up and thanked the Lord. I only pray that what we did accomplish cleared the path for those behind us.

I've never regretted leaving our apartment in the 6th arrondissement, but I do sometimes wonder about that alternate existence in the City of Lights. We, all of us, were not only the stars. We were the night—the dark sky without which no star can shine. In Paris, we ruled the heavens, but I never saw coming home as a fall. We marched with Martin. Locked arms with the likes of Fred Shuttlesworth. Worked alongside women like Rosa Parks down South and Dorothy Height up North. As a young woman when I left Harlem, I wanted to see the world, but it was when I came home that I *changed* it.

Katherine leans down to whisper, "You alright, Mama?"

"I'm fine, Kitty." I smile and squeeze my daughter's hand. She will be our legacy, along with all Cal's music students. I taught voice and led the church choir. We set down roots, planted ourselves in this community, and grew like longleaf pines. For so many here, we were shelter and we were shade.

When I was young, I wondered where I would find my home. Was it in the nocturnal haunts of Harlem? London? The French Riviera? Paris? For years I chased the music, thinking anywhere I could sing could be my home, but I was wrong. Home is not a song, and it's not a place. It's people. It's community. It's the bond of blood and the friends we choose. It is that feeling—that knowing you are never alone. I've lost those I held dearest—my first love and my last. My daddy and my mama. The friends I laughed and lived alongside, all gone, and still, I'm not alone. Love lingers and I feel them all with me even now. I can almost see Tilda standing at my side, wearing a wicked grin and her rent-red dress. Almost hear Cal's trumpet, blowing like the Angel Gabriel's. Even death cannot steal, even time cannot erase, the peace I found in all the people I have known and loved.

The ceremony ends, and after a while, the crowd dwindles until Katherine and I are the only ones left standing on the side of the road.

"I guess we better get on home," she says, tucking her arm through mine. "It sure is a pretty sign."

It glows and glints, fired up by the setting sun. The raised text sketches only the briefest of details. That I was born. How I lived, and soon, I guess it will say I died. My memory reads between the lines, fills in the gaps, keeps my secrets, and I am content.

Maybe I didn't ever gain the fame of that other life, but this little roadside sign in a small Alabama town—it says I was *here* and it will tell my story.

BONUS EPILOGUE

Neevah

"What was your favorite part about making *Dessi Blue?*"

It was a reasonable question the first time someone asked me... oh, ten hours ago. Now with the setting sun casting marigold shadows through the hotel suite windows and my body practically trembling with fatigue, hearing it for the twentieth time today is a nail this well-meaning journalist hammers through my pounding skull.

"Um, it was..." I flounder, unable to find the pat answer I've delivered every other time during today's press junket.

"I think we're done here."

The curt response comes from Canon on his stool at the end of the row. Three cast members sit between him and me, but I feel his stare, his focus as if he were seated right beside me, breathing down my neck.

Him breathing on my neck or any part of my body would be welcome right now, but first... work. If I don't get my shit together and answer these last few questions, he'll shut this interview down, and even more rumors will start.

"No, I'm fine," I tell the young journalist/blogger/influencer with her wide eyes, obviously a little starstruck by the impressive cast and intimidated by our famously taciturn director.

"Neevah," Canon cuts in, leaning forward to look past Trey and the other two actors, a frown stamped on his bold features. "You can take a break. We got this."

"I'm fine," I grit out through a forced smile.

Am I flagging? Yes? 'Bout to collapse as soon as this interview is over? Abso-fucking-lutely.

But I'm the star of this movie. I *am* Dessi Blue, and this is my big break. The whole cast and crew worked so hard to get to this point. *I've* worked hard for as long as I can remember to reach this moment where I'm the lead in one of the biggest movies of the year. I endured a grueling shoot over months while living through the worst health crisis of my life. I'm not letting the team down when faced with a few questions. I'm not letting *myself* down, and Canon needs to respect that.

"How much longer? Let's wrap this up," he snaps, glaring at the poor girl…Percy, I think was how she introduced herself. All the people who interviewed us today have run together into one big blob of names and faces. I probably wouldn't recognize one of them if they walked back through the door at this point.

"Like I was saying," I continue as if Canon isn't trying to shut this shit down expeditiously. "My favorite part of the process was working with this amazing cast. What a blessing for my first feature film to be with such a stellar group of actors."

"You got your start on Broadway," Percy says, pressing her advantage lest Canon swoops in again. "As I was watching the screener, I couldn't help but think this part was made for you. Your vocal performances, the choreography. Did you feel your previous experience prepared you well for this opportunity?"

"Perfectly," I reply. "I couldn't have written a part for myself better than this. And speaking of the vocal performances and the choreography, shout out to Monk—"

"You mean Wright Bellamy, the music supervisor?" Percy clarifies.

"Yes, Monk really tested me vocally, but I grew so much as a singer being under the direction of such a gifted musician. And Lucia, our choreographer." I whoosh out a breath and shake my head. "I've never worked harder or been prouder than I am of what she pulled out of me as a dancer."

Percy finally redirects her questions, moving on to Trey seated beside me. She asks about transitioning from Nickelodeon, which makes him roll his eyes since his days as a child actor are so far behind him, but he answers politely anyway. Like the professional he is. Like we all are, except

Canon peers down the line, brows drawn together like an anxious parent instead of the man helming one of the decade's most epic biopics.

Stop, I mouth, sneaking him a discreetly pointed glare.

Instead of stopping, this man stands, walks behind the line of stools set up, and comes down to my end. Percy stumbles over her question, flicking a curious glance to Canon before refocusing on Trey.

I stiffen when he leans forward to whisper in my ear. "Babe, you okay?"

I'm going to ignore all the swoony, melty things that happen in my body when I hear the concern threading that deep, rich voice. I turn my head just enough to meet his dark eyes.

"I'm fine," I hiss. "And this is unacceptable, Canon. Go sit down."

"Do you really think I give a fuck what she or anyone thinks if you need to stop for the day? After all we've done, *I'm* exhausted and I don't even have—"

Before he can say *lupus,* I press my fingers over his lips. A mistake for two reasons. One, because touching him there reminds me of the life-changing work that mouth accomplished between my legs last night. Two, because Percy gives up any pretense of not being riveted by the sideshow we have become.

"Is everything okay?" she asks.

"Of course," I offer with what I hope is a reassuring smile. "Canon knows I've been under the weather and wanted to make sure I'm feeling fine."

"It's been a really long day," Canon says, his tone gruff. "I was just… concerned."

"Tell me if I'm overstepping with this next question," Percy ventures.

"I'm already sure you are," Canon says dryly.

Percy gulps, but bravely plows ahead. "Ms. Saint, you've spoken openly of late about your journey with lupus, but we haven't touched on it here. And the other thing we haven't discussed is the very public relationship between you and your director."

For a moment, you could hear an ant piss it's so quiet. Yes, Camille exposed our relationship on that podcast, her vindictive ass, but like they say: What the devil meant for evil…Being outed ended up being a turning point in our relationship, a way for Canon and me to openly acknowledge how we feel about each other. But we don't discuss it, and our publicists always make sure anyone interviewing us knows we don't want to. The work of the cast and crew shouldn't be overshadowed. Canon is especially protective of me being respected for my talent, not whom I'm dating.

"That is definitely overstepping," Canon says after a few seconds drawn tight with tension.

I close my eyes and bow my head.

Oh hell.

"I'm going to address your question," Canon goes on, to my surprise. "Because I'm tired of answering the same shit over and over today and not talking about real things. Neevah's soaring talent—that's a real thing."

I open my eyes and slowly turn my head until I can study his profile, the dramatic slope of high cheekbones and the flared arrow of his nose.

"Neevah acting and dancing and singing her ass off, while managing a chronic illness, and humbling us all with her work ethic," Canon says softly. "That's a real thing."

His words cast a spell of care over me, and my muscles relax, the tension of holding myself tightly all day loosening. His wide, warm palm presses to the small of my back. That pressure against my body, the love in it, the intimacy—I want to lean into that touch; surrender to the pull of this man the universe saved for me.

"I'll leave it to Neevah to address her health if she chooses to," Canon goes on. "I haven't spoken about our relationship much, not because I'm ashamed of it, but because I'm so proud of her. I want people to see her as an artist in her own right and not get it twisted that somehow her decision to be with me *after* she had secured the role and done the work has any bearing on all the praise she deserves."

The room is silent again, this time tinged with our collective awe because even though Canon asked the cast and crew to get tested for matching when I needed a kidney transplant, what he just said is probably the most they've heard him articulate about his feelings for me.

"Wow," Percy breathes, looking down at her phone to make sure it's still recording. "That's . . . thank you for being so forthcoming."

"It's not that we have anything to hide," Canon says, squeezing my shoulder. "This is our job. This project has consumed the better part of our lives for the last year, some of us for even longer. The work, everyone's work, should stand on its own, and not suffer any detraction because of rumor and conjecture about our personal lives."

"I'm sorry if..." Percy bites her lip and sighs. "I didn't mean to intrude. Everyone wonders."

"And it's not everyone's business," Trey says, reaching over to squeeze my hand. "Ask any of us. Neevah and Canon have been nothing but professional. And what Neevah pulled off for this film, while managing lupus, it's astounding."

I squeeze his hand back and blink away tears. The whole cast has been incredibly kind. Filming literally shut down while I had a kidney transplant. All our work could have been sabotaged by my illness, but their support never wavered. I won't forget that.

"As you can see," I tell Percy with a wobbly smile, "we've become very close as a cast and making *Dessi Blue* has been the best experience of my life. I wake up every day grateful for what I have, that I had lupus and it didn't have me and it didn't steal my lifelong dream."

"Do you mind if I ask how you're doing?" Percy queries, before rushing on. "If you don't feel comfortable, it's fine. I'll edit the question out."

Canon's hand makes the subtle slide from my back to the curve of my hip, a soft squeeze of support.

"No, I'm in a really good place." I clear my throat. "Knock on wood. I'm taking the meds recommended by my doctor. I'm pretty regimented with my diet and exercise. Stress can be a trigger for flares."

I glance up over my shoulder at Canon where he still stands behind me, feeling the love in his eyes as if his arms are wrapped around me.

"Thus Canon's concern about me overdoing it." I look back to Percy, releasing anxiety in a long breath. "I definitely overdid it when we were filming, and I had a real health crisis, but I'm much better."

"Is there anything you want others living with lupus to know?" Percy asks.

Those days in the hospital—the kidney transplant, losing my hair, lesions, dialysis—all of it rises and breaks through the surface of my thoughts. For a moment, none of this feels real. My smooth, unblemished skin. The thick luxury of my hair braided into a regal natural style. The glossy rigor of press junkets and red carpets and premieres. This feels like a fantasy that never happened. The steady beat of my heart trips, and I panic as if the reality is still me at death's threshold, the odds stacked against me, debilitating pain and fatigue robbing me of strength.

But then…

Canon cups the side of my throat with one hand, brushing his thumb across my nape in a caress so gentle, yet firm, it anchors me in this moment. In this reality where I *won*. Where I beat the odds and lived another day to keep on fighting.

I swallow back the emotion scorching my throat to answer her question. "I want them to know that I'm no different from them, even though lupus manifests differently for us all. What I mean is, I have a diagnosis that is potentially life-threatening, but I'm still living my life. I don't let it stop me, and I work hard at not letting it stop me. Staying on top of diet, exercise, remaining in consultation with my doctor. There may be times you don't think you'll make it. We live with the possibility, but we *live*. We find joy. We follow our dreams. Chase our passions."

I reach up to cover Canon's hand at my throat with my own.

"We find love." I flash him a besotted smile and then return my attention to Percy. "We can't control everything, every outcome. It's futile to try, but we can live our life to the fullest. We can live with a grateful heart. We can love deeply and outrageously. Nothing and no one can take away our capacity for love."

"Girl, stay still."

Takira's words come out slightly jumbled around the hairpins shoved between her lips.

"I *am* still," I say, pouting only a little bit. "It's taking a long time. Are we almost done?"

"What are you, six?" she teases, sliding a pin into the intricate loops of my braided updo. "It's taking the time it takes. Beauty moves at its own pace."

Takira meets my eyes in the hotel's bathroom mirror. "You been squirming since you sat down in this chair. Is it impatience or nerves? Tonight is a big night, huh?"

I close my eyes and sigh. She got me. Of course, she knows. She's seen me at every stage of my career. It's fitting that she's the one preparing me for my first big premiere.

"Maybe there are a few nerves." I accompany the admission with a chagrined look. "Sorry if I'm being bratty."

Takira scoffs and sprays sheen over the finished hairstyle. "You 'bout the least bratty chick I know. You have a lot you could complain about, Neeve, but you never do."

Takira holds my gaze in the mirror, resting her hands on my shoulders.

"You did it," she whispers. "And I'm so proud of you, sis."

Tears well in my eyes because it seems like only yesterday she and I stood together in a small dressing room. I was a Broadway understudy, and she was the only one I trusted with my hair. With the truth about my condition. I had no idea the man who would change my life forever sat just beyond the curtains, waiting for me to take the stage. So much has changed, and yet Takira and me—we're the same.

"You better dry them tears," Takira says, fanning her own wet eyes. "After all the time I spent getting that makeup just right."

I choke out a laugh and stand, turning to pull her into a hug.

"You got nothing to be nervous about," she whispers, patting my back. "You've done all the hard work, Neevah. Now let the world shower you with the praise you deserve."

"Kira." I tighten my arms around her. "Thank you for everything. I couldn't have done this without you."

"Thank you for bringing me along. I've gotten to see my work onscreen in one of the biggest movies of the decade. Not bad."

"Not bad at all," I agree, smiling and landing a kiss on her cheek.

"Now let's get you into this dress."

The cast got rooms in the hotel where the press junket took place today. It's close to the theater and most of us just stayed here to get dressed for the premiere. Takira walks over to the rack of dresses several designers sent for our consideration and pulls off the one we chose.

"Boy, Canon's tongue gon' fall right outta his mouth when he sees you wearing this."

The white, one-shouldered Elie Saab gown contrasts starkly with the gleaming brown of my skin. It molds to every curve faithfully—cupping my breasts, cinching my waist, clinging to my hips, thighs, and ass. It flares at the knees, belling to my ankles. Borrowed Harry Winston diamonds glitter at my ears, neck, and wrists. Takira even pinned a few in my hair.

"How do I look?" I turn in a little circle, a smile already splitting my cheeks.

"Like a woman who has the world at her feet." Takira clasps her hands together under her chin. "Damn, I'm good."

I swat her arm and laugh. "Get outtta here and go get your own self red carpet–ready. Is Naz coming?"

"Yes." She flashes that smile that seems reserved specifically for the NBA baller who swept her off her feet. "So glad he didn't have a game tonight. I'll see you at the theater."

Takira packs her makeup and styling tools, admonishing me the whole time to be careful not to ruin the perfect image she pulled together tonight.

"Your man ready?" she asks, hefting the bag over her shoulder.

"He's mighty quiet in there." I tip my head toward the corridor that leads to the bedroom we've shared in this suite. "I better go check on him. You know this is his least favorite part of the business."

"Good idea." She inspects me from top to bottom one last time and puts a staying hand on my arm, waiting until I meet her sober eyes.

"Everybody gonna see you shine on that screen and on that red carpet tonight, Neeve. What makes you glorious isn't even what you do on that screen, but what it took for you to *get* there. You're a survivor and I'm so proud of you."

"You must really not care about this makeup." I hiccup and fan at my watery eyes. "Saying stuff like that."

"Suck it up and keep it dry." Takira laughs, blows me an air kiss. "Love you."

"Love you, too."

Once she's gone, I turn to face the mirror. My breath catches, and even though I watched Takira building this elegant vision piece by piece, seeing the luminous whole startles me. The woman is a vision swathed in glamor. Delicate and glowing from the crown of her head to the soles of her very expensive shoes. For a moment, I don't recognize myself in the reflection, but then I study closer. It's in the eyes that I find myself. There is the world-worn weariness of a fighter, the resolve of someone who has lived through some shit. If I were to lift this gown, you'd see the scar from my kidney transplant. You'd see a few blemishes from particularly stubborn rashes and lesions. You'd see the marks of battle.

My stomach, which has felt a little floaty and nervous all day, settles. My heartbeat steadies. After all I've made it through, what is the red carpet? What is the scrutiny of a thousand eyes tonight? I have dragged myself back from death's door. Who cares if people speculate that I'm here because I'm dating Canon? Nothing critics can say will diminish me.

"Shit."

The softly uttered expletive draws my eyes up to meet Canon's in the mirror. He stands in the doorway, devouring me at a glance. His gaze roams with hunger and tenderness over every dip and curve and flash of skin.

I send a seductive grin over my shoulder, hoping to lure him to me. In a few long-legged strides he eliminates the distance between us, coming to stand so close I feel enveloped by the warmth of him. I turn in his arms, and he slides one hand to the base of my spine, fingers splaying over the curve of my ass.

"Are you sure we have to go to this thing?" He bends to drop soft kisses along the slope of sensitive skin between my neck and shoulder, leaving a fleet of goose bumps in his wake.

"This *thing*," I say, glancing up at him through a sweep of mascaraed lashes, "is the biggest movie of your career and mine. The thing we've worked so hard on for so long. The whole world gets to see it tonight. So, yeah. I'm pretty sure we have to be there."

"I'll make a deal with you."

"A deal? You're negotiating with me to get you to your own movie? Let's hear it."

"We do the movie premiere."

"So far so good."

"But we leave as soon as possible. Just show our faces at the after-party long enough to satisfy the studio execs and our publicists and all the people who've been bugging me all damn day, but then we go."

I think of all the reporters we've met the last few days. Of the endless interviews and photo shoots and everything that's been demanded of us to get here. It's easy to miss how big this moment is. Easy to go through all the motions and not let it sink in. Sneaking off with Canon sounds like the perfect way to end this night.

I tip up onto my toes and press a quick kiss against his lips. Canon's hands tighten at my hips, and he pulls me closer, bends as if to recapture my mouth. I intercept the kiss with one raised finger.

"If you ruin my lipstick," I whisper, "Takira's gonna whup your ass."

He chuckles, shaking his head and settling for a kiss to my temple.

"Okay. I'll save all the kissing for after the premiere as soon as we can get out." He pulls back to peer down at me, brows lifted. "But do we have a deal?"

I pass a finger over the faint smear of gloss coloring his lips and grin. "Deal."

Canon

The entire audience stands to applaud *Dessi Blue*. It's the end of a journey that started on a rural Alabama road. Started with me squinting through the summer sun at a tiny plaque much too inconsequential to commemorate the life of such a fantastic entertainer. The injustice of Dessi's obscurity stung so sharply it compelled me to make this movie about her.

It also led me to the love of my life.

Neevah and I didn't arrive together for the premiere. No photo ops of us holding hands or shouted demands for us to pose together on the red carpet. We didn't sit beside each other in the theater. Neither of us wanted to distract from the movie or from the rest of the cast by sparking more speculation about our relationship.

The invisible thread that runs from her heart to mine, though, pulls taut all night. Straining when she moves, agitated by the distance as if not being with her is the most unnatural thing in the world. Miraculously it is.

It sounds sad now, but devotion to my work was the closest thing I'd experienced to true love.

Until her.

And now not even the craft I've poured my life into comes close to what I feel for Neevah.

It was so gratifying to watch all the photographers and reporters scrambling to get photos of her when she arrived. She was breathtaking, and the light I saw in her from the very beginning shone so blindingly tonight, she'd halfway won over the skeptics with her presence alone. But then they saw her become Dessi Blue. There is such a melding onscreen of Neevah and Dessi that it's difficult to tell where one ends and the other begins. She embodies the character. Neevah found the role of a lifetime, or rather this role found her. I found her, and I'll never let her go.

"It's not creepy at all the way you watch your girlfriend like a stalker," Monk says from beside me, taking a long draw of his old-fashioned at the after-party.

"Where *is* Verity tonight?" I crane my neck, pretending to search the crowded room. "I thought I saw her talking to that agent from—"

"Okay." Monk's expression morphs into an irritated frown. "One day it won't work, you know. Using Ver to get me off your back."

I slide a smug smile his way and knock back what's left of my Macallan. "But today is not that day, my friend. Today is not that day."

"How's it feel to have a hit on your hands?" he asks, steering us further from the subject of him and his old flame. "That standing O. The critical response so far. Early Oscar buzz. You worked hard for this. You're always so intense, but I hope you're savoring it."

"I am." I nod, allowing a brief smile. "It's one of the biggest nights of my career."

"Then why do you look like this is the last place you want to be?"

Because I'd rather savor it with Neevah and no one else around for a little bit.

I grunt a nonresponse and try to catch Neevah's eye so we can get the hell out of here. Our lives have been chaos leading up to this night. Between the aggressive shooting schedule, Neevah's health issues, getting filming *back* on track, post-production, and now all the promotion and release hype…it's been hard to find a rhythm for our life together. But that ends tonight.

"Neevah's family made it?" Monk asks.

"Yeah, they did." I glance across the room where Neevah and a few cast members chat with a reporter from *Variety*. "Her mama, sister, niece. Hell, even that brother-in-law she used to date came."

"Shit, therapy works wonders, huh?" Monk lifts his brows, obviously impressed by the progress her family has made.

"They've still got a ways to go, but things are good enough that they show up for each other. That means a lot to Neevah, and what makes her happy makes me happy. I think they've gone back to the hotel. Neevah's meeting them for breakfast in the morning."

Which is just as well since tonight is about *us*. I'm going to give her five more minutes before grabbing her and leaving.

Monk glances over my shoulder and a wide smile overtakes his face. "If it isn't the woman of the hour."

A cool hand slips into mine, slim fingers intertwining. Neevah's scent drifts up to me, at once somehow arousing and soothing. When I glance down, her face is lifted to me and glowing with a smile that is equal parts joy and wonder. All my impatience dissipates. She deserves every minute of tonight. I've done so many events like this, and the schmoozy, boozy part of a movie release is always my least favorite. As soon as the film has been seen, I'm ready to jet and then be on pins and needles until the box office numbers come in. But this is Neevah's first movie, first time doing any of this. My plans for tonight can wait if Neevah wants to stay.

Monk hugs her and Neevah loops one arm around his neck, but never releases my hand.

"I can't help but think that none of this would be possible without you," she tells Monk.

"Um, need I remind you both that I'm the one who saw Neevah's potential that first night onstage," I say, feigning indignation. "I'm the one who fought to cast her. I directed the movie."

"Yeah, baby." Neevah playfully rolls her eyes. "You were there, too."

We all laugh, but I touch Monk's shoulder and say with all seriousness, "I really do owe you the biggest debt."

"For bringing your Dessi Blue to you?" Monk asks, some of the teasing lingering in his tone.

"For bringing my Neevah to me," I correct softly, looping an arm around her waist to pull her closer.

"Oh, God." Monk groans, closing his eyes. "I think I liked you much better miserable than this cotton candy happily-ever-after shit."

"Don't knock it 'til you try it." Neevah laughs.

Monk's smile melts as his gaze drifts and locks with Verity's across the room. She's decked in a tight black leather dress with cutouts flashing golden brown skin. Her makeup is dramatic—smoky eyes and bold red lips. She looks gorgeous, and when she sees Monk, annoyed. With a quick frown, she looks away, turns her back.

"Not likely," Monk mutters. He determinedly relights a grin, brighter and more forced than his previous ease. "I think Imma bounce."

The tightness around his eyes and mouth clearly telegraphs this isn't the time to tease him, so I just fist bump and let him slip away and out of the ballroom without further comment.

"I thought we had a deal," Neevah mutters once we're alone. "That we'd get outta here first chance we get."

It's completely the opposite of what I expected her to say and startles a laugh from me.

"Don't you want to stay a little longer? It's your big night."

"It's *our* night. And we've given enough of it to everyone else." She drops her head to my shoulder, seemingly unaware of how many eyes have turned to study our linked hands and the unmistakable intimacy of her pressed into my side. "Take me home."

Throwing caution to the same winds, I bend to kiss the top of her head, forcing myself not to snarl at the photographer who just stole a picture of us.

"I don't care," Neevah whispers, mischief glinting in the gold flecks of her brown eyes. "Everyone knows anyway."

And suddenly I don't want to hide it anymore either. If anyone sees what Neevah did in *Dessi Blue* and still questions her talent or whether she deserves to be there, fuck 'em.

I press my hand to the silky skin of her back left bare by the dress she's been torturing me with all night. "Then, baby, let's go home."

~

"This isn't home," Neevah says, frowning when we pull up to the Galaxy Studios lot.

"It *was* our second home for months," I counter with a grin.

I wave at the guard in the booth who knows me by sight and doesn't bother asking for ID as he motions me through the gate.

"What are we doing here, Canon?" Neevah asks, but her frown has been replaced by anticipatory curiosity. "What are you up to?"

"We celebrated their way." I park the car and kill the engine. "Now let's celebrate ours."

"Ours?" she asks, stepping out of the car carefully in her stilettos and silken finery when I open her door. "Or yours?"

I shrug, taking her hand and leading her down a street on the lot we both know by heart. I don't bother answering because I might give too much away.

"Whatever you're up to," she says, turning to walk backward a few steps and holding my gaze, "I'd rather be up to it with you than anywhere else in the world."

"I feel the exact same." I pull her back to my front, cross my arms at her waist, and we keep walking. "You were amazing tonight."

"It was surreal." She shakes her head, her soft hair brushing my chin with the motion. "It's hard to believe any of this is real."

Ironically, we're strolling past facades, fake cities, manufactured mountains, elaborate microcosms created as homes for the fantasies we sell. Finally, the last few familiar steps take us where I've been wanting to be all night. We turn the corner, and Neevah stops abruptly, her fingers tightening on mine at her waist.

"The Savoy," she breathes, looking up at me over her shoulder, surprise and delight on her face. "It's still here."

"Yeah, this set piece is too elaborate and too well-crafted to just tear down after one use." I walk over to the wall and flip up more lights, illuminating the huge replica our production team built with such care and attention to detail—the marble stairs, mirrored walls, cut-glass chandeliers, bandstands, and the mahogany spring-loaded dance floor. If I close my eyes, I can see Neevah twirling, twisting in a rainbow sea of costumed dancers; hear Lucia's strident voice slicing over music from a bygone era, demanding another take. Expecting no less than perfection.

"Galaxy spent a lot of money on this and will use it for something else," I say. "Even if it's slightly repurposed. For now, it's still our Savoy."

In the center of the ballroom floor, a small high table is set, covered in a white linen cloth. A silver bucket stuffed with ice cradles a bottle of champagne.

"A private celebration, huh?" Neevah kicks off her high heels and practically skips over to the table. "No glasses? We drinking straight from the bottle?"

I reach down to the floor, grabbing two champagne flutes from a small tote left there by a thoughtful person I'll thank later. "Got the glasses right here."

I follow more slowly, my pace deliberate to counter my heartbeat, which is *racing* unreasonably fast.

She lifts the bottle of champagne from the bucket to read the label. "And it's the good stuff."

"Only the best for you." I take the champagne and pour it into the two glasses I hold by the stems. "Allow me."

I flick a searching, alert glance from the bubbly liquid filling the flute to her face.

"A toast." She holds the glass, her eyes dancing. "To Dessi."

"To *you* and Dessi," I amend, kissing the lips of our flutes together and lifting my glass to drink.

She goes to take her first sip, but pulls the glass away with a frown.

"What the—"

She peers down into the glass of golden liquid, and her eyes widen, flicking from the champagne to my face and back again.

"Is that..." She can't seem to catch her breath, her chest lifting and falling in rapid inhales and exhales. "Canon, I... are you..."

I take the glass from her trembling hand and fish out the ring floating in the cold champagne. The flawless square diamond sparkles, capturing and releasing light from chandeliers overhead. I place the glasses on the table, watching and waiting for my heart to slow and my tongue to release the words I rehearsed like one of the actors I usually guide. Our breaths sound loud and ragged in the silence. If I pressed my hand to her heart, would it be stampeding like mine has been ever since we stepped onto this set? I knew the reason I brought her here, the question I would ask, and that her answer would change our lives forever.

I do something I never thought I would, but for Neevah...anything. I drop to one knee and suspend the ring in the space between us, grasping it between two fingers. The makeup Takira so carefully applied, that has held all night, is marred with the tears streaking Neevah's cheeks.

"Neevah, I've never wanted anything more than I want a life with you," I say, swallowing the heat of my emotion. Nothing I've achieved, lost, won, compares to this moment with her.

"In the grand scheme of things," I continue, struggling to steady my voice, "I know we haven't been together that long, but if there's one thing the last year has taught me, it's that life is short. Nothing is promised."

"Yes," she shouts.

"And I want to—"

"I said yes, Canon!"

"Yes, what?" I frown.

"Yes, I'll marry you."

"Neeve, I haven't even asked. You're accepting without even letting me get the question out?"

"Redundant! Why else would you be on your knee holding a ring?" She laughs through tears. She swipes her thumb at the corner of my eye. "And why else would you be crying? You never cry over anything."

Am I crying? I blink at the wetness clumping my lashes. *Shit, I guess I am.*

"There's only one other woman I've ever cried for in my entire life," I tell her. "And that was my mother. You are worth these tears. You deserve more than all that's in my heart, but I'm offering it to you for the rest of my life."

At those words, Neevah closes her eyes, and the tears trickle beneath her lashes. God, I wish my mother could have met her, could have known this woman who feels like the missing piece of my heart.

"She would love you, Neevah." I choke out a laugh. "She'd find a way to take credit for us. Like she dreamt you up for me, prayed you into my life. Something. And she'd be right because that's the only way to explain how I found you."

I wrap one arm around her waist and draw her into me. "It had to be a miracle."

"It feels like she's with us sometimes." Neevah shakes her head as if to dismiss her own whimsy, but goes on. "I felt her with us tonight."

Fuck, now I'm crying for real. Not just tears standing in my eyes, but surrendering and sliding over my cheeks. "I felt that way, felt her tonight, too."

Neevah settles her weight on my bent knee and kisses my tears away.

"You're such a softie," she whispers against my jaw.

"Only for you." I huff a laugh, sniffing.

"That's what makes it special, that it's only for me."

"So I have your permission to be an asshole to everyone else?" I smile into the soft, scented curve of her neck.

"Could I stop you?" She giggles, the sound so happy and soaring it lifts my heart with it.

"No, probably not." I shake her a little. "Damn, Neeve. This is the most anticlimactic proposal ever. If you don't—"

She presses a finger to my lips, cutting me off. "I said yes."

"To a question I never got to ask."

She shrugs her shoulders, the burnished brown skin gleaming in the light of chandeliers. "So ask me."

Now that I have to actually pose the question, it lodges in my throat. I can't get the words out, and I've pitched impossible ideas to studios determined not to make them and gotten a yes. Yet I can't form my lips around this simple question. Only nothing feels simple about the question. The rest of my life and all my happiness hang in the balance of this moment.

"Neevah Mathis," I say, abandoning her stage name because none of this is for show. It's finally just for us. "Will you marry me?"

"Yes, Canon." She gasps the words, beaming, eyes shining with promise. "I will."

Her acceptance, hearing the words that launch our new life together, breaks me down in a way I don't think I've ever experienced. I've always been reserved. Maybe that resulted from growing up in the shadow of my mother's mortality, living with a heightened awareness that I would lose her someday soon. And when I did, it devastated me so deeply, I pulled a shade down over my heart to protect it from that kind of pain again. Neevah, nearly from the beginning, ripped that barrier away with her smile, her warmth, her compassion. On the surface, she may seem like the last person I should choose because all her life, she'll face challenges with her health, too. But she's perfect for me. She's the only one who could have coaxed me from those shadows, back out to love again, because the rareness of her makes any risk worth it. Even risking my heart. The urgency of our love, of her life, forces me to pause and to savor. To appreciate life beyond my work. And isn't that what Mama wanted most for me?

Neevah brushes her thumbs across more of these damn tears I can't seem to hold back. I shake my head, frowning because *what the hell?* I had this all planned out, like I meticulously plan everything, and nowhere did I account for my own tears. But fuck it. Tears roll freely down Neevah's cheeks, too. She frames my face with trembling hands, and dips to skate her lips over mine. It's our first kiss of the night, and of all the firsts we've had today, this is my favorite. Our lips brush and cling lightly, and then the kiss deepens, our tongues tangling and tasting the salt of tears and the sweetness of joy. She presses closer until I imagine I feel her heart pounding that rhythm life has conspired against us finding.

It's the rhythm of *you, me, you, me, you, me.*

It's the heartbeat of forever.

ACKNOWLEDGMENTS

This book! It officially takes the crown as hardest book I've written to date. And I have to thank so many people who've helped along the way.

First and foremost, I have to thank the women who shared their journey of living with lupus and those whose family members have lupus. Wanda, Bianca, Camille, Ladonna, Sandi, and Daisy. You opened your hearts, told your stories, and taught me so much. I cannot say thank you enough, and your fingerprints and heartbeats are all over Neevah's journey.

To the "industry insiders" who spoke with me about filmmaking, thank you. Your insight was invaluable.

To Joanna. Where do I even start? You are the first eyes on everything I write, and your support is priceless. Thank you AGAIN for not pulling punches and for always caring about my work as if it's your own. Your friendship is one of the greatest treasures I've found along this journey.

To my beta readers, my promo team, the amazing readers in my Facebook group and beyond—thank you for supporting me, loving my work, and for always having my back.

To my hubby and my son, you guys put up with a lot for this one. Thank you for being patient with me when I lose myself in these worlds I create. I promise I'll always come back! LOL! And I'll try to shorten my stay there. :-)

You, Sam, are my infinity x immeasurable.

NOTE: The verbiage in chapter fifty-one was taken from public signs posted in London's tube stations during the Blitz of WWII.

YOUR BOOK CLUB RESOURCE

READING GROUP GUIDE

AUTHOR'S NOTE

Reel is a work of fiction, but it's inspired by the energy and excellence of countless Black creatives from the past and present. Dessi Blue is a composite of the amazing women I encountered during my research for this book. Her recipe for greatness is a dash of Billie Holiday, some Ella Fitzgerald sprinkled in, and a heaping scoop of Ma Rainey and Bessie Smith.

It was important to me that Dessi's journey reflect the realities of the era in which she lived. Both the outrageous abundance of talent like James Baldwin, Louis Armstrong, Sarah Vaughan, Duke Ellington, and so many more; but also the challenges these brilliant artists navigated. For example, the scene when Dessi is forced to perform in skin-darkening makeup. I wish that had sprung from my imagination, but Billie Holiday actually faced that dilemma in Detroit, and had to go onstage, just as Dessi did.

Facts inspired several other details in the book. *The Chicago Defender*, arguably the most influential African-American newspaper of the early and mid-twentieth century, sent two young women overseas, cousins Roberta G. Thomas and Flaurience Sengstacke, who reported their experiences traveling Europe as young Black women. In the book, this prompted Cal's reporting as the band traversed the continent. The all-Black production of *Macbeth* actually happened as it does in *Dessi Blue*. Touted as the play that electrified Harlem, it seemed the perfect setting for Tilda and Dessi's meet cute! The time Dessi and Cal spend in London during WWII came to life as I learned more about Adelaide Hall, a New York performer who moved to London, where she worked and lived much of the rest of her life. She is believed to hold the world record for most encores, a whopping fifty-four while entertaining the troops during WWII with the sound of Nazis dropping bombs in the distance. She released material over EIGHT DECADES, and in 2003 the *Guinness Book of World Records* listed her as the world's most enduring recording artist. We should all know her name.

Reel is a love story, but also a love *letter* to the scores of Black creatives whose work and accomplishments have gone largely unacknowledged and unsung. In many cases, they sacrificed so much for little gain in their lifetimes. But *we* have gained, learning from and being inspired by their example. They blazed a trail with their talent, discipline, and dedication. To quote Dessi, they were not only the stars. They were the night—the dark sky without which no star can shine. How brightly they shone, leaving us a legacy lit by grit and enduring grace.

And I say thank you.

PLAYLIST

Scan here for the *Reel* playlist.

AUTHOR INTERVIEW

Q: What inspired you to write about both the Harlem Renaissance and the current Hollywood Renaissance?

A: *Reel* is a love letter to creatives of color who brought us so much joy and high art under sometimes awful circumstances living in a country that saw their skin before their gift. I drew from the energy fueling projects like *The United States v. Billie Holiday* on Hulu, *Ma Rainey's Black Bottom* on Netflix, and *Sylvie's Love* and *One Night in Miami* on Amazon. There is a burst of creativity and production among creatives of color we haven't seen at this level maybe since the Harlem Renaissance. It is accompanied by newfound creative agency and power, enabling us to tell our stories unfiltered, through our lens and with our voices. I see this story as a slice of what is happening in broader culture, and I'm excited to add my perspective through romance storytelling. I want to shine light on this movement and what it means, not just for communities of color, but for everyone.

Q: You wove the story of Dessi Blue into Neevah and Canon's story. Was it difficult to craft this style of story within a story?

A: I had never written a screenplay. I actually bought a copy of the script from *The Cotton Club* to see the format for a movie in the period in which I was writing. The most challenging parts were figuring out how much of Dessi's story to reveal before that thread would start to distract from the primary love story. And then how to fit that into the natural flow of the story. Meaning, in a way that organically intersected with the action occurring in the contemporary storyline. It was surgical and I adjusted both storylines as I went along to ensure that flow.

Q: What can we expect in future books in the series?

A: You can read Takira's story in "The Close-Up," a novella. Monk and Verity will get a full-length novel titled *Score,* and Evan's story, *Seam,* will follow a little later.

DISCUSSION QUESTIONS

1. Kennedy Ryan crafted a unique structure for this book. How did you feel about the intertwining of the novel and the movie script? Past and present? How did this enhance or detract from the reading/listening experience?
2. What did you like most about the book? What did you like the least?
3. Were there any quotes (or passages) that stood out to you? Why?
4. Which character or moment prompted the strongest emotional reaction for you? Why?
5. Were there times you disagreed with Canon's or Neevah's actions? What would you have done differently?
6. Were there any plot twists that you loved? Didn't like?
7. Neevah and her sister, Terry, have a complicated relationship. How did you feel about its evolution throughout the book?
8. What specific themes does Kennedy Ryan explore throughout this novel?
9. How does Neevah Saint grow and change throughout the story? How is her personality and confidence impacted as the story evolves?
10. In what ways does this book hold a mirror to societal issues?
11. If you were to ask Kennedy Ryan a question about the book, what would it be?
12. Even though this book is classified as fiction, there is a lot that is grounded in reality. Did anything surprise you?

APPLE COBBLER RECIPE

"It's just cobbler, right? I have enough willpower to eat dessert and get out of here without anything happening. Don't I?"

FILLING:

6 medium tart baking apples (Granny Smith, Honey Crisp, Gala, etc.), peeled and sliced
½ cup brown sugar
2 teaspoons cornstarch
1 lemon
½ teaspoon vanilla extract
1 teaspoon cinnamon
1 teaspoon ground nutmeg
Pinch of salt

TOPPING:

1 cup flour
2 teaspoons baking powder
¼ teaspoon salt
½ cup sugar
¾ cup milk
6 tablespoons melted butter
2 teaspoons vanilla extract

Preheat oven to 350°F. Grease 9 x 13 baking dish and set aside.

In a large mixing bowl, combine apples, brown sugar, cornstarch, juice from the lemon, vanilla extract, cinnamon, nutmeg, and salt. Toss together and pour into baking dish.

In a new medium mixing bowl, whisk dry ingredients together (flour, baking powder, salt, and sugar). Add wet ingredients (milk, melted butter, and vanilla extract). Whisk to combine and pour over filling.

Bake for 40-45 minutes until crust is golden brown. Serve warm.

ABOUT THE AUTHOR

New York Times and *USA Today* bestselling author **Kennedy Ryan** writes for women from all walks of life, empowering them and placing them firmly at the center of each story and in charge of their own destinies. Kennedy and her writings have been featured in NPR, *Entertainment Weekly, USA Today, Glamour, Cosmo, Ebony, TIME,* and many others. The audio edition of *Reel* received the prestigious Audie® Award, and her Skyland series is currently in development for television at Peacock. The co-founder of LIFT 4 Autism, an annual charitable book auction, Kennedy has a passion for raising autism awareness. Dubbed the Queen of Hugs by her readers, she is a wife to her lifetime lover and mother to an extraordinary son.

Find out more at:
KennedyRyanWrites.com
Facebook.com/KennedyRyanAuthor
X: @KennedyRWrites
Instagram: @KennedyRyan1
TikTok: @KennedyRyanAuthor